To Khonnik

A TRIAL OF LACE AND BONE

KALISTA NEITH

A Trial
OF
Lace
AND
Bone

BOOK TWO

KALISTA NEITH

First published in the United States of America in July 2023 by Ammewnition Studios LLC

www.kalistaneith.com
ISBN 978-1-957303-10-9 (ebook)
ISBN 978-1-957303-05-5 (hardback)
ISBN 978-1-957303-08-6 (paperback)

Book cover design by Seventh Star Art
Character Art by Tonyviento and Zoe Holland

To be kept up with all things in the realms Of Chaos and Darkness please visit www.kalistaneith.com and sign up for our newsletter.

This book is dedicated to my readers, my Morally Gray Hoez, and those of you who gave Yoshi a place in your heart... You know who you are.

Thank you from the bottom of my black heart. I would have nothing without you.

Trigger Warnings

Attempted Murder
Attempted Non-Con (of a male)
BDSM Hunter/Prey
Blood
Death
Degradation
Enslavement
Kidnapping
Memories of SA
(a male's memories)

Occult/Magic
Pregnancy and birth
Sexual Themes Throughout
Sexually Explicit Scenes
Sexual Harassment
Threat of Death
Torture
Vampires
Violence

The Realms of Chaos and Darkness

Artithia

A series of floating continents serving as the capital of the five realms.

Necromia

Home to the immortal and the short-lived who carry soul shards.

Anaria

Referred to as the commoner's lands. This realm is considered a territory of Necromia. Home to the short-lived who do not carry soul shards also known as Anarians.

Hell

A closed realm containing the souls who have yet to return to the Darkness.

Chaos

The mysterious realm of the Familiar, keepers and caretakers of Chaos and Fate.

Soul Shards

A small marquise-cut crystal worn as jewelry, serving as an exterior indication of the power housed within an individual.

Day-Blood
The weaker of the soul shards, indicated by the white tendrils within the clear to grey mist surrounding the soul shard.

Dark-Blood
The stronger of the soul shards, indicated by the black tendrils within the gray to black mist surrounding the soul shard.

Shard of Darkness
A rare soul shard unmatched in strength, indicated when the black mist obscures the soul shard within it.

KALISTA NEITH

A TRIAL OF LACE AND BONE

AMMEWNITION STUDIOS

ARTITHIA • ANARIA • NECROMIA • HELL • CHAOS

ACT ONE

OPENING

One

Faye was an imposter. Flexing her hand, sharp purple tendrils edged in swirling black mist obscured the soul shard at the center of her index finger. She'd lost count of the times she had accompanied Sparrow to Necromia wearing a counterfeit ring. This felt no more real than the jewelry her sister once charged. Each morning she expected the misted jewel to fade into an empty crystal depleted of its borrowed magic. But this time, instead of veiling herself as a darkblood, she became a Queen.

Something she never wanted to be.

Faye's teeth chattered, her black hair tossing in the autumn breeze. The cold descended over her, curating a host of unwanted memories through her mind. Alister's crushing grip around her throat allowed freezing water to tear the air from her lungs as distorted whites and golds glimmered through the liquid surface, phasing in and out as she struggled.

Death will come for me, but not today, her thoughts had chanted.

She tensed and squeezed her wrist, attempting to suppress the choking memories.

"Are you well?" Rune asked. Her vampire shifted closer as they strolled along the dirt road.

Faye nodded,, rubbing her hand briskly over her arm. "I'm fine."

Rune thinned his lips and shrugged out of his jacket. "No one is here, vsenia. You do not need to pretend with me."

He settled his coat over her shoulders and drew her hair away from the collar. His warmth seeped into her, thawing the icy images. Hugging the cashmere wool closer, she squeezed her arms to her side. The scent of amber and sandalwood enveloped her senses as she glanced at her mate with a smile. "I know. Thank you."

It'd been two weeks since Rune's blood debt was paid. Two weeks since Alister submerged her in a coffin. Faye's aversion to the cold percolated her recollections, leeching the heat from her bones. She'd kept it to herself, hoping her sensitivity would fade. The memories trapped her within nightmares she couldn't escape.

Rune captured her hand and gently pulled her to a stop. "We can return home if you wish, love. I could draw you a hot bath. I know how the cold affects you."

Faye shook her head and pulled him forward. "I've been putting this off. Sparrow went running her mouth. So, I need to introduce you to Aunty Clara."

Her vampire glanced up and exhaled. "We can reschedule dinner. Tell her the High Council summoned me at the last moment."

"No." She laughed.

Returning to her childhood home would be good for her. Perhaps it was a necessary break after Alister petitioned for her Formal Announcement. It ignited a chain of events which ended with her hurled into dark-blooded society.

Rune phased them to the outskirts of her village, where they purchased sweets for the children at Aunty Clara's house. Everyone stilled at his approach. Tension settled through her shoulders when their untrusting gaze slid to her.

Faye had expected them to keep their distance from Rune, but it hurt when the people she'd grown up with suddenly saw her as an enemy.

Like she was a dark-blood, Faye thought, looking down at her ring once again.

She pushed the thought aside. Aunty Clara wouldn't look at her differently. Faye bumped her hip against Rune. "I want her to like you." And after the Shadow Prince made an appearance in her village, Faye was positive everyone would run to the elderly woman eager to share their gossip with the town's mother hen.

If Faye left now, she would never hear the end of it.

Rune gazed down at her, a hint of sadness darkening the blue of his eyes. "I believe that particular ship has sailed, love. I treated you unkindly—."

"None of them know. So, shut up about it," Faye said in a hushed tone, widening her eyes in an unspoken threat. Sparrow managed to keep quiet about it. *Fates help him if her vampire ended up telling on himself.*

Rune pulled her closer. "You know I am sorry, and I shall spend the rest of my days making it up to you. Your judgment is the single influence which bears weight on my soul."

He had a strange way of speaking, but his words cut straight to her heart. She hugged his arm and sighed, "I love you."

"I love you, too," Rune said as he lifted his chin. "We are nearly there. Though, I do not understand why we are walking."

"You can't just magic us in there. You'll scare them," Faye said as the peak of Aunty Clara's red roof rose over the hillcrest. She reached for the bag of caramels and hard candies Rune insisted on carrying after purchasing it from the village.

Small children ran across the lush green lawn as teenagers sat on swings idly in conversation. A few little ones caught sight of her and squeaked with delight, calling for the others. They crowded the gate like excited little birds, chorusing questions.

"We missed you," one pair of twin girls said in unison.

"What did you bring us, Faye?" a little boy asked.

"Who's that?" repeated among the children while they blinked up at Rune.

"Can you read us a story?" asked another.

Faye forced a smile, once reserved for the dark-bloods who deigned to speak to her and shook the bag of sweets. She widened her eyes in an exaggerated surprise and gasped. "You need to eat dinner before you have dessert."

"We're allowed to have snacks," a little boy with short, curling black hair said with crossed arms while Rune opened the gate. "One piece is a snack." Sparrow said the same thing thousands of times. Her sister always found a way to sneak bites of chocolate while Faye helped prepare dinner. A simpler time when there were no responsibilities, only the laughter they shared.

"It's Bayle, right?" Faye asked as she mussed his locks. He came to Aunty Clara's house last winter, if she remembered right.

He pushed her hand away and straightened his hair. "Bayle Alexander," he crowed proudly.

"You're so much taller. I hardly recognized you. If Aunty Clara says you can have a snack, I'll give you one," she said, knowing full well Aunty Clara would agree to no such thing.

The children turned and ran toward the house, chirping for the elderly woman.

Faye intertwined her fingers with Rune's, strolling over the manicured lawn. The earthy scent of the nearby forest soothed her. Memories of Aunty Clara sitting atop the porch steps cutting her fruit washed away the cold intrusive thoughts of Rune's brother. A calmness blanketed her as she gazed over the repairs and additions Rune facilitated. It didn't matter how many years passed or what her future held. This would always be home.

Another gust of wind slipped between the lapels, and Faye pulled Rune's jacket tighter. He smoothed his hand down her back, and the coat warmed, staving off the chill.

"You need to teach me how to do that," Faye said, admiring the rose-gold colors filter through the sky, arching over the trees.

"Phasing first," Rune replied as they approached the front door.

Faye opened it, the rich aromatic scent of beef stewed with onions, rosemary, and nutmeg wafting through the air. She'd never realized how much she took these freshly prepared meals, surrounded by family, for granted until she moved out. Helping in the kitchen had been a chore during her childhood, and now it was one of the things she looked forward to most when visiting. She stepped inside, a host of overlapping voices and clanging kitchenware greeting her.

"Faye!" Kimber waved happily from her place at the worn dinner table, cutting potatoes while Aunty Clara inspected three simmering pots with her hands on her ample hips.

"She said no," a young blonde girl complained, drawing Faye's attention to the room's far end. She sat at the smaller children's table designed to accommodate shorter limbs. Bayle sat beside her, winding a black curl around his finger as he nodded in disappointment.

"What's the matter with you? It's not good to eat candy before dinner," Aunty Clara scolded.

Faye laughed at the elderly woman.

Aunty Clara wiped her hands on a towel, and Faye rushed forward to hug her.

The smaller, plump woman held Faye momentarily, then patted her bottom as she craned her neck at Rune. "He's a big one."

The smile she forced earlier came naturally this time, and she turned to stand beside her and said, "Aunty Clara, this is Rune. Rune, Aunty Clara."

"Delighted to meet you," Rune said with a slight bow.

"Stop it," she chided, waving her hand. "I'm too old for all that court rubbish."

Aunty Clara took Faye's hand and reached for Rune's, holding their palms side by side. She squinted, reading their palms. Faye mouthed, *Sorry,* to Rune as Aunty Clara scrutinized them, mumbling to herself while smoothing her thumb over the lines in their hands.

"Your brother is terrible. I hope you fix him good," Aunty Clara muttered.

The blood drained from Faye's face. "You saw?"

She pursed her wrinkled lips. "I'm old, not dumb. Everybody saw. Why do you think they call it The Eyes?"

Faye tried to step back, but Aunty Clara's grip held fast.

"Stop moving. Next, you're going to tell me you don't wear this ring," she grumbled, turning Faye's hand over momentarily. She lifted Rune's palm toward her. "He is rich, but gold marks are not everything. Rich is no good if he doesn't love you."

"I am hers to command and love her more than anything," Rune said solemnly.

Aunty Clara eyed him, weighing his words, before she continued to scrutinize their palms. Faye's cheeks heated as the seconds awkwardly passed by in silence. Kimber's giggles from her place at the table did nothing to help.

She patted her wrinkled hands over theirs with a nod before releasing them. "Your love is good. Strong. But you have to watch her," Aunty Clara said to Rune. She held up Faye's hand, showing Rune how the joint of her thumb arched back. "Her thumb is curly; this means she likes to be the boss. You need to listen to be happy." She looked toward Faye this time. "And you." Faye pointed to herself. "Yes, you. It's not good to be the boss all the time."

Rune chuckled, and Faye swatted his side.

"Why are you hitting him? You two, married, be nice to each other," Aunty Clara huffed.

"No," Faye said in a rush. "This is my boyfriend. We're not married."

Aunty Clara glanced between them and dusted off her flour covered apron. "You two. So silly."

Faye caught Rune's gaze and mouthed, *Sorry.*

She is delightful, vsenia, Rune purred through her mind.

"Can I help with anything?" she asked, looking around the kitchen.

"I'm finishing the last of the potatoes," Kimber said as she stood. She took her cutting board, sliding the white cubes into a steaming pot.

Faye set the bag of chocolates and caramels on the table. Kimber opened it, while Aunty Clara monitored the stove.

"Hey, you need to wait until after dinner," Bayle huffed at Kimber's feet before crossing his arms and presenting his best 'stern' face.

"No, I don't. I'm a grown-up," she said, popping a caramel in her mouth and smiling at him.

Kimber was all grown up. The tall brunette had blossomed into a beautiful young woman. The shy little girl she'd met all those years ago was gone. When Kimber first arrived, she instantly took to her and Sparrow, following them endlessly during their teenage years. Faye gardened with her, explaining different herbs and how to apply them. Sparrow, on the other hand, taught Kimber how to get into all sorts of trouble.

The plump, old woman swatted Kimber's bottom, and the tall brunette yelped, covering her rear. "Stop teasing the kid," Aunty Clara reprimanded before returning to her stove.

Faye giggled. Her nerves were melted away by the loving recollections she'd gathered within these walls with Aunty Clara.

Kimber moved to the opposite side of the table before sneaking another caramel. She winked at Faye, popping the treat in her mouth.

"Aunty Clara said you can't have candy before dinner," Bayle insisted.

Kimber widened her eyes and made a fist. "Quit snitching on me," she said through her teeth.

"Don't act like Kimber. She's the worst one," the elderly woman grumbled, simmering pots and adding more thyme and a dash of nutmeg to the stew.

"The worst one is going to clean up before we eat," the tall brunette announced. She leaned on the table and pointed at Faye. "Don't leave. I have so many questions."

"Never," Faye said, poking her fingertip before she strolled down the hall out of sight.

The edge of Rune's sleeves extended past her hands. She curled them in her fists and took a deep breath while Aunty Clara was busy with dinner.

Rune narrowed his eyes as she took another before relaxing her hands. He glanced at the hallway, and his voice flowed through her mind. *She reminds me of the blonde harpy.*

A hint of a smile appeared on Faye's lips. Rune inched closer, running his fingers through her dark hair. The children chattered among themselves, seated at their table. The novelty of her guest took a backseat to coloring books and stuffed animals.

She leaned toward him and whispered, "I thought the kids would be scared of you."

"They don't know who he is," Aunty Clara answered as she continued to stir her pot before grinding black pepper into it. She turned toward Faye and said, "I wasn't always old, you know. I belonged to a court when I was your age."

Her day-blood soul shard twinkled as the gray mist churned in on itself. Faye was curious to hear what gossip she would dish over dinner. Bayle slowly approached Rune, drawing Faye's attention.

"Can you read us a story?" he asked shyly, fiddling with his hands.

Faye patted the table. "I'll read you a story after dinner, buddy."

Rune took her hand and brought the backs of her fingers to his mouth. Faye flushed at the warmth of his firm lips. The casual intimacy with a man she trusted was a dream she worried would evaporate with her soul shard.

Rune leaned toward the boy. He glanced at Faye over his shoulder before whispering as though the two of them were conspiring against her. "Bring me your favorite book."

The boy beamed, disappearing down the hall, and Faye could only stare at Rune. He arched a brow, and she blinked. In her imaginings of their family, he'd been loving but formal. A stoic figure. This playful side of him reminded her of Voshki. Faye bit the inside of her lip, wondering which of her men Rune's demeanor stemmed from.

"You don't have to read to them," Faye said quietly.

Rune stood and straightened the cuffs of his shirt. "If I keep the young occupied, it affords you the opportunity to catch up with your caregiver."

"Children," Faye corrected.

The corner of his mouth lifted, and Rune silently strolled to the smaller table. The boy returned a short time later with a large pop-up book. Rune took a seat, struggling to fit on the small chair. Faye delighted in seeing him attempt to catch his balance. Resting his arms across his knees, he held the book out for the children to see as they crowded around him.

"He's good with the kids," Aunty Clara said, leaning on the back of Faye's chair. "You going to tell this old lady how you really met? Don't tell me the Shadow Prince was strolling through Anaria and tripped over you."

Faye sighed and gazed up at Aunty Clara. The woman was like a mother to her. The best lies began in truth. "Sparrow and I snuck into the Hunter's Moon Ball. I ran into him."

Aunty Clara shook her head and sucked her teeth. "She is always getting you in hot water."

"He's the one who fixed your house. All this," Faye said, waving her hand in dramatic sweeps. "I wouldn't date him. He did this to prove he cared for the things I valued."

"That doesn't mean he cares; it means he's rich. And you be careful. I know about the vampire bite-bite."

Faye flushed, mortified. "Aunty Clara."

"Don't *Aunty Clara* me. You take care, or you're going to have *this* running all around your house," she said, pointing at the children crowding around Rune. She stepped forward and pulled the collar of Rune's coat to peer at her neck.

"Stop." Faye laughed, pulling the jacket tighter around herself. "I don't have 'bite-bite' marks."

"Your Aunty Clara cannot live forever, you know. I worry about you. Maybe I don't trust him, but I see how he looks at you. He watches you very closely. I don't know if it's love yet, but it's something. Your sister has her wing boy. You have the white-haired vampire boy."

Faye burst out laughing. Rune was thousands of years her senior, but he was still a boy to her. The gray hairs framing her face claimed she could.

"You don't have to worry about me," Faye said, imagining Rune with the children they would have one day. He turned the pages reading to the little ones upside down as they gawked at the popped-up pictures of dragons and castles.

Aunty Clara pinched her chin, upturning her face. The corners of her eyes wrinkled as she observed Faye. "Did he kill the brother?" the elderly woman asked, touching the tops of her cheekbones.

Faye tensed as her heart raced. Cold constricted her lungs.

"I don't want him to kill his brother," she said weakly.

The plump woman nodded, sensing her trauma. "You always take care of everyone else—"

"I'm fine," Faye bit out, leaning back in her chair. Rune glanced in her direction. His gaze shifted from her to Aunty Clara and back again before returning to his audience as he turned the page.

A chill spread over her back, siphoning the warmth Rune gave her. Faye rubbed her hands together and took a deep breath. She didn't want to think of the icy water filling her lungs. *Not here*, Faye thought as she ran her fingers over the uneven surface of the aged table Sparrow carved their names into. This was her sanctuary.

"You're stubborn. I saw his face. Hate like that doesn't die—you kill it," Aunty Clara hissed before returning to her simmering pots. "And you need to eat more. You're so skinny. He doesn't feed you with all that money?"

Irritation bristled Faye as she tightened her arms to her side.

Obstinacy didn't drive her. She'd made a choice. The simple life she longed for vanished when she acquired her shards.

And him, Faye thought, admiring the feared Shadow Prince as he read to small Anarian children.

"I am fed plenty," she answered, remembering the time she refused to eat. From the moment she was in his home, even with his hatred, he tried to take care of her.

He owned her heart, and she chose to protect him. Her vampire had been willing to be labeled a whore for her safety. Faye refused to allow him to do such a thing and opted instead to face his brother and pay the blood debt between them.

Through terror and pain, they were together—Fated and matched.

Two lingering truths she held with absolute clarity. A love for a man she had never imagined existed, and…

The strong protect the weak.

Two

Rune spent the evening as a spectator while the Ra'Voshnik listened to Faye spin a tale of how they met, glossing over the months Rune had been unkind. He had partaken in the blood Faye's caregiver deemed 'red wine,' forbidding the young from touching it. It only made the brunette harpy more curious to take a whiff and subsequently scrunch her nose at him. Now the Ra'Voshnik slumbered deep inside his mind, uninterested in the physical world without Faye's presence.

The sound of his queen's slow, even breathing filled the quiet night. She slept curled onto his chest, draping her leg over his body. Observing his queen with her family did nothing to loosen the guilt rattling in his chest.

For all his strength, he failed to protect her.

She'd suffered because of him. Endured his brother's murderous rage. The nagging thought laced itself through the edges of his mind during his quiet hours. An ever-present list of scenarios he could never change or confirm as true.

Faye's breath accelerated suddenly. Her skin chilled beneath his touch. A manifestation of her magic, bleeding her nightmares into her waking moments.

"Faye," Rune called, rubbing her back as she shivered.

The Ra'Voshnik roused with his words, rushing to its queen.

Rune called her name again as her breath fogged, her body heat siphoned from her night terrors. Faye's eyes closed tight, her brows pinching together. She kicked, clawing at him. Rune sat up, pulling her into his arms. He wove a warming spell through the sheets, pulling them over her.

Frost began to crawl up the thin windows framing Hell's sky. "Vsenia!" Rune roared.

She choked, and her eyes snapped open, her body shaking in his grasp. Faye's shrill scream lanced his ears, and she raked her nails across his face.

Let me rise! She thinks you're Alister. The Ra'Voshnik bashed itself against his awareness as the veined misted shadows stretched beneath his gaze.

Faye's wide eyes darted, assessing the room as her lips parted. Her hands tremored as she touched his cheek. She withdrew immediately as her lightning-streaked midnight eyes shimmered with unshed tears.

"I'm sorry," she choked, before hugging him lightly.

Rune encircled her in his arms and crooned, "I am well, love."

Her tears trailed down his neck, branding his failure. Each shuddering breath was a reminder of his queen's pain—his inability to alleviate the suffering she hid behind a smile.

Tell her she has claws like a kitten and can't hurt us, the Ra'Voshnik growled, prowling the edges of his mind.

Rune ignored the creature and added a second layer of warming spells to his dark sheets.

"I'm so cold," Faye whimpered as her voice trembled.

"I know." Rune pressed a kiss to her temple. "I have you."

He pulled the sheets over her shoulders, offering her the depths of his unending devotion until her memories melted beneath her skin. Memories she carried because of him.

Every time she has a nightmare, I'm going to rip a bone out of the frail-blood, the Ra'Voshnik growled through his mind.

Rune stifled his exhalation for patience, fearing Faye would believe she was the source of his frustration. *Killing him will upset Faye,* Rune countered.

His dark queen carried enough of a burden on her slim shoulders. Rune refused to allow the crass creature to add to it.

It gave a low laugh. *I'll extract our queen's retribution for centuries, carving it from him. The frail blood will beg for death, but he'll live.*

Rune didn't bother replying. The night terrors his queen suffered dredged up ancient, stained memories of his own. They clawed at the edges of his awareness, seeking light he would never offer. He knew what it was like to wake in terror. To attack those closest to him. Because in the bitter hellscape of his mind, he could not discern family from enemy.

Safety from danger.

His queen would not suffer alone. He would be her anchor in the abyss of her nightmares. He could do nothing else. Would do nothing else…

The fault of her torment rested squarely at his feet.

Tears fell from Faye's lashes with tight shuddering breaths, streaking her throat. She attacked him. Mistaking the man she loved, for her assailant.

"I'm sorry," Faye said, her voice breaking.

Rune gathered her in his arms and stood, dragging the sheets with him. The beat of his heart against her cheek grounded her. His scent calmed her. She closed her eyes, taking another breath and when she opened them, they stood near the hearth in his study.

A blue glow fanned over the angles of his face as hellfire blazed to life under the mantle. Heat radiated over Faye's side, and she lifted her hand, fingers wrapping his face. His injury knitted together before her eyes. The veined, misted shadows were disrupted by her touch as she followed the thin pink line with a feather light caress.

"I am the one who is sorry," Rune softly whispered against her hair. He adjusted his grip, lowering them to the floor.

Faye pulled her knees to her chest and leaned into him.

Her vampire kneaded the tension from her muscles, working his way down one side of her spine and up the other.

"The Ra'Voshnik is worried," Rune said.

She nodded, and he carried her awareness into his mind. Her eyes adjusted to the faint shift in perspective.

The Ra'Voshnik sat beside Rune with his back to the fire. He bundled the heated silk around her feet before meeting her gaze.

"Tell me to hurt him, love," Voshki purred. She knew he promised a massacre from the way his muscle ticked in his jaw.

Faye narrowed her eyes and bit out a single command, "No." She shoved her foot against his thigh to emphasize her point. "I made a *promise*."

"The blood debt is paid. You are not obligated to see him again," Rune said.

Faye lowered her gaze, comforted by the men she loved. The checks and tallies they used to measure right and wrong were a vicious cycle. Rune shattered Prinia's mind, and Alister demanded her life as payment. The outcome made no difference. The animosity between both brothers would persist whether she survived or perished.

"I promised him," Faye breathed. She needed to wipe the slate clean. A heavy feeling festered in her soul, digging its claws into the life and happiness she found. Tainting it with mirrored comparisons of the love Rune ripped from Alister.

"I promised to kill him. Does that count for nothing?" Voshki teased with a grin.

Faye leaned forward, and Voshki mimicked her movements with a predator's grace. She took his face in her hands, staring into his black eyes. "Violence is not the answer."

He arched a brow and canted his head the same way Rune did. "But it could be."

"Be silent," Rune growled behind her.

"Behave," she said to Voshki before turning toward Rune. "And you, be nice."

His breath warmed her neck as he whispered, "As you command. Are you warm enough?"

Faye nodded, unwilling to part with the heated silk or their embrace. The pop and crackle of the hellfire soothed her.

"It's the middle of the night. You should return to bed. I can pet your hair," Voshki offered.

It was a sweet notion. But she was exhausted, and sleep scarcely returned to her after a nightmare.

"I can't sleep."

Voshki lifted his chin at Rune. "Show her the nonsense you're putting together."

"Be. Silent," he grated.

Faye leaned back and smiled at Rune. "Are you planning a surprise?" Then to Voshki. "Is it romantic?"

Voshki's smirk lit his dark gaze. "He's been collecting villages for you."

Collecting villages? Faye turned back to Rune and bit her lip.

"I have been working toward your wishes. It would be simpler to show you."

Voshki stood in a fluid motion and offered his hand. He guided Faye to her feet, and she separated one of the sheets. Her offering fell short when she found Rune dressed in his customary black suit, mirroring the Ra'Voshnik.

"You weren't wearing that when you came to bed." The man slept naked.

"He always has a spare suit waiting," Voshki answered. "Hates being under dressed."

Rune growled at Voshki while he chuckled. Faye dismissed their odd behavior as a private joke she wasn't privy to. Rune moved behind his desk, offering his chair. Faye sat in his seat, and he unrolled a heavy, pale parchment.

"I hired a cartographer to help me find the simplest path to organize your realm."

Your realm. Her chest tightened, and panic pierced her veiled illusions. The scope of what Rune suggested suffocated her under its weight. Her hesitation solidified a truth she couldn't hide from.

Two sides of her would always be at war.

The dark-blooded queen, her soul shards proclaimed her to be, would forever be at odds with the Anarian heart beating beneath her power.

Three

Faye gingerly touched the darker lines, forking through valleys and rivers. Its surface reminded Faye of soft leather. She gazed at the map depicting Anaria and its untouched terrain.

Less than a year ago, she'd been nothing more than a peasant. A simple Anarian. Despite her tumultuous courtship, she was very much the same person at heart. Doubt crept through her mind. A lifetime of insecurities hooked into her subconscious. Once she began this path, there would be no turning back.

Faye's actions would reshape the realms.

"We will ride from the south and take the eastern path." Rune's elegant fingers traced over the bumps and ridges.

Faye nodded before pausing on a marker. It identified a simple village she would always call home, Alexander. Rune brushed her hair behind her shoulder, caressing the side of her neck. Her vampire claimed he couldn't taste her emotions, but he was too attentive. Always asking what troubled her. Assessing the weight upon her shoulders when she yearned for the equality of her people— the *simple* Anarians. Reassuring her when uncertainty whispered through her mind.

Hell's ever-twilight sky streamed in through the intricate wrought iron window stretched across the back wall of his study. The edge of Rune's long white-blonde hair illuminated in a gentle glow.

"Why are we taking a carriage instead of phasing to the villages?" Faye leaned back in his chair and smiled teasingly before adding, "Are you planning a romantic trip through the countryside?"

Rune smirked, leaning on his desk. "Phasing to these villages would mean I have visited them previously. Unfortunately, I have not spent much time in Anaria."

"I'd be happy to take you on a countryside picnic." Voshki mirrored Rune on her left. She gave a vibrant smile at his offer, and her beautiful hunter stood taller.

Rune thinned his lips before continuing, "Our trip will serve a dual purpose. We will see each village and verify if a ruling court has been established. If they are unoccupied, you will establish your court over them."

Faye frowned. Alexander was a poor village even by Anarian standards. The families depended on each other, banding together for generations to ensure their survival.

"I want to protect them, not tax them," Faye said.

Farming and raising livestock were common, but rumors had spread every year. Someone entered the vampire auctions. If they were chosen, they were offered contracts. A trade of body and blood for coin. The riches they sent their families allowed their town to flourish. For a time. The coin only went so far.

Sparrow tried to drag her to one. Faye refused, afraid to see the desperation in so many faces. What they would offer in trade to ensure their family survived the winter.

Anarians suffered yearly, and the dark courts never cared because there was nothing to gain. One of the few things Faye was certain of in the ruling courts was how they taxed their cities then used the income to fund their lavish courts.

"Eventually, they will be taxed, but only once they are established. The funds are collected to maintain the cities and villages.

I suspect funds will flow toward them initially, not away," he said gently.

Faye blinked as her brow drew together. The cost to rebuild Alexander would be more than she could obtain over a lifetime. This man planned on financing every village and town in Anaria as though it were a few spare silver marks.

"How rich are you?" Faye asked, remembering Aunty Clara's words from dinner last night. *That doesn't mean he cares; it means he's rich.*

He canted his head, giving her a questioning glance as though to ask, *Truly?*

She widened her eyes, silently demanding an answer.

"*We…* are exceedingly wealthy," Rune said as though he'd just informed her, *yes, the sky is blue.* He turned his attention back to the map, tapping a finger on the outskirts of Anaria. "I would focus our efforts on the smaller villages who may need more care, then move to the larger towns."

Faye pressed her lips and peered at the fine parchment. "If we start at the towns, we could help more people faster."

"The larger villages have more resources. The impact on the smaller villages will be greater once we install healers and repair buildings," Rune explained.

Faye supposed he had a point.

Rune slipped his hands into his pockets and smiled. "We will be doing exactly as Belind had with Necromia. After your court is—"

"Our court," Faye corrected.

He laughed, lighting his pale blue eyes. "No, vsenia. I am your Consort, but you are the Queen. The court is yours to command. As am I," Rune said, tracing the backs of his index and middle finger across her cheek.

His feather-light touch *almost* took her mind from his archaic court principles.

Almost.

"The three of us are partners in *our* court," Faye decreed.

"Yes, my queen." They spoke in unison. A teasing tone from Voshki and reluctance from Rune, but their smiles warmed her. Faye wet her lip wanting to return to bed and spend the day curled up in their arms.

Rune lifted his chin toward the map. "After you establish yourself as the ruling court over the villages, I will draw up the necessary documents for the High Council to claim Anaria."

Faye leaned back in his chair, staring at him and his expectant gaze. "I don't speak dark-blood."

Voshki laughed as Rune said, "You will claim Anaria as your own. Become the realm's Queen."

"What?" She felt like a girl playing dress up. Rune wanted her to become a *real* Queen—over a realm.

"You wish to protect your people. This," Rune gestured to the map, "is the most efficient way to do so."

"In a month's time, you will be Anaria's Queen," Voshki added.

"A month?" Faye asked. Counting the number of villages on the map, there were fewer than two dozen of them. "Surely, we can visit more than one town a day."

Voshki flashed his fangs with a wide grin. "This," he said, tapping his black-tipped claws on the map, "will take no more than a week. The High Council won't convene again until next month."

"How do you know so much about this stuff?" Faye asked. Rune had suppressed him his entire life.

"I know everything he does. We have the same body even if the Shadow Prince never learned to share."

"An unfortunate tie," Rune added.

The Ra'Voshnik's warm breath fanned her ear as he grew closer, his smile widening against her neck. "I could even tell you what he fantasizes about."

She shuddered at the thought of her teeth dragging over a highly sensitive spot on his neck.

"How he'd like to bind your wrists and have you on your knees while he fucks your pretty thro—"

Rune's growl silenced Voshki's words.

"Lies will not garner her favor," Rune grated.

He straightened, fixing the cufflink of his suit. "Lying to yourself doesn't make my words any less true."

Faye looked back at the map and took a deep breath, exhaling slowly while her males glowered at each other. "Stop it, both of you."

She touched the border, the word *Anaria* was depicted in a beautiful script and highlighted with a flourish. This was her home. For so long, she wanted this. A chance to make a difference. The strong were meant to protect the weak. It was a bone-deep truth, resonating from her very being. What Rune proposed wasn't how she expected to protect her people. She was still adjusting to the assembly of her court—Now, she was expected to claim an entire realm. Royal blood didn't run through her veins. She was reaching for a crown she had no right to. In a hushed tone, Faye said, "I don't want to be a Queen. I want to protect them from being mistreated."

Voshki took her hand, and Rune gently squeezed her shoulder. "You think of them as your people. I believe it is fitting."

They *were* her people. She was one of them. Faye read the names of forgotten towns and villages Necromia refused to acknowledge. Perhaps through her, they would have a Queen who cared for them.

Saw them.

With Rune's help, she could offer them protection. The title was a means to an end. An end that stopped others from laying claim to her people and realm. An end to the cowards who sought to exploit the weak and powerless.

No, Faye thought. She would stand between Anaria and the dark-bloods who took pleasure in cruelty. She would rebuild their villages and allow them to live with dignity. And for her people...

She would become a Queen.

Four

Ruling Anaria meant more than a crown. It was a duty Faye would protect with her life. One the High Queen wouldn't offer freely. Her expression fell as she imagined standing before the High Council. The High Queen's dismissive demeanor swept over her.

The high bitch's taunting, melodic voice never left her. Faye had begged for her freedom in this very room, and the High Queen's answer turned her thoughts bitter.

You're in his realm, dear. Feel free to call your court to war against the Shadow Prince.

A seat on the High Council was entangled with the crown she sought to wear as a shield for her people. She looked to Rune. He had told her his brother Jareth represented Hell after he refused the position. Maybe she could abdicate in the same way.

"Can I let Sparrow sit on the High Council?" Faye pursed her lips, tipping back and forth on her heels.

"As amusing as that would be, I believe you should take your place among them." His smirk slipped into a frown as he leaned his hip to the desk. "There will be those who oppose you. You will need to be swift and brutal."

"Or leave them to me," Voshki purred, his seductive tone at odds with his predatory smile.

Their words soured her expression as the grandfather clock near the mantle ticked quietly. "It doesn't have to be that way. I don't want to rely on fear and violence to vindicate my actions." Faye ran her fingers over the black surface of Rune's bloodroot desk. Smooth and polished, the exact opposite of the kitchen table she grew up with. "We have the opportunity to show the dark courts a better way to rule. With mercy and compassion. Anaria could be a realm where dark-bloods, day-bloods, and Anarians live as equals."

"Change will always be met with opposition," Rune stated.

A show of force was always necessary with dark-bloods. They reigned with an archaic series of checks and tallies. Justifying their violence as a necessary example until others were too frightened to oppose them—or they became tallies themselves on an endless score-card.

Fear would never be part of her reign.

"I'll need to meet with Alister," Faye muttered. Speaking his name sent a chill down Faye's spine. The frigid bite of the water he'd held her beneath lingered with her.

Sadi agreed to train her in Familiar magic. She needed to control the newfound power she inherited in order to allow her to retrieve Prinia's mind from Chaos. The Familiar suggested visiting Alister's wife before they began. A connection to a person made it easier to reach them. Though, Faye wasn't sure how to establish the tie she desperately needed. Alister spent centuries caring for a body his wife's mind no longer inhabited.

A love he lost because of Rune's cruelty.

"How is he?" Faye asked.

Her vampire's look softened, and Faye's heart stung. Guilt gnawed at her from every angle. Rune had been astoundingly cruel, but he wasn't the same man he'd been eight hundred years ago. He loved her and would help her protect Anaria. Her tangled heart wouldn't allow one act to forgive the other. She needed to bring Alister's wife back to him to heal the ache in her chest.

"His distance is not your doing. There is much to settle between my brother and I."

Settle wasn't a word she'd use to describe the blistering history between Rune and Alister. Warring parties didn't settle… they destroyed each other. Prinia was the only path to peace between them.

"You should rest." Rune rolled the map and returned it to its leather case. "I will arrange the visits to your villages. After which, I will escort you to Alister and Prinia."

Rune phased Faye and the Ra'Voshnik to their bedroom and slipped out of his jacket. His queen preferred to sleep between them in his mind after a nightmare. The creature tucked Faye into their bed before retrieving another set of sheets, allowing Faye to remain cocooned in her silk.

The Ra'Voshnik disrobed, and Faye giggled when it leaped over her, stretching across the space at her back. On top of the sheets. *Uncivilized creature.*

Faye wrinkled her nose, peering at Voshki over her shoulder. "You're not going to get cold?"

It purred, rolling onto its side to drape an arm across her waist. The creature rubbed the side of its face between her shoulder blades. "You, my queen, are warm enough for all of us."

Rune stripped and joined his dark queen. The Ra'Voshnik grumbled as she lay her head on his chest.

"She only sleeps on you because she prefers me," it said.

Faye tangled her legs with the creature. "I love you both." She yawned and murmured, "Equally."

Rune closed his eyes as her nails grazed over his side. He purred, content in these small moments and satisfied to hold her until she fell asleep.

Her lashes brushed his chest as she traced small circles over his side. "What will we do… if the High Queen won't surrender Anaria?"

"We kill her," the Ra'Voshnik answered on the heels of Faye's question.

Rune exhaled in an attempt to gain patience, turning his head toward the creature who blissfully ignored him. He could count the times he'd felt envy during his endless centuries. A strange emotion to harbor for the Ra'Voshnik and his queen's easy kindness toward it. She forgave its vicious demeanor and demanding speech. Rune didn't delude himself, knowing he garnered no such favor with their queen. Keenly aware of his numerous misdeeds. He had been the one who treated her ill. The one who drove her away with cruelly spoken words to save her. Between himself and the Ra'Voshnik, he had been the monster.

"Anaria is unoccupied. It will be a simple exchange," Rune assured her. The villages had nothing to offer a dark court, and without resources to tax, even day-bloods held no interest. Lyssa would surrender the realm at his ask. He shielded his queen's home realm from The Crumbling for the better part of eight centuries. If she owed him any favor, it would be this. "Sleep, vsenia," Rune murmured. "Leave the details to me."

The Ra'Voshnik hummed its agreement. "I'll keep you company while the Shadow Prince buries his nose in books." It would like that, wouldn't it? Leaving all the work to him. The creature would spend its days at Faye's feet if she humored it. There was much work to be completed, a multitude of tasks to breathe life into his queen's vision. Her idyllic realm would face heavy opposition.

He would become an instrument of her will. A weapon and shield used to secure her reign.

Perhaps then he would be worthy.

Five

R une skimmed through the latest book from Morbid's library,
finding nothing of value in regards to his queen's heritage.
Loose pages and aged documents littered the small desk across from
his four-post bed. He closed the book and set it on the neat pile
stacked perpendicular to the bloodroot edge.

His focus had suffered under his growing apprehension surrounding his brother. It had taken Alister three days to reply to the
letter he'd penned on Faye's behalf. Three days of his queen anxious-
ly waiting to receive a reply. Rune had a mind to phase to his brother's
home and remind him Faye was granting him a kindness.

He'd held his tongue, aware his anger would serve no one and
upset his gentle queen.

Rune arranged Faye's visits to Prinia with their tour of Anaria.
They would begin today after his night breeze completed her morn-

ing ritual. He drew her a bath each morning after he showered. The requested temperature bordered on scalding, but she eased into it and remained until it pinkened her tanned skin.

He hoped her nightmares would lessen with time, but the passing days only amplified their frequency.

His queen stepped out of their bathroom, swallowed by his black bathrobe. It dragged behind her as she toweled off her hair. *Let her keep it. She looks better in it than we do,* the Ra'Voshnik purred. Pride radiated from the creature as it glided through Rune's mind. While Rune respected Faye's wishes, his possessiveness was something he and the creature both shared. The entirety of his being rested in the hands of his dark queen, and she was his.

Ours, the creature grated.

Rune rested his ankle over his knee. His queen kicked the material gathered at her feet off to one side, explaining, "Yours is fluffier than mine."

"They are made of the same material." There was something entirely too pleasing seeing her walk in his clothing.

Faye's bare feet quietly padded over the stone floor as she made her way to her closet. Her towel was discarded to the doorknob. "These are new," she called. She held the sleeve of a full-length cashmere wool coat, leaning back on her heels to inspect it. Curious fingers pawed through the black fur lining of the second jacket before abandoning her latest gifts to face him.

"You were cold during our walk to your caregiver's home," Rune said as he got to his feet.

His queen stood beneath the smoke quartz chandelier in her walk-in closet, surrounded by a host of colorful garments he procured for her nearly a year ago. He remembered the first time she refused to wear anything in that closet.

"Can I ask you something? But I need a real answer, not *I'm yours to command,*" Faye said in a deeper voice, mimicking his accent. Did she think he sounded like that?

"Are they not to your liking?" Rune asked, retrieving her towel to return it to its rightful place in their ensuite.

"No, these are beautiful. Thank you," Faye said as she dressed. She leaned in the doorway of her closet, looking at the jacket folded over her arm. "Do you... do you want children?"

Rune canted his head at her question. Did she worry he would not sire her young? As though he could deny her anything. "I am aware you desire young, vsenia. You will have everything you wish for."

"I know what I want. What do you want? You're old... three thousand years is a long time. More than enough to have a family if you wanted one," Faye said, her voice slowly fading into a whisper.

Tell her you want a legacy with her, the Ra'Voshnik urged, rising to the surface.

Legacy, a word his mother used to describe offspring. Rune's chest tightened as Faye hugged the coat closer. She blinked rapidly as tension spread over her slight frame.

"Vsenia," Rune said gently, taking her into his arms. She didn't return his embrace, clutching the garment she held.

"I want a family. I've always wanted a family, but I don't want you to just... go along with me because it's what I want," Faye said quietly.

"We come from very different times, love." Faye stiffened, and the Ra'Voshnik raked its claws over his awareness. *Let me rise, you're upsetting her. Tell her you want young with her. I do if you don't!* Rune lifted Faye in his arms and sat at the edge of their bed. He arranged her on his lap and held her loosely. Fabricating a tale where he dreamed of offspring with a dark queen might alleviate her fears, but the lie would only hurt her in the long run.

He purred softly and brushed his lips over her temple. "When I was still in my youth, I wanted what my parents had: a queen I could devote myself to and young to carry our legacy if she desired them."

The ancient memories faded, the emotions associated with them losing their color as the centuries passed. The choice he resigned himself to lifetimes ago did not. It persisted over his endless life, resurfacing from time to time to haunt him.

Faye rested her head on his shoulder as he continued. "I invoked my blood at fifteen. I was too young to properly pledge myself to a queen. My mother threw a ball for prospective suitors from noble houses who were my age."

His mother had meant well, hoping his introduction would sow friendships, and as he matured, he would follow the queen who best suited him.

"They feared me." Rune remembered stepping into the opulent ballroom dressed in his first tailored suit with painful clarity. Hundreds of guests stilled, their gazes fixed on his Shard of Darkness. "The taste of their emotions was overwhelming, and I immediately understood two things. Fear would be my sole companion if I continued my lessons with Saith, and to quell the fear emanating from each guest, I would need to shun my power and prove I was not a threat."

Rune contemplated stepping back, weighing the life he expected against the reality his mother's guests showed him. His life altered in the space of a few hours. "Word of my soul shard spread quickly. Two vampire hunter guilds joined forces in an attempt to assassinate me before I could grow into my strength. They infiltrated the ball, murdering a number of our guests and injuring my mother. I came to my decision while I hunted the guilds. I chose to protect the family I had instead of risking my court for one I may have in the future."

Faye's silence answered him.

"I am woefully ill-equipped for off-spring. My experience with young is limited to my brother Jareth, and I did not spend much time with him while Saith mentored me." Rune curled his finger under her chin and gently lifted her face.

The Ra'Voshnik roared at the unshed tears collecting on her lashes. *If you turn her from us, I will dedicate the rest of my days to finding a way to kill you.*

Veined misted shadow stretched beneath his gaze as Rune tenderly brushed her tears away. "I do, however, have a quick learning agility. We will navigate raising our young together."

Faye drew his hand away and muttered, "You didn't answer my question."

"I will never lie to you, love. I am not against young, but I never saw them as part of my path. You are a gift I never expected. I thank the Darkness every day for you, vsenia. I only hope, when you bear my sons, you do not begrudge me for their pale coloring." Faye giggled and leaned into him, soothing the ache in his chest.

"But my hair is black," Faye countered.

Rune chuckled, relieved to hear the pained sorrow lifting from his queen's voice. "So was Michelle's."

Faye wrinkled her nose at him. "Did you just call your mom by name?"

"Immortal customs, we call our parents by name when we reach our second century," Rune explained.

"We're not doing that. If I make it to their second century, they are calling me mom the whole way through," Faye grumbled.

Rune laughed and held his hand up in apology when Faye glared at him. "I will happily follow any custom you desire."

Faye played with a length of his hair, pulling it through her fingers. "So, you think we'll have white haired children?"

"My brothers and I are the very image of our father. I suspect his lineage will continue through the generations."

"Well, I think you're handsome," Faye said, sliding off his lap.

Only because you look like me. The creature calmed with their queen's mood as it spewed opinions Rune never requested.

"Courting you would have been far more difficult if I were not to your taste," Rune teased.

Faye wandered to his desk and picked up a bleached leather-bound tome. She flipped the book open to a random page. "You're always reading these. What are they?"

"Saith created my father using a woman called the Elysian Queen. I am researching her origins."

Faye recoiled. "Was he your... grandfather?"

"Saith? No," Rune said. "Magic requires balance. Creating a life meant extinguishing another."

Faye closed the book and returned it to its place, misaligned. "Do a lot of dark-bloods use magic like that?"

"Creating races?" Rune asked as he moved beside Faye, straightening his books. Faye nodded and he answered, "Saith was the only person I am aware of who found success in his particular endeavors."

"He sounds like a horrible person," his queen commented, quietly.

Rune couldn't disagree with her assessment. "He was unkind to many."

"He killed people and used them as ingredients for his spells. He's not unkind. He's evil," Faye corrected as she donned her fur-lined coat. "I'm sorry. I know he mentored you, and you were close."

All my efforts on you will be wasted.

Saith's parting words played through his mind, and bitterness settled in Rune's mouth. "He discarded me in the end." *And took everything from me.*

"He was using you," Faye said, adjusting his lapel. "You're better off without him."

"I belong to you now," Rune whispered.

She spared him an appraising glance and patted his chest. "I guess I'll keep you, but I think we're late for our tour of Anaria."

"They will wait," Rune crooned as he outstretched his hand. "Shall we?"

Six

She placed her hand in his, and her surroundings faded to black in an instant. The next moment they stood beside an open carriage hitched to a large black horse. Faye retreated instinctively, distancing herself from the beast as smoke curled around its nose. Flames whispered from its nostrils and around its mouth, ebbing and flowing with each breath. Faye's hand tightened over Rune's as her gaze trailed lower. Its massive hooves burned as well.

"We are not riding in this," Faye said, letting go of his hand and stepping back. Searching for an alternative, she went into the stables only to find more fiery beasts similar to the one attached to the carriage. She walked out to find Rune with both his hands in his pockets, smirking as a small man clicked his teeth and patted the horse's neck. She pointed to the beast and hissed, "That horse is going to terrify the villages."

The flames died out, and Rune hugged her to his side. "They are called Nightmares," he whispered.

"Shadow Prince." The man bowed and turned toward her. "Lady Faye."

She tried to be polite with her smile, but the idea of getting on a horse-beast-whatever-drawn carriage terrified her. The man opened the carriage door, waiting for them to enter. Faye surveyed the conveyance. Without its flames, she supposed it looked like a horse. Right. *It's just a very large, muscular horse, except it has fangs protruding from its mouth. And flames. And smoke.* Faye took a deep breath and held Rune's hand as she stepped into the carved, walnut carriage with him following suit. It was identical to the other dark-blood carriages she'd ridden with Sparrow, but the roof had been replaced with a small awning to keep the sun away.

The coachman clicked the reins, and the carriage pulled forward. Fading away were the heads of the fiery beasts as they hung from their stalls, unphased, and they watched with large dark eyes until the view disappeared entirely. Dense fog surrounded the carriage before the color reappeared.

Faye leaned closer to Rune. "What's happening?"

"Phasing the carriage is taxing. It makes for a slower transition," Rune explained.

The mist cleared to uncover beautiful fields surrounding a stream which later cut into a forest in the distance. She'd teased him earlier, but it did feel romantic. A quiet ride through the countryside with the man she loved. She breathed in the fresh, clean air. It felt like the meadow which lead into the forest she adored back in Anaria. She preferred the richer, earthier scents of her forest, but this was a close second. Faye leaned her head on Rune's shoulder and glanced up at him. He gazed down at her, then resumed examining their surroundings. Seemingly scrutinizing every hill, field, and tree.

Faye squeezed his arm. "What are you looking for?"

He didn't look at her as he stated, "Being able to traverse the land is advantageous during times of war."

Her eyes narrowed. "War?"

"Phasing," Rune explained.

Faye quirked her lip and exhaled. *Dramatic male.* She returned to the blissful view. "We won't be at war."

Rune lifted her hand. His firm lips warmed the bend of her fingers. "I serve as your consort and executioner. Darkness willing, we will never need my latter talents."

A faint roaring sounded while they made their way around the forest. The steep face of a mountain towered above the trees. Faye leaned forward, watching the woods give way bit by bit. She imagined a waterfall flowing down the cliffside, thundering into a clear pool beneath it.

The blood drained from her face as the sky panned into view. A wall of turbulent storm clouds stretched into the cerulean sky in the distance, beyond another mountain range. The hairs on her arm stood on end as she leaned back, squeezing closer to Rune.

"We are perfectly safe, and there are no villages within The Crumbling's reach."

Faye angled herself to face the hills and fields. The faint roaring crept over her skin like a great beast growled behind her, ready to swallow her whole. She kept silent, drawing comfort from Rune. Thankfully they rode away from The Crumbling, and Faye's nerves calmed as the sound faded.

They followed the road over a bend, and rooftops peeked over the next hill. "Which village is this?"

Rune answered, "Streck."

Faye smiled as they approached. The buildings were older but maintained. People stood in small groups talking. Barefoot children chased a fat brown hen. It reminded her so much of her village, the way she grew up.

Her smile fell when they caught sight of her and ran. Women gathered the children, rushing them into the nearest houses. Door after door closed as the lively village stilled to nothing. A silent reminder of the truth.

Faye glanced up at Rune. "Maybe I should have come alone?"

"I would prefer to escort you." Rune said, studying the soundless square.

"There's no real place for you to hide with that flashy hair," Faye teased. She sat forward, expecting the coachman to veer to the edge of the village, and realized he meant to ride straight into it.

"Stop. You're going to scare them more than they already have. Pull to the side, and don't ride into the villages," Faye said, then added, "Please."

She exited the coach and patted Rune's arm. "Stay here, big guy." He shot her a disapproving stare but obeyed. Faye headed for the aged building. A crescent moon intersected by a staff was painted on the door, a common healer's insignia. Villages were small, tight-knit communities. The healer would know who she needed to speak with. Faye knocked before pushing the door open.

A woman stared at her wide-eyed, tucked into the corner of the room, dropping a bundle of dried herbs. Faye smiled and said, "Hi, are you the healer?"

She nodded but moved no closer, slowly gathering her fallen herbs. "Yes, my lady."

Faye stepped into the small room containing two beds and a desk. She glanced over the rack of jars and ointments against the wall, surprised they were well stocked. Faye folded her hands, giving the woman space. "My name is Faye. What's your name?"

"Deni, my lady," the woman answered too quickly. She fidgeted and swallowed, glancing over the small space to put the herbs in one of the cupboards she had sitting next to the far-left cot.

Faye left the door open and stepped away from the entryway. "Faye is perfectly fine. I would like to help your village. I came to see if you have a ruling court."

Deni lowered her gaze, flattening her back into the wall. "We don't have anything to give, my lady."

"No," Faye said, holding her hand up. "I'm not here to take anything. I want to keep your village safe. We want to install healers."

The woman's doe eyes softened, stepping closer as she said, "Like Alexander."

Faye smiled brightly. "Yes. Exactly. We want to do that for all the villages."

The woman took another step forward and peered through the door. "Is that really the Shadow Prince? You're his queen, miss?"

Miss was better than lady. *Small steps,* Faye reminded herself. "We're partners. He's helping me keep the villages safe. We're stopping at all the villages to take inventory of what's needed. How many families are here?"

Deni became more comfortable as she spoke of the families that inhabited her village. The healer coaxed some of the others out. Faye observed, taking notes in a small journal of the number of people who lived in each home, the amenities they were afforded, the food available to them, and how many children resided here. The people warmed up to Faye but remained skittish around Rune. She sighed. I *should have had him wear something normal.*

The next village, Briar Grove, fled at the first sight of Rune. By the fourth, she'd given up trying to introduce him. Thirty centuries of reputation wouldn't be overwritten in a day.

Faye leaned against Rune as she watched the scenery pass by. The sunset streamed oranges and golds over the sky. Another day slipped away from her. The passing hours constantly reminded her Rune would remain the same, and she would age.

She shifted beside him, pushing the thought away. She wiggled into a more comfortable spot and said, "I didn't think these visits would be so tiring."

Rune ran his fingers through her hair. "You carried yourself well."

She narrowed her eyes as the field they passed turned red. She'd never seen flowers like these. Clusters of smaller red flowers balled at the top of long green stalks with long crimson whiskers arched past them.

"What are those?" she asked.

"Spider lilies."

An interesting name. Turning her attention to the multi-story country house with a cozy white wraparound porch facing the field of flowers. Faye searched their surroundings and found no other houses. This home stood silently alone among the spider lilies. Faye turned toward Rune, and he answered her unspoken question.

"This is Alister's home."

Seven

The mention of Alister's name riddled Faye with tension. She'd spent hours preparing to see him again. The sharp steel of his blade dragged across her mind, burning the side of her neck where it had once been. Alister couldn't penetrate her shield. He couldn't hurt her—*he couldn't*. But the memories lingered. Choking the air from her lungs, burning like the frigid water he forced her beneath.

The coach turned the corner, and Faye's gaze tracked the front door as they came to a stop. Slow breaths passed her lips, attempting to calm her racing heart.

Rune leaned toward her, bringing her hand to his lips. His kiss warmed the night chill from her hand. "You are safe. Nothing will harm you," Rune murmured.

Her vampire would kill his brother if Alister came for her, and the truth stung her heart. Rune's family was splintered by his past.

A shadow cast over his life, concealing the future Faye desperately wanted with him.

The door opened, and Alister stepped out toward Rune. "Brother," Alister grated, his deep voice filled with gravel. His pale stare fixed on her next, and she flinched. "Faye." A muscle ticked in his jaw as his gaze returned to Rune.

The coachman opened the door to their carriage. Rune exited first and helped Faye down.

She took a deep breath and swallowed. Her heart thundered as she fought the urge to shrink behind Rune. *Look at the bigger picture,* Faye reminded herself. Peace was worth her fear and discomfort. But it couldn't compare to Alister's in Rune's presence. She studied the man shrouded beneath the shining anger he wore like armor.

In contrast to her vampire's finery, Alister wore plain clothing. They would be considered fine by Anarian standards, but nothing she would see in Necromia. His long white-blonde hair was tied with a strap of leather behind him. He wasn't as terrifying without his three swords. Though Faye was positive his weapons were close by.

Alister stepped back into his home, gripping the door until his nailbeds went white. "You must be tired from your travels."

Hesitation sank its claws through Faye's heart, halting her from entering Alister's home. The enclosed space felt more like a trap than an invitation. Rune took a subtle step forward and laced his fingers through hers. He guided her to his side until he stood between them, acting as a barrier.

Faye's breaths grew shallow as they followed Alister through a small foyer into a larger living room. His furnishings were simple, giving his home a warm, lived-in feel. Alister's wife sat in the middle of a settee. Faye's chest constricted when she caught sight of Prinia. Her vacant, clouded gaze stared into nothing. There was no hint of emotion, no light behind the murky film coloring her dull eggshell eyes.

Her malady rested at Rune's doorstep. Faye held everything she'd longed for while Prinia and Alister suffered. Guilt gnawed at her, coloring her love for Rune in a painful light. If Faye had been brave enough to pursue her heart, it might have been her body sitting empty-eyed instead of Prinia. Fate and circumstance separated their situations, trading one brother for the other.

Faye wouldn't abandon her to fate.

Alister narrowed his similarly pale-blue eyes at her coat but didn't remark on it. He gestured to a pair of chairs opposite of Prinia and took his seat beside his wife. He and Rune looked so much alike. She searched for differences between them and found nothing discernable. They mirrored each other perfectly, save for their demeanor. Rune wore a cold mask of neutrality while restrained fury roiled beneath the surface in Alister. It glimmered in his face, bordering hatred. His day-blood soul shard twisted with his rising emotions.

He stiffly poured himself a glass of wine from the pastries and refreshments on the low table between them. He placed it at the oak edge, making no move to drink it. Glancing between them, his gaze settled on Rune once more. He made a fist, then splayed his fingers out before repeating the motion, the cracks of his bones echoing. "It is… difficult having you here."

"Neither of us trusts the other with our chosen," Rune said, wasting no time with his answer.

Faye shot Rune a glance, but he continued to glare at his brother. *Rune*, she hissed into his mind. This wasn't the way to peace.

"He dragged a sword across your throat," he said out loud.

Faye's hand lifted at the memory, and she stopped midway before reaching her neck. She pressed her nail into the pad of her thumb, refusing to run her fingers over the column of her neck to assure herself she was uninjured.

She wet her lip and met Alister's rage-filled gaze. "You've wronged each other, but you're family. Doesn't it count for something? Can we agree to start over?" Faye asked, her voice a steady contrast to the trembling dread creeping through her mind.

Their deafening silence filled the room. Her fear gave way to irritation, which morphed into frustrated anger as the moments passed with each beat of Faye's heart. The two of them were so fixated on their animosity for the other. Concerning themselves with repaying the other's pain rather than correcting their wrongs.

"Darkness, tell me you're not as old and stubborn as he is," Faye bit out. Her growing impatience made her bold.

"A family trait, I'm afraid." Alister answered coldly.

Faye selected a pastry topped with thinly sliced strawberries, muttering, "I prefer Jareth to the both of you."

"You would be hard pressed in your pursuit." The corner of

Rune's mouth lifted when she turned his way. "My younger brother favors males."

She paused glaring at Rune's sarcasm. "I wouldn't mind sharing one with him, but fate saddled me with a vampire as stubborn as he is old," Faye grumbled, before taking a bite.

Alister chuckled. The sound was so much like Rune it shook Faye from her anger.

She set the tart down on a small plate. Centuries of wrongs wouldn't be overwritten with a visit and a promise. *Change takes time,* she reminded herself. She only hoped the strain between them would ease once she healed Prinia. "I would like to visit and read to her. If I become a familiar voice, she might listen when I call for her in Chaos."

Alister turned away, taking a breath. His features softened as he took Prinia's hand. He spoke softly, keeping his focus on his wife. "I read to her often. I'm not sure if it reaches her."

The anguish in his eyes pierced her apprehension, slicing to her heart. "Tell me about her. How'd you two meet? I avoided Necromia before I carried my shard. I still do," Faye confessed.

Alister returned Prinia's hand, folding them in her lap. He carefully tucked a strand of hair behind her ear and said, "I oversaw most of the court's correspondence and petitions when Belind ruled."

"Did she ask you to help in Anaria?" Was the high bitch's mother a true Queen and loved all her people? Hope bloomed within Faye, misting over the chill beneath her skin.

"Belind involved the court if the complaint warranted her intervention. I reviewed them and distributed the documents to the ruling Queens in the corresponding cities. A few petitions came from Anaria. They were simple things." Alister glanced at his day-blood shard. "I assisted in their villages, helping rebuild homes. Laying traps for the dark-bloods who would prey on them."

"I met Prinia when I was rebuilding her father's roof." Alister smiled faintly. "She made me lemonade every day."

Faye's lips parted. He helped Anarians? The same man who lifted her by her hair and slid his cold blade across her neck. She couldn't imagine a day-blood showing up in Alexander, let alone helping them. She hated to admit it, but she would have avoided him. Distrusting his intentions for the very shards he wore.

Prinia approached him with... lemonade?

Faye glanced at his motionless bride, imagining Prinia bringing him a cool drink as he climbed his ladder. "That must have been some lemonade."

The sides of his eyes crinkled, and the sneer he addressed Rune with softened into equal parts of happiness and sorrow. "It was terrible. The most awful concoction I've ever had." Alister glanced at his wife. "I finished with her village after two weeks and found myself looking for other things to do there, in order to keep her company. I made any excuse to return and see her again."

She slowly blinked her large vacant eyes as he said, "I couldn't take my mind off her."

Faye would have her village be among the first she and Rune repaired. Prinia would want to see her home even if it changed after all this time.

Her chest tightened as she asked, "Where is she from? Does she have relatives?" Generations would separate her, but she would want to be reunited with her family.

The light in Alister's pale blue eyes faded. "She's an only child. Her parents returned to the Darkness long ago. Her village no longer exists."

Faye's heart ached for stripping him of his pleasant memories. "Is there anything that could reach her? Even a small reaction?"

He looked to the assortment of beverages. Moments ticked by in silence, and Faye couldn't help but wonder if he silently wished for another glass of Prinia's lemonade.

"She closes her eyes when she feeds. I don't know if it's a response or something all vampires do." Alister glanced accusingly at Rune.

Blood was critical to her mate. "Blood might be the best way to reach her."

"No," Rune grated, squeezing her hand. "She may seize upon you."

"She doesn't seize." Alister's voice roughened, becoming more gravel filled with his rage. Any ground Faye gained with him vanished as his attention settled on Rune.

"Apologies—"

"Shut up." The brothers glowered at each other. "I know you.

You say *apologies* when you're insincere. *I am sorry* when you are." Alister said, mimicking his brother's marked accent.

Rune swallowed. His lips parted but immediately closed. He turned his head a fraction as veined misted shadows stretched beneath his gaze. Arguing with Voshki, Faye gathered. After a time, he exhaled and admitted, "I am uncertain of Faye's mortality."

"Prin isn't going to attack her." Alister dismissed Rune with a look of disgust. "Her fangs don't drop. She doesn't bite. I cut my wrist and bring it to her lips. She drinks like you do when you're unconscious."

"Stop fighting. We all want the same thing." Faye bit out. She squeezed Rune's hand. "Blood is the best way to reach her."

"This is unwise," Rune grated.

"Trust me," Faye whispered. This had to work. It was her only opportunity to mend the cracks between them. At his nod, she turned to Alister. "What do I do?"

"Sit beside Prinia," Alister said as he called a small knife, outstretching his hand. Faye tensed, her breath locking in her throat. She blinked, willing herself to calm, while realizing his mannerism was identical to Rune's. Alister frightened her. Prinia was nothing but a victim of her vampire's mistakes.

She glanced down at the pastries, searching for courage. "Can you leave the knife there? I'm not ready to be at arm's reach."

Alister stood, shifting his attention to Rune before his gaze returned to her. "He stays there."

"You are mistaken if you believe I need proximity to kill you," Rune growled, his eyes flooding black, like ink through water, before the pale blue returned.

Faye stood and brought her hand to her consort's face. "Stop," she said gently. When he turned toward her, she added, "Please."

He closed his eyes and took a breath. The veined shadows beneath his gaze receded.

Moving to stand beside Prinia, she kept an equal distance between her and Alister as he walked to the edge of the couch.

Faye took the knife and winced as the blade nicked her skin. A thin trail of red welled across her wrist. She looked to Rune, who nodded, and brought her wrist to Prinia's mouth.

Her large eyes slid closed as she exhaled, akin to a sigh. The warmth of her mouth pressed onto Faye's wrist. Each pull brought a soft scrape over her skin, followed by a touch of her tongue. Prinia's teeth were surprisingly dull, without a hint of fangs.

Faye glanced at her vampire. Tension riddled him, but to his credit, he remained seated. She smiled at him reassuringly. "She's not biting."

Prinia's sickly complexion faded with each swallow. Her skin brightened, illuminating from within. A bright pink blush colored her cheeks.

Alister leaned closer but didn't approach. "I've never seen her like this."

Rune leaned back in his chair, setting his ankle over his knee. "She should always look as she does now. I gave her my blood that night because she looked starved. You need to feed her darker blood, brother."

"You will not touch her," Alister growled.

Silence stretched between them, and Faye wondered if their pissing match would continue after she returned Prinia to her body. She prayed not.

"Draw your power to you. Housing it within yourself will charge your blood, making it more potent," Rune said idly.

Faye nodded, feeling her reserve far below her. Her magic was sluggish to answer. Disobedient and lazy as she dragged her dead weight higher.

"The two of you should be on guard with Lyssa." Alister looked away, slipping his hands into his pockets. He quietly scrutinized the flower arrangement at the center of a long rectangular table beneath a picture window.

Faye gently moved her wrist away, and Prinia went still, opening her eyes. She was pretty before, but with these new changes, she was breathtaking. Her fawn-colored hair seemed thicker, taking on a glossy shine. The pink color on her cheeks bloomed over her full lips.

She returned to Rune's side as Alister took his place at Prinia's. He placed his finger under her chin, tenderly lifting her head to look at him. His lips parted, and hurt hardened his eyes but quickly faded to an empty sadness. He released her, and she lowered her chin to stare straight ahead.

"Lyssa pointed you out at the Artithian Princess's wedding,"

Alister said, meeting Faye. "When I failed to kill you, she suggested I request your formal acknowledgment."

That fucking bitch. The High Queen wanted Rune and maneuvered others as weapons. Faye's power coiled with her emotions. It woke, coming to life as tendrils of power rose from it, searching for an outlet. For prey.

Faye shoved the urges away, burying them. The violent impulses pulsed beneath her skin, burning away the lingering icy waters. She rejected them, freezing over her veins as she struggled for a fragile ounce of control. This power was hers, and she would learn to harness it, mold it. She wouldn't allow it to use her.

"Thank you," was all Rune offered as he healed her wrist.

"I'll work to bring her back to you," Faye promised.

"If you bring her back to me, I will be in your debt and at your disposal," Alister replied.

His words were touching, but it was her and Rune who were indebted to him. Her mate wronged him terribly, and she couldn't begin her life with Rune if this remained broken. "I do this because we're family."

Alister's look softened by degrees. "I'm honored."

"Save the pretty words until after you have met her harpy sister," Rune said with an arched brow.

Alister smiled at Rune, and her mate's eyes widened for the briefest moment. "I will love anyone who brings you discomfort."

Rune raised his chin at Prinia. "She will be strong when she wakes."

Alister trailed his fingers through her hair. "I just want her to wake."

Faye took the opportunity to reach for Prinia's mind, unnerved by the abyss meeting her. Her own awareness was minuscule by comparison. Faye's breath hitched as she glimpsed into the fathomless sea occupying Prinia's consciousness. Deep blue faded into black, obscuring its waters and dangers.

Faye swallowed and sent a thought into the ever-expansive emptiness, spearing it into those hidden depths.

I know you're in there. I'm going to bring you home.

Eight

Faye groaned, tightly closing her eyes as Rune slipped from their bed. The shower started moments later, disrupting her sleep further. The man woke too early and kept her up entirely too late. She grumbled a second time even louder to make sure he heard her annoyance and rolled over to clutch his pillow. They'd spent the past week visiting every village in Anaria on their list after visiting Prinia. Rune drafted and submitted the necessary documents. In a few days' time, she would stand before the High Council on the platform called The Eyes and petition for Anaria. She sighed, wiggling into a comfortable position. Faye let the sound of falling water slip into the background. Her breathing became even as Hell's twilight blanketed her.

The bed shifted, and Faye's brows pinched. She cracked her lids to find Rune sitting beside her. The cut of his court-tailored suit molded over the powerful body concealed beneath it. "Shall I run you a bath?"

She smiled, caressed by his deep, accented voice. Faye arched her back, stretching her arms over her head. "No. I'm getting up. Damian has been hounding me to start training again. I'll meet him at seven."

The corner of his mouth lifted. "It is nearly nine, vsenia."

"What?" Faye sat up and rubbed the exhaustion from her eyes. "Damian's going to kill me." He would expect her to run extra laps for missing his morning session.

Touring Anaria and her nightmares left her exhausted. The days were strung together, and the strain began to feel normal, oddly enough. With her tours finished, she wondered how much longer the nightmares would continue plaguing her. Their severity began to fade, and slowly she'd been able to get back to sleep wrapped between Rune and Voshki. She longed for a morning she could wake feeling rested and fresh.

The strap of her nightgown slipped off her shoulder. Rune brushed the back of his finger over her collarbone, gliding his touch to the fallen lace. Faye closed her eyes as his hand slipped under her strap, straightening the garment.

"I have noticed you stopped drinking your contraceptive tea."

Heat spread over Faye's cheeks. She had forgotten to take it a few times, blaming the vile hour of the morning she'd been forced to rise. "I was going to bring it up after things settled with your brother and the High Council. But you're too attentive," she said, patting the side of his face.

"I could stop drinking my tea. It is rather bitter." Rune chuckled. "You desire young. There are healers who assist with things… taking root."

Faye leaned forward, brushing her lips over his in a feather light kiss. "Stop calling them young. They're children."

"Forgive me," he rasped, leaning closer.

"We could do things naturally and see if you can get things to take root on your own." Faye laughed.

Rune caressed the side of her face, threading his fingers through her hair. He pulled her in, and Faye closed her eyes, melting for him. His thumb smoothed under her jaw, lifting her chin. He kissed her deeply and thoroughly with slow, languid strokes.

He pulled back a moment before she was going to tug him into bed with her. By his sly expression, the dick knew it too.

"You need to be fed before I... How did the blonde harpy put it? Ah, yes. Before I tie you to the bed and ravage you." He brushed the side of his face against hers. A light animalistic caress.

"Or... we could spend the morning alone. You could ravage your queen, and I'll have breakfast while I soak in the bath my loving, *devoted* consort draws for me." Faye brushed her hair past her shoulder and turned, offering him her throat.

He purred, drawing her against him. His cock pressed against her thigh, long and hard. His warm breath fanned over the side of her neck as he groaned, "And how would my queen wish to be ravaged?"

"I'm sure my attentive male will think of something."

Rune grazed his fangs along her throat, taking in her scent. His night breeze through plum blossoms. Faye arched her back, wrapping her legs around his waist. Rune groaned, detecting notes of her arousal. This wouldn't do. He needed her wetter.

Desperate for him.

A breathy sigh slipped past her lips as he palmed the back of her thigh, caressing lower. Rune gathered her night gown and drew the satin she wore beneath it down her thighs.

The Ra'Voshnik prowled through his mind, brushing the surface to view their queen through his eyes. It waited in silence, knowing the act bought the creature the same courtesy when it was with their queen.

An unspoken bargain Rune favored.

He hooked the back of Faye's knee and dragged her to the edge of the bed with a growl. The little startled breath she gasped hardened him even further. Vampiric instinct commanded he pin her and ruthlessly drive his cock into her wet heat. Fuck her hard, demanding her surrender and her throat.

Rune gnashed his teeth. "Spread your legs for me," he rasped before lowering himself to his knees.

Faye smoothed her foot into the front of his jacket. She propped herself up with an elbow, pushing his jacket over his shoulder. "You're overdressed."

"Noted," Rune replied before roughly stripping it off.

She dragged her heel up his back, untucking his shirt, and laid back in silent invitation. Rune closed his eyes, brushing the side of his face over her inner thigh. A soft purr rumbled from him.

Her body was his home. Her mind his haven. Each moment with the dark queen fate gifted him only deepened the depth of his devotion. Intensifying until his existence before her faded into a pale shadow.

He parted her gently, coating his tongue in her sweet desire. She moaned, drawing her legs together. Possessive instinct silenced his thoughts, demanding he trap his prey beneath him. Rune growled, capturing her thighs. He would spread her wide and take his time with her. Teasing her clit and fucking her with his tongue until she begged for his cock.

Faye's hand tangled in his hair as he kissed and licked her delicate flesh. She rolled her hips into him each time he drew her clit between his lips. Panted when he purred, tonguing it until he drove her to the very edge of her pleasure.

He eased the pressure, smiling as her hand fisted into his hair. She lifted her hips and pulled him lower.

"Rune, please," Faye begged. He kissed her, refusing the friction she demanded. He closed his eyes, licking through her folds. Darkness, he would never tire of the breathy way she cried his name. The desperation to come.

Faye shuddered when he flicked the tip of his tongue over her clit. She made an exasperated sound, he cataloged as a growl, and yanked his hair harder. "I'm going to tie you up and edge the fuck out of you."

Rune purred again, pressing just where she needed him.

For a moment.

He kissed her and met her lightning-streaked midnight gaze. "Hardly a threat when you do it so often, vsenia."

Faye's hand slipped to the side of his face, her fingertip brushing over his mouth. Rune parted his lips, showing her what he could be doing.

"You're not playing fair," she breathed, before pressing the pad of her finger to the point of his fang.

Her blood was exquisite, dark, and rich, laced with raw power. It electrified his senses, narrowing his focus until she was the sole occupant of his world.

"Be still, and I will make you come harder than you ever have," Rune murmured. Faye tensed as he bared his fangs. He paused for a moment, reassuring her. "This will not pain you. Trust me, vsenia."

His queen relaxed beneath his touch. A quiet response to his statement. He spread her, drawing her clit between his lips while lashing her with his tongue.

"Rune," she cried, grasping the gray silken sheets on either side of her.

Come for me, he crooned through her mind. The tip of his fang pricked where he knew she was most sensitive.

Faye's back bowed, and a strangled cry tore from her sweet lips.

Rune licked and sucked, purring against her. He drew out her orgasm, intoxicated by her blood mixed with her arousal. The rhythm of her heart, her breathing, the way she strained against his hold as each wave of pleasure crested over her. His queen had yet to experience what a fully trained male was capable of. Rune smiled to himself.

It was time he educated her.

She trembled as he reached beneath her nightgown. He palmed her breast, squeezing as he tugged and pinched her nipple. He drove her pleasure. Each touch curated and intentional.

Faye tensed as her next orgasm crashed through her. Rune devoured her, savoring every sound she made. The pad of his thumb sliding over her entrance, monitoring the intimate flutters of her pleasure.

Darkness, the way she would feel around his cock. Rune lifted his gaze, wanting to see her. Watch her come apart beneath his mouth.

His queen stole his breath with flushed, sweat slick skin. Beautiful. She drew a sharp breath but didn't exhale.

Rune roughened his purr, pressing two fingers into her. Her mouth opened in a silent cry while she tremored beneath his touch. He stroked into her deeper. Harder.

Breathe, vsenia.

Faye exhaled and drew a short, ragged breath.

Deeper, Rune instructed, speaking directly to her mind. He curled his fingers the way she liked, drawing out her release before repeating himself.

She moaned again and again.

Rune held his queen in her pleasure. His eyes slid closed as he lost himself, savoring her taste. He memorized every breathless cry and roll of her hips. The way her nails dug into his arm while she begged so sweetly.

He'd lost track of time when Faye dragged her heel up his back and pushed against his collarbone.

"I can't. Rune, please," Faye screamed.

He kissed her, tasting her one last time before he released her. Rune ran his hand over his mouth as Faye climbed into their bed. She lay on her side, drawing her knees up.

A purr rumbled from him at the sight of her wet, delicate flesh. Hardly a view to curb his aching need. Rune joined Faye, grasping her ankle, and straightened her leg before turning her on her stomach. He tucked her other leg beneath her to lift her ass for him.

Faye's arms were carelessly thrown above her. She looked peaceful with her head turned to the side. A serene expression painted across her quiet features. The rapid breaths through her parted lips betrayed her.

Rune unfastened his pants and groaned, pulling his cock free. His length throbbed as he leaned over her. He guided himself into her soft flesh, cursing in High Tongue as she stretched to take the head.

Their fingers intertwined, and Rune caged her beneath his body, thrusting as she took more of him. He gently brushed the side of his face against hers, taking her with long, deep strokes.

She turned her head up, meeting his lips on a desperate kiss as she arched her back. Rune chased his pleasure. Tension set through his shoulders and back. He fucked her harder, thrusting savagely. Growling in anticipation of his own release.

Faye dropped her shoulder, offering her throat, and he sank his fangs into the smooth column of her neck. Possession and need crashed within him, and Rune drove into her a final time, spending deep inside her. He groaned, releasing his bite. Pouring more of himself into Faye with each pulse of his cock.

I'll be expecting the same silence when I fuck her later tonight. The Ra'Voshnik's voice slipped through his mind like a falling ribbon.

Rune blinked, catching his breath. *I doubt she will need your affection this evening,* Rune replied.

A growl voiced the Ra'Voshnik's disagreement. His mind filled with thoughts of Faye writhing on the creature's cock and fangs. *She prefers me.*

Rune said nothing. He preferred focusing on her pleasure, finding it far easier to hold his instincts at bay if he wasn't inside her. He smiled as Faye drew their laced fingers to her lips.

"I love you," she said with a breathy sigh.

These small moments he shared with his queen branded his soul. Rune nuzzled the sensitive skin behind her ear as he whispered his devotion.

"I love you too, vsenia. Command me as you will."

Nine

Faye needed to begin her lessons on Familiar magic. She glanced at her vampire and asked, "Do you know where Sadi is?"

Rune tilted his head a fraction. "Everyone is in the great room having their midday meal by the sound of it."

"Right," Faye said, picking up a towel to dry her hair. "I'll pick at some fruit so Sparrow doesn't interrogate me." Her expression lightened as Rune straightened his jacket. "Are you ever going to wear normal clothes?" Faye asked as she struggled to close the pin at the top of her blouse.

"This is normal attire," he said, smoothing his lapel. "And sharing a meal with your consort. How scandalous. Allow me…" Rune turned her around as she held her hair. His fingertips brushed her neck as he closed the latch.

"Thank you." Faye's cheeks heated as they made their way to the others. "When has Sparrow ever not mentioned us doing something illicit?"

Hellfire lit the edge of his white-blonde hair as they passed the simple sconces lining the gray stone corridor. "Your sister's need to sexualize everything is a reflection of her nature, not yours."

Her blush deepened as memories of Rune holding her thighs apart surfaced through her mind. "But we *were*," she whispered.

Rune lifted a brow, and the corner of his mouth lifted. "Beside the point."

Faye shook her head lightly, taking a deep breath as she buried her indecent thoughts. Her court's voices carried into the Hall. Faye walked in to find Damian and Sadi sitting opposite Sparrow and Vashien. Her sister flashed a toothy grin, and Damian lifted his glass. "Missed you at breakfast, dove."

"Where've you been all day, bitch? I was about to break into your room," Sparrow grumbled.

"I slept in," Faye answered.

Sparrow snorted. "Slept in, huh? Is that what we're calling it now?"

Faye swallowed as Sadi looked her up and down. The Familiar lifted her chin and sniffed before her eyes set with tension.

"Darkness, woman," Vashien chided, thumping Sparrow with his membranous wing. "She's been awake—touring Anaria—while you're still snoring."

Can she smell what we did? Faye directed the thought to Rune's mind as she took her seat. She knew vampires had a keen sense of smell. Did Familiar?

A vial I added to your bath stripped my scent from you. A Familiar's sense of smell is more attuned to poisons than people, Rune answered as Sparrow leaned toward Vashien.

She ran her finger down the inside of his wing, where it met his back. Vashien's wing snapped back the next instant. "You're asking for it," he growled. Her sister dropped an elbow on the table and propped her head up before batting her lashes at him.

Rune spoke to her mind. *I am afraid the lack of my scent is also telling. However, I believe you prefer this option.*

I do, she answered back. Faye's cheeks flushed as Rune pulled out a chair. His schooled expression gave nothing away. She cleared her throat, and Vashien apologized. Faye glanced over the table for something light to nibble on. Chocolates shaped in orange slices were fanned in a circle over a small plate. She smiled, taking one. "Did Sparrow tell you I liked these?" Faye asked Rune as she bit her sweet.

Her sister wrinkled her nose. "Fuck, no. That shit is disgusting."

Damian laughed, lifting the small plate. "I brought them, dove. They're my kitten's favorite," he said, holding the chocolate oranges to Sadi.

The Familiar narrowed her eyes, smirking as she selected a piece. "Please have them. I don't mind sharing my belongings with you."

Faye's hand twitched as she finished her piece of chocolate. Sparrow snorted, rolling her eyes at her evil twin. Rune wasn't a belonging, and her consort was *not* Sadi's to share. Faye bit her tongue, refusing to acclimate to their twisted dark-blooded views of love. She didn't own Rune—Would never own him.

She loved him.

Sadi held the small plate of chocolates out to her with a coy smile. Faye gazed down at the sweets. As much as she hated to admit it, she needed the Familiar.

Faye reluctantly took another slice and said, "I've been visiting Prinia. When you have time, I'd like to start our lessons."

Since visiting Alister, Rune phased her to his home each evening. She let Prinia drink from her wrist and called into her mind, hoping she somehow heard her. So far, Prinia had only answered with a hollow stare.

Sadi admired her nails. "Do you want to begin with Familiar magic or healing?"

Faye bit the inside of her lip, considering for a moment. "Won't I need both to heal Prinia?"

Sadi shook her head, skewering another small cut of meat with the knife she used as a utensil. "Prinia's a vampire. Her body heals on its own. You'll need Familiar magic to bring her mind back to her body."

"I want to heal Prinia first."

Sadi laid the edge of her knife against her lower lip and smiled. "We'll go to the Hall of Empty Eyes in two days."

"You are beginning in the Hall?" Rune asked, concern darkened his voice.

Sadi sipped her honeyed wine. "It's where we all start." She looked at Faye. "You need to worship fate and be free of doubt in order to enter our temples."

Free of doubt. Familiar arrogance, Faye assumed. "How do you worship fate?"

Sadi drew her brow up and together, her beseeching eyes feigned a look of sympathy. "Familiar *serve* fate. Sight is the gift we receive for serving Chaos. We need to accept the path carved for us."

Sparrow snorted, pointing her fork at the Familiar. "So, let's say you know you'll die tomorrow. Or, better yet, Damian was going to die. You wouldn't save him?"

"My sweet kitten would save me," Damian crooned, grasping her throat. He leaned into her and stilled a moment before their lips touched.

Sadi gave a small laugh and spared him a habitual kiss before shaking off his hold. "I could hint at his path. Warn him. But altering his fate?" Sadi shook her head. "Twisting his path would impact every life he touches. Every life they touch in return. Consequences are an endless tie." Sadi cupped the side of Damian's face, running her thumb over his cheek. "And I would lose my Sight." She leaned closer, whispering against Damian's lips, "Your dick is good, but it's not that good."

Sparrow choked as Faye asked, "You can lose your Sight?"

"Sight is the reward for serving Chaos. When you no longer serve, she takes her power back." Sadi's midnight eyes gleamed with a passion Faye had never seen.

How did they trust and accept an intangible path? The entire concept of absolute faith was daunting. Faye wanted to believe they weren't tied into a predetermined life. That fate could be changed. If she needed to blindly accept the path carved before her, could she save Prinia?

"Do all Familiar serve Chaos?" she asked.

"No." Sadi laughed. "And fewer survive the initiation."

"But they never advertise who serves," Damian added. "It's more fun to leave people guessing."

Knowing that few Familiar were able to wield the magic their kind were notorious for eased Faye's mind a touch. This fact didn't make her evil twin any less dangerous. Sadi embodied everything the

Familiar were feared for. She reached into minds, imprisoned people in their own bodies, and happily forced them to relive their darkest fears.

"What's the initiation?" Faye asked, positive she wouldn't like the answer.

Sadi flicked her hand as though it were nothing. "Rune brought you through your Ceremony of Blood. Familiar who wish to serve Chaos complete our rite differently. Both ceremonies are scheduled on the same day. On our twentieth year, we request willing males or females to participate in our rite."

"Familiar just take volunteers." Sparrow stared dreamily at Sadi.

"Our rituals are sacred. You will not speak of this," she warned.

Sparrow sat up straighter and nodded.

The Familiar twirled her glass, sweeping the dark liquid to the lip of her fluted glass before stilling her hand. "We invoke our blood and select the partners who will breach us."

"Partners?" Sparrow leaned forward as her green eyes gleamed, nearly falling from her seat.

Sadi shrugged. "Familiar take multiple partners often."

Sparrow glanced at Damian. He arched a brow as he drank his coffee. "Want to join our bed, dove?"

Faye tensed. Was he serious? At his words, her sister immediately looked to Vashien.

He didn't even glance up from his meal, mumbling into his plate, "She looks exactly like your sister, no."

Sparrow's shoulders fell as she turned her attention back to Sadi. "Multiple partners would help hold you above the Darkness. Like how we all helped Runey hold Faye."

Sadi laughed over her glass of sweet wine. "We don't hold them above the Darkness," she said, pressing her hand to her chest. "You embrace fate and plummet?"

Faye paled. They let their women plummet. Now she understood why Familiar were largely thought of as insane. Their rituals were madness. It was a wonder any of them survived. Her rite nearly killed Rune, and he'd been prepared.

"How do you stop?" Sparrow asked.

Faye peered at her sister. It was a rare occurrence for Sparrow to be more interested in conversation than food.

"Accepting fate opens Chaos to us. We receive Sight and an altered version of magic. It slows our decent, and we rise to our physical bodies." Sadi's hair and clothing began to float and sway around. "Our magic is unlike yours. We touch the intangible, see the past, and weave the future."

"And after the rite is completed, we have an orgy to celebrate," Damian interjected.

Faye pinched the stem of her glass, slowly turning it. She didn't remember her fall, but she was positive she didn't embrace fate and dive freely. Why would Chaos gift her with Familiar magic when she wasn't one?

"I'm through my rite. How will I prove I accept fate?" Faye needed this magic to heal Prinia and erase the debt darkening her life with Rune.

Sadi rapped the metal claw of her articulated ring on the table. "You'll need to enter the Hall of Empty Eyes."

Damian visibly shuddered. "Best of luck to you, dove. Never catch me in there."

"What's the Hall of Empty Eyes?" Sparrow asked.

"A temple," was all Sadi would say.

Ten

Sparrow ushered Faye away from him for *girl-talk* after their midday meal, and Rune returned to his study. He took a seat, reaching for the last book in the latest set of bone-bleached volumes he borrowed from Morbid's library.

Hours passed, and he closed the book. His concentration suffered as Sadi's words echoed in his mind. She was a gifted Familiar who worshiped fate and regularly visited the Hall of Empty Eyes. Her visions guided Belind's court in times of war, and he depended on her insight.

Trusted her.

So why did this gnawing worry fester in his chest when he thought of Faye accompanying Sadi into the Hall of Empty Eyes?

Because few who enter Chaos ever leave, and we can't reach her if she is in their temples, the Ra'Voshnik growled through his mind. *We need to go with her.*

Rune exhaled. He'd never seen their temples. His travels through the strange realm were isolated to Morbid's home and more recently an odd library. The Familiar King didn't close his realm in the same manner Rune did. Morbid permitted travel into Chaos, but when the coach companies requested guides for Chaos, he'd laughed, offering no assistance. Phasing was limited to places individuals had visited previously, leaving Familiar as the only ones capable of bringing people in.

And their guests seldom left.

I don't trust that fucking cat with my queen, the Ra'Voshnik bit out. *If she hurts Faye—*

"She will not," Rune answered aloud.

Compulsive hostility bled through Rune's mind. *We both know Familiar die attempting rituals in hopes of entering their temples. What do you think will happen if an uninitiated mind walks through their doors? This will be the price.*

The creature offered him an illusion of Faye. Her lightning-streaked midnight eyes clouded and vacant.

Rune's fangs lengthened, and he banished the image. Rage feeding from the memory of his brother attempting to drown Faye in a coffin too close in his mind. He couldn't lose her. Not after he'd spent his life wishing for her. Rune's power thrummed beneath the surface, needing to obliterate the threat to his queen.

Yes, kill her, the Ra'Voshnik ground out. If Sadi was dead, she couldn't escort Faye anywhere.

Darkness, there was something wrong with him. The protective rancor stinging his mind aligned with the creature's flawed logic. Rune scrubbed his hand over his mouth, needing his queen's presence to ground his mind.

He stood, mentally reaching for Hell. It answered, divulging Faye's location. His queen was in the private gardens housing the medicinal herbs he'd brought to Hell all those months ago.

Rune phased, strolling through the crystalline courtyard. He made his way to the wrought iron gate leading to the grounds Faye claimed as her own.

A cool night met him as he stepped over the threshold and into the outer gardens. Unlike his ever-twilight plane, the small patch of Necromia his father wove into Hell followed its realm's time and seasons. Fall would soon give way to winter.

Small balls of hellfire illuminated the space in a blue hue. He'd installed the stone lanterns to counteract Faye's poor night vision. The sweet scent of black roses lent their fragrance to the evening air. The manicured plants were pleasant but didn't compare to his night breeze.

He followed the walkway to Faye's inner sanctuary. The tightness constricting over his chest eased when he spotted her, and the Ra'Voshnik purred. She was here.

Safe.

His queen sat with her back to him beside her garden, wrapped in a fluffy blanket. Rune cleared his throat, announcing his approach. Faye turned toward him. Her soft smile didn't reach her eyes, and she quietly turned her attention back to her garden.

Rune took a seat behind her, needing her closeness. He rested an arm over his bent knee and peered over her shoulder, searching for the dead plant souring his queen's mood. Nothing was amiss. He canted his head, glancing lower at the harvesting basket on her lap.

Empty.

"You look troubled," he said gently.

She turned to her side and leaned against him. Rune held her close, offering her unspoken comfort. Her silence sank its claws into his chest, burrowing deeper with each passing moment.

"Speak with me," Rune murmured before pressing a kiss to her hair. "Have your nightmares returned?"

The dreams disturbed her sleep, but thankfully, she no longer woke to icy skin and frosted glass. The creature disagreed with Rune's assessment, focusing on a more recent point of tension.

We should take Anaria for her, the Ra'Voshnik whispered through his mind as a lover would. Imaginings of Lyssa driven to her knees before their queen filled his mind.

Rune dismissed the creature's fantasies, and he lifted Faye onto his lap.

She reached under his jacket, smoothing her hand over his side. Another beat of silence passed before she breathed, "I'm afraid."

"You have nothing to fear. I will not allow harm to come your way," Rune vowed. He would decimate those who endangered his queen.

Faye shook her head, pushing off his chest. Turmoil stormed in her lightning-streaked midnight eyes. "I'm afraid I won't be able to reach Prinia."

Guilt hollowed a pit in his soul. Faye carried the atrocities he committed, suffocating under the weight. She was too kind. Soft. He clasped the back of her neck. His eyes closed as he leaned forward until their foreheads touched. "It will take time, vsenia."

A small laugh escaped her lips, but the sound was filled with sorrow, abrading his soul. "Time is something I don't have. How can I have a life with you—a family, while Prinia is lost?"

His heart sank with her pain. Rune gently swept the moisture from her lashes. "We will have an eternity, one way or another."

He desperately wanted her immortality to sit, making her undying. Immortals approaching their prime commonly injured themselves in some small way. A small cut on the forearm or thigh. Immortality was accompanied by accelerated healing. Their injury healed within a few hours, signaling their bodies had ceased aging, preserved for eternity.

He prayed to the Darkness for Faye's immortality. But if this wasn't their fate, he would worship her until the Darkness took her and awaited her return.

She will be immortal, the Ra'Voshnik growled. *Nothing will take her from me.*

Rune pulled Faye closer, holding her against him. "I am sorry." Simple words wouldn't repair the chasm his wrongs left on Faye's heart. He'd tarnished the love she offered so freely with arrogance and pride. "I am unable to make this right. It pains me to see you shoulder my misdeeds."

"We'll get through this together," Faye said, hugging his arm to her chest. "Do you know anything about The Hall of Empty Eyes?"

"Familiar are a secretive race. I know The Hall is where Familiar go to receive visions… and many Familiar die attempting the ritual granting them entry. My knowledge beyond that is limited," Rune explained.

Faye glanced up at him. "Morbid's part of your court. You haven't been to Chaos?"

He chuckled as his hand settled on her hip. "The extent of my travels through the Familiar realm is Morbid's home and, more recently, a library."

She narrowed her eyes. "Never visited Sadi's house?"

The Ra'Voshnik growled, brushing the surface of his awareness. Faye's gaze lowered a fraction, watching the veined misted shadows stretch beneath his pale eyes.

"No," Rune answered. "She resides in her father's manor and has rooms in Lyssa's estate as well as my own."

Faye dropped his gaze as her expression soured. He leaned closer, brushing his thumb along her jaw as his fingers threaded into her dark hair. Rune was no fool. It was plain to see Sadi's presence weighed on his queen. How could he explain knowing and trusting were not the same as wanting. In seventeen centuries, he'd depended on Sadi, relied on her visions, gone to war countless times with her at his side, but he never desired her.

Never wanted. Anyone.

Not until he caught the scent of his dark queen. His night breeze through plum blossoms. In those first moments, a flame bloomed in him. He'd been strung taut, desperate in his search for her.

Darkness, she'd made his fangs ache, and he'd merely scented her.

How could he convey an eternity of unanswered yearning? The bitter ashes left in his mouth after lifetimes of watching those around him find comfort and passion while he felt nothing. His queen had little use for words. However, he hoped his actions would eventually convince her.

"You are the only woman I have ever pursued with intent. There is only you, vsenia. Now and always."

Faye leaned into him, and Rune purred at the soft touch of her lips. He whispered to her, welling his reverence and devotion.

"I am yours. Command me as you will."

Eleven

Hellfire crackled in the hearth, softly illuminating the den in its blue glow. Faye leaned on the armrest with her legs tucked underneath her, reading the latest erotic romance by her favorite Familiar author. She turned the page, smiling as the main character seductively bit into an apple and drove her love interest out of his mind. She often read to distract herself. Her latest anxiety: lessons with Sadi. And while her evil twin didn't often shake her confidence, this time was different.

Movement pulled Faye's attention from her book. Her sister sprawled over her chair and kicked her feet. Her blonde curls cascaded over one armrest with her knees bent over the other. Sparrow clicked her nails together as she steepled her fingers.

"I should go with you," Sparrow said quietly before meeting Faye's gaze.

"I'm reading," Faye said, frowning and closing the book on her finger. Sparrow widened her eyes at her, and Faye shook her head. "I'm lucky she's taking *me*, hooker. She's not going to take you."

"Bitch, I'm a Familiar. I'm allowed in Chaos," Sparrow insisted. When Faye didn't respond, she added, "She's in love with your man. You need someone watching your back."

She sighed at her sister's uncharacteristically serious tone, eyeing the cover of her book. Her relationship with Sadi was tenuous at best. At first, she looked forward to expanding the family she'd found through her court. She foolishly believed Sadi helping her form her court and incapacitating Alister meant they had found some common ground to build a friendship.

Her evil twin remained clipped and aloof, making it painfully evident she only tolerated her existence beside Rune. She knew Rune had no romantic interest in Sadi, but her sister's words drove her to reconsider.

Not her mate, but the Familiar who would teach her how to wield this foreign magic.

Faye cut a glance at her sister, pushing her suspicions aside. "Don't be a bitch, there isn't a way around this. I need her."

She wanted Prinia restored. Needed it. She hid the truth, burying it deep. Alister and Prinia were trapped in an unending cycle. Guilt gnawed on a piece of Faye's heart. Reopening her raw, bleeding wound when she imagined her life and family with Rune. Only to recall the part he played in Alister's misery.

The sound of Sadi's heels entered the room before she sauntered in with Damian behind her. Her tulle and black silk barely covered her ass. And her corset looked uncomfortably tight.

"Where do you buy your whore couture?" Sparrow remarked as she folded her hands.

Sadi looked down at herself and dusted the lace of her plunging neckline before lifting her gaze. "From a designer who wouldn't waste their time on you."

Sparrow snorted, rolling her eyes, and Damian slipped his arm over Sadi's hip. He pulled her close and rasped, "Now, now. Play nice, kitten."

Sadi momentarily curled her lip to hiss at him.

"I want to go with Faye," Sparrow blurted out as she righted herself.

Sadi strolled to a sitting table decorated with an arrangement of black roses. She breathed in the sweet bouquet before turning to Sparrow. "No."

Faye knew Sadi would never allow her sister to accompany her, but it stung. Abandoning her book, Faye swallowed and got to her feet. She glanced at Damian and asked, "Are you coming with us?" *Please be coming with us.*

Sadi laughed, returning to Damian's side. She scratched her nails over his dark stubble, staring lovingly into his molten silver eyes. "The empty-eyed vessels would tear you to pieces."

A chill skated down Faye's spine. *The empty what?*

"I fight real opponents," Damian purred to Sadi. He turned, leaning back on his heel. "You, chickadee, are training."

"*Spaaa*-Row," her sister answered, dragging out the syllables of her name.

He shrugged with an arrogant grin. "They're both small fat birds. Same thing."

"I'm about to fuck your life," Sparrow said before leaping to her feet.

Faye laughed until Sadi's midnight eyes met hers. She paled, silently hoping the Familiar wasn't rifling through her thoughts at this exact moment. Her evil twin's plum-colored lips curled into a knowing smile, and she outstretched her hand.

"Chaos is waiting."

Faye inhaled sharply at her first glimpse of Chaos. Thunder crashed overhead as arcs of lightning sang through heavy, gray storm clouds.

A simple, solitary building stood tall and thin against the churning sky. Its large double doors monopolized the face of the building, the side of it spanning back no more than twenty feet. Faye took in her desolate surroundings: a lack of vegetation, uneven ground, and the strangest rocks she'd ever seen. Her chest tightened as she realized *what* she stood on. Bones covered the ground. Bile rose in her throat.

"Don't worry, the rain never falls," Sadi said, strolling toward the temple.

She took in a deep breath, willing her stomach to unknot. "Why is the ground covered in bones?"

Sadi turned gracefully and shifted the remains littering the ground with the toe of her boot. "Why is the ground in Hell crystal?"

"Are these the people who didn't survive their initiation?" Faye regretted asking the question the moment it left her mouth. She didn't want to know.

Sadi laughed. "Darkness, no. Chaos is ever changing. We have few constants." Sadi waved her hands around as she said, "The sky, our temples, and the bones. Everything else will change each time you visit."

Faye stared out over the macabre landscape. *These weren't real bones*, Faye reminded herself. A snap crunched beneath her feet, and she glanced upward. These were *definitely* rocks, just rocks in Chaos.

A heavy creak drew Faye's attention. Sadi stood at the entrance as one of the doors opened wide behind her. Faye took long, leaping steps over the rock-bones and hurriedly climbed the stairs.

Sadi leaned against the door frame, gesturing to the hallway within. "Your first lesson will be entering the Hall of Empty Eyes."

Faye peered in. A hallway much longer than the building itself waited inside. She took a deep breath, silencing what her senses screamed were wrong. She was in Chaos, the realm of madness. Nothing would make sense here.

Mirrors covered each wall as a plush-red carpet runner extended the length of the floor. Besides the eerie silence, nothing prevented her from entering. How was this a test?

Faye made no move to step over the threshold and glanced at Sadi. "What happens when you enter?"

Sadi pointed. "Empty-eyed vessels will line the mirrors. If you serve Chaos, they answer your questions."

"And if I don't?"

Her maroon-stained lips swept up in a predatory smile. "They will find your insecurities and doubt, tearing at your mind." Sadi stepped over the threshold and glanced back at her.

Waiting.

Faye wished she could bring Sparrow to tie a rope to her foot. She didn't trust Sadi to pull her out of the temple if her eyeless friends decided to rip into her mind.

She looked down, staring at the polished granite threshold. Inches separated her from bringing Prinia home and mending the ache in her heart. From starting her life with Rune without guilt.

Faye swallowed. She needed to be without doubt. Faye thought of Alister reuniting with Prinia. Their quiet happy life in the cottage overlooking the flowers. She thought of Rune and the family she would have with him.

She stepped over the threshold, bracing for pain—And blinked when nothing happened. Did she have to be in the temple completely? Faye held fast to her mental images and stepped into the hall. A moment passed, and she shared Sadi's expression of shock.

"That's quite the surprise," the Familiar said.

Faye smiled with relief, turning as the mirrors began to change. The reflection blurred, refocusing.

Rows of ashen, naked bodies stood in the mirrors, shoulder to shoulder, moving as one. Each turned toward her as they slowly swayed back and forth, watching her with vacant, empty eyes.

Her heart raced, and Faye took a fearful, retreating step away from *them*. She struck the edge of the closed door with enough force to rattle it, knocking herself off balance. Faye fell outside the temple and scrambled backward, stopping at the edge of the steps.

"What are they?" Faye's breaths quickened as she struggled to contain her panic.

Sadi stood a few feet from the doorway and looked over her shoulder at the mirrors. She searched the reflection before turning to face Faye with an arched brow. "The empty-eyed vessels didn't attack you."

Faye's heart hammered in her chest as she got to her feet. She leaned to look past Sadi into the hall. The mirrors lined the simple walkway, feigning innocence as the glass panels stared back.

When her ass was outside, Faye thought grimly. She glanced toward Sadi. "Do they come out of the mirrors?"

"No. When a mind breaks, it comes to Chaos. When their physical body dies, they become part of the realm. Chaos and Hell are sister realms, serving the same purpose, capturing stray energy, and returning it to the Darkness."

They weren't the same. Hell glittered with remnants of borrowed power until it faded into the Darkness. *People* were imprisoned in Chaos, not whisps of power. Just like Sadi. A clever reflection of herself. One filled with deceit. She needed to focus. The only way to help Prinia was in this temple.

Faye took a tentative step into The Hall. The reflections blurred, slowly refocusing again until rows of empty-eyed vessels turned to stare at her. Their clouded stares unnerved her, grasping at her most primal instincts—Run from this place.

Sadi stepped into her, an uninvited spectator to her thoughts, staring at the side of her head. Irritated, Faye leaned away. "What are you doing?"

Sadi frowned, tapping the clawed point of her articulated ring on her bottom lip before pointing at Faye. "They aren't attacking you?"

This bitch expected her eyeless friends to attack her. "They're just... staring at me," Faye said with more bite than intended.

Sadi gave her an appraising glance. "They see you. That's a good thing." Faye disagreed with the Familiar's sentiment wholeheartedly but nodded. "I didn't think you would get in. You're not Familiar, and I see doubt in your mind. Why aren't they attacking you?"

Faye stepped away, creating some distance between them. "Why don't you show me what I must do before they change their minds." *Or I change mine.*

Sadi shrugged, strolling further into the Hall. Faye forced herself to follow.

"This temple is one way we view the future. We ask a question, and the empty-eyed vessels part to show your answer," Sadi explained.

Rows of ashen bodies filled the length of the mirrors, standing shoulder to shoulder. Dread slithered down her spine. The vessels remained where they stood but turned their heads, tracking her movements. Faye cringed, seeking interest in anything but the mirrors. The belts of leather strapped over the length of Sadi's thigh-high boots suddenly became intriguing.

"Do they talk?" Faye asked.

"When they speak, it's typically the last thing you hear. They echo every insecurity you have until nothing is left of your mind. Until it shatters your core," Sadi said, stopping so close to the mirrors her skirt brushed the glass.

"Do you see what I do, or are the reflections different for each person?" Faye would much rather the vessels concentrate on Sadi than her.

"Visions are individual. We can't see what the other is shown. Have you been calling into Prinia's mind?"

Faye nodded, focusing on Sadi's lace choker this time.

"Calling a soul from Chaos isn't a vision. If you manage to coax Prinia forth, we'll both see her."

Faye tensed when the vessel standing closest to her twitched his hand. She took a half step away, unable to shake the eerie feeling he could reach through the glass and drag her in. "How do I call her?"

"It's like phasing. Picture Prinia instead of a place. Instead of your body transferring to your consciousness, your query will be summoned."

Faye made a fist, tapping the nail of her index into the heel of her palm. She concentrated on the man before her, opting to stare at the small hollow base of his throat to avoid his clouded vacant eyes. The man jerked his neck unnaturally, and a chittering noise sounded behind her. Faye stiffened as her mind screamed to run, but she remained still. They filled either side of The Hall, surrounding her. Trapping her. The air in her lungs became thick.

Faye stabbed her nail into her palm before counting to five, desperate to calm her mind and focus her thoughts. *One.* This was the path to bring Prinia back. *Two.* A new beginning for Alister. *Three.* An opportunity to mend the rift between Rune and Alister. *Four. Five.* She reached forward with her mind touching the mirror, moving past it. The cavernous abyss continued endlessly. She expected to feel the Vessels. Nothing brushed her awareness.

"This feels like Prinia's mind," Faye muttered.

"You're feeling Chaos's Heart. When minds break or escape to Chaos, their path remains open so the soul may return to the body."

Faye closed her eyes, blocking out the empty-eyed vessels, her fear, and the climbing dread of being in this hall. She pictured Prinia.

Prinia. Faye speared her telepathic thought, singing through the psychic abyss like an arrow. She pushed harder, repeating the message she sent each time Prinia drank.

Come back. You're safe.

Cold silence answered her, and Faye opened her eyes. She failed, Prinia ignored her call. Her mouth slackened as her shoulders slumped. How was she supposed to face Alister? His heartache and pain drove a knife between herself and Rune. How many years would Alister be forced to care for his wife but never truly be able to touch her— Sip their morning coffee on the porch in the house Alister built for her…for their future family.

Instead, he listened to the sound of a hollow home. Alone.

She tensed. The answer stood before her the entire time. Prinia wouldn't answer her or Sadi. They were no one to her.

But Alister…

Her heart raced as the vibration of his sword, dragging across her throat, seized her mind. *No,* Faye thought. The man who attacked her wasn't the Alister Prinia would know. Faye closed her eyes and focused her thoughts, picturing Alister sitting with his wife. How he loved and cared for her.

Things she wouldn't know, Faye realized.

She thought of Alister perched on a roof. The sleeves of his shirt rolled past his elbows as he hammered in planks of wood. The excitement Prinia must have felt when he climbed down the ladder. The smell of the lemonade she offered him—

"Faye," Sadi hissed in a hushed whisper.

She opened her eyes and couldn't breathe. The empty-eyed vessels parted and revealed Prinia, standing a few paces from the mirror. Her dark eyes were wide and fearful but clear. A beautiful deep brown. It reminded Faye of rich soil.

Holding perfectly still, Faye whispered, "What do I do?"

"She needs to come closer. Bring her consciousness into your mind. We'll go to her body after that."

"How do I do that?" Faye asked as Prinia took a step back.

"Reach for her mind the same way you would when speaking through a communication thread."

Before she could begin, Prinia turned and ran.

"Bring her back," Sadi hissed.

Faye outstretched her hand, pushing her mind into the abyss beyond the mirrors. Her fingertips grazed the glass, but it wasn't solid. Faye pulled her hand back and ever-widening rings rippled over the mirror as though it were water.

She didn't have time to think. She needed to act. Faye splashed through the mirror, chasing Prinia. Sadi screamed Faye's name, and

Faye slowly glanced behind her, her mouth going dry.

Faye's body lay sprawled at Sadi's feet as she pounded her fist against the glass.

Twelve

Faye's body lay empty on the floor of The Hall of Empty Eyes. Did she trap herself here like Prinia?

"Come back!" Sadi screamed. Each strike of her fist distorted the magic, rippling against the glass.

Alister's wife sprinted further into the blackness, her silhouette fading with each passing moment. He waited eight hundred years for Prinia. If Faye was trapped outside of her body, she wouldn't let it be meaningless. Whatever she'd done could wait a few minutes. Prinia answered her, and Faye had no guarantee she would respond a second time.

Faye tore after the fleeing vampire, sprinting through the dark.

She gained on Prinia, thanks to Damian's grueling regiment, over-taking her quickly. Faye reached for her arm. Faye's fingers slid across the fitted sleeve of her dress, catching her wrist as Prinia screamed.

"It's okay. I'm a friend of Alister," Faye said softly, attempting to soothe her.

Prinia wailed, ripping free of her grasp. Faye managed to recapture her arm, holding fast with both hands. She planted her heels on the ground as Prinia dragged her off balance.

Darkness, she was strong.

"He's waiting for you," Faye shouted.

Prinia whirled on her, and Faye's breath locked in her throat. Blood tracked from her eyes, slipping down her cheeks.

Tears.

"He's coming!" Prinia cried. Her eyes darkened, and her canines lengthened. She ripped out of Faye's hold, then lunged forward, taking them both to the floor.

Faye shoved a hand under her chin and turned her head to the side. Prinia snapped her fangs—Teeth slicing her cheek. Blood trickled down the side of her face, and Prinia's eyes darkened with hunger.

Faye braced her arms between herself and the much stronger vampire. Power screamed to the surface, coiling within her before lashing out. A flicker of magic knocked Prinia away before her fangs found Faye's neck. Panting, she outstretched her hand and splayed her fingers wide, pinning Prinia with her will.

The smaller woman hissed, flailing desperately. Terror contorted Prinia's soft features as Faye righted herself. She shrank against the ground, cowering. Fresh bloody tears flowed over her pale cheeks. "Let me go. Don't take me to him."

A growl sounded behind her. Distorted yet familiar.

Faye gasped as she turned to find her mate.

Was this how Prinia saw Rune?

A phantom of the Shadow Prince stood a few paces from them. Veined misted shadows swayed beneath his dark gaze. Voshki's expressive eyes Faye loved were absent. His focus, hardened and empty, belonged to a starving animal.

And his mouth.

Razored teeth lined his cruel smile. His lips and chin smeared from the continuous flow of blood.

Faye lifted a shield around herself and Prinia. *This isn't real,* Faye thought, clinging to her thin hope. This was Prinia's version of Rune. Faye's heart raced as she turned her back on the hellish version of her mate crouched beside Prinia.

"Alister sent me. Your husband," Faye said, placing her hand alongside Prinia's and releasing her mental bonds.

"He's going to get me." Prinia shook her head, drawing her hand away as she curled into a tight ball. Her slim shoulders shuddered with each broken sob.

Faye didn't know how to comfort or make her understand she was a friend. She only knew she couldn't leave Prinia here with her nightmares.

"Alister told me about you," Faye began, stroking a length of her fawn-colored hair. "How you met when he was fixing your father's roof." Prinia opened her eyes, then narrowed them. Seemingly frustrated. Faye smoothed away her red tears. "He said you brought him lemonade."

Prinia's gaze shifted behind her, and she immediately shrank to the ground, terror paralyzing her. The twisted depiction of Rune loomed nearby. Darkness, she'd been running from him through this abyss for centuries.

Faye moved closer, blocking her line of sight. "Hey, look at me." Faye lay next to her, bringing her face inches from hers. "I won't let him hurt you."

She took a shuddering breath and crawled against Faye, ducking her head. "Don't let him hurt me."

Faye nodded as her heart broke. "I won't let him hurt you."

"Don't let him hurt me," she repeated. Her soft voice muffled against Faye's neck. Fury rose with an anger so cold; it numbed every part of her. The ice cracked as it circled, clashing with her own feelings of betrayal and guilt. Guilt for loving a man who terrorized and attacked his own brother's wife.

She would protect Prinia. The Shadow Prince she feared was no more. Rune was a different man—A better man.

But every ragged breath and broken sob fanned her deep-seated hatred for dark-bloods. It was why she had avoided them for so long. Faye held her as she cried, stroking her cheek. When Prinia's sobs slowed, Faye brushed her fingertips over her brow to her temple. "We need to go," she whispered. "I'm going to bring you to a safe place."

Prinia tensed, crimson tears brimming in her dark eyes. "He finds me when I hide."

"I won't let him find you," Faye promised.

She slowly got to her feet and guided Prinia up. She banded her arms around Faye, tucking her head under Faye's chin. She couldn't see their feet, and their steps were slow and awkward, with Prinia tangled around her.

They managed an easy pace, heading back the way they came. The vision of Rune had vanished, and Faye suspected it was because Prinia wasn't thinking of him. She kept quiet, worrying this place summoned Prinia's fears to torment her. The endless abyss stretched around them, unnerving Faye. She concentrated on the light from the mirrors far off on the horizon.

By the time they approached the mirrors, Faye's ribs had ached beneath Prinia's tight embrace. She spotted Sadi standing at the glass with her hands flattened against it.

Prinia stopped suddenly, nearly knocking Faye to the ground, a few feet from the rows of ashen bodies. "No! They tell him where I am."

Sadi's eyeless friends rocked side to side quietly, focusing on the Familiar.

"He won't come if I'm with you," Faye said, taking a step and waiting for her to follow.

Prinia tensed, her arms tightened until Faye's ribs groaned, but took a half step. Then another. Slowly inching forward until they stood before Sadi.

"We're going to step through now," Faye whispered against her hair.

Prinia nodded, and Faye perceived the rapid beat of her heart. "Away from him. Somewhere safe," Prinia muttered.

Faye stepped into the glass. The surface rippled as she passed through. Her vision darkened for a moment. Faye opened her eyes and found herself staring up at the arched ceiling in The Hall of Empty Eyes.

Sadi perched over her, roughly shoving her hair away. The Familiar stared at Faye's face but focused on something past her head.

"Are you injured?" she asked, searching her eyes.

"I'm fine," Faye answered, pushing Sadi away. She stood searching for Prinia. A faint tapping sound chilled her spine.

No.

Prinia stood on the wrong side of the mirror, her palms pushing against the glass. Her bloody tears fell, scrawling angry red lines across her pale moon-kissed cheeks.

Her vision of Rune materialized from the shadows behind her.

"No!" Faye leaped forward. Sadi's arm caught her waist. But it was too late. She touched the mirror as her awareness passed through it.

Prinia rushed to her with a broken sob. She squeezed her close and buried her face in Faye's neck. "They told him to find me."

"It's okay. I'm here," Faye murmured. The nightmarish version of Rune dissolved as Prinia calmed down from shaking in her arms.

Faye turned to Sadi, still on the other side of the mirror. Her chest constricted at the sight of the physical body she left behind, hanging limp in Sadi's arms. Her eyes were as vacant and clouded as Prinia's. She reached for her own mind and was met with an endless abyss.

"How did you get through?" Sadi hissed.

"I don't know," Faye answered, thinning her lips. "Can you bring her consciousness into your mind?"

Sadi set her body down and flattened her hand to the glass. She stared at Prinia briefly, her fingers curling as they pressed the glass. Sadi pulled her hand away with a sharp breath. "I can't feel her. She never answered me when I summoned her."

Faye looked down toward Prinia as the blood tears stained her face. "She's a friend. You can go with her." Faye nodded encouragingly.

Sadi shook her head. "I don't feel her consciousness… or yours," she said, glancing down at Faye's still body.

Faye glanced down at the smaller woman. She refused to abandon her and reached for the depth of Prinia's mind.

Her heart fell.

She didn't feel Prinia's consciousness. There was only blackness. The endless, cavernous abyss.

Faye wouldn't leave Prinia to this emptiness. Captive to her fears. "Get her body. I'll help her walk through the mirror like I did."

With a curt nod, Sadi vanished.

Thirteen

Rune turned the page, needing the text to distract him. He'd lost his place for the sixth time, glancing at the grandfather clock beside the black marble mantle. He and the creature had been on edge since Faye left his side. She'd been nervous about her lessons with Sadi, and Rune suggested she read her newest book to calm her mind.

Because books are your answer to everything, the Ra'Voshnik groaned. *We should have accompanied her.*

We cannot enter their temples. Our presence would hinder her lessons, Rune said smoothly through his mind. The fool creature was a puppy at their queen's heels.

Rune flipped the page, nearing the end of an identical set of books he borrowed from the Familiar library. The Ra'Voshnik rose closer to the surface, peering at the High Tongue script through his eyes. A short, low growl vibrated through it. *Why are you wasting time looking for her race? Our queen has her shards.*

Rune exhaled, closing the book. *Do you truly believe Faye carries her power by chance?*

The Ra'Voshnik glided lower, slipping to the depths of his mind as it snickered, *You should research more important things, like why the sky is blue. Or why you drink blood.*

Rune ignored the creature, leaning back in his chair. The times and rule predating Saith were strange. The realms were divided into provinces, each ruled and governed by a king. Much like the courts claimed towns now but without a High Queen above them. Rune begrudgingly opened the last book in his borrowed set as he tuned out another outburst from the Ra'Voshnik. His research progressed slowly with the bothersome creature's constant presence in his mind. He would have worked his way through Morbid's library in a few months if the Ra'Voshnik had been silent.

Sadi's voice lanced through his mind. *I need your assistance. Come to Alister's home.*

The Ra'Voshnik growled as Rune stood, struggling to collect his thoughts. She and Faye were gone over an hour. Rune's mouth went dry. Had Faye been successful? Rune phased, and his surroundings faded, refocusing on his brother's living room.

"I am coming with you," Alister said, standing between Sadi and Prinia.

Rune stiffened. Where was Faye?

Sadi leaned forward and hissed at his brother. "You are wasting time. Give me her body. I don't know how long Faye can hold Prinia there."

A plethora of questions filled Rune's racing mind. Prinia answered Faye? But if his queen had been successful, where was she? His fangs lengthened as realization dawned on him.

Sadi *left* Faye in The Hall of Empty Eyes.

The Ra'Voshnik clawed at his awareness, fighting to surface. *Get to Faye now!*

Sadi moved to step around Alister, but he moved with her, blocking her path. "Take me with you."

"You can't enter our temples," Sadi grated through bared teeth.

Rune didn't have time for this. "Brother," he snapped.

"No!" Alister bit out, pointing at him. "You will not take her from me a second time."

The Ra'Voshnik's panicked aggression bled through his mind. Sadi gripped Alister under his chin. Her clawed ring pressed into his cheek. "Give her to me before I lose my patience and snap your neck."

"Take us to Faye!" Rune bellowed. His untrained queen was alone in Chaos. His stomach knotted as he struggled to draw a breath. It took Sadi moments to decimate a mind. How long could his night breeze last if the temple's magic turned on her. He couldn't lose her. "Take us to my queen, now."

Alister nodded sharply, and Sadi bared her teeth at his brother before phasing them to Chaos. They materialized deep in the Familiar's realm before The Hall of Empty Eyes. Rune pushed his senses past himself, feeling for Faye. She wasn't here. Rune reached for her mind as his hands tremored.

He couldn't sense her.

Where is Faye? the Ra'Voshnik shouted. *If anything happened to her...* The creature's blinding rage clouded Rune's thoughts.

"Now, give her to me. You cannot enter our temples," Sadi ordered.

"I don't care about your fucking temples." The heavy door groaned as Alister pushed it open.

"You cannot enter with doubt in your mind!" Sadi replied, matching his rancor.

"I am without doubt!" Alister bellowed, his voice echoing through the hall. He stepped over the polished wooden threshold and immediately drew a breath. He collapsed, seizing on the blood-red carpet.

Rune used a flicker of power to pull Alister out of the temple, but nothing happened. He reached for Alister's twitching leg, and Sadi shoved him before he made contact.

"Don't touch him unless you want to share his fate," Sadi said as she lifted Alister by the back of his collar and unceremoniously tossed him at Rune's feet. She turned and lifted Prinia into her arms, taking a final look at Rune. "The empty-eyed vessels will attack Prinia once she is back in her body."

Sadi pushed the door with her shoulder, revealing a mirror-lined hall. Rune's heart leaped to his throat as the Ra'Voshnik roared. Faye was sprawled on the floor, her black hair spread over the crimson carpet. He took an instinctive step toward her, and Sadi spoke without looking at him.

"Do not enter the temple. If you force me to choose, I will leave her to fracture." Her tone was icy, honeyed in a threatening promise he knew she would keep.

Rune held the Ra'Voshnik at bay as it thrashed and screamed, desperate to reach their queen. Sadi stepped over the threshold, and Rune muttered to the creature, hoping he spoke the truth.

She will return Faye to us.

Faye held Prinia surrounded by the empty-eyed vessels. They looked like living corpses. She thanked the Darkness they didn't smell and kept their distance. Faye wasn't sure she could withstand one of them touching her. Feared if she began screaming, she'd never stop. They stared ahead, moving as one in a slow, eerie rhythm.

Minutes passed, and a low creak filled The Hall. Prinia tensed at the sound, and Faye sucked a breath as Prinia's claws pricked her back.

"I am without doubt!" a gravel-filled voice echoed through the Hall.

The empty-eyed vessels moved in unison, snapping their heads toward the door.

"Frail-blood."

"Worthless."

"Pathetic weakling."

The insults overlapped, again and again. They blended with a wet, tearing sound Faye had heard once before—When Vash skinned rabbits for a stew at his tavern.

Prinia hyperventilated as she cowered against Faye, covering her ears.

Faye needed to be strong for Prinia. "It's going to be okay," she said. Praying she wasn't lying.

She turned, catching sight of the empty-eyed vessels behind her. They stood with their heads tilted back, and their mouths opened wide. None of them spoke, yet the voices continued to slither from their unmoving lips. Faye's heart hammered faster as Prinia trembled in her arms.

It all stopped at once, their heads snapping back to the hallway, staring ahead as they swayed.

Sadi glided down the hall, cradling Prinia in her arms. She shoved Faye's body out of the way with the side of her heeled boot. Faye ignored how her evil twin treated her body like a pile of discarded laundry. She didn't have time to care. Faye guided Prinia closer to the mirror and gestured to her body. "He can't hurt you over there."

Prinia blinked up at her. "He won't find me?"

"He won't, and Alister is waiting for you," Faye promised, taking her hand and nudging her toward the glass.

"Ally," Prinia muttered. She crept closer. Her fingers touched the glass, and the surface rippled. She stepped through, and Faye stiffened. The mirror's depths engulfed Prinia, but nothing emerged on the other side of the glass. Her hand slipped from Faye's as she crossed the threshold completely.

The vessels jerked again, snapping their attention to Prinia. The cutting words and wet tearing sound began anew. Prinia spasmed in Sadi's arms. Blood leaked from her eyes and nose.

They continued, tracking her movements as Sadi sprinted down the Hall.

"He doesn't love you."

"Peasant mortal."

"Insignificant pet."

The words aimed at Prinia cut Faye deep. Her own doubts surfaced. Rune would abandon her when she aged. She tensed, waiting for the eyeless things to turn on her. The vessels went silent, swaying in their slow rhythm. Waiting.

Faye steadied her breathing. Prinia was safe. Faye closed her eyes. Rune wouldn't leave her. He loved her. Faye pictured the family she would have with him. The life they would make together. Now with Prinia safely on the other side, maybe they could start anew.

The sound of dozens of shuffling feet startled her. Faye opened her eyes, and the empty-eyed vessels parted, revealing...

Children.

A boy and a girl, no more than five years old, dressed in court finery. The boy was a blend of her features with Rune. Her black hair and Rune's pale blue eyes. The girl took after her but bore Rune's coloring. Her young angular face was framed in white-blonde hair and the same pale blue eyes as her brother.

This was her family.

She stepped closer to them. Her hands shook as she cupped each of their faces. They silently gazed up at her. They were hers. To love and protect. Tears misted her lashes as she smoothed her thumb over their cheeks and stepped back.

Faye would take Anaria and shape it into a haven for her future children. Her cause began with Prinia. Faye refused to accept a world where the weak were punished and the strong thrived without consequence. She would protect her people.

Faye committed their faces to memory. For a moment, she wanted to stay longer with them. Her hand pressed the watery glass before turning around, looking once more at the children who filled her heart with so much hope. Hope she hadn't felt for a long time. She understood Rune's strange words now.

Legacy.

Their children would be her legacy. Faye pressed her lips to hold in her tears and returned to her body.

She would see them again soon.

Fourteen

Rune stood at the threshold; his brother's limp body draped across his arms. A steady flow of blood trickling from his nose and mouth collecting into a small puddle on the stones.

"You are injured." Rune's gaze lowered to Faye's cheek the moment she exited the temple.

She touched her face and winced. Prinia's fangs sliced her. The pain numbed in the presence of her fear.

"It's nothing. I'm okay," Faye insisted, glancing between Alister and Prinia.

She perceived the depths of their power, but it felt wrong. Faye focused on the jagged feeling and tensed when her surroundings began to fade.

The instant she stopped concentrating on the feeling of broken glass, her vision returned.

"Are you well, love?" Rune asked, still holding his brother.

Faye nodded, walking closer to Sadi. She cradled Prinia in her arms. Red tracks lined Prinia's face, but she had stopped bleeding. "There's something wrong with them. When I focus on it, everything fades."

Sadi adjusted her grip on Prinia and narrowed her eyes at Faye.

"Stop trying to read my thoughts." Faye flicked her hand, positive the Familiar trespassed within her mind. Sadi leaned closer and sniffed her hair. Faye stepped back, flushing at the intrusion. "Get off me," Faye hissed.

Sadi leaned back on her hip, unphased, as Faye glared at her.

"Your surroundings fade when you look into people. It allows us to see their power and manipulate it. These two fractured their cores," Sadi said before turning her attention to Rune. "Take us to Alister's home. They'll heal faster in a setting they're accustomed to."

Rune nodded, and their surroundings darkened for a moment.

As soon as Faye's vision cleared, she couldn't breathe. Terror dragged her beneath the icy memories haunting her mind. They were in a room. Alister's room. Three swords were mounted above a large sleigh bed. So far from where she stood, but the glint of the silver blade made her throat close. The same one Alister dragged across her throat before he nearly drowned her. The razor-sharp edge nicked what little control she had left. Faye was frozen, bound over her conflict to save Prinia or run from the man who submerged her in an icy grave.

Faye's skin chilled as her breaths grew shallow.

A warm, tender touch heated her body, removing her from the images replaying in her mind. He closed the distance between them and pulled her close.

Rune whispered against her hair, "Thank you."

This— This was why she kept going.

Faye leaned into him. She clenched her jaw to still her chattering teeth and silently prayed Sadi was too busy to notice her shivering.

Do you want my coat? Rune asked her mind.

No. Faye glanced at the bed, willing her mind to understand that Rune's brother couldn't hurt her. She was safe.

The slate between Rune and Alister, clean.

Alister and Prinia could begin again. An eternity of morning coffee while they gazed over her flowers. She hoped, in time, they would share some of their mornings and reunite as a family. Sparrow would gossip while Prinia and Faye giggled. Her twins would play in Prinia's field of red spider lilies.

Her attention drifted to Sadi. The Familiar sat beside Prinia, staring off into the distance.

"What's she doing?" Faye asked.

Rune turned his head. "She is healing them."

Faye breathed in Rune's scent of amber and sandalwood, glad to be away from her evil twin's eyeless friends. "Can I help?" Faye asked, unsure if Sadi could hear her.

"You will need to learn to heal and siphon before you can begin stitching cores. I have much to repair," Sadi said, still glassy-eyed.

Heat swept up her legs, and Faye jerked.

A warming spell, vsenia, Rune spoke in her mind.

Faye stifled a moan as it moved further up her body, like she was lowering herself into a hot bath. It stopped at her neck, and she sagged against Rune.

From the safety of his arms, Faye focused on the broken, jagged feel of Prinia and Alister's magic. Maybe she could help.

Alister's bedroom faded. The darkness was replaced with an expanse similar to the place she found behind the mirrors. The same void surrounded her, but the floor was covered with a rolling black fog. It covered her ankles and obscured the floor beneath it.

Sadi stood in the space Alister's bed occupied, but all Faye could see were two objects floating side by side.

The one on the right was a beautiful crystal vase embedded with spider lilies. Deep fissures cut through the flowers allowing its dark, glittering contents to leak out. Instead of dripping to the ground, the churning dark mist suspended near the cracks, amassing into faint hints of the night sky. Faye bit the inside of her lip. Was this Prinia's magic?

Beside her was a pale thunder cloud. It took up much more space than Prinia, and there was no vase containing it. Faye's lips parted as her lungs constricted. The shimmer didn't come from the lighter gray mist cut in white tendrils, but slivers of glass floated within the wisps of Alister's strength.

Alister destroyed his core. How could Sadi fix this?

"Don't venture to the Hall of Empty Eyes without me." The Familiar's voice came from far above her, even though she stood a few feet from Faye.

Sadi strolled to Alister's shattered magic. Her clawed, articulated ring reflected the glow from the shards of glass beneath it. She flicked her finger above it one way, then another. The shining slivers followed her movements, bunching at the edges of his pale mist. The pieces were so small Faye couldn't make out what his vase originally was.

"I have no intention of visiting the talking dead," Faye said quietly.

Sadi's midnight gaze met hers, the Familiar's eyes wide with fear. "You heard the empty-eyed vessels speak?"

Faye gasped when fingers harshly gripped her face. A point of metal dug into her jaw, and Alister's room snapped into focus. Sadi stood inches from her, holding her under the chin and palming the back of her head, staring into her temple.

"Let go of me," Faye grated as Rune pulled Sadi's hand away.

"Be mindful of how you handle my queen," Rune grated, tossing her wrist.

Sadi waved him off and asked, "What did they say?" Her voice became raspy lined with a desperation Faye had never seen from the evil twin.

"When I was with them—"

"What do you mean *with them*?" Rune growled. What little color he held, drained from his face. He looked to Sadi as Faye explained her encounter with the empty-eyed vessels.

He caressed the side of her cheek, searching her eyes as though he would never see her again. Fear darkened his pale blue eyes as the veined misted shadows stretched to graze the tops of his cheekbones. "You are reckless, vsenia. I could have lost you."

She tried to comfort him with her touch, but it did little to soothe him. She turned toward Sadi and said, "There was a wet, tearing sound. They called Alister frail-blood and told Prinia he didn't love her."

Sadi folded her arms with a confused scowl. "She has Familiar magic but wields it differently." She turned back to Alister and Prinia. "Her mind is in much better shape than I expected. The fool will take longer to mend than his wife. I'll need a few days."

"Why is his core fractured more than hers? The vessels didn't speak to him for very long." Prinia was there for far longer, even if Sadi raced her out of the temple.

"He's a day-blood. His core is weaker. Rune turned her. She's no day-blood," she replied, not bothering to keep the irritation from her voice.

"Can I arrange anything for you?" Rune asked.

Sadi sat beside Alister, staring off into the distance once more. "No. Damian will be arriving shortly." She seemed to focus on Rune, and a ghost of a smile whispered over her lips. "Don't enter Chaos without me. If we weren't there to pull them out, the empty-eyed vessels would have destroyed their minds. Don't make me explain to Rune why only a shell of you remains."

Faye was safe. Rune desperately clung to the thought.

Tear the cat's skull from her shoulders, the Ra'Voshnik growled. The creature urged him to wrap his hand around Sadi's slim throat and pluck her head from her body.

Be silent. He would speak with Sadi and reign in her unorthodox teachings. For now, he needed his queen's closeness to blunt his fear. If he lost her—

We would reduce Chaos to shadows and ash. Nothing will separate her from us. The Ra'Voshnik prowled closer, growing agitated as Prinia's rose-water scent mingled with his night breeze. *Get that stench off her.*

You will offend our queen, Rune answered. His dark queen commanded that he made peace with his brother. Insulting Alister's wife would garner no goodwill between them.

The Ra'Voshnik chuckled, floating through his mind. *She likes when I bathe her.*

Rune ignored the creature's inability to read a situation and offered Faye his hand. "Shall we?"

Faye glanced down at his hand then back at the bed. Her shoulders tensed, and Rune stepped into her, taking her hand. Darkness, she was so cold. "There is nothing else to be done, vsenia. You brought her back. She needs time to heal, love."

His queen nodded and leaned into him.

Rune phased to the inner gardens of his home and lifted Faye into his arms. Her black hair gleamed in the sunlight. A pang of guilt stung him. Hell didn't suit her. She belonged in the light, framed by the twin willow trees swaying on either side of the spring in her picturesque garden.

"What are you doing?" Faye asked.

He drew a breath as her icy fingers slid between the buttons of his shirt. "Warming you, my frozen queen," Rune said, momentarily glaring accusingly at her offending appendage.

"Rune, no. You can't. I'm still dressed," Faye argued.

He stepped out of his shoes and waded into the steaming spring. Faye objected, squirming in his arms. When she failed to free herself, she lifted her feet to his shoulder and growled, "I have boots on."

Tell her I don't give a fuck about a pair of shoes, the Ra'Voshnik growled through his mind.

His queen ceased her struggles as he lowered them into the pool. She closed her eyes, leaning into him. Short breaths passed her parted lips, caressing his throat. He turned and carefully placed her feet on the spring's stone border.

Rune held her until her breathing returned to normal.

Bring her into our mind or get out of my way, the Ra'Voshnik growled.

Demanding creature. Rune began unlacing her boots as he said, "Your Voshki would like to spend time with you as well."

Instead of answering, her mind brushed his outer barriers. Rune smiled, pulling off her boots. "Your skill is improving."

He opened his mind and his night breeze slipped through his awareness. Her delicate scent settling over his senses.

Rune recreated the garden, his mind mirroring their bodies. The Ra'Voshnik appeared beside him. Lengths of its white-blonde hair hung loose over its bare chest. Rune's gaze lowered, assessing the degree of the creature's lack of dress.

A dark chuckle flitted through his mind. *Did you expect me to sit in my suit like you?*

The creature cupped the back of Faye's neck and crooned, "Lie back, vsenia."

Faye leaned up, and Rune closed his eyes as her soft lips met his throat. The kiss was an apology and a sign of his queen's forgiveness.

The Ra'Voshnik guided her to lie her head on the crook of its arm. It gently stroked her face, beginning with her jaw and ending at her hair line. Rune was certain Faye believed the creature touched her out of affection. Which may have been true but wasn't its primary motivation. It was possessive in a way Faye would not appreciate or understand. Rune held it back from saying all it desired. And he wasn't sure if Faye would be so happy with her *Voshki* if she heard everything it had to say.

The Ra'Voshnik used the mystical elements to cleanse Prinia's scent from their queen with water.

"If you ever scare me like that again, I'll put you over my knee and spank your ass red," the Ra'Voshnik rasped, tapping the tip of her nose to punctuate his threat.

Rune growled, "Still your crass tongue." She tolerated the creature far more than he did.

"She likes my crass tongue," the Ra'Voshnik said, smiling wide enough to flash its fangs. Rune rolled his eyes.

Faye grasped either side of the creature's mouth. "Be nice."

Rune couldn't discern if the Ra'Voshnik tossed its head or Faye shook it. Rune ran his hand over Faye's thigh as the creature freed itself from her grasp. "I would ask you to be more cautious with your dealings in Chaos," he began.

"How about, don't leave your body to go running through mirrors," the Ra'Voshnik grated, tracing its claw over her throat. In a softer tone, it added, "I thought we lost you... we both did."

Faye sat up. Her lightning-streaked midnight eyes met Rune's for a moment before lowering to the steaming water. "I had to go after her..."

"Vsenia—"

"I couldn't risk it." The tone of Faye's voice grew. Her stormy gaze pleaded for understanding. "She only answered because I projected Alister. She came for her husband but found me and Sadi instead. I lied to draw her out." She looked down, seemingly choking back the last of her words.

He bore his queen's pain. Yet there was nothing he could do to alleviate her anguish when his deeds were the cause. "I am eternally grateful you led Prinia out of Chaos. But you position yourself at risk in place of others too easily."

The Ra'Voshnik curled a finger under her chin, guiding her until she faced him. "Measure the realms against your life. If you are lost, I will reduce the realms to shadow and ash."

"We don't. Destroy. The realms," Faye punctuated each word with a stab of her finger to the creature's chest. She leaned forward, taking Rune's hand in both of hers. Her thumbs slid over the back of his hand, soothing his stricken mind. For once, he and the creature were in agreement.

"I'll be more careful. I promise."

Fifteen

Sparrow played with the skirt of the pastel blue dress Faye wore. She tossed the gauzy material back and forth before posing it dramatically. Faye laughed and pushed Sparrow away, taking her place in front of the mirror.

"This is cute, bitch," her sister said, inspecting the layers of blue organza flowing over her hips. It was so light in color; it could have been easily confused for white. She settled on an elegant dress designed in simple lines with an empire silhouette laced bodice. The restlessness and anxiety prickling beneath her skin amplified with each passing day. It was almost time for her dream to come to fruition.

The Court of Chaos and Darkness had been installed over every village in Anaria. She rubbed the back of her neck, willing the knotted muscle to relax. With every village in Anaria under her court, she would stand before the High Council and petition for her realm.

Reaching for a crown I have no claim to, she thought.

Sparrow leaned against the free-standing bloodroot mirror. Her green eyes glimmered in Hell's ever-twilight. "Isn't Runey going to get jealous? You're marrying a realm before him."

Faye flushed. "He's not— He hasn't… It's not even white."

The petite blonde snorted and fluttered her hand. "Bitch, you may as well be married to tall, pale, and scary. You announced him as your consort in front of the High Council. Vash said you're *dark-blood* married."

Dark-blood married? Were they husband and wife in Rune's eyes? No. He never asked her, and she wouldn't assume. She never imagined being married. Let alone to a dark-blood. She imagined him pressing his chest to her back, holding her against him. His familiar purr would rumble in her ear as he whispered, *Wife.* Her lips curled into a smile.

"Look at you! You want to be Mrs. Shadow Prince," Sparrow teased in a sing-song voice.

"I made him my consort to end his blood debt," Faye said, dismissing her daydreams. Did Rune even believe in marriage? Or was it like the difference between *I love you,* and *I am yours to command?* He'd given her so much. She could give him this and do the dark-blood thing.

"What the fuck is his last name? Sacary? Sacarcrow?"

"Sacarlay," Faye volunteered, over-emphasizing the consonants to end her sister's senseless butchering of Rune's name.

"So, when are you doing the real thing?" Sparrow asked, wagging a finger at her pale blue gown.

Faye dropped her shoulders and folded her arms. "It's not white." She huffed, picking up the skirt and walking off the pedestal. "I need you to focus. High Council. Me. Asking for a realm. Remember?"

The muscles in her neck twinged, and Faye winced. She adjusted her hem and fell into the closest chair. Darkness willing, the High Queen would sign over the realm. She was no Queen to her people. Faye hoped she would be relieved, ecstatic to be rid of the realm she ignored. Alister's warning replayed through her mind, unsettling her.

"Stop worrying. Runey said it would be a simple exchange,"

Sparrow said with a shrug. "If she fights, we take it. Simple. Exchange."

"Right." Her sister headed toward the bathroom, and Faye glanced down at her ring. The mist surrounding her soul shard obscured the marquee crystal within it like a Shard of Darkness. The tendrils within her mist differed. Instead of black marking it a dark-blood, hers were a sharp purple, mirroring the Darkness itself.

If the High Queen contested her petition, Faye would be forced to bring her court to war with what remained of Lyssa's. She prayed it wouldn't come to that.

Two knocks in quick succession drew her attention. Faye turned to find Rune standing in the doorway, with Vashien a step behind him.

"Come on in, your shadowy highness," Sparrow yelled from the bathroom while curling her hair.

Rune silently strolled toward her, and she smiled up at her vampire. He canted his head, approaching her. "Are you well?"

Faye folded her hands in her lap, and her shoulders slumped. "A little nervous."

"Anaria will be yours before sunset," Rune assured her.

He leaned down, and a length of his white-blonde hair fell forward, grazing her collarbone. Faye's lids slid closed as his lips touched hers. Rune pulled back a fraction, threading his fingers through her hair, and a breathy sigh escaped her.

"There is no need for nerves," he whispered, before pressing a kiss to her temple.

"I'm just asking for a realm," Faye answered in the same fashion, sliding her hand down his side. Planning had been the easy part. The late nights she shared with Rune and Voshki, pouring over maps and strategizing how to best protect her people. She saw her goal clearly.

Executing her vision, however, was another thing entirely.

"It will be a simple matter. If there is opposition, I will halt their intent." Sparrow had said the same thing. Faye didn't want to solve their problems with violence. Rune straightened and offered his hand. "Shall we, love?"

Faye placed her hand in his. She took a breath before standing up. They materialized in a box seat far above the High Council. The view silenced her imposturous thoughts. The airy basilica sparkled in whites and golds. Tall pillars of marble lifted the domed ceiling high

above the rowed seating. From Rune's balcony, she had an unob-
structed view of the endless sky Artithia was known for. It stretched
all around them, painted in azure, lapis, and cerulean. Picturesque
white clouds floated softly, capturing the sun's rays in crisp golden
highlights.

Sparrow and Vashien appeared behind her a moment later.

"Runey catered," her sister chirped, gracelessly flopping into the
chair beside the circular table. She stuffed a grilled fig in her mouth,
acting as if she had received the best orgasm of her life. Faye glanced
over her shoulder. Leave it to Sparrow to notice food instead of the
breathtaking view. Faye leaned onto the railing, observing the crowd.
Masses shuffled below them. It wasn't as crowded as it had been
the last time she stepped into this building, but it still was a popular
affair. The High Council members sat at their table, flipping through
and arranging their own stacks of documents.

Rune's hand met the small of her back and offered her a glass
of pomegranate juice. "You should take a seat. I suspect we will be
moved to the end of the roster, considering what happened the last
time you stepped into The Eyes."

Faye took the glass, sitting in the oversized, black, upholstered
chair beside Rune. People were watching them. Faye glanced down,
overlooking the other golden rail. A mass of onlookers whispered
among themselves, discreetly pointing at her and Rune. Faye crossed
her legs and studied her soul shard. Her smile turned bitter.

She'd been an outcast, living at the edge of society without a
shard. Seen as little more than an animal by those gifted with magic.
Now she was living at the edge of society *with* a shard. Nothing had
changed. She felt just as isolated by the black misted ring adorning
her index finger cut in sharp purple tendrils. It proved her power far
eclipsed Rune's with the single shard she displayed.

I'll get used to the scrutiny, Faye silently reminded herself. She focused on the ornate table between their pair of chairs instead of her
onlookers and made a small plate of cut fruit and pastries. She bit
into a plum tart, and the crowd quieted.

Jha'ant cleared his throat and stood, opening the meeting. Faye
would guess he stood as tall as Rune, but his shoulders were much
broader. He shifted his large white feathered wings and sat down,
slipping on a pair of reading glasses. The Artithian King called a set

of names Faye didn't recognize. She nibbled on fruit as the day wore on, watching court appointments announced.

The petitions unfolded, and Sparrow made no attempt to hide her commentary. "Yes. No. Darkness, no. Yes, but it will dissolve within a year. That's a terrible idea. Are they serious?" Sparrow tried to grab Faye's attention, but Faye tuned her out. She continued watching a woman decline her Queen's request to name her consort. Dark-bloods and their strange customs. It all seemed backward. Why would they come here with petitions instead of talking to the person in question?

Faye leaned toward Rune, taking his hand. "Is Sadi here, or is she still with Alister and Prinia?"

"Sadi is in her family's seats." Rune leaned closer and pointed down a series of large balconies. "She and Damian will stand with us."

She recognized Sadi's thigh-high belted boots and Damian's long black hair streaked with red. Instead of chairs, an elaborate chaise dominated the space. Sadi reclined with her head on Damian's lap while her booted feet laid on the railing. Faye frowned. By the way her skirts were positioned, Faye was sure her neighbor was getting an eyeful.

"She doesn't care if people can see up her skirt?" Faye asked.

Rune spared Sadi a passing glance. "She is Familiar." His attention returned to her like his answer was explanation enough for her behavior.

"We will be called soon." Her vampire rose, offering his hand.

Faye stood, shielding herself and Sparrow.

Her sister rubbed her arm, scowling at her. "Is this *really* necessary?"

"A precaution," Rune stated. He phased the four of them to the walkway in front of the raised platform before the High Council called The Eyes. Sadi and Damian materialized behind them.

The High Queen straightened her back and sat taller, raising her chin. The embodiment of regal pride and arrogance. She overlooked Faye, casting a sweeping glance at Rune.

Faye pulled her shoulders back, prickling at Lyssa's display. The High Queen regarded Rune as an object. An ornament to parade and stow at her convenience. But he was none of those things. Rune had told her love was a mortal sentiment. Immortal emotions ran deeper.

Their affection was displayed through ownership and devotion.

It was as twisted as the scores they collected against one another. A metal point pressed into her finger as a hand closed over hers. Faye turned her head and pulled away, but the grip held.

Sadi smiled at the High Queen as she lifted Faye's hand. She curled her fingers and ran Faye's nails down Rune's back. Black flooded the High Queen's gaze, like ink through water before dissipating.

"She looks cross with you." Sadi laughed. The Familiar bounced the claw of her ring against her lower lip. "Can you taste her emotions from here? Which is stronger? Betrayal or jealousy?"

Sparrow poked Faye in the ribs, joining in Sadi's game. "Kiss him."

Rune quirked a brow the same moment Faye hissed, "Stop."

"You don't have fangs, or I'd tell you to feed on him while she watches," Sparrow added, sourly.

"Sparrow," Vashien growled in a hushed whisper. Damian's low laugh sounded from behind her.

"Your dove never ceases to surprise me," Damian nodded at her sister, pulling Sadi against him.

Rune exhaled. "I would remind you we are in a crowded building with sensitive ears. Lyssa among them."

"I spelled our space. Our words will travel no further than our ears." Sadi smiled, reaching up to drag the clawed tip of her articulated ring along Damian's jaw.

He bit down, pulling it from her finger. He held the finger gauntlet in front of her and growled. "Keep prodding me with this, and I'll shove it somewhere you won't like, kitten."

Faye stiffened at Damian's abrading tone, but Sadi only grinned up at him, sliding her jewelry into place. And she thought Rune and Voshki were *creative* with her.

Sparrow snorted. "You don't have to lie. We all know Sadi will shove that somewhere you won't like."

Faye flushed, but Damian only smirked. He gripped the front of Sadi's throat, and she tilted her head back, giving him more access. "My docile kitten does nothing of the sort," Damian crooned, swiping his thumb over her lips. "Do you?"

Sadi bit the tip of his thumb, holding him with her teeth while she beamed up at him.

"Never pinned you as the submissive type." Sparrow laughed.

"Takes a special touch," Damian said with a wink as he dropped his hand.

"Can you teach me the quiet spell?" Sparrow asked.

Sadi nodded, raising her brow as Jha'ant addressed the crowd. "The last order of business is a petition from Lady Faye Alexander, Queen of the Court of Chaos and Darkness."

Faye froze as her nerves returned all at once. She forced a controlled breath and stepped onto the raised platform. Her heels seemed to echo through the silence, and she stilled at the center of The Eyes, standing tall. The High Queen refused to acknowledge her, and Faye raised her chin in defiance.

Faye smiled at Jareth and Morbid, then addressed Jha'ant, repeating the words she rehearsed with Rune for the past week. "I am the ruling court over every village in Anaria. I petition the High Council to recognize my rule and dominion of the realm."

The High Queen laughed, and Faye's power flickered, radiating up her back.

"You are a mouthpiece for the Shadow Prince's rule." She waved her hand dismissively, turning her hazel gaze to Rune. "If you wish to hunt in the peasant lands, you need only ask. Do as you please Rune. It seems you acquired a taste for..." She glanced back at Faye, her lashes lowered momentarily as her hazel gaze raked her head to toe. "Inadequacy."

Anger woven into rage coiled within her, spreading throughout her body. The flicker of power sharpened, the sensation heating up beside her shoulder blades. Her wings begged for release. She stepped toward the High Queen and grated, "I will protect my people from the dark-bloods who see Anaria as a hunting ground."

The vampire queen squared her shoulders. "You are nothing more than a peasant blood whore." A coy smile crossed her lips as she leaned back in her chair. "Does the Shadow Prince drink from your neck or thigh?" She lifted her hand, admiring her nails as she continued, "I preferred the inner thigh." She arched an eyebrow this time. "He has a talent with his mouth and hands."

"Lyssa—"

The High Queen raised her voice, speaking over Rune. "You are a product of his vanity since he could not be seen with such a debased creature beneath his title and breeding."

Lyssa was suddenly ripped from her chair, suspended a foot in the air by an invisible force. She sucked a breath, going rigid. Her eyes went wide before dark crimson flooded her gaze. Veined misted shadows swayed over the tops of her cheekbones as the High Queen bared her fangs.

"I've grown tired of your tongue," Sadi spoke with sweet venom, peering at Rune as she twisted the High Queen's spine until she screamed. "Apologize to the Shadow Prince."

Faye turned toward the Familiar. She floated in place. Her hair and clothing swayed around her as though she were submerged in deep water. Faye felt Sadi's power snake through the High Queen, choking her magic. Holding it out of reach.

"Rune!" Lyssa cried.

"Release the High Queen. Anaria belongs to me," a woman's voice Faye didn't recognize rang through the domed building as screams and panicked voices overlapped each other. It was followed by the sizzling crack of magic and will colliding.

Balanced on the back of a chair, a dark-haired woman stepped above the others. Steel gray eyes trained on Faye, but the woman made no move for the dagger strapped to her thigh.

"The peasant lands belong to the Court of Lace and Bone."

Sixteen

The Queen of Lace and Bone phased into The Eyes beside Faye. Rune's fangs lengthened with aggression as his power shaped to his will. He knew Delilah and her sadistic tastes. A phantom hand cruelly closed over her throat, ripping her away from Faye. He'd nearly lost his queen the last time she stood in this fucking place.

Never again, Rune growled, stepping onto the raised marble platform.

Rune simultaneously shielded himself and slammed his prey to the ground. Her skull struck the marble with a sickening crack and the Ra'Voshnik rose to the surface, bleeding through his eyes. It approved of Rune's methods, purring, *Kill her. I'll get Faye to forgive you.*

Delilah unsheathed the dagger at her thigh as Rune dragged the dark-haired Queen to her feet. She clutched the blade's handle, and the depth of Rune's magic seared her fingers. Faye had forbidden him from killing, but he could mold a lesson from pain. She screamed as her hand charred, and the abandoned weapon clattered on the white marble among the ashes.

She came to a stop at Rune's feet, and he stepped on her neck. He wanted to kill her. To tear her head from her body in such a way her spine would come with it. A message to anyone who opposed the will of his queen. He peered down at the sadistic female, leaning forward to inflict pain but not crush her windpipe.

Kill her, the Ra'Voshnik roared as Rune fought the overwhelming urge to separate her head from her shoulders with a twist of his heel.

The panicked screams overlapped the crescendo of shoving bodies and stomping feet quieted in the space of a breath. Rune turned, ready to snap the bones of anyone who dared to openly challenge him with a flicker of his mind—and smiled.

The crowd stood eerily still. Each person stared ahead with a blank expression. Sadi had snared their minds. She floated a foot above the ground, her hair and clothing drifting around her as though she were submerged in deep water. He and Sadi worked together like this countless of times over the centuries. She'd held armies while Rune systematically dispatched their leaders, efficiently making their kills.

His attention returned to the seething queen beneath the sole of his polished black shoe.

She clutched her burned nub of a wrist and hissed, "What happened to you? Why are you allowing this mockery?"

The corner of Rune's mouth lifted and the Ra'Voshnik brushed the surface. The Queen of Lace and Bone stilled as veined misted shadows stretched beneath his gaze. "I am the will of my queen."

She bared her fangs and struggled against him. Through labored breaths she bit out, "You were the best of us."

"There are no Anarian villages under your court's care, Delilah," Rune stated with a false sense of calm, shifting his weight until she began to choke.

"Anarians have nothing to tax. The only thing they're good for is bloo—"

Rune ended Delilah's tirade with a sharp thrust of his heel, crushing her spine. He straightened his jacket before looking at his queen, and his chest constricted.

Faye's shoulders rose and fell with labored breaths. Tension riddled her as revulsion painted her features. She pressed her hand to her middle, taking a step back.

Away from him.

He killed her. Faye choked on the thought. *She's immortal*, Faye told herself. *She would rise again*, but all Faye could see was Rune stomping down on her throat and the sickening crunch of bones. Her stomach knotted, and Faye scanned the crowd struggling to breathe. Sadi and Rune went against her wishes, making her court no better than the dark-blooded vultures she sought to protect her people from.

"Stop," Faye shouted at Sadi.

The Familiar tilted her head and smiled, as though she were listening to a beautiful melody. She lifted her hand and flicked her wrist, raising her index and middle finger. The wet sound of bones cracking filled the silence and bile rose in Faye's throat as the High Queen screamed for Rune.

"Stop!" Faye yelled.

Sadi's midnight eyes gradually focused on Faye, and she lowered to the ground. Her long black hair and clothing settled around her. The crowd shifted, unsettled but able to move again.

Her evil twin sneered at the High Queen.

Rune spelled his voice to carry through the domed building. "Bow before Faye Alexander—Queen of Chaos and Darkness, Ruler of Anaria."

"Get away from my mother!" A red-haired woman charged at Sadi, brandishing two blades the length of her forearm.

A blast of dark power knocked her to the ground and sent her tumbling into the High Council's table. Sparrow stepped into The Eyes dusting off her hands. "I don't know who you think you are, but you're fuc—"

The High Queen moved in a blur, but Rune was faster, catching her by the throat. Sparrow's eyes widened. She took a step back, examining the black-tipped claws aimed at her throat. "Good save, Runey."

Faye's power crackled, burning through the space between her shoulder blades. Her wings shot free, weighing down her back. Magic flowed past her in an ominous aura, mirroring the Darkness. An unquenchable dark rage colored Faye's mind. The High Queen would have killed her sister if Rune had not intervened. Faye took a step toward Lyssa, fixating on the thought of twisting the vampire queen's head from her body.

Faye exhaled a sharp breath, turning away. This wasn't her. Frustration welled in her. Her mind turned against her as her power breathed to life, soaking her in terrifyingly foreign urges and instincts. Her power felt like a living thing seeking an outlet. Demanding she drew a sweet symphony of screams from the High Queen.

Pleasure and violence blended in Faye until she couldn't differentiate one from the other. She made a fist, her claws cutting into her palm. The heady feeling of power pulsing through her veins overpowered the pain.

Rune tossed Lyssa with a flick of his hand. She landed easily, her violet corseted gown sweeping the floor. She straightened and hissed, "You would abandon your court—Your *family*, for what? A peasant blood whore."

Faye clenched her teeth. She didn't trust herself when so much of her power brimmed at the surface. Couldn't let herself inadvertently hurt someone.

Rune remained unmoved, addressing her with a calmness Faye didn't possess. "You will speak of my queen with the greatest respect. Should I find you in error a second time, I will take your fangs and offer them to her as a trophy."

The High Queen paled, taking a step back.

Faye's hand brushed her gown. Red marring the pale blue. This would not be how she began her reign. Violence and bloodshed would not be tools she used to vindicate her actions. She took a steadying breath and faced Jha'ant. The man squeezed into his chair and tucked his wings tightly to his back. His widened eyes and slacked jaw stabbed at her heart. He was afraid of her.

Faye raised her chin, pushing aside her feelings, and concentrated on her realm. Her people depended on her. She would not allow them to suffer under a dark-blood's boot any longer.

"I am the Queen of Chaos and Darkness. I am the ruling court over every village and town in Anaria. I request the High Council recognize my rule and dominion of this realm," she spoke the words, beginning her rule.

The Artithian King's attention snapped from the High Queen to Rune. The notch in his throat bobbed. He inclined his head, holding Faye's determined stare.

"The High Council recognizes Faye Alexander, Queen of Chaos and Darkness, as Ruler of Anaria."

ACT TWO

MIDDLEGAME

Seventeen

Rune knelt, gazing up at the Queen he placed before the realms, the High Council, and the strands of fate. He would be her consort and executioner. An extension of her very will.

Hers to command until the Darkness dragged him from her.

Faye straightened her back and studied the crowd. The corner of his mouth lifted. She moved like a predator, singling out prey. "Anaria is mine. Each of my subjects are members of my court. If my people are mistreated, I will bring retribution to your doorstep."

Rune smiled at the words they'd rehearsed, awaiting her signal to stand.

The Ra'Voshnik prowled his mind and growled, scenting their queen's blood. *She's injured.*

She couldn't be. Her shields were intact. Rune inhaled slowly, sifting through the psychic scent of magic clinging to him.

Darkness, he hated the scent of other women on him. His fangs sharpened, and he stilled. There was no denying the scent calming his mind. His night breeze through plum blossoms laced with her delectable blood. Tension left his shoulders, and his focus sharpened onto his queen. The blood must be her monthly courses beginning. Rune ignored the Ra'Voshnik's disagreement and admired the woman fate gifted him.

Her iridescent wings glimmered, lighting the marble around her in shades of pink, blue, and purple. His gaze followed a thin layer of black mist cascading down her membranous wings and dissipating at her feet.

Dark and radiant. The queen he had wished for his entire life.

Faye turned toward him. A small streak of red stained her pastel gown. Transferred from her palm, Rune realized, as a drop of crimson fell from the curve of her dainty claw.

She strolled toward him. Her chin held high. Her wings shifted, bathing him in their glittering reflection. Lightning-streaked midnight eyes met his, and his queen uttered a single command. "Rise."

Rune stood, turning his back on Lyssa. He closed the distance between himself and Faye, offering her his arm. "Shall we, my queen?"

Faye slipped her injured hand into the crook of his arm, her claws pricking the sleeve of his suit. Strain lined her eyes, and her shoulders were drawn back by more than the weight of her wings. He parted his lips and inhaled, forgetting his mate's emotions could not be read so easily.

He moved forward, escorting her to the pathway leading away from The Eyes.

Are you well? he asked, unsettled by the growing tension between them.

Her voice flitted through his mind. *Where are we going?*

A show of dominance. We must walk out of the building. Phasing is construed as fleeing, Rune answered as her court paired off and followed behind them.

Faye stood tall as they walked, her iridescent wings softly shifting behind her with each step. She upturned her face as they stepped into the sunlight.

Rune phased them home, materializing in the great room. The

blonde harpy bounded up the ornate staircase, oblivious to her sister's mood. She lifted her arm once she reached the top and yelled, "Don't take forever. We have sparring."

Faye's hand slid down his arm, pulling his wrist lower to intertwine her fingers with his. Without a word she led him down the hall leading to their bedroom.

You've upset her, the Ra'Voshnik growled. It brushed the surface of his awareness; certain it could mend what he had done.

Only Rune wasn't entirely sure how he offended her. Faye won her realm. He silenced Delilah. Perhaps she was upset Lyssa attacked her sister. If his queen wished for retribution, he would gift her Lyssa's offending appendage in a carved wooden box.

The black mist flowing down Faye's wings deepened until they became the Darkness, holding their shape. Sharp purple tendrils lit the churning mist as it slowly dissipated, revealing Faye's bare back.

Her hand slipped from his as they entered their bedroom. He closed the door, shielding the room from prying ears.

Let me rise. She prefers me, the creature grated.

Rune ignored it, turning toward his queen. "Have I offended you?"

Faye turned and peered at him with her mouth agape. "Offended me? This—You went against everything we talked about."

The bite in her words struck him. He'd done as she asked, obeying her will and sparing fools he should have killed. "The situation escalated. I settled it."

Faye folded her arms and gazed out the window, muttering, "Settled it. Sadi turned everyone into puppets."

"Vsenia," Rune said gently. He strolled to the tall narrow window, allowing her space. She stood silently for a long moment, eyes glazing over and peering over his crystalline realm as she had when he first sequestered her in Hell. "Speak with me," he whispered. Rune frowned at her continued silence. "Help me understand, vsenia."

Ask her forgiveness, the Ra'Voshnik growled.

The creature was too short-sighted to see past its own nose. Apologizing did nothing if he didn't understand what caused his queen's ire.

Faye swallowed, and her shoulders fell. "All of you... even my sister." She winced and glanced down, slowly unfolding her arms.

"You all went against what I asked." Red stained the crook of her arm and transferred to her gown. She cradled her injured palm, looking down at her dress. "Fucking hell," she cursed under her breath.

Veined misted shadows stretched beneath Rune's eyes, the Ra'Voshnik lingering close to the surface. Longing thrummed from it as the creature urged him to comfort their queen.

Rune took her hand, smoothing his thumb over the cuts. He mended her injuries, whispering, "The Queen of Lace and Bone is a vampire. I snapped her neck to silence her. She will rise in a few hours." She didn't react to his words as he continued, "Sadi held the crowd but left no lingering effects. Your sister…" He healed the last laceration and thinned his lips. "I have no rationalization for the blonde harpy."

Faye wiggled her fingers, testing the healed skin. "I don't want to be like them. I don't want *us* to be like them," Faye whispered without looking up at him. "I'm not going to act like a dark-blood."

His young queen held the best intentions, but goodwill and kind intent were not what dark courts were built on. Dark-bloods wouldn't stop a millennia of bloodshed because Faye didn't agree with their methods.

"Vsenia, you *are* a dark-blood," he murmured, drawing her into his arms. Rune sighed relieved she allowed it. The Ra'Voshnik purred as she leaned into him, resting her head on his chest. "Fear of retribution is what will protect your people, love. You cannot have one without the other."

Faye leaned away, staring up at him. "We can do this without bloodshed. Violence isn't the answer."

If you're violent enough, it is, the Ra'Voshnik argued.

Rune exhaled. She would hesitate, softening her blows. Dark-bloods like Delilah wouldn't return Faye's kindness. His queen's heart was far too timid, a weakness others would be all too happy to exploit. "Vsenia, you need to strike at enemies. They must fear challenging your will."

Faye shook her head. "No. They're children throwing a tantrum because they lost a realm where their actions had no consequences."

He could offer her understanding, if not, agreeance. This would end badly, but he could shield Faye. Protect her. "You are my queen, and I will always bow to your will. You have the noblest of intentions, but you move in error."

"This isn't a mistake," Faye said softly. "We can do this the correct way."

Her wishes would paint a target on her back, inviting others to oppose her court. *We will protect her,* the Ra'Voshnik growled. Rune agreed. He was vicious enough to protect his mate and her court. If she wished to rewrite protocol, he would be her line in the sand. "I am yours to command," Rune vowed.

Rune's scent of amber and sandalwood comforted her. The tension Faye carried through the day melted away in increments as he held her in silence.

"If you are well, I need to bathe," Rune said quietly.

Faye's brow pinched, and she pulled away. His black suit looked impeccable; nothing was amiss. As always. Her gaze stopped at the slightly darker stain inside the crook of his arm.

"I'm sorry. I didn't mean to get blood on you," Faye said, brushing her fingertips over the dark spot.

He chuckled, stepping away from her as he slipped out of his jacket. "Magic leaves a psychic scent. I have no tolerance for the musk of other women on me."

Faye quirked her lip at him. *Really?* When he didn't immediately reply, she stood on her toes and sniffed his collar while he loosened his tie. "I don't smell anything," she whispered, before falling back on her heels.

"I can," Rune purred. He raised his chin toward their bathroom and crooned, "Shower with me."

Faye lifted her head higher and blinked at him. "I think you're looking for an excuse to see me naked."

"An exquisite perk of being your consort," he said.

The corner of his mouth lifted into a smirk, and he silently strolled away. Her dress pooled on the floor, and Faye frowned at the sound of spraying water. He started the shower without her.

"This man," Faye grumbled to herself. She stepped out of her heels and padded to her mate.

She leaned in, holding the doorframe. A smile spread over her lips, and Faye swallowed a laugh. Her poor vampire scrubbed himself with a cleansing oil, running it through his hair.

"Do they smell *that* bad?" she asked, wiggling her fingers at him in greeting when he glanced her way.

She stepped into the glass enclosure, admiring the hard plains of his body. How the muscles of his chest and arms flexed as he tipped his head back to rinse his white-blonde hair.

Rune straightened to meet her gaze and stepped into her. She flushed under his predatorial gaze… suddenly wanting to run. Her lips parted as she imagined him catching her and pinning her beneath him. The steam rose in wisps around them, and she soaked in the heat of his body. Her hair clung to his damp chest as he encircled her in his strong arms.

"Yours, is the only scent I care to be covered in," he purred.

Her gaze fell to his lips, and he smiled. His canines lengthened to sharp points.

Rune gripped the backs of her thighs, lifting her against him. His lips brushed her throat as he guided her legs around his waist. Faye jumped as teeth grazed her earlobe, and he rasped, "Your sister is expecting you."

Faye wrapped her arms around his neck, pulling him in. At his mouth, she whispered, "She can wait."

He palmed her ass and turned, guiding her into the hot water. Faye sighed, squeezing her thighs over his ribs. She arched her back, lifting her breasts to him as the water rinsed through her hair down her back.

"If the harpy shuffles my books again," he growled, pulling her against him. Rune nipped and licked her throat until Faye lost her breath and rolled her hips, desperate for him.

He pulled back, and when she opened her eyes in protest, he purred, "I will edge you for the same amount of time it takes me to reorganize my study."

Faye dragged her nails across his back, and he groaned. "You could be quick."

Rune canted his head. "You wound a man's ego."

Faye raised her brows and pouted in a feigned look of sympathy.

"I will tend to you tonight when I can take my time," he promised, setting her on her feet.

Eighteen

Rune dried his hair and escorted his queen to the courtyard. A gray stone archway opened into his crystalline realm. He was surprised to see Sadi seated across from Vashien near the refreshment table. Perhaps her open hostility was beginning to cool.

The creature's dark laughter swept through his mind. *You're not that lucky.*

Sadi did have a temper, but she was loyal. A difficult trait to come by—nearly impossible among immortals. Rune silently regarded the winged male who stood between himself and Faye on more than one occasion. The corner of Rune's mouth lifted. He'd even stepped between himself and the blonde harpy, knowing Rune could reduce him to shadows and ash with a simple thought.

He liked the winged male but pitied him for his choice of women. He supposed it was happenstance he and Sadi were seated together since their chosen circled each other in the crude sparring circle Damian designed in the courtyard.

The blonde harpy lunged at Damian but stopped mid-swing when she caught sight of Faye. Damian shook his head and twisted his wrist to spin his sword in idle circles. "Going to smack you the next time you drop your guard, dove."

Sparrow snorted and fluttered her hand at him. She turned to Rune and said, "Since Faye is the Queen of Anaria are you the King, Runey? You are, right? Since you're 'dark-blood married' and all." Her eyes widened at Faye. "Darkness, you're the Queen of Hell, bitch."

Yes, she wants to be married. Did you forget she was talking to her sister before we went to collect her realm from the bird king? The Ra'Voshnik asked, floating comfortably through his mind.

Rune ignored the creature and exhaled. "I have no desire to be king of anything. I am the will of my queen."

Sparrow rolled her eyes and gestured around her. "You're the King of Hell."

The Ra'Voshnik scraped its claws across his awareness. *You can't ignore me. If you won't ask her to marry you, I will.*

We will speak of this at a later time, Rune bit out. He followed Faye to the iron benches beside a small table topped with drinks and snacks the blonde harpy constantly kept on hand.

He poured Faye's tea as he spoke. "I took my father's mantle after his death because I was the strongest."

"That's usually how kingliness is passed down," Sparrow said, waving the tip of her sword at him in a tight circle.

Thank you, Faye mouthed as he offered her drink. These small moments warmed his heart with emotions he'd thought he would never experience. She'd changed him, and he craved her presence above all others.

You can crave her at a jewelry store. We should be looking for her ring right now, the Ra'Voshnik growled.

Be silent, Rune bit out. The creature tested the limits of his patience. He refrained from dragging it to the recesses of his mind because his queen held affection for it.

It's not affection. She loves me, the Ra'Voshnik chuckled. *Prefers me to you—if you're honest with yourself.*

Rune schooled his expression and replied, "There is nothing to rule. I accepted the title because a Shadowman needed to maintain Hell's floor."

Sparrow gave him an unimpressed look. "A shadow what?"

"My father was a Shadowman. Saith created him as a caretaker of Hell. The realm is stitched into our veins." Rune tapped the crystalline ground with his shoe. "Hell's floor is a construct of my father's design. The realm fed on him to maintain it when he lived, and I have taken his place."

"So, Hell is eating you?" Sparrow crinkled her nose at his nod and asked, "What happens if you stop?"

Rune suspected the errant power trapped beneath the crystal ground would be unleashed across his realm but was reluctant to test his theory. His father, Julian, devised Hell as it stood. Rune worried if he unraveled too much of his father's design, he would be unable to restore it.

"It would be disastrous," he answered.

Sparrow snorted, rolling her eyes. "So back to the wedding—"

"Anaria is our primary concern," Faye said over her sister.

Damian quirked his lip. "Made some enemies today. Delilah was quite unhappy with you, dove."

"Was that the red-hair bitch or the black-haired bitch?" Sparrow asked, tipping her sword one way then the other.

"Delilah rules the Court of Lace and Bone." When Sparrow's brow came down, Vashien added, "The black-haired one."

"The red heads are Lyssa's twins. Gabriel and Morgan," Damian said. "Keep your shields about you. You made enemies of all three."

"Let her send her court. I will return them to her," Rune crooned.

"In mangled pieces," Sadi said in a deceptively sweet voice.

"No." Faye met each of their gazes. "We are not killing. We're setting an example."

Sparrow snorted. "Stop being so nice. They swung first, you're allowed to stomp on their necks now."

Faye winced and guilt ate at Rune. He'd offended her, operating outside of her will. She wanted to rule without bloodshed, and he would protect her, while obeying her desires. "My queen wishes to rewrite protocol. We will be a more civilized dark court."

Damian frowned and shrugged as he inspected the edge of his

blade. "I could pay the Court of Lace and Bone a visit without my queen's knowledge. Rough them up a touch."

In the past, he would have agreed, accepting Belind's silent instructions. But Faye was different.

He quietly wondered where the woman who struck him with a weighted metal candleholder after he kidnapped her had gone. If she used the same ferocity, she'd fought him with, her court would be established in a few weeks. Rune exhaled. His gentle queen dug her heels into her concept of right and wrong, despite his warnings and better judgment.

Rune spoke, giving them each an unspoken command as Faye's consort and executioner. As the male fate chose to protect her.

"We will obey the will and desire of my queen."

Nineteen

S parrow remained diligent during the past week, meeting Damian
to train each morning. Her sister insisted she join the *fun,* but Faye
chose to focus on her magic. Sadi and Rune both assured her that
learning to control her power would be taxing, but she felt inadequate. She could do so little, and the effects lingered, leaving her
exhausted for days.

Each day she woke in the early afternoon and found Rune
reviewing documents on the small desk in their room. The bitter animosity between Alister and Rune no longer tainted the happiness she
found with her vampire. The slate had been wiped clean, and she felt
lighter after Prinia's rescue.

Even the night terrors plaguing her dreams faded slowly. She
suspected her apprehension to the cold would never truly go away,
but she slept through the night for the first time in ages, waking up

between Rune and Voshki, warm and at peace.

Faye strolled into Rune's study. His ornate glass backdrop filtered the soft light of Hell's ever-twilight sky, basking the edge of her vampire's hair in a gentle glow. Today was her first official day of being Queen. Rune smiled as she reached his desk and slid a stack of letters toward her.

"What are these?" Faye picked up the first envelope. The elegant script read:

To the Queen of Chaos and Darkness.

Rune didn't answer, only watched her expectantly.

Faye broke the burgundy wax. Her heart pounded faster as she read the words over and over again. "This is a day-blood." And they requested admittance to her court. Hers.

She'd known Anarians would come, desperate for any protection from the dark-bloods who preyed on them. A year ago, she would have petitioned for her place within the safety of a benevolent court, then begged for her village's entry.

Those with magic could never understand the fear she buried every time Sparrow dragged her to Necromia. A moment. A moment was all it took for a dark-blood to kidnap her, trap her in their dark court, and force her to become their pet. And in some ways, she did get kidnapped and trapped. While she didn't become Rune's pet, the danger was all the same. But Rune was different and yet, in many ways, all the same.

Day-bloods couldn't comprehend the suffocating feeling of being weak, of never truly having control. Faye swallowed her bitterness. Why would one of them want to associate with the lowly Anarians they considered animals?

Faye set the letter down, opening the next. She looked to Rune. "Are they all requests?"

"You have dozens of requests. Perhaps the harpy could be of use? She seems to delight in reading documents addressed to you," Rune teased.

Faye bit the inside of her lip, studying the letters. "There has to be a misunderstanding." She placed it back down, eyeing the shimmery texture of the seals. "Do they think I'm going to hand over my villages and let them rule?" Why else would a day-blood ask to migrate to her realm?

Rune's playful expression fell as he thinned his lips. Her vampire shifted his chair back and held his hand out to her. Faye let the letters fall on his desk. This wasn't what she wanted. Anaria was hers, and she would protect them all.

His deep, accented voice caressed her. "Vsenia." The warmth of his hand surrounded hers, and Rune drew her onto his lap. "You offer safety to the weak," Rune said, holding her loosely.

"Day-bloods have no interest in Anaria. My realm only looks attractive because they can't get a foothold in Necromia." A place where the dark-bloods ruled, and the strong reaped no consequences for their actions. Faye swallowed her hateful thoughts. Day-bloods wanted nothing to do with her realm before Faye blanketed Anaria under her protection. An invitation she extended to *her* people, not them.

"What you are offering will be coveted by many. There will be many day-bloods and dark-bloods requesting to join your ranks. Courts are more than power, vsenia. They are safety and protection." Rune held her against him as he reached forward to retrieve the letters she had abandoned.

He held the request in front of her and explained, "Each of us holds a range of strength. Our courts and system of retribution allow lighter shards to band together and collectively fend off a more dangerous threat. A dark-blood could easily harm a single day-blood but will think twice if the consequence of their actions yields the retribution of a court twenty strong."

"You don't think they want to come here to be *Anaria's dark-bloods.*" Faye eyed the stack of letters he left in easy reach and spared him her skepticism. Rune chuckled, and Faye thumped his chest. "It's not funny. I'm being serious."

"I am sorry, love." He brought her hand to his mouth and kissed the back of her fingers. "I believe they desire the safety associated with belonging to a court, and you..." A gentle purr rumbled quietly from his lips. "Are the Queen of the darkest court in history."

She wore a darker shard than him, but she was no fool. Having the Shadow Prince as her consort afforded her court the merciless reputation he spent lifetimes cultivating. His words played in her mind. His promise when she woke with her shards.

I will be the consequence for striking against our court.

She longed for equality between the Anarians, day-bloods, and dark-bloods. Which meant she needed to stop looking at the day-bloods and dark-bloods as enemies. She couldn't afford to let her bitterness color the realm she wanted for her children.

Faye studied her nail beds and asked, "What do I do if they ask for villages?" Courts ruled over the cities and towns in Necromia. Would they expect the same thing to happen here?

The corner of Rune's mouth lifted into a smirk, and his eyes lit with humor. "You are the reigning Queen, vsenia. Your word is law. Simply tell them no."

She gathered the stack of letters, and hesitantly took the day-blood request Rune held. "Do you think he'll see the Anarians? Treat them as equals?"

"If they wish to join your court, they will acquiesce to your will."

A mental tether scratched the edge of Faye's mind, and her brow pinched. She welcomed Rune into her mind, unsure why he wanted a communication tether when he could speak to her.

And if they won't bow, I'll take their legs.

Their voices were identical, but Faye recognized Voshki. She leaned closer to Rune and whispered, "Behave."

Her vampire glanced upward and exhaled. "You are being rude."

Says the man hogging our queen, Voshki grated.

A growl rumbled through Faye's mind, and she giggled. "I think he has the communication tether set up so I can hear both of you."

"Wonderful," Rune said, drumming his fingers over her thigh.

Get out of the way, I want to sit with our queen, Voshki purred.

Voshki's veined misted shadows stretched beneath Rune's pale blue eyes. She ran the pad of her thumb through them. The shadows swirled in different directions, disturbed by her touch. She pressed a kiss to the corner of his mouth and whispered, "I'll sit with you tonight. Rune is showing me court things."

The kiss was for me, Voshki grumbled. The communication link snapped a moment later, and Rune shook his head.

"The creature has grown bolder since becoming acquainted with you," he sighed.

"Voshki isn't a creature," she said.

Rune closed his eyes and tilted his head to run an index over the center of his forehead. "I have lived with *it* longer than you have."

He gazed down at her with the same look of annoyance she wore when Sparrow rattled on about something she shouldn't have done but was unreasonably proud of. For as old as they were, the two of them squabbled like teenage boys. Voshki was more to blame than Rune, but she trusted him implicitly. Her beautiful hunter wouldn't act without her direct approval. Even if he reminded her of a cat, bringing her the mice and birds he caught to show his affection. Sparrow joked Voshki showed his love with violence, and Faye reluctantly agreed. The man wanted to solve even the simplest problems with abject murder.

"Be nice to each other?" Faye hadn't meant for it to come out as a question. Her plea was met with silence. "Please," she added. The two of them shared a body. They couldn't escape each other. Getting along should have been a priority thousands of years ago.

Rune remained silent, and Faye resigned herself to his answer. *He's really old. Baby steps,* Faye reminded herself as she stood, taking her letters to sit across his desk. She broke the dark green wax seal of the next envelope and began to read.

"You will need a staff. A secretary, at the very least. There are several more requests," Rune said.

Faye blinked up at him. "I have more?"

Rune waved his hand, and a large, wired basket filled with letters appeared on the end of his desk. "More are coming by the minute."

As Rune spoke, more letters appeared above the basket, falling into it. "I'll get Sparrow to help me sort these," Faye said as another group of letters appeared and fell. Faye met Rune's gaze and added, "Maybe Vash too."

Twenty

F aye took the wire basket and hurried to Sparrow's wing. More
requests appeared and tumbled out of the basket, scattering across
the stone floor. She couldn't help but laugh as she retrieved them.

"Allow me," Rune said, promptly vanishing the basket and letters.

"Thank you," she said, getting to her feet. They turned the corner,
and Faye yelled, "Hooker."

"Bitch," Sparrow answered.

Faye found her in the den, seated at the dining table. She held a
cold compress to her shoulder and poured a shot of vodka. Faye wrinkled her nose as Sparrow threw back her shot and filled a second.

"What happened to you?" Faye asked.

"She dropped her guard," Vashien answered from behind them.
He walked to Sparrow with a jar of white salve.

"That fucker *threw me*," Sparrow interjected.

"Do you need Sadi to mend your injuries?" Rune asked.

Sparrow rolled her shoulder as Vash massaged in the ointment. "No, I already healed it. It's just stiff."

"I have something that will make you feel better," Faye said as she sat down. She drummed her hands on the table and glanced up at Rune.

Her vampire called the basket and Faye shook the requests. Sparrow lifted her chin to peer at its contents. "What's this shit?"

"We have requests to join our court," Faye said, unable to keep the excitement from her voice.

The petite blonde promptly picked up a letter, cracking its wax seal. Rune chuckled as Sparrow lifted her gaze to him momentarily. She set the letter aside and opened the next. "You are one popular bitch." She rapidly opened the letters, each detailing the same thing: a request to join her court.

"Open these," Sparrow said as she placed a messy pile of letters in front of Vashien.

He caught Faye's gaze and held up the envelope addressed to her with a frown. Faye laughed softly, reaching for her own pile as more folded parchments appeared and fell on her hand.

"There are too many for me to read through alone," Faye explained.

"When are you getting your castle in Anaria?" Sparrow asked.

Faye glanced up from her letter to stare at her sister. "I'm not getting a castle."

"His shadowy highness isn't buying you a castle?" Sparrow cut a glance to her vampire and snorted. "Runey, how could you?"

Rune exhaled deeply and took his own pile of requests. "It pains me to agree with the blonde harpy, but she is correct."

Faye slouched, tucking her feet under her chair. He couldn't be serious. "I don't want a castle," she grumbled, glaring at her sister. Next, she would want her to string diamonds through her hair like the High Queen. "And no, I don't want a crown," Faye said before Sparrow could rattle off her list of demands.

Her sister wilted with a huff. "You're a Queen. Don't be boring."

"Vsenia, we are not asking you to change," Rune reassured her.

"The fuck we're not. You're a Queen now, bitch. Not just his queen. A *Queen*, Queen," she said, pointing at Rune before splaying her fingers to make small circles at Faye. "You need a castle, preferably bigger than the high bitch's. And multiple crowns. And wing jewelry—Did you know Artithians have wing jewelry?"

"Be silent," Rune chided.

Sparrow opened her mouth wide and hissed at him.

Vashien's membranous wing curved around her sister's seat and yanked her closer. The chair dragged loudly against the stones, and she wrinkled her nose, staring at him. A smaller hiss escaped her lips.

"Leave Faye alone," Vashien said, pulling her sister's blonde curls into her face before mussing it further. "You don't get to be Queen through her."

"Your court will need an estate to serve as your stronghold," Rune added.

Faye bit the inside of her lip. He was so cautious, approaching everything like they were preparing for an inescapable battle. She didn't need a stronghold.

"Build your shit in Anaria," Sparrow grumbled. Her sister leaned forward and her blonde curls fell over her shoulder as she rubbed her bottom. "I think I still have a crystal in my ass from when Damian threw me."

Vashien cracked the wax seal on the next letter with a sharp twist of his wrist and paused, thumping Sparrow with his wingtip. "You should've been shielding yourself."

She threw an elbow at the much larger male, and he only stared down at her. "Keep siding with cat boy, and I'll bite your dick next time you want me to *play nice*."

Faye didn't mind knowing all her sister's euphemisms, but it had been easier when Sparrow kept a man for a few weeks at the most. Faye studied the request in her hands, convincing herself she didn't know '*play nice*' meant Sparrow let Vashien tie her hands behind her back and fuck her mouth. And she definitely didn't see Vash's cheeks flushing burgundy.

"I could purchase the land near your home, outside Alexander, but an estate will take months to complete," Rune offered.

"You want to be close to Aunty Clara, don't lie." Sparrow's bright green eyes lit with excitement. "*Aaaaaaaand* we could train at Aunty Clara's house. You get to visit the little beasties, and I get soft grass for my tail. It's perfect!"

Faye glanced at Rune, and he nodded, saying, "I will make the arrangements."

"Do not," Faye warned, pointing at her sister, "show up at Aunty Clara's house with swords and shit. I need to ask first."

Sparrow made a rude noise and fluttered her hand in her direction. "Bitch, she lets you do anything." She tilted her head back and forth, whining, "You're her favorite."

Faye rolled her eyes and the four of them opened letter after letter. The sound of rustling paper filled the space between them. Faye motioned to the requests Sparrow stacked in two piles. "Why are you separating them?"

Sparrow tapped the smaller pile. "Day-bloods." Then the larger one. "Anarians."

"That's a good idea." Faye sifted through her open letters pulling out the day-bloods she had.

Rune held out a letter to Faye, and Sparrow snatched it.

"Give it back, hooker," Faye hissed, kicking at her sister under the table but missing entirely.

Sparrow met her gaze, and her eyes gleamed as she shook the page. "You just bagged your first dark-blood, bitch."

Faye's snatched the letter back. Her lips parted. A dark-blood shared her vision?

Sparrow gave her a toothy grin. "Maybe Silver Leaves will want to join you too."

Rune arched a brow and glanced at Faye. "I was trying to set her up before you came along and kidnapped her." Faye kicked again, this time connecting with Sparrow's shin. "Ow, bitch. His shadowiness did kidnap you. Tell me I'm lying."

Her sister leaned forward to rub her shin, and Faye went back to reading without answering.

"Don't be so boring. It'll be a hell of a story to tell your kids." Sparrow tapped a sealed letter at Rune. "Have you stopped drinking your contraceptive tea yet?"

"I'm about to take the letters away from you," Faye said.

"No! I want to know who's joining our court." Sparrow moved her pile of letters out of Faye's reach and glared at Rune "She never kept secrets from me until you showed up."

"It's private," Faye said curtly.

Sparrow huffed, blowing a curl out of her face. "You're going to make me an aunt. I should get to know."

Faye glanced at her sister. Her expectant expression left her speechless. "I don't know what's going on in that kitty cat brain of yours, but this is private."

Sparrow gave Rune a pleading glance, and he chuckled. "You know I do as she bids."

Her shoulders slumped as she went back to her letters. "You better tell me after you tell him."

"You'll be the first we tell," Faye promised. Her sister only snorted at her. She narrowed her eyes and glanced at Rune. "Do you think Sadi will be okay to continue our lessons at Aunty Clara's house?"

"I am certain it will not be an issue," Rune replied.

Sparrow took another pile of documents. "What's she teaching you?"

Sadi wasn't really teaching her anything because Faye struggled to do the basics. She'd thought her power would obey her. Sparrow had such an easy time of it after she invoked her blood.

"I'm practicing drawing my power toward me." And failing. She couldn't take a small piece of her power and lift it. Her magic was a great lazy beast who refused to listen to her. She'd struggled to drag its dead weight to her body after she woke this morning, and the ordeal left her exhausted.

Rune added his letters into Faye's sorted piles. "It will come in time. The practice is for your benefit."

Sparrow snickered. "I bet he said that in bed too, huh?" Her sister frowned when she didn't reply. "Know what comes after your orgy moon?" Sparrow asked, opening another letter. Faye glared at her sister. When she learned how to manipulate her powers, the first thing she was going to have Rune teach her was a silencing spell.

Her vampire leaned back in his chair and gazed lovingly at Faye. "I am aware of my mate's birthday."

Sparrow eyed him suspiciously. "How old will she be, your fangyness?"

"Stop," Faye hissed.

"I'm testing his *devotion*," Sparrow said.

A warm smile spread over his lips. "A quarter century and a year."

Sparrow quirked her lip. "Say twenty-six like a normal person."

Faye laughed, placing another letter in the Anarian pile.

Sparrow clapped and pressed her hands together. "You know what we should do? Go back to the Hunter's Moon ball and reenact how you met."

"You'd get escorted out of the High Queen's ball the moment you set foot there," Vashien said dryly.

Faye straightened her documents as Rune said, "I will not be attending. Lyssa seems to have… misplaced my invitation this year."

Sparrow threw her hands in the air and Faye groaned, closing her eyes. "Even more reason to crash her party," her sister insisted. "I'll sight shield her again. You both meet by the food station. Then I'll trip her into you. Orrrrrr—"

"We are not welcome. I will not trespass into her ball," Rune said simply.

Sparrow lips spread into a toothy smile. "You'll just be trespassing on Faye in your bed?"

Vashien coughed, and Faye cracked her lids.

Her sister propped her head up with her hand and pouted. "Something must happen. The vampire brothels charge triple that night."

Faye's face heated, and she stood, announcing, "I'm going to take a nap. We're not having this discussion." The Hunter's Moon would rise next month, and she needed to talk to Rune and Voshki about it. The thought of them lusting for her beneath the red moon intrigued her. She might have to ask Voshki what Rune liked since he was always too concerned with her pleasure. The few times she'd seen her stoic vampire undone, ignited her blood. She craved seeing him past his reason.

"Give me something," Sparrow whined. "Does the red moon let you keep it up all night?"

The corner of Rune's mouth lifted. "You could request Vashien to escort you to a vampire brothel."

Vashien immediately shook his head. "It's the biggest night of the year, and it's gotten a lot busier since your sister's court formed. I need to be at work."

Sparrow squinted at each of them.

"I hate all of you."

Twenty-One

R une excused himself a few minutes after Faye's departure. He vanished the requests and thanked Sparrow and Vashien. The continuous flow of letters would need a staff to review. He would speak to Faye regarding it after she woke from her nap.

He phased to his study and took a seat behind his bloodroot desk. Bookshelves lined the wall opposite the fireplace. He turned the page of the latest volume he'd borrowed from the Familiar library. He'd read dozens of books, their blank covers silently mocking him. He supposed he should be grateful. Morbid refused to give him the information he required outright, but the identical leather-bound tomes remained in order.

Small mercies, he thought to himself. However, he was no closer to uncovering the origins of the Elysian Queen after months of toiling.

An identical set of books was piled at the far edge of his desk as he fell into an easy rhythm listening to his queen's breathing as she snored softly. Faye would deny it vehemently anytime her sister brought it up, but a smile tugged at his lips. What she considered a flaw he found endearing.

The blonde harpy's commentary replayed through his mind. Her thoughtless words made his dark queen retreat to their bedroom. He knew when Faye bound herself to him after announcing her court, any dark-blooded immortal would see them as a devoted pair. However, his night breeze held other customs and desires.

Marriage and children among them.

Things we could easily give her, the Ra'Voshnik grated, disapproving of the distance separating it from Faye.

The grandfather clock near the mantle chimed, and Rune glanced up from his desk.

You've been here for thirty minutes. Return to our queen, it growled.

The creature had a singular mind. Its focus always toward one thing: their queen. It listened to her easy breathing from their bedroom, growing more agitated with each moment it suffered from the lack of her proximity.

Rune typically read while Faye dozed on his lap, but he had other affairs to attend to once he was certain Faye was in a deep sleep.

She is resting, Rune replied.

The Ra'Voshnik circled his mind impatiently. *She's nocturnal. We should adjust our sleep schedule to her.* She wasn't nocturnal, but she did tire easily. It forced her to nap during the day more often than not.

Rune skimmed the last few pages of the tome he was currently reading.

Faye sighed and a rustle of sheets followed. Rune glanced toward the bookshelves and listened as her breathing became slow and steady once more. He thanked the Darkness for gifting him such a wonderous woman. With their previous conversations, he found himself hoping Faye carried his young but held his tongue on the matter each time her monthly courses began. He dismissed her fatigue as a symptom caused by the stress of forming her court, especially with the influx of new requests to join.

He'd never contemplated siring young, but imagining white-haired little ones with lightning-streaked midnight eyes made his chest ache.

The Ra'Voshnik ran its claws over Rune's awareness. *Don't delude yourself. We both know I'm fathering our queen's young.*

Rune didn't answer, silently wondering if his sons would mirror his father as he and his brothers did. He'd ordered a selection of fruits and honeyed tea for Faye and had it delivered on the nightstand beside her. Satisfying his queen's needs was his primary focus. And his most pressing task involved finding a suitable ring to offer her.

Had she been raised in a dark court, he would have procured a diamond ring whose fiery glitter would shame the very stars. But her taste and temperament ran opposite of the typical dark-blooded queens. He'd observed her, learning her inclinations. What she valued.

But trinkets weren't among them.

The single piece of jewelry adorning his queen was the ring housing her soul shard. He had nothing else to measure her preferred style against. No hair combs, pendants, or bangles for him to search through and compare. Her few hair sticks were wooden with small floral charms attached to them. Devoid of jewels.

Only one person could help with such a task. Rune reached for his realm feeling for Sparrow's location. Hell answered, and his brow pinched. The blonde harpy was in Faye's gardens.

Finally coming to your senses and going to ask her to marry us? the Ra'Voshnik asked, pleasantly floating through his mind.

Rune phased to the outer courtyard, narrowing his eyes against the late afternoon sun. Magic sustained the black roses, holding them in perpetual bloom for more than eight centuries. He plucked a flower and silently strolled toward the gate leading to his queen's sanctuary.

"Harder," Vashien groaned. A splash followed and he rasped, "That's my best girl."

Rune halted his steps and the Ra'Voshnik came seething to the surface, riddled with animosity. *Kill him. He called Faye his best girl.*

Calm yourself. He is speaking to his female, not our queen. The large male knew better than to incline Faye with any type of sexual connotation. Rune extended his awareness beyond his body and discovered the mental perimeter Vashien set up before the iron gate. A pang of guilt stung him, but he didn't have days to wait for the perfect opportunity to arise.

Rune strolled to the mental barrier and outstretched his hand.

"Stop, someone's here," Vashien growled.

Give him to me! I'm going to rip his wings off his back and mount them in the great room, the Ra'Voshnik's roared.

Rune reached for the winged male's mind. *Apologies for the interruption. I am in need of Sparrow's assistance on a matter.*

Is Faye alright? Vashien's voice pitched up in concern.

She is well—

Call Faye your best girl again and your suffering—

Rune cursed in High Tongue, dragging the creature into the recesses of his mind, and silencing it.

Apologies, Rune grated.

Vashien didn't answer immediately, and Rune waited. After a long pause he said in a hushed whisper, "Rune is asking for you."

"Come on in. You shadowy cock blocker!" Sparrow yelled, followed by the sound of splashing. "What are you doing?"

"You're not dressed," Vashien snarled as Rune stepped into the inner courtyard.

Sparrow stood on the stone seating in the spring, lifting herself out of the water to her waist. "I have a bikini on," she hissed, pointing at herself.

"You're in a thong!"

Sparrow rolled her eyes. "He's a million years old. He's seen ass before."

Vashien's wing snapped around her, dragging her back into the water.

The corner of Rune's mouth lifted. "Is she your first Familiar?" Rune asked, attempting to keep the amusement out of his voice. By Familiar standards, the minimal strips of red fabric crisscrossing over the blonde harpy were conservative.

Sparrow shoved Vashien's wing away and folded her arms over the stones bordering the spring. "Best five years of his life," she answered.

"We're not at five years yet."

"We're past four," Sparrow retorted and stuck her tongue out at him. Her attention returned to Rune, and she asked, "How many Familiar have you been with?"

He casually glanced over the articles of clothing strewn over the azalea plants. *On either side of the spring.* "My mother resided in Chaos when she was mortal. She adopted much of their culture."

"Your mom, huh? Nothing to do with Sadi?" Sparrow pressed.

Rune hummed, narrowing his eyes at the towels hanging in his willow.

She followed his gaze and fluttered her hand at him. "They're fine," she assured him.

He exhaled, bringing his attention back to the petite blonde. "I have never touched her in that way." He couldn't fathom why she and Faye fixated on Sadi. She was his oldest friend. Steadfast and loyal. She never feared him or coveted him simply for the status his title provided.

He'd never held romantic inclinations for the Familiar Princess.

You didn't have any romantic inclinations for Lyssa either, but you bowed all the same! the Ra'Voshnik roared from its shackles. Rune ignored the creature.

Unlike Lyssa, Sadi would never ask it of him.

He lifted his chin toward the winged-male. "Vashien would have better luck crawling into my bed."

Sparrow gasped and turned toward her male. "Hear that, Wing Daddy? You have a chance."

"No, thanks. I'm sure you bite a lot harder than she does," Vashien said, rubbing the side of his neck.

Sparrow ogled the water droplets sliding down the tendon in his throat. Her gaze roamed over her male's heavily muscled physique. Rune cleared his throat, and the little blonde harpy drummed the grass, staring up at him. "You came to ask me what to get Faye for her birthday, huh? I have a personal shopper's fee, just so you know."

"I would like to know the type of jewel Faye would prefer in an engagement ring," Rune replied.

The blonde harpy shrieked and clapped, hopping in the water. Rune winced, rubbing his ear.

Vashien lifted himself out of the pool, wrapping the towel around his waist while Rune took his measure, quietly assessing what position he held in his previous court.

He approached Rune, clasping his hand in a firm shake. "Congratulations, that's great—"

"I need to plan a bridal shower. I was already planning a baby shower." Sparrow's eyes widened, and she fell silent for a breath. "Darkness, is Faye pregnant? You knocked her up, didn't you? That's why you need to get married suddenly." She lifted herself out of the pool while spewing her theories, each more intrusive than the last.

"The stone, harpy," Rune said dryly while adjusting his cuffs.

Sparrow opened and closed her hand. "No, baby first." She pointed to her empty palm. Rune exhaled and glanced at Vashien. He shrugged. "Vash isn't going to save you from me, fangs. You tell me if my sister is pregnant, and I tell you the rock she likes." Rune thinned his lips, and the blonde harpy nodded at him with a toothy smile. "She likes a very specific gem, and I'll give you a hint. It's *not* a diamond."

Rune folded his arm, pinching the bridge of his nose. "Do you know the jewel Faye would prefer?" he asked Vashien.

"You better shut all the way up," Sparrow hissed, holding her hips.

Vashien hefted his broad shoulders and lifted his hands, stepping away from Rune.

"My queen is not pregnant," Rune sighed.

In true Familiar fashion, she narrowed her eyes and quirked her lip. She leaned closer, jutting her chin out as she peered up at him. "You promise?"

Rune placed his hand over his heart and inclined his head.

"Okay," she muttered before pointing at him. "I'm trusting you."

She called a plain wooden box and lifted its lid. Rune arched a brow as she sat cross-legged, removing handfuls of articulated rings before growing frustrated and dumping its contents onto the grass.

"She likes Alexandrite. Not because we grew up in Alexander." Sparrow continued to pick through the pile with the claw of her gauntleted ring. She lifted a gauntleted Familiar ring with intricate scroll work and held it up.

Rune leaned down, glad for her offering. He peered at the tear drop cut stone. It changed from green to purple as the sun hit its facets, depending on how he angled the ring.

"She likes it because it reminds her of her favorite leafy baby," Sparrow said, pointing to her sister's garden. "See that Jeweled Thorn? Big leafy fucker in the middle? She saved for three months to buy it. Had it since she was eighteen. You better thank the Darkness it didn't die when she broke up with you."

Rune knew she valued her garden but didn't realize she had a plant she favored for nearly eight years. Rune studied the ring and strolled toward the plant. He never would've made the correlation. Whenever Faye tended to her garden, his focus was always on his dark-blood queen. He reached out, touching the Jeweled Thorn. It had a deep green stalk which blended into a rich purple hue on its curling thorns and leaves.

"You should take me with you." Rune glanced over his shoulder at her, lifting a brow. "I'll help you pick out a ring for her, your shadowy highness."

"That will not be necessary," he said, letting go of the plant.

"That ring she's wearing now. The *only* ring she wears." Sparrow hopped back into the pool and tapped the dark gray misted soul shard embedded in its articulated metal. "I picked that shit out. Just saying."

"We should have a congratulatory drink after I get dressed," Vash said, collecting his and Sparrow's clothing.

"What? No, no. You can go drinking after *we're* done," Sparrow argued.

"I'll be a few minutes, sunshine." Vashien smiled at her warmly and vanished.

Sparrow crossed her arms over the stone border and pointed at Rune, "My shopping fee just went up exponentially."

Twenty-Two

R une shielded the room from prying ears and observed the large
Artithian sitting across his desk. He was tense. His wings tucked
tight to his back. Rune poured two glasses of bourbon and slid a
glass toward the winged male.

This was not a social call.

Vashien scrutinized his glass before swallowing the contents
in a single gulp and poured another. He spoke, inspecting his glass.
"When you came into the garden, there was another voice, but it
didn't speak like you."

Now it was Rune's turn to drink.

Let me surface. I'll introduce myself, the creature growled.

"I am a Pure Blood. What you heard was the Ra'Voshnik. I
would appreciate if this information did not move past you." Rune
didn't care for his nature being exposed, but his queen was bound to

divulge his secrets to her sister. Who in turn would tell her male.

"Is it your bloodlust?" Vashien asked, narrowing his eyes.

The Ra'Voshnik raged to the surface, bashing itself against Rune's awareness. It reached for Vashien's mind, and Rune subdued it before it could ground a mental tether.

I'm just going to rip off his wings, it bellowed, struggling to reach its prey.

Faye will not forgive you if you kill her sister's male, Rune growled.

He'll live. They'll grow back! It roared in answer.

The color drained from the winged male's face as veined misted shadows stretched beneath his gaze.

Rune raised a finger as he dragged the creature beneath the surface. *Calm yourself, or I will restrain you.*

It prowled his mind, stringing together profanities in High Tongue. Rune watched it for a moment before returning his attention to Vashien, who appeared to be on his fourth glass of bourbon.

"The Ra'Voshnik has its own consciousness and apparently takes great offense when called bloodlust." Rune chuckled while saying the last.

"Noted." Vashien rubbed his hands together and ran his thumb over his palm before glancing up at him. "Is it dangerous?"

Exceedingly, the creature snapped.

"To Faye," the winged male finished.

The Ra'Voshnik was shocked silent for a moment, before growling, *He's fucking dead.*

"Ah," Rune said with a smile. "I can respect you are worried for your friend. We are both hers to command."

Vashien leaned forward and in a quieter tone, as though it would somehow stop the Ra'Voshnik from hearing him, said, "So, Faye does know about it."

Rune laughed, placing his hand over his chest.

"Faye named it."

Vashien parted his lips, but no words came. The winged male's brows pinched as he blew out a breath and swirled the contents of his glass. He glanced up, meeting Rune's gaze and said, "I'm sorry. I needed to know she was safe."

Rune had grown to respect the male. True loyalty was difficult to come by, and Rune repaid it in kind.

He inclined his head and said, "I pose no danger to my queen."

Tell him I'll pose a danger to him if I catch his scent on Faye, the Ra'Voshnik snapped.

Rune ignored the creature and studied the larger male. "You served in a dark court before opening your establishment."

Vashien ran his hand through his hair. "It was a long time ago, but yes."

"What position did you hold?" Rune asked. His heavily muscled physique read a guard. A station within the courts, but not high enough to reap the opulent lifestyle.

"I was like you—*not like you*, like you," Vashien stammered out. He sighed, putting down his glass. "I was an executioner and consort."

Rune canted his head, puzzled. Both were coveted positions in their own right, and Vashien held two. "Why would you leave?"

Did his Queen perish under his guard?

Vashien shifted in his chair. "You're a consort to a woman who loves you. I became an executioner during my first century. I accepted the position of consort in my second." His smile faded as he said, "I thought he'd been sincere, but I was mistaken. He used me to pull the attention of the person he really wanted."

"I am sorry," Rune said, too familiar with the pain of being used and discarded.

The winged male shook his head. "I left because I didn't have the stomach for court politics and their agendas. I could never trust their intentions. I'm much happier running my tavern."

"Until a blonde harpy made herself at home in your bar." Rune laughed.

Vashien's smile returned, lighting his eyes. "I've had nearly everyone I know ask how I ended up with her."

Rune shrugged. "Opposites attract?"

"It's not that," he answered, gazing over Rune's head at Hell's sky. "Sparrow doesn't have an agenda. I don't have to second guess her intentions or wonder if she means what she says."

"She does overly express her mind," Rune agreed.

Vashien nodded, meeting his gaze. "And I love her for it." His smile turned sheepish as he rubbed the back of his neck. "I was going to ask her to marry me during the new year festival. But now she'll just say I'm copying you."

"Apologies." Rune chuckled as a bundle of letters appeared in a mesh basket. He untied the twine and began sorting the letters.

Vashien sipped his bourbon. "I asked Aunt Clara for her hand, and she said if I want that wild girl, she wouldn't stop me."

Rune canted his head. "Is this another custom? I am not acquainted with the machinations of marriage."

"Yes," Vashien said, setting his glass down. "You need to ask for permission to marry. You would typically ask the father, but Aunt Clara is the only parental figure Faye and Sparrow have."

Rune supposed this request was similar to the way dark-bloods sent letters of intent to a court, stating their desire to pursue a member romantically. "Are there any other steps I should be aware of?"

"Get Aunt Clara's permission. Get Faye a ring. The actual proposal is critical. Make it a romantic surprise for Faye, and don't tell Sparrow. She won't be able to keep it a secret," Vashien said, counting his fingers. Rune nodded and Vashien lifted his chin at the folded parchments. "Is Faye ready for her first High Council meeting?"

Rune wasn't fond of leaving Faye and Lyssa in the same room, but his brother Jareth and Morbid were there.

"She is understandably nervous, but I think her nerves will soothe in time," he said, separating the letters into stacks addressed to himself or Faye.

He paused, recognizing his brother's elegant script. There was no magic woven into the wax seal. Rune flipped it over, curious as to why Alister would address a letter to the Queen of Anaria.

To hide it from us. If he's trying to lure her into a trap, I'm going to make him suffer, the Ra'Voshnik's voice dripped with menace.

Rune set the letter aside and narrowed his eyes at the next.

"Something wrong?" Vashien asked as Rune broke the wax seal and opened the document.

Rune thinned his lips. "The Court of Lace and Bone attacked the shipment for Faye's estate."

Vashien leaned forward and tensed. "Was anyone hurt?"

He shook his head. "No one was harmed, but the lumber and stone were destroyed." Rune folded the parchment and collected Alister's letter.

The winged male studied the letters. "Faye needs to fight back."

The wisest course of action would be a swift and brutal retaliation, but Rune knew her heart. His queen was far too gentle and would not act since no one was injured. He only hoped when her hand was finally forced, the consequences of her kindness would not be too severe.

"I will speak with her," Rune said as he stood. "Were you in need of further assistance?"

Vashien tilted his glass. "No, but I might have to tell my managers I won't be in and sleep this off."

Rune laughed softly, strolling past the winged male. "I am certain Sparrow will favor spending a day in your company."

"Not if I'm trying to sleep," Vashien answered as Rune turned into the hall.

He made his way to his queen, and the Ra'Voshnik paced impatiently. The door opened with a soft click, and Rune stepped in, closing the door behind him. Faye clutched his pillow tangled in their sheets.

Rune sat at the edge of the bed and stroked Faye's hair. Hellfire danced in its metal sconce above his nightstand, highlighting her dark hair in shades of blue.

Faye took a deep breath, stretching her arms out over his lap. She groaned, peering up at him and abandoned his pillow in favor of his thigh.

"Are you hungry?" Rune asked, stroking her cheek.

She grumbled, wiping her eyes. "I'm getting up."

Rune smiled as his queen rolled over and rubbed her face on his leg, the same way he imagined a cat would.

"Why am I so tired," she said, flopping her arm across his lap.

Let her rest. We can hold her while she sleeps, the Ra'Voshnik added hastily.

Rune smoothed his hand down her back and Faye sighed, squeezing closer to him. "There are a few documents in need of your attention after you have eaten."

Faye pushed herself up and cast a sidelong glance at the letters he held. "High Council homework?"

"No. One is from Alister," Rune said, stopping when his queen tensed. He drew her closer, holding her against him. He smoothed his hands down her arms and silently thanked the Darkness her skin hadn't chilled.

"You do not need to read it. Burn it if you wish," he murmured against her hair.

Faye leaned into him, hugging his arm to her chest. "It's okay. He just catches me off guard sometimes. I want to know how Prinia is doing."

"I have not read it. Would you like me to open it?" Rune asked. Faye nodded and he cracked the black wax seal, readying his brother's letter behind her.

"He is requesting an audience and says Prinia is asking for you," Rune said against her hair.

Faye's breaths became measured. Forced, long gasps of air to ground herself under stress.

"You are not beholden to them," Rune whispered, tightening his embrace. Her night terrors diminished significantly in the weeks since she reunited Prinia's consciousness to her body. Rune would not allow them to begin anew. "If you are not ready to see him, you do not have to."

"I—I want to see Prinia," Faye said, the tension ebbing from her slim shoulders. "What was the other letter?"

"The Court of Lace and Bone attacked a materials shipment for your estate."

Faye stiffened and pushed away from him to meet his gaze.

"Was anyone hurt?" she asked, searching his face as her heart began to race.

"No," Rune answered gently. He took her hand and Faye rubbed the base of her throat, glancing around the room as her heart rate slowed. "Vsenia, this is an act of aggression. We need to strike back."

"No one was hurt. Just… ignore her. Delilah is a child throwing a tantrum for losing a realm that was never hers."

"I would ask you to reconsider. She will not stop."

"She's everything I despise about the social hierarchy strangling my people. If I destroy anyone who thinks differently than I do— anyone who opposes me—I'm only proving her and every dark-blood like her, right. They believe the only way to rule is through violence and fear."

Faye squeezed his hand, silently begging for his understanding. He saw the path his queen walked clearly. Her intentions were pure.

However, Delilah was no child. Young did not possess the machinations of sadistic brutality and torture the Queen of Lace and Bone delighted in. Experiences Faye hadn't lived in her quarter century of life.

Rune nodded. He would be her sword and shield.

Faye's lightning-streaked midnight eyes gleamed as she leaned into him. "We can show them a better way to rule. Together."

Twenty-Three

It had taken Faye two days to gather her courage and requested an allocation of her caretaker's yard for training. Rune opened the red-painted gate for his queen and the blonde harpy. The young crowded around Faye, jumping for a box of confections she held out of their reach.

"She was just here!" Sparrow huffed, shooing the young ones away. The midday sun pinkened the blonde harpy's fair shoulders. "You act like she's not here every other week bringing you snacks."

"You're just mad she loves us more than you," Bayle snipped.

Sparrow opened her mouth wide, hissing at the group, and Rune suppressed a grin.

"Don't teach them that," Faye bit out, elbowing her sister.

The harpy scrunched her nose, rubbing her side. "I didn't swear."

"Because Aunty Clara would beat your ass." His queen cut her a sideward glance.

Sparrow snorted. "You're trying to bring your evil twin here. I'm not the influence you should be worried about."

Rune stilled as a young male hugged his leg and said, "Hi," before running off to rejoin his friends.

Faye giggled, and Rune arched a brow. "Is this a common greeting?"

A willowy girl with unusual hair hugged his queen's waist. It reminded him of a sunset. Faye dropped her arm around the young girl and gave her a squeeze. She glanced toward him as the girl ran off as well and said, "For the little ones, yes."

Kimber waved at the sisters. She rushed across the manicured lawn as his queen quietly said, "Don't say anything, I still have to ask Aunty Clara."

"Like she's going to tell you no. You're the favorite," Sparrow answered with a smile as she waved in the same manner.

Kimber stopped in front of Faye and knelt in an exaggerated curtsy. "Your majesty."

Faye stiffened for a moment, then relaxed into a smile.

The brunette harpy didn't notice. She linked arms with Faye, lifting the pink box out of her hands. "What did you bring me to eat in front of Bay Bay?"

Rune canted his head. "Your male?"

Kimber widened her eyes at him and scrunched her nose. "*Nooooo*. You met Bay Bay. Little shit with curly hair. About this tall." She straightened her arm beside her and held her hand out.

He didn't reply as the women climbed the steps. While the parallels between the harpies were humorous, Rune was certain the young Bayle appreciated his renaming as much as he did.

The blonde harpy held the door open with her hip, motioning him to join them.

Rune stepped inside and found the house matriarch ladling a hearty broth filled with small chunks of beef and vegetables into pie tins. Faye added the crust, crimping the edges with a fork.

His gaze fell to the harpies seated across from each other, eating the sugar-glazed cookies he'd purchased in Necromia.

He'd thought to use the trip as a rouse to escort Sparrow to a jeweler. The harpy picked out a diamond studded bracelet as vengeance for interrupting her tryst with Vashien. Then promptly informed him he needed Aunty Clara's permission to marry Faye before he could buy a ring.

Marriage was a host of strange ceremonies, all of which were performed in a specific order. He'd never placed much weight into the mortal vows, but he understood the sacrament was important to his queen.

And so, they became important to him.

Rune supposed he should be happy the blonde harpy had the sense to vanish the bangle. He wasn't sure how he would explain the gift to Faye.

He caught sight of Bayle. The boy stood near the hall with his cohorts, glaring daggers at Kimber. She stuck her tongue at them in turn.

The boy has fire. Pity he won't carry a shard, the Ra'Voshnik said.

Sparrow had grown up in this orphanage, but the likelihood of a second dark-blood in their midst was minuscule. Rune reached over the blonde harpy liberating the box of treats from the harpies' clutches.

He opened the box, displaying the contents to Aunty Clara. "If the young promise to eat their midday meal, will you permit them a snack?"

"This fucking traitor," Sparrow hissed, hunching her shoulders forward to protect her small plate of cookies.

"Don't teach the kids to talk like that," the elderly woman snapped. She narrowed her eyes, peering at the sugared cookies painted in bright colors. The ladle clanked in her large pot, and she wiped her hands on her worn apron.

Bayle's dark eyes gleamed as he watched her expectantly.

"Are you going to eat all your lunch?" Aunty Clara asked pointedly without looking at the boy.

He nodded vigorously, a black curl falling in front of one eye.

She nodded at Rune before continuing her task.

"One," Rune said, holding up a finger as he placed the box on the smaller table. Bayle rushed to the table, followed by nearly a dozen little ones. Rune raised his chin at his entourage. "Are you their leader?"

"He's the worst one," Aunty Clara muttered.

The boy straightened his back, meeting Rune's gaze. "I am."

The creature's laugher trailed through his mind. *He's puffing up at you.* After another fit of laughter, it said, *Darkness, do you think Faye will let me keep him? He can teach my young to stand up to you.*

Rune ignored the creature and crouched, lowering himself to the boy's height. "A true general will place his men before himself."

Bayle looked at the pink box, then looked back at his friends. He stepped to the side, and the group descended on the treats. After a few moments, Bayle stepped into the group and took a green cookie.

"It's not for me," Bayle said. Rune narrowed his eyes. "My second in command isn't feeling well. She's sleeping. So I'm making sure she gets one."

"He loves her," Kimber teased.

The boy glared at her, "You're just mad no one loves you or your horse booty."

The brunette harpy pressed her hand over her heart, feigning injury. "Words hurt, you little gremlin." Bayle shook his head and started down the hall. Kimber called after him, "Can you bring me a cookie too, Bay Bay?"

"That's not my name!" his young voice bellowed.

Faye glanced over her shoulder and flashed Rune a smile. This home was so different than the way he'd been raised. The young had lessons but not the strict regimen he'd been raised beneath. Faye would want their young here to play with the other little ones. Rune frowned. They wouldn't receive the court training necessary to fulfill his queen's dream. She wished for a realm where courts would be made up of every caste. He would add court protocol to their lessons.

"I'm getting an estate built soon," Faye said, sliding the finished tin with the others. "We chose some land past my old cottage."

"Well, sure," the elderly woman replied, transferring the dishes into the oven. "You're a Queen now."

Faye lowered her gaze and examined her cuticles. In a small voice she asked, "Can I use the far end of the yard until everything is built?"

The plump older woman waved her hand as she took a seat. "Just make sure the kids don't get hurt."

"Runey's going to teach her how to phase," Sparrow volunteered.

The corner of Rune's mouth lifted as Faye wrinkled her nose. "You need to learn too."

Aunty Clara made an exasperated sound. "So lazy, that one. Good luck teaching her."

Rune chuckled as Sparrow's expression pinched. Her plate of cookies vanished and reappeared on the kid's table.

"Hey!"

"If you weren't so lazy, you could phase them back," Aunty Clara scolded.

Kimber scooted her plate of sweets out of Sparrow's reach and the blonde harpy hissed.

"The two of you should clear the space you would like to utilize. I will shield it, so the young ones are not able to happen upon anything that may injure them," Rune said to Faye.

She glanced up at him. The ever-present guilt lingering through his mind lifted a fraction. His queen's lightning-streaked midnight gaze was aglow with ease and comfort. She managed to walk through the worst of her pain, and he would happily commit atrocities to spare her from suffering a second time.

Kimber wrinkled her nose, tapping her nails on the table. "What do you need to hide from the kids? You're just teaching Faye magic."

"I have sparring lessons," Sparrow said, leaning over the table.

Rune couldn't help but smile as Kimber unceremoniously stuffed the pink cookie she held in her mouth. He arched a brow when the brunette harpy proceeded to lick the two remaining on her plate before sticking her tongue out at the petite blonde.

The Ra'Voshnik laughed. *If we lick Faye in front of the winged male, will he stop rubbing his scent on her?*

Doubtful, Rune replied. He suspected the male's scent was transferred from Sparrow. The two were inseparable, and there were few moments the blonde harpy wasn't covered in Vashien's scent.

The Ra'Voshnik grumbled as Faye stood and collected her sister. "I'll meet you out there," she said to him over her shoulder.

"I want to spar," Kimber whined, following the pair.

The door swung closed with a soft click, and Rune reached for Aunty Clara's mind. *May I have a moment?*

The plump elderly woman's brow pinched as she craned her neck to meet his gaze. She shook her head and dusted the loose flour from her apron. *What are you afraid of people hearing?*

Rune tensed, preparing to silence the Ra'Voshnik. The creature remained quiet, and Rune silently thanked the Darkness.

You are the family my queen has chosen. I would make her my wife and humbly ask for your blessing.

Aunty Clara straightened to face him. Her mouth tightened into a thin line. *You're already Queen and Consort.*

Rune smiled. *My queen is unfamiliar with court machinations and holds other traditions closer to her heart.*

The old woman silently inspected him, and Rune swallowed. Was there recourse if Faye's aunt denied his request? He needed this done in Faye's customs to please his queen. Long moments passed, and her voice sounded through his mind.

You didn't buy her a diamond, did you?

Rune cursed in High Tongue. He had not thought to come to Faye's matriarch for the information he needed. He'd been forced to seek out the blonde harpy instead—And paid the ransom she demanded.

I have learned she favors Alexandrite, Rune answered.

Aunty Clara nodded, turning to her sink. She turned on the faucet and began rinsing the large pot.

If she tells you yes, you have all the blessings you need.

Twenty-Four

Faye shielded her eyes from the sun and watched Aunty Clara's door, waiting for Rune to emerge. She wondered if Rune was trapped in a room with Aunty Clara after touching one of her pots. She dropped her hands and turned toward her sister.

They settled on the stretch of grass opposite the stables against the fence in the front yard. The overlapping chatter of children playing and the warmth of the sun soothed her. The haunting memories plaguing her these past months seemed smaller. Her night terrors, a shadow shrinking from the light surrounding her.

"Is the Shadow Prince teaching you to fight?" Kimber asked, swatting Sparrow's wrist and holding her hands up in played combat.

Sparrow snorted. "I don't think Runey knows how to hold a sword."

"We have other friends teaching us, Damian and Sadi—"

"You don't have to be nice to her evil twin," her sister interrupted. Kimber slipped her hands into her back pockets and glanced between them. Sparrow sighed dramatically, rolling her neck on her shoulders. "You'll see when the bitch gets here."

Rune materialized beside Faye, and Kimber jerked, taking a step back. "Sorry," Faye said, holding her hand out. She leaned into her mate, running her hand under his jacket and over his side.

"Can you please walk until everyone gets used to you?" Faye asked, smiling at her pale-eyed vampire.

He tucked a strand of hair behind her ear. "Phasing is today's lesson. It will be unavoidable."

"But you won't be poofing on people and scaring them, dick," Sparrow hissed beside Kimber.

Rune inclined his head and said, "Apologies."

"It's okay. This is something we need to get used to." Kimber linked arms with Sparrow and met Faye's gaze. Her lavender-gray eyes gleamed as she said, "We're going to have day-bloods living with us."

"Bitch bagged a couple of dark-bloods, too," Sparrow said, giving Rune a toothy smile. "Tall, pale, and scary has some competition."

Faye smiled, intertwining her fingers with Rune's as her heart swelled. The realm she envisioned bloomed around her, beginning with her home. Rune and Voshki offered her everything she could possibly desire. Respected her and listened, even when they disagreed with her methods. They would usher in a new type of court. A new way to rule.

And they would do it together as equals.

Sparrow tugged on Kimber's arm. "Let's go. You don't want to watch the love birds play 'magic'."

"You should learn too, hooker."

"Phasing is simple—" Sparrow snorted, interrupting Rune, and he cut her a glance. "A skill you should have mastered years ago."

Her sister huffed, crossing her arms. "Fine. Get on with it, your shadowy highness."

"I'm going to see if Aunty Clara needs anything. I'll see you guys later," Kimber said with a wave.

Rune stepped away from Faye to stand between herself and Sparrow. "Phasing is projecting your mind to a location and summoning your body to follow."

Faye stifled a giggle as Sparrow closed her eyes and touched her temples. "I'm thinking of Vashien in the shower."

"Not a person. A place. One you have been to before. Choose a location you are well acquainted with." Rune exhaled, meeting Faye's gaze. "Close your eyes and picture it. This should be a simple task for you. The more power you have, the easier phasing is."

Faye bit the inside of her lip, hoping he was right. The shards she carried mirrored the Darkness itself, but all her strength was useless—Like having a sword that far outweighed her.

It didn't matter how sharp the blade was or how finely it was crafted. It meant nothing if she couldn't lift it.

Faye closed her eyes, searching her mind for a familiar location. She took a deep breath and thought of her room in the cottage outside Alexander. She could see her dresser and the sunlight streaming in through the window over her bed. The small rug concealed the floorboard she pried loose to hide her gold marks.

"I see it. What do I do now?" Faye asked.

"Focus on the details. They will become clearer," he said.

Faye glanced over her room. She went to her dresser, trying to recall what would be on it. A thick layer of dust covered it. Maybe if she opened the drawers. She grasped the drawer handle and froze. It felt so real.

Vsenia? Rune's deep, accented voice swept through her mind.

Faye stared at herself in her mirror and broke into a wide smile. *I phased!*

Concern trickled through their mental tether. *You returned to your cottage?*

She ran her finger through the dust blanketing her dresser and glanced back at her bare bed. *I'm in my old room,* she replied.

His chuckle rolled through her mind. *I expected you to select a closer location. Near the fence, perhaps.*

Faye closed her eyes, picturing Rune and Sparrow standing in a sunny stretch of grass. She saw the newly painted fence. Felt the sun pouring warmth over her shoulders. The sound of children laughing carried toward her.

Images of Rune and Sparrow flickered, then solidified as the large front yard came into sharp focus. Pride filled Faye, and she pressed her hands together, bringing them to her lips. Relief nearly brought tears to her eyes. Her magic finally obeyed her. Even if only in this small way, it validated her.

"That was easier than I thought it would be," Faye said, phasing to stand beside Sparrow. She grasped her sister's hands and squealed, "Darkness! I can do it."

"It is typically easier for the darker shards to learn to phase. They have more power to burn, stumbling through the act. With your strength, you could bridge realms with relative ease." Rune looked impressed.

Sparrow snorted and closed her eyes. "I hate you."

"If you just practiced and took lessons, you could do it too," Faye teased, poking Sparrow's side.

"I have been taking lessons, bitch," she whined. "It never works."

"Another approach may be necessary in your case if you have taken multiple lessons." Rune strolled to the fence post and called the small plate Aunty Clara took from Sparrow. He frowned at the empty plate and set it on the post. He called the pink box next and placed a pastel blue and green cookie on the dish before vanishing the box again.

He took a few steps from the treats and motioned for Sparrow to join him. "Food seems to motivate you. Stand here but envision yourself closer to the post and pick up the cookie."

Sparrow stared and reached her hand out multiple times, pinching at the air. Sparrow's shoulders slumped after her sixth try. "How long do I do this?"

"Until you phase there and pick up the confection you are visualizing," Rune chuckled.

Sparrow turned to glare at him. "I hate your ass." She returned her attention to the plate and pinched the air with more force.

Faye stood on her toes and tipped her chin on Rune's shoulder. She ran her nails over his ass and asked, "When can you teach me to phase your clothes off?"

Sparrow's image flickered as she turned to them. "You can phase her clothes off?"

Rune thinned his lips. "You should be more concerned with the fact you flickered. It is a sign of a failed phase." Rune crossed his arms, leaning back as he examined her. "I am unable to decern if you are truly focused, and Faye's words distracted you, or if you are over complicating a simple act, and the distraction helped simplify your will."

Sparrow turned to Faye. "Go back to the kinky shit. He phases your clothes off?"

Faye giggled in answer, ducking behind her mate, and Sparrow glared up at Rune.

"Teach Vash your tricks."

Twenty-Five

Faye phased back to Hell after they finished at Aunty Clara's house. Sparrow's lesson had been unsuccessful, but her sister seemed more determined to learn since Faye could now phase.

Rune brought her into his mind when they turned in for the night. She fell asleep between him and Voshki but woke restless. It wasn't the night terrors impeding her sleep. The Hunter's Moon would rise in a few weeks, and her anticipation kept her awake.

She'd moved while she slept. She was still curled on her side, but her head was on her pillow instead of Rune's chest.

Her vampire slept peacefully with his hand nestled on her inner thigh.

Voshki slept behind her, holding her against him. Her waist flushed with his chest. The open back of her nightgown allowed his lulling breaths to caress her in an easy rhythm.

Faye glanced up at Rune and smiled. He was stunning in Hell's gentle half-light. His features relaxed.

Faye untangled her arm from his, searching his face. Satisfied she hadn't disturbed him; she lightly ran a nail over the back of Voshki's hand. He inhaled lazily, tightening his hold as he rubbed the side of his face between her shoulder blades.

Her eyes rolled over Rune. She was nervous Voshki woke him, but when she realized he was sound asleep, she dragged her nails across Voshki's forearm. Harder.

Voshki adjusted his hold, his black-tipped claws grazing between her breasts. He pushed off the bed and rested his chin on her side, arching a brow.

She suppressed the giggle bubbling in her throat. She'd never seen Voshki like this. His wholly black eyes were heavy-lidded. Even the veined misted shadows stretching beneath it seemed to move slower.

Faye widened her eyes, and he rolled his head to one side as his brows pinched. *Fates,* she grumbled to herself. His mind brushed the edge of her awareness, and Faye thanked the Darkness. Voshki's predatory senses fell over her, systematically prowling her mind. Hunting her. He pounced, enveloping her consciousness with his. Offering everything he was. His vicious protectiveness. His submission to her will.

The desolate loneliness her presence abated.

She smiled at her beautiful hunter, the man who loved and accepted her before she'd ever met him.

Why are you awake, vsenia? It's late. Voshki purred through her mind.

Can Rune hear us? she asked in return.

He smirked and nipped her side. *Are we keeping secrets from the Shadow Prince?*

Can he hear us or not?

Like this no. Voshki chuckled. *You can differentiate our minds when you're here with us. If you reach for the body, both of us will hear you. We can recall each other's thoughts and memories if we look through them. So, if you want to confess you love me more than him, I'll be sure to let him know.*

Faye jabbed her nail into the space between his thumb and index. Voshki's dark laughter floated through her mind.

I love you the same, she insisted.

But you prefer me. That's why you curl up to him at night.

I sleep on my left, Faye scolded.

A beat of silence passed, and Voshki glanced up in contemplation. He pressed his lips to her gown and said, *I'm claiming his side of the bed tomorrow.* Rune's silk sheets rustled as Voshki lowered himself behind her.

Faye bit the inside of her lip, gathering her nerve. She rushed the words before she could change her mind. *Tell me what he likes.*

Voshki traced the curve of her breast. *You want to know what he thinks about when he fists his cock in the shower?*

Heat carried over Faye's cheeks. *He does not.* Does he?

He's not half as civilized as he pretends to be. Voshki tightened his hold, his corded muscles flexing around her. Faye remained quiet, and he continued, *The Shadow Prince prefers blood over the flesh. He fantasizes about pinning you and taking your throat. Fucking you hard while he drinks.*

Faye stared at Rune's sleeping face. Maybe she was worried over nothing. *Sooo, he's doing what he likes. I thought he was holding back.*

He is vsenia, Voshki laughed. *He's never fucked you. Not the way he'd want to.*

He likes it the way you do? Faye asked.

Voshki was considerably rougher than Rune, driving into her with enough force to jar her body. Faye's nipples hardened beneath her nightshirt as their last encounter played through her mind. He growled against her throat, gripping her hair with one hand and the headboard with the other. Her legs spread wide around his lean waist.

He inhaled and purred through her mind. *Careful. He's going to scent how wet you're getting for me and wake up.*

Faye pressed her thighs together. Would it be so terrible if he was awake?

The Shadow Prince is easy to please. Offer him your throat, let him tongue your pretty cunt, and ask him to fuck your mouth.

Heat pooled between her legs as her breaths grew shallow. *I don't want him to tend to me. I want to tend to him.* Worship him the same way he worshiped her.

Oh, he enjoys it as much as you do. Maybe more. Faye turned to meet the liar's gaze, and Voshki grinned at her. *We both think you're absolutely exquisite there.*

Voshki's gaze lifted past her. *He's waking.*

Rune slowly opened his eyes, realizing his hand was squeezed between his queen's thighs. Other nuances registered as the sleep cleared from his mind. He'd grown accustomed to waking with her subtle scent surrounding him, but it was her arousal his body reacted to.

His fangs sharpened, and he hardened in an instant for her.

"You are not usually awake this early," Rune rasped.

He lifted his arm as Faye clutched him. Her dark silken hair spilled across his chest. The creature held her against it, awake and just as hard for their queen. Rune wondered why it hadn't offered to tend to Faye.

You were asleep. It seemed rude, the Ra'Voshnik grated. Not that it had ever stopped the creature before.

Faye scratched his side as she shifted herself into a more comfortable position. The bite of her little nails rousing his vampiric instincts further. He buried the urge to spread her legs wide and drink from her toned thigh.

She remained silent. "Are you well?" Had the creature upset her?

She favors me. You're the one who continuously upsets her, the Ra'Voshnik countered.

Faye traced her fingertips down his side, stopping at his waist. "I was thinking about the Hunter's Moon."

Rune held her lightly, not caring for the hesitation in her voice. Frightening his queen was the last thing he wanted.

"You will not have to trouble yourself. I can weave a spell to burst my heart," he said gently.

Faye shoved him, gaping. "I don't want you to kill yourself."

He ignored the creature as it rolled onto its back in a fit of laughter.

"My control will be tenuous. This course is for the best. I will rise in the morning." Rune felt his words would assure her.

"The Hunter's Moon is sacred to vampires," Faye breathed. "I want you to have your night."

Rune was touched by her compassion. The Hunter's Moon had little effect on him the past year, but he suspected it was because he had been out of Faye's proximity. Her intentions pleased him, but she couldn't understand what she would be subjecting herself to. And he would never allow himself to lose control.

"I am a Pure Blood, vsenia. My instincts are not gentle," Rune explained. "Vampires are aggressive. Sex is centered around blood and possession. The moon exaggerates these traits, none of which, align with your inclinations."

Faye climbed up his body, her lips touched his in a soft kiss. Rune stroked her back as she trailed her affection along his jaw.

"You've been everything I needed. Let me be the same for you," she whispered.

Rune relinquished control so she might find herself. Discover her tastes and settle into what she favored. He needed no such space.

He pulled her closer, nuzzling the spot she liked behind her ear. "I would rather do without than have you submit to something you did not truly want."

She sighed, turning her head to expose the length of her throat. Rune exhaled, watching the flutter of her pulse point. His fangs ached, needing to sink into her giving flesh.

"I asked Voshki what you liked."

Rune blinked, subduing his carnal urges. He did not need the creature filling her head with trivial flights of desire. Fantasies passing as quickly as they arose. He leaned back and glared at the Ra'Voshnik over Faye's head. It pretended to fist its cock and rolled its hips suggestively, mouthing, *I told her.*

Rune cursed in High Tongue and Faye cupped the side of his face, returning his attention to her.

"Don't be upset with him. I'm the one who asked." Her lightning-streaked midnight eyes searching his.

He covered her hand with his. She did not have to do this. "Vsenia, I am content. Truly."

She leaned into him and stilled a moment from his lips.

A soft laugh escaped him, and Rune asked, "Yes, my queen?"

Her thick lashes lowered, and she asked, "Do you want me?"

Rune purred, running his thumb along her jaw as his fingers threaded into her hair. His lips met hers, and she deepened the kiss.

The minx licked his fangs, and he groaned at the taste of her blood. Dark, rich, and utterly intoxicating.

She palmed his cock, and Rune thrust into her hand.

His queen pulled back as he opened his eyes to find her smiling coyly at him while idly running her nails down his shaft.

"I don't want you content. I want you satisfied."

Twenty-Six

Rune stilled Faye's hand and rolled onto his side. His features were molded into a controlled mask. He remained quiet, and she leaned forward, touching her forehead to his. She closed her eyes, whispering, "I don't want you to discard parts of yourself because you think we won't align." Faye pulled back and gazed into his pale blue eyes. "This is who and what you are. I don't want a convenient version of you. I want all of you. Every piece."

He exhaled, running his thumb over her knuckles. "Vsenia, you do not realize what you are asking for."

"Then show her," Voshki grated.

The hard muscular plains of his chest warmed her back, and Voshki hooked his chin over her shoulder. A length of his white-blonde hair fell over Faye's arm.

"Bite her. Fuck her hard. Give her a demonstration of the

Hunter's Moon." Voshki turned toward her and purred, brushing the bridge of his nose along her cheek. He gazed at Rune and grinned. "She'll tell you if she doesn't like it."

Rune leaned up, caging her between their bodies. Faye's lips parted as her heart raced. Heat pooled between her thighs as he gazed down at her. A hunter examining his prey. He remained still, searching her face. Always analyzing, considering the best course of action. She didn't want him to think. She wanted him to feel.

To be honest with himself.

Faye leaned up, nipping his bottom lip before she gripped the front of his throat and pulled him in. Voshki nuzzled the side of her throat as Rune deepened their kiss. She pressed her tongue to his fang, offering him a taste of her blood. Rune groaned and she opened wider, submitted to each stroke.

When he pulled back, Faye followed. Desperate for another taste. Needing them to take as much as they'd given her. Her hand skimmed down Rune's chest, and he caught her wrist.

His pale gaze met hers. "Is this truly what you want?"

Her nails bit into the hard plains of his chest as she moaned, "Please."

Voshki's black-tipped claws grazed her thigh as he slowly lifted the hem of her nightgown. "Do you want us both, or should I return you to your body?"

Faye arched her back, pressing the curve of her ass into Voshki's erection. "Show me what to expect during the Hunter's Moon."

"You can expect us to fuck you until dawn," Voshki purred, his arm circling above her waist. Faye gasped as he dragged her backward, out of Rune's reach. He lifted her in his arms and stepped off the bed.

"What are you doing?" she hissed.

Voshki chuckled, carrying her to Rune's side of the bed. "You, vsenia, are going to learn how the Shadow Prince likes his cock sucked while I fuck you."

Faye's lips parted, and she stared up at Voshki. Heat spread from her cheeks, pinkening the tops of her ears.

"You look hesitant," Rune said, studying her from the edge of the bed. Their dark silken sheets draped across his lap.

Voshki set her on her feet before her solemn vampire. Faye

frowned. He was thinking too much. She stepped into him, gliding her fingers along the side of his throat. A smile pulled at her lips as his eyes slid closed. He lifted his chin, leaning into her touch.

She tangled her hands through his hair and leaned closer as their lips met in a brief touch.

A silent invitation.

"Let me be what you need," Faye whispered, wrapping him in her arms.

His breath skimmed over her shoulder, and Faye shivered. She waited while he held her loosely. Silence stretched between them, and Faye's heart sank. He cut away so much of himself, believing he spared her from the darker aspects of his nature.

She craved them, wanting what lay beneath the centuries of court polish. She turned toward him, brushing her lips along his jaw. He'd told her once vampires appreciated aggression. She fisted his hair and gripped the front of his throat, *like she meant it.*

His purr reverberated beneath her touch, and Faye dragged his lower lip between her teeth. Her grip tightened in his hair, forcing him to meet her gaze. She smiled at his lengthening fangs and whispered against his mouth, "Fuck me the way you would, if I was one of your kind."

His fingertips smoothed up her back and into her hair, grazing her scalp. A tingling sensation whispered down her spine, over her shoulders to her breasts. She sighed as her nipples tightened to peaks, pressing against her lavender nightgown.

Rune fisted her hair, stripping the blissful euphoria from her mind. She drew a short breath as he angled her head to one side. She squeezed her thighs together, craving this side of him. She wanted him to take everything he wanted. Faye dropped her shoulder, tempting him further. Submitting to his will as he'd done for her countless times.

Needing him to take from her.

A breathy sigh slipped past her lips as he kissed and nuzzled her throat. The pad of his index finger traced her nipple in slow, agonizing circles. His gentle caresses were at odds with the cruel grip holding her hair taut to her scalp.

Rune only allowed her one view, the gray stones stretching over the arching ceiling. She closed her eyes, letting his touch consume her.

Her nails dug into his muscular shoulders. Darkness, she ached for him. Wanted his length thrusting inside her.

His breath warmed the side of her neck, and Faye moaned, waiting for his fangs to pierce her. Desperate for the feigned sensation of his cock stretching her to accommodate his size.

Voshki growled, and Faye jerked, drawing her arms to her sides. He spoke harsh words in a language she didn't understand while tracing his claws over her waist.

Tension thickened the space they occupied.

Faye turned toward Voshki. "What did you say?"

He looked at her and grinned viciously before crooning, "I told him if he doesn't want to show you what he likes, I'll be more than happy to teach you."

Faye reached behind her and scratched her displeasure across Voshki's thigh. He leaned into her, purring in response.

Fucking vampires. "You're not helping."

Even if she returned to their physical bodies, she wasn't truly alone with Rune. At least this way, she could manage the remarks Voshki pelted Rune with. She loved him, but the man had no sense of restraint.

Or patience, she thought dryly.

She touched Rune's cheek, reclaiming his attention. "Ignore him," she breathed. "Should I get my rope for you? You can tie me up."

She pictured herself with her forearms bound together across the middle of her back in the same elaborate harness she had restrained Rune with so many times.

Faye kissed him, running the tip of her tongue over his fang. He groaned, pulling her closer.

"Teach me how to take you so you can fuck my pretty throat," she begged.

Rune's hand caged her neck as a low growl rumbled from him. He pinned her with his pale blue eyes. Faye smiled at the predatorial glint darkened with desire. "You can stop us whenever you wish." At her nod, the corner of his mouth lifted. "Then strip."

Twenty-Seven

Faye's skin thrummed in excitement. She would finally see Rune without his court polish. She lifted the lavender nightgown over her head, tossing it on the warm stone floor. Rune's shoulders tensed as the cotton and lace glided over her hips next.

Voshki retrieved Rune's pillow before returning to her. She narrowed her eyes, and he said, "It's for your knees."

Faye bit the inside of her lip, lowering her gaze to the cushion Voshki provided.

She knelt before Rune and swallowed, examining their dark sheets draping his considerable length. Did he really mean to fuck her throat? He occasionally stroked the first few inches into her mouth, but he'd been gentle with her. Voshki had been more forceful but measured his thrusts to keep her from choking.

Rune's fingers slid through her hair, and Faye closed her eyes.

She leaned in closer as he gathered her hair, fisting it into a high ponytail. Heat pooled between her thighs. It was a throbbing empty ache she needed to be filled. She rose onto her knees, sliding the silk sheets away. Needing him inside her.

Faye wrapped her hand around the base of his cock. Rune purred in a low groan. She licked and kissed the head before taking the tip into her mouth. Black-tipped claws glided up the backs of her thigh, and Faye moaned around Rune's length.

"Like that, vsenia. Suck harder," he rasped.

He pulled her in while rolling his hips forward, driving more of himself past her lips. Faye dug her nails into the hard muscles of his thigh, eager to appease his fantasies.

Taking more of him.

Rune leaned back on his arm and thrusted upward, holding her in place.

"Look at me," he rasped, stilling his thrusts as he guided her down his cock. He didn't stop until the head pressed the back of her throat. "Be a good girl, and open your mouth wider."

Faye lifted her gaze, and Rune cursed in High Tongue. She moaned, sucking harder, afraid he would stop after seeing her tear-misted lashes. Instead, his brow pinched, and he tipped his head back, groaning as the head of his cock nudged the entrance of her throat.

"Work him into you," Voshki purred, easing her legs apart.

Faye glimpsed the predator beneath Rune's polished facade. The veins and tendons in his arm stood with each shift of his tensed muscles over his sculpted body. Harsh possession reflected in his pale blue eyes. A hunter beset on his prey as he groaned with each inch he pressed into her mouth.

The head of his cock squeezed into her throat, cutting off her airway. He tilted his hips up. Faye blinked, holding perfectly still. She focused on the hard muscles beneath her hands, attempting to relax around his length.

Faye stared helplessly. His gaze was more erotic to her than having him in her mouth. She submitted to her vampire. His darker instincts made her slick with need as he fucked her mouth, heating her blood as he lost himself in his pleasure.

He held her there a moment longer and withdrew enough for her to breathe.

"The only thing I envy is the Shadow Prince's ability to touch you more intimately than I can," Voshki said in a hushed tone, tracing the underside of her breast with the curve of his claw.

The backs of two fingers glided through her folds as Rune dipped a fraction deeper, and Faye tensed.

"Moan for me, or I will fuck your mouth harder," Rune growled. "Would you like that, vsenia?"

Faye lifted her chin, driving his cock deeper in response—and choked.

Everything stopped.

Rune's grip on her hair.

Voshki's stroking touch.

Her vampire immediately withdrew and sat forward. Concern softened his features as he cradled her face in his hands. He smoothed the pad of his thumb over her lashes, brushing away her tears.

"I am sorry. I was too rough with you," he murmured.

Faye took his hand and pressed her lips to his palm. "I wanted to take all of you. I was the one who got impatient and choked myself. This was my fault, don't be sorry."

Rune canted his head, his expression masked in aristocratic etiquette. Faye could still taste him, her lips swollen by his use. She wasn't going to lose the ground she gained tonight. She forced his cock deeper than she knew how to take, but Faye was eager to try again as she used his own words against him.

"Did you truly think I was done with you?"

The uneasy smile Rune had been giving evaporated. She leaned back against Voshki's muscular chest, rumbling with laughter as they stared at her vampire. He caressed the side of her jaw, turning her to face him. Faye parted her lips as he pressed down on her chin. He kissed her deeply, his tongue stroking hers until she moaned into his mouth.

He pulled away with a smirk, sliding the backs of his fingers along her throat. "You're not going to be able to take his entire cock in one night. We have time if you want the Shadow Prince to fuck your pretty throat under the Hunter's Moon."

Faye rose to her knees and leaned into Rune, flattening her hand over the center of his chest as she pushed him back. The sculpted muscles over his torso bunched and flexed as he obeyed her, reclining back on his arm.

His eyes glazed over as she stroked his thick cock and slowly took him past her lips. Rune purred as she found her rhythm, working him with her hands and mouth.

Strong hands settled over her hips and his claws lightly traced over her awareness. Faye took Rune deeper and opened her mind to Voshki. The broad crown of his erection glided through her slick folds and nudged at her entrance.

Do you want to ride my cock or my face, love? Voshki asked.

Faye rocked back against him, pressing his length into her. She moaned, moving between them. Taking one deeper as the other withdrew, returning in a steady rhythm. She whimpered, rocking harder as she chased her pleasure.

Darkness, she was so close.

Faye's lids fluttered closed as Rune's hand tangled through her hair. The corner of his mouth lifted into a smirk while he nodded to Voshki behind her. The predatory glint in Rune's gaze returned with a vengeance. Faye's inner walls squeezed around Voshki's cock.

"Fuck her harder. Make our queen come. I want to feel her screaming around my cock," Rune growled.

Phantom mouths closed over her nipples and clit, teasing her hard peaks, sucking them, and nibbling with a whisper of teeth. The tension built within her crested and snapped as she came. She cried out while they continued fucking her.

The sensation at her clit purred relentlessly, and Faye screamed as another orgasm crashed through her. Rune thrusted harder, stroking into her throat.

"Look at me while I fuck you, or I will torture your clit until your legs give out, vsenia," he grated.

Faye blinked away her tears and gazed up at him, sagging with relief when the vibrations between her legs stopped.

"You are more than I ever wished for. More than I dreamed of," Rune whispered as his hand left her hair. He brushed away her tears and caressed her jaw. The front of her throat.

She didn't pull back, letting him possess her. Wanting to please him.

Voshki's grip tightened over her hips. He thrust harder. Faster. Faye arched into him as his chest pressed against her back. He growled, driving into her a final time. His cock pulsed as he came deep inside her.

"Fuck," Voshki groaned, pulling out of her.

Faye sucked harder, needing Rune to come for her. She didn't have time to react as he lifted her and bent her over their bed in a fluid motion. He growled, pulling her hair taut and shoving her legs wide.

"Rune," she breathed, arching her back for him.

Cool silk pressed against the side of her face as her vampire pinned her with a cruel grip in her hair, and the other at her waist. He thrusted into her savagely, the wooden frame creaking beneath her.

Faye lifted her ass, taking his hard rhythm. Each brutal stroke wound the tension growing in her tighter, driving her into the next orgasm. She couldn't move. Couldn't pull her legs together with Rune standing between them. He was rougher than Voshki, fucking her mercilessly.

Darkness, she loved it.

Rune's fangs sank into her neck, and Faye came once more. Screaming her release while Rune took his pleasure. The grip on her waist bruised as he drove into her a final time and cursed in High Tongue, releasing his bite. His breaths were heavy in her ear while his cock pulsed inside her.

Voshki stretched over her side of the bed, his face upside down in her view. He brushed a strand of hair from her forehead and smiled before asking, "Did you like your taste of the Hunter's Moon, vsenia? I know the Shadow Prince did."

Rune purred, pressing his chest into her back. He kissed and licked his bite, drinking from her while he rocked against her in a kinder rhythm.

"Yes," Faye answered, tangling her hands in Voshki's white-blonde hair. She urged him closer. He leaned in, taking her mouth in a claiming kiss. Faye pressed her tongue to his fang, and Voshki groaned, sucking on the tip.

He pulled back and glanced at Rune. "Let her up."

Her vampire's grip on her hair loosened, and he rubbed his fingertips over her scalp. Tingles spread along her body, and Faye's eyes slid closed with a breathy sigh. Voshki chuckled and whispered to her between soft kisses.

"I need your lips around my cock, vsenia."

Twenty-Eight

Faye inspected her reflection. Her peach silk dress flowed to the floor, tailored with exaggerated split sleeves. Faye smoothed her hands over her middle, her fingertips catching over the pleats sweeping from her bust to her waist. Today was her first High Council meeting. She wasn't sure what to expect, but she wanted to appear approachable.

Her nerves scraped for what was scheduled after her High Council meeting.

She'd granted Alister an audience. The communication between them so formal, she found it strange. Alister was her mate's brother after all, family. It was entirely impersonal, but she preferred it to Alister showing up unannounced. She tensed with the memory of him stalking toward her in the kitchen as if they were still there.

When everything in her screamed to run but mistook him for Rune.

Her vampire would escort her to Alister's home. If she could weave fate, she would choose to not see him for the rest of her life, but she needed to see Prinia.

"Knock, knock. Is Runey naked?" Sparrow sang, before strolling in without waiting for an invitation.

Rune turned toward her from his seat at his small desk and exhaled. "I am not sure when I began sharing space with you."

Sparrow snorted, fluttering her hand at him. "The exact moment you started sharing space with her," she said before leaping toward their bed.

Her sister froze in mid-air and was gently placed on her feet by an unseen force. Rune smiled, flashing his fangs. "Stay out of our bed."

Sparrow shook a series of rose gold chains at him. The delicate links clicked together in a soft rasp as she walked toward her. She reached in front of Faye to loop the intricate belt around her waist. Her sister fastened it tightly and arranged the looping design. "I can't have you going to your first High Council meeting looking boring."

Faye turned and the metal shimmered in the light. It was pretty but reminded her of a harness. A single thin chain with three sweeping lengths flowed over each hip and one dipped in the front.

"My baby bird is going to fly on her own," Sparrow said, beaming as she looked her over.

Faye supposed she should be glad her sister didn't tackle her and stuff her into a corset.

"Shall we, love?" Rune asked, strolling to her.

Faye nodded, placing her hand in his.

"Have fun. Don't be boring—and don't take any shit from the high bitch," her sister fired off, while waving goodbye.

Faye glanced up at Rune when her surroundings didn't fade.

The corner of his mouth lifted, and he rubbed his thumb over the back of her hand. "Your phasing has progressed well, take us to the High Council."

"Oh." Faye blinked and collected herself, picturing Rune's box seats. The golden railing. The gorgeous view of the endless cerulean sky. She reached out to touch the rail, and her hand closed over the cool metal. Faye smiled as her heart leaped, and Rune pulled her closer. She giggled, running her hand over his chest, overjoyed to share her small wins with him.

"Your seat will not be here today," Rune said against her hair.

He vanished, and Faye glanced down over the railing. Her vampire stood behind the curved table and pulled out the vacant seat between the High Queen and the Artithian King. The audience meandered below. As Faye glanced over their faces, she found several of them watching her.

She swallowed, looking away and concentrated on the space beside Rune. Her surroundings slowly dissipated, engulfed with an inky blackness. It snapped into sharp focus, and Faye stood beside her place at the table.

"Thank you," Faye said, taking her seat.

Jareth leaned forward and waved at Faye cheerily. His hair was styled in disheveled-chic, giving a careless, approachable air, but Faye knew it was painstakingly arranged. A white-blonde lock strategically hung over one eye. He smiled, and Faye wondered how this ball of sunshine could be related to her solemn vampire.

"These meetings are really easy. We just sit here. You didn't forward a drink preference, so I looked through Rune's menu the last time you were here," he said, pointing at a wine bottle and cham-pagne glass near a few papers in front of her. "Pomegranate juice."

"Thank you. That was really thoughtful," Faye said as Rune poured her a glass.

"Well, you put up with him. It's the least I can do," Jareth teased before sitting back.

I will not be far, Rune spoke into her mind as he ran his fingers through her hair.

He vanished and Faye's gaze lifted to the golden railing, three stories up. Her vampire poured a flute of crimson wine, ignoring the crowds' stares and murmurs, focusing on her instead.

You don't have to stay here. If you have other things to do, I'll be fine, Faye said. She wasn't ecstatic to be seated next to the High Queen, but Morbid and Jareth were here.

I have nothing more pressing than remaining at my queen's side, he purred.

Faye smiled and sipped her juice. She glanced at Lyssa as she set down her drink. The High Queen ignored her existence, entirely. She straightened a stack of pages much thicker than Faye's. She turned toward the Artithian King, and his bundle of pages eclipsed hers several times over as well.

She couldn't see Jareth's documents without leaning forward, but there was nothing in front of Morbid. The Familiar King rested his boots on the table and tilted his chair onto its two back legs.

The Artithian King shifted his white feathery wings and leaned toward Faye. "Has the Shadow Prince made any progress on The Crumbling?"

Faye was struck silent by his question. She wasn't sure. Rune went to The Crumbling every few days, but she didn't know exactly what he did. She didn't want to paint her vampire in a bad light, but she didn't have an answer Jha'ant would find acceptable.

"Stop pestering Faye, you have Rune's report," Jareth interjected. To her mind he said, *The mortal king worries… a lot.*

Faye searched the Artithian King's face. Strain marked his eyes. While he was far younger than everyone at the table, he looked older. Faye understood mortality. Jha'ant was responsible for the safety of his people. He had a right to be concerned with a threat looming over his kingdom.

And hers.

A chill ran down Faye's spine. She'd taken the realm from the High Queen but didn't think of the additional responsibilities. She reached for Rune's mind in a panic. *If the High Queen withdrew her shield protecting Anaria, we would have heard, right.*

Amusement flickered across their mental tether. *I have shielded Anaria and Hell for some time.*

You've been shielding Anaria? Faye stared up at him, relieved. Her comfort soon turned bitter. He shielded the realm and let the high bitch take the credit? *Don't say the people should look up to their queen.*

She leaned toward the Artithian King and reached for his wrist. He jerked and Faye smiled, squeezing his arm reassuringly. "He's doing everything in his power. I worry about The Crumbling too. If he makes a breakthrough, he'll send his reports right away."

"Thank you," Jha'ant said with a kind smile and stood.

The Artithian King cleared his throat and opened the meeting. The crowd quieted as he called the first pair listed on Faye's agenda.

Faye observed as the day went on. Pairs and courts stood in The Eyes, and after their petitions were either accepted or denied, the

High Queen or Jha'ant turned a page over, separating it from their documents.

The High Queen turned over parchments for some Artithians, and Jha'ant turned over some pages for people without wings. Faye guessed they lived within their corresponding realms, which would explain why Jareth didn't separate any documents as Hell's High Council Member.

Hell had no citizens.

Faye suspected Familiar handled their affairs more privately within their own realm. She glanced at Morbid, wondering why he was here if his people would never submit a petition.

He met her gaze and winked.

She turned her attention back to The Eyes, and as her list of names whittled down, she silently chanted a mantra to ease her nerves.

Alister can't hurt me. I need to see Prinia.

Twenty-Nine

The meeting concluded, and Rune stood, observing the High Council. He didn't care for the bird king requesting information from his queen, but Faye seemed to develop a budding friendship with Jha'ant.

She glanced at the small stack of pages, across from her empty glass tinted with pomegranate juice. The Artithian King leaned in at the same time, quietly instructing Faye to leave the glass but take the documents for her records.

Rune blinked. Perhaps he judged the feather-winged male too harshly.

Faye glanced in his direction, and he tilted his head, indicating for her to join him. His queen vanished and materialized beside him. Her phases were smooth, her image never flickered. He couldn't be prouder. She mastered the skill with relative ease.

She interlaced her fingers with his and leaned into him. Her hand slipped beneath his jacket and across his back. Murmured voices broke out over the audience below, and Rune wondered if his queen realized she would be a source of gossip for days to come.

"Can you take us to Alister's house? I… don't want to phase there," Faye said quietly, scratching his lower back.

The Ra'Voshnik growled at her hesitation, and Rune found himself of the same mind. His gentle queen wouldn't allow him to cancel his brother's audience. Her kind heart bled too easily for his brother's wife.

"Of course, love," he whispered to her. "Shield yourself."

Faye nodded as a black light streaked in purple flashed over her. She clutched his arm as their surroundings faded, and Rune brought them to the field of Prinia's strange red flowers. An enormous greenhouse stretched above them. He gazed up at the intricate wrought iron framework and reluctantly admired his brother's devotion.

This structure of spelled glass would allow Prinia to spend her time in the light as she did when she was mortal. The sun's rays stretched over the spider lilies, and their sweet fragrance curled around them.

Rune smoothed his hand down Faye's bare back, pulling her closer. "You do not have to see him if you are not comfortable."

"I'm okay," Faye answered.

When his queen told him she was fine or okay, it typically meant the opposite. Rune kept silent as she began rubbing his forearm in an attempt to self-soothe.

He reached for his brother's mind, hostility bridging their tie. Rune's fangs lengthened as the Ra'Voshnik prowled closer to the surface.

He asks for an audience but expected us to send Faye alone? the creature growled, fantasizing about the sounds he could coax from Alister, while it opened his throat.

The door clicked open, and his brother stepped out. Rune blinked, struggling to keep his expression neutral while the creature's dark laughter filled his mind.

His brother had cut his hair shorter than Jareth's and dyed it black. "Your hair is… different," Faye commented.

Alister glowered at him, running his hand through the dark

strands. "I didn't appreciate the look of fear in my wife's eyes every time I entered the room. Our father's blood was strong, we all look like him."

His queen swallowed and stiffly stepped toward his brother. "How, how is she doing?"

"Skittish," Alister answered. His expression softened as he addressed Faye. "I've darkened our home. Light frightens her. Her night vision is better than mine, but I make do."

"Has she been outside?" Faye asked, looking upward.

Alister glanced over her flowers and some of the strain left his gaze. "She's come out once during the night."

Rune fell instep behind his queen and his brother raised his hand, pointing at him. "*You* are not welcome here."

"Did you truly expect me to send my queen, unaccompanied, into an enemy's home?" Rune snapped.

"You attacked my wife!" Alister roared, taking a threatening step toward Rune, causing his black hair to fall into his eyes.

Rune growled and Faye took his face between her hands.

"Stop! Stop. Look at me. Rune," Faye yelled the first and softened each word until she whispered the last. "We need to move past this hatred. There is nothing here, except pain."

Rune remained silent as the Ra'Voshnik circled his mind, voicing its displeasure in a string of obscenities. Faye nodded at him, stroking his cheek. "Please… Do this the right way."

He squeezed her hand and brought her fingertips to his lips. In all the time he'd known her, he'd never wanted to deny her will more than he did in this moment. Faye was shielded, and his brother wasn't strong enough to hurt her.

He was strong enough to drown her! the Ra'Voshnik snapped. *Do not leave her side.*

Rune agreed with the creature, but his queen desired peace. Peace in her lands. Peace between the castes… between him and his brother. He was hers to command and would submit to her wishes. Hold her values as tightly as she did.

"I will not be far." Rune's gaze raised to his brother. "If I hear—an ounce—of distress in my queen's voice, I will tear your home to its foundation."

Faye tensed, stepping away from Rune. A fraction of her tension slipped away when he didn't follow. The brothers glowered at each other, but she would take what progress she could.

Like the brothers, Prinia would take time to heal. Faye couldn't fathom running from a nightmarish version of her mate, being chased through endless darkness for eight hundred years. They each bore scars, and Prinia wouldn't shake off what she'd suffered in mere weeks.

Alister opened the door and stepped inside, while Faye froze in place. Her heart began to race as she forced herself to follow. She added a second shield over herself, inhaling deeply through her nose. *Alister wasn't going to attack her,* she chanted, even as her gaze darted through the confined space, searching for a gleam of metal. The memory of his blade gliding across her neck flooded her senses. The edge hadn't slit her throat, but she could feel the pressure. The vibration as it dragged across her windpipe.

Faye squeezed the front of her throat, desperate to override the lucid memories. She reached the threshold and slowly exhaled through her mouth. Hesitation stilled her for a moment before she turned toward Alister and lowered her hand. "Don't spell the house. Let Rune hear us."

Alister looked past her at Rune and nodded.

Faye stepped into the small, dimly lit foyer and Alister led her up a stairway. She glanced at him as they climbed in silence. He looked like a different person with his hair cut short and dyed black. Maybe she should have asked Rune to cut and dye his hair when her night terrors prevented her from sleeping.

"Can I ask you… a question?"

Alister turned to look at her as his brows drew down.

"Perhaps," he grated with strained politeness. She swallowed, and Alister shook his head. "I'm sorry." His tone lost the bite it held with Rune, taking on glimmers of regret. He stopped and leaned on the rail, meeting her gaze.

Silence stretched between them. She wasn't going to tell him it was okay, or she forgave him. He tried to drown her in a coffin while Rune watched. What he'd done left her scarred with night terrors for weeks. A simple *I'm sorry* didn't erase her pain.

Alister dropped her gaze, turned, and continued up the steps. "My brother and I have a long history. You didn't deserve what I did to you. Prin has been asking for you, and I am truly thankful you agreed to see her."

After they neared the top of the steps Faye quietly asked, "Does she recognize you?" She mistook Rune for Alister in the grip of her nightmares. But her trauma was a speck of sand compared to Prinia's suffering.

Alister paused, his hand on the door handle. "She has moments of clarity on her good days. Prin hasn't invoked her blood. Her magic is erratic, manifesting with her emotions, and she's adjusting to being a vampire. Don't be frightened if her eyes go black. She doesn't drink deeply so she feeds often."

"Oh," Faye said as heat rose to her cheeks. "I can visit after she... feeds?"

Alister turned to face her and rubbed the side of his neck. "I've tried offering her blood. She's repulsed by it, until she's thirsty enough. If her eyes go black…"

"The visit is over," Faye finished for him. She wouldn't want an audience when Rune drank from her. It was a private intimacy she treasured.

Alister grinned and nodded. "Yes." He paused, glancing at the door. "She's also conjured a shadow beast, larger than a hellhound. It guards her and makes her feel safe. Whatever you do, don't run from it."

He opened the door before Faye could reply.

Thirty

Faye froze as a growl reverberated from the dark. How big was a hellhound? Her mind filled with images of a dog matching the fire-breathing hell pony Rune called a Nightmare. Alister entered the room and Faye forced herself to follow.

Strategically placed candles blazed to life. They lit the space enough for Faye to avoid tripping over furniture, but she couldn't make out anything else. The room grew colder with each step. The blackness shrank the space, leaving the home Alister built for his wife, hollow and empty.

"Prin," Alister called into the dark.

The growl subdued into a happy whine as heavy paws padded toward them. Faye tensed and followed Alister into the next room, looking for the manifestation of Prinia's terror.

A large shadowy beast bounded at Alister, constructed of

shadows twisted into the loose shape of a massive wolf. Its glowing red eyes left a hazed trail as it touched its nose to Alister's chest. It wagged its tail once and pranced happily at Alister's feet.

She frowned when he didn't interact with it, making his way to an adjoining room instead. The shadow creature turned its head toward Faye, and she froze. Her mouth went dry as its glowing red eyes fixed on her. *Don't run from it*, Faye told herself. *Don't run.*

"Wait here. I'm going to see if Prinia is having a good day," Alister said as the darkness swallowed him.

Faye stared at the shadowed hellhound. It took a half step toward her and tilted its head. She bit the inside of her lip, praying to the Darkness it didn't want to use her as a chew toy.

Don't run. Don't. Run.

"Prin. You have a visitor, sweetheart. Do you remember Faye?"

The hellhound turned toward Alister's voice and padded out of the room. Faye's shoulders sagged as she fought the urge to flee. She squeezed her wrist, taking a few measured breaths before she found the courage to follow Alister deeper into his home.

A single candle lit the sitting room. Prinia sat in a plush chair near a dead fireplace with her knees pulled to her chest. The candlelight illuminated her silk slippers and bright blue skirt tucked into the bend of her legs.

She curled into herself, taking up less space. "It's too bright in here, Alister. He'll find me."

The light snuffed out before Prinia finished her sentence, and Faye's vision blurred in shades of blue. She rubbed her eyes as Alister said, "Night vision."

He crouched next to his wife, taking her hand. "He won't find you. You're safe, sweetheart."

She turned, leaning into him, and jerked when her gaze leveled with Faye's. Her dark eyes were clear, free of their clouded stare.

"I remember you. You keep him away." Prinia's shadow beast whined, nudging closer to her chair. It moved with her as Prinia stood and tilted her head at Faye. The shadowed hellhound mirrored its master's movements. She took a small step closer, her conjured beast in step beside her.

Faye swallowed, fighting the urge to back away. "I remember you too. You have a beautiful dog."

Prinia smiled brightly, and Faye caught sight of her subtle fangs. "Would you like some tea?" Her expression deteriorated into confusion as she rubbed her forearm, turning toward Alister. "Do we have tea?"

"We can check." Faye volunteered before Alister could respond. She'd brought balms and creams for aging members of her village. They depended on their families to care for them, and Faye learned early on it was better to walk with them in their memories than force them into the present. "And if we don't have tea, we can make nice glasses of water."

Prinia brightened again and leaned into Alister, wrapping her arms around his waist. She rested her chin on his chest, gazing up at him. "We're safe now. He won't come when she's here. She commands him."

Her shadow beast whined and approached Faye.

Please don't bite, Faye chanted in her mind as she extended her hand. She knew its teeth couldn't penetrate her shielding, but her near drowning had proven shields wouldn't stop it from shaking her like a stuffed toy.

Its nose touched her hand, and Faye was surprised by its warmth. The shadowed beast stepped into her, rubbing itself against her waist as it passed by. Its shadows swirled, disturbed by her touch. The same way the veined misted shadows beneath Voshki's gaze did.

Alister gently caressed the side of Prinia's face. "Why don't you have a seat and visit with Faye while I will make us some tea." He kissed her forehead and said in a lower tone, "I'll make a plate of the cookies you like."

He left the room and Prinia's smile faded as she searched the room.

"We can sit here until Alister comes back," Faye offered as she gestured toward a small oak sitting table.

"Yes," Prinia said, nodding to herself. She leaned toward Faye and inhaled deeply through her nose. "Did you fight him? You smell like him."

Faye frowned as Prinia clutched her hands to her chest and tucked her arms tightly at her side. She should have realized Prinia would smell Rune on her. Reaching for a different subject Faye said, "Have you made Alister lemonade recently?"

Prinia relaxed and smiled, twisting her wedding ring—a gold band etched into the shape of flowers. It circled her finger beside another holding a round cut diamond. The beautiful setting was quietly elegant but hidden without light to reflect its radiance.

"When I met him, I thought he was so handsome. I brought him drinks as an excuse to talk to him. He was a day-blood. I didn't want to bring him water. So I made him lemonade. He didn't tell me I was making it wrong until much later." Her smile widened as she took her seat. "I add water to it now."

Alister drank lemon juice with sugar?

"I'm sure he appreciates it." Faye laughed.

"I cried the night he finished my father's roof, but he came back the next day to repair a fence." Prinia turned and her face lit up.

Faye turned, expecting to find Alister, but a lonely doorway greeted her. She glanced at her host as she blinked at the vacant space. Faye wondered if she was seeing a memory. A moment later footsteps carried into the room, and Alister entered, carrying a tray. Were her senses as sharp as Rune's since he was the one who turned her?

Alister poured the tea and sat as far from Faye as possible while remaining beside his wife. Faye pulled her cup closer, glad for the distance as the hot liquid warmed her hands. Prinia's shadowed hell-hound rested at her feet while she nibbled on a yellow cookie. Alister repositioned his cup a few times before saying, "I would like to assist with your court."

Faye swallowed, staring at him. The hard edges of his expression had fallen away, leaving a vulnerability she didn't recognize. "Your brother is helping me, but thank you."

Alister taped his fingers on the table and exhaled. "I don't expect you to trust me. I'll have to earn that, and I have every understanding you are only here because of Prin. My brother has always held the position of executioner. He has never handled the internal workings of a court. I have."

"He is my consort. Why do you want to join a court he is an integral part of?"

Alister gazed at his wife. "Because if your court existed eight centuries ago, we would have had a place to belong." He turned toward Faye, meeting her gaze. "Do you truly think I'm the only day-blood to fall in love with an Anarian?"

Faye crossed her ankles, tucking them under her chair. She's never thought past Alister's marriage. If others longed for a realm who accepted them without judgment. Where they were more than the sum of their shards.

Prinia pulled her lip back and licked the top of her mouth. "I think these cookies are bad. They taste funny."

"I'm sorry, sweetheart. I'll go to the market and bring you another tin." Alister took the crumbly yellow cookie, dotted with a red circle at its center, and placed it on the small porcelain dish. Prinia dusted her fingers, wearing the same expression Bayle did when Aunty Clara told him he couldn't have a snack.

"I'll need to speak to your brother about it," Faye said, sniffing her treat. She took a small bite, and her brow pinched slightly. This tasted like an almond cookie. Maybe Prinia got a bad one?

Alister slid Prinia's tea closer and said, "If you allow me to assist the Court of Chaos and Darkness, I will need a space for Prinia he cannot enter."

"I understand," Faye said. She wasn't thrilled at having Alister in her estate, but this might be the first step in mending things between the brothers.

Prinia choked, coughing into her teacup. It slipped from her hand, and Alister caught it before it cracked against the table. "It tastes bad," she cried.

Alister dabbed her mouth with his napkin, and she crawled onto his lap. He cradled her against him and murmured, "I know, love. It's okay." Prinia quieted, and he turned his attention to Faye. He glanced down momentarily before his brow furrowed. "I never thanked you for bringing my wife back to me."

Faye forced a smile. They'd all left scars on each other, but maybe they could begin again.

Prinia wiggled closer to Alister and inhaled deeply at his throat. A purr rattled from her as black covered her eyes.

Faye stood and turned her back to them. "I'm going to go, but I'll visit Prinia again."

Alister spoke as she phased.

"Thank you."

Thirty-One

Rune stood among the spider lilies, bathed in sunlight before a picturesque home he wanted to reduce to kindling.

Violence crackled beneath his skin. Faye was strong, carrying a far darker shard than his own. She was more than capable, but it didn't mean he wanted to relegate her to fight her battles alone. He was her shield and her sword—her very will.

Yet, his queen chose to lay down her armor and weapons to enter Alister's house.

The Ra'Voshnik drifted at the edge of his mind, brushing the surface as they both listened to the conversation occurring within. *The frail-blood wants to join Faye's court,* it growled.

And Faye would allow his entry for Prinia's sake.

Asking her to deny him entry will upset our queen, the creature said quietly.

Rune's brows lowered. *That is the first sensible thing I have heard you say.*

The Ra'Voshnik pondered his praise, and satisfaction rolled off it. *You should ask her to deny him. You upset our queen regularly, there's no point in both of us losing her favor. I'll put a good word in, so she'll forgive you.*

Rune exhaled. He should not have attempted to converse with the creature.

Did you forget we exist in tandem? I don't need your conversation to know your mind. Rune's fangs sharpened, and he resisted the urge to drag the Ra'Voshnik into the recesses of his consciousness. The creature tsked at him. *Our queen sees us as equals. If you aligned yourself with her views… you could garner the affection you're so desperate for.*

Be silent, Rune growled, focusing on his queen's voice behind Alister's walls.

Faye appeared beside him a short time later. He stepped into her, curling a finger under her chin. "Are you well?"

"I'm fine," his queen replied. Her smile brightened her gold-streaked eyes, and he allowed his tension to ease. She stood before him, unharmed. "Let's go home. We have some things to talk about."

"I heard," Rune said quietly, inspecting her for injuries.

She squeezed his hand. "I'm okay, he didn't do anything." When Rune met her gaze she added, "Take me home."

Rune phased them to his study and the fireplace blazed to life. Faye glanced at the petitions piled up in the mesh basket and led him to the settee. He smiled and murmured, "We have not sat here in some time."

He sat lengthwise and guided his queen to curl up against him. He stroked her hair, and the Ra'Voshnik purred through his mind. His queen's proximity soothed him like nothing else. His beautiful night breeze.

Ours, the creature grated.

Rune tempered his response, focusing on the woman in his arms. She shifted against him and sighed. "I'm missing my book."

"So you are," Rune purred.

"This dream was nice, but I looked forward to the ones where you held me in my sleep, the most."

The corner of Rune's mouth lifted. Between the new responsibilities to her court and serving on the High Council, he would carve out time for them. Her mortality vexed his thoughts. If this was the path fate allowed them, he refused to look back on the decades he'd been gifted to find them wasted on mundane tasks.

"I will gladly hold you until the end of my days," he whispered against her hair.

She was quiet for long moments, worrying her lip. Rune soothed her, content to listen to the crackle of hellfire until his queen curated her words.

After a while she said, "Alister wants to join our court."

Tell her to refuse him, the Ra'Voshnik countered.

Rune ignored the creature and spoke in a soft voice, "The only wants I consider are yours, vsenia."

Faye's shoulders fell and examined her nails. "He said if our court existed back then, he would have come to us with Prinia. He wants the same things I do. It's just…"

His brother had planned to deliver her waterlogged body in the coffin he drowned her in. "Forgiveness and understanding are not mutually exclusive concepts. You can give one without offering the other." Rune was deeply intimate with this truth, and his brother would never receive his forgiveness.

"Was he good?" Faye asked, before quickly adding, "With the paperwork for court."

"Alister spoke truthfully. He did handle Belind's court documents for many centuries, but you are not obligated to him. Hire a staff if you wish, it does not have to be him."

"But he was good at what he did," Faye said flatly.

He won't be if I take his hands, the Ra'Voshnik grated.

Rune pulled her closer, but she wouldn't meet his gaze. "If I have to hire a hundred clerks to run your court smoothly, I will. Do not ask me to witness your pain and do nothing."

Faye leaned into him, comforted by his warmth. "I thought it would be easier… after I brought Prinia back. I thought I would stop feeling his hand on my neck after the nightmares faded." She hugged his arm tighter and whispered, "I still feel the water when I see him. I try to keep it quiet because I want you to be brothers again."

Rune purred softly and stroked her hair. The gentle vibrations lulling her. "These types of wounds scar, but never truly heal, vsenia. Immortals have centuries to inflict and accumulate a great deal of unseen injuries. Centuries of animosity stand between Alister and I. It will not be mended in a matter of weeks."

Or her lifetime, Faye feared.

His lips pressed to her hair. "I know you are concerned for Prin-ia. Perhaps I can ask if the two of you can visit alo—"

"No." Faye's voice was lackluster. "She gets confused without Alister. He is her anchor."

Rune caressed the side of her face. His careful touch sent tingles down her back. He coaxed her chin up, and she met his gaze. "I cherish the kindness in you, but you give too much, vsenia."

"I can't abandon her."

"I know," he pressed a kiss to her forehead. "I will support whatever you decide… and perhaps we should find a kinder subject to speak on."

Faye smiled and tugged on a length of his white-blonde hair. "My brain hurts, you pick."

He gazed down at her and smirked. "My queen's birthday is in approximately two weeks. Would you mind terribly if I asked for a hint of what to get you?"

She relaxed in his embrace and laughed. "You're building me an estate. I think that covers my birthdays and new year festivals for at least ten years. Maybe twenty."

"I suppose I could bribe the blonde harpy into telling me," Rune countered.

Faye pushed off his chest and sat up. "If you keep calling my sister a harpy, I'm going to bite you."

Rune leaned up, stopping when his lips were a moment from hers. "Hardly a threat to one of my kind."

Faye leaned in, brushing her lips over his in a sweet kiss, before getting to her feet.

"And where are you off to, love?" Rune asked. His gaze raking over her with a predator's intent.

She grinned, lifting one shoulder. "I might be going to tell my sister to keep her mouth shut when you ask her what to get me."

"I may come hunting for you in fifteen minutes," he crooned.

"I'm going to have to talk her out of whatever wild plans she has for my birthday. So, I need at least two hours," Faye said, walking backward toward the door. "Think you can occupy yourself until I come back?"

He nodded and said, "Tell the blonde harpy I send my regards."

Faye made her way to Sparrow's wing and turned the corner. "Hooker," she called, playing their game of echolocation.

"Bitch," her sister answered. "Wing daddy is shirtless in case tall, pale, and scary is with you." Faye heard Vash's hush murmur but couldn't make out the words. "Well, you're a lot bigger than him, baby. I don't want his shadowy highness getting intimidated."

Faye knocked on the doorframe without looking in. "You okay in there?"

"Come in, I don't know why he's being a baby," Sparrow answered. "She's seen you without a shirt on plenty of times."

Vashien donned a shirt while Sparrow lay sprawled over the bed, peering at her upside down. He thumped her with the edge of his wing and counted off on his fingers. "At her hot spring, in the kitchen in the morning, *not* in our bedroom when she's fated to a Pure Blood." He shifted his wings as he adjusted the shirt glancing between them. "Have your girl talk. I'll be in the den."

Faye lifted her hand and Vashien slowed to a stop. "I'll be quick. I know you'll be working that day, but can I ask you both to stay in Necromia on the Hunter's Moon. Give us until late the next day?"

Sparrow shrieked and rolled to her feet. "Something does happen. What is he going to do to you?"

"Please keep her in Necromia," Faye said to Vash.

"She can't phase, and Hell is a closed realm. She couldn't get a ride back if she tried," Vashien said as he walked past Faye.

"You're supposed to be on my side!" Sparrow yelled.

Vashien turned toward her sister. "She's family, I don't want to accidently hear anyth—"

"While Runey is defiling her?" Sparrow finished.

Faye snatched the closest pillow off a chair and hurled it at her blonde curls. "Shut up."

"No, you're kicking me out of my home. I want details," her sister whined, flopping back onto her bed.

"She's all yours," Vashien said before vanishing and Sparrow huffed at the empty space.

Faye sat beside her and patted her thigh. "Do this for me, please."

"*Fiiiiine*," she groaned. Her eyes suddenly narrowed, and she asked, "You're not planning on tying him up, are you?" When Faye didn't answer she threw her arms over her head. "You have two trained males. Two. Tell them to make you come until you pass out."

Faye pushed her sister's leg off her. "I'm going to ask you for something, and you cannot freak out."

"Is it lingerie collars? I know all the stores Vashien goes to," Sparrow said, proceeding to name off shops along with their districts.

Faye grabbed Sparrow's wrist. "Okay, I need that too, but stop. Are you calm?"

Her sister jostled her hand and threw her head back dramatically. "Just tell me."

"I need the drink you use after you play nice with Vash," Faye said, ready to clamp her hand over Sparrow's mouth if she got overly excited. Her green eyes widened, and Faye pointed a finger at her.

"I'm calm. This is me calm," Sparrow sang, splaying out her fingers in front of her. "Did you let him? Did he get it all the way down there?" she asked in a whisper, pointing at her neck before tapping the hollow. Faye scowled at her, and she lifted her hands in surrender. "Okay, okay. I'm sorry. I'll teach you how to make the tea if I get to go collar shopping with you."

She expected Sparrow to demand the she describe Rune in detail, or to surrender some sordid detail. This was easy, but she had to pretend to be put out, or her sister would want more.

Faye frowned at her and grumbled, "Fine."

Sparrow squealed, hugging her. "This is going to be so fun."

Faye untangled herself and stood, glancing back at her sister. "Tomorrow?"

"Tomorrow," her sister answered.

She phased to her gardens before Sparrow could question her further. The sun had set, and the lush green space was lit by the small lanterns Rune placed for her. She glanced up at the moon, wondering what the space would look like bathed in a red glow.

Her vampire was a predator, but she wanted to make it more

than three steps before he caught her.

Faye phased though the gardens, preparing for their game.

Thirty-Two

Faye cut beef into cubes beside Kimber while Aunty Clara inspected her simmering pots. Oregano, bay leaves, and other aromatics spiced the air. Younger children dashed past the screen door, chasing a fluffy white cat across the yard.

"One of those kids is going to fall on her," Aunty Clara said, wiping her hands on her apron. "I don't want to hear that one crying when she gets hurt."

Kimber laughed, and a smile crept over Faye's lips. Sparrow had played tag with the children for years. Jumping on their backs and swatting at them before she ran away. Her sister wouldn't get hurt, but Faye wouldn't disagree with Aunty Clara's grumbling.

Preparing the meal helped distract her. Nerves warred with her excitement as they approached midday. She had her first lesson with Sadi today. Her ability to phase increased her confidence, but her magic's sluggish response to obey her will left her uneasy.

After the lesson, Rune would take her to the hot spring she had abandoned since taking up residence in Hell. Wanting to include the hot spring in her estate, Rune offered to learn what she wanted to be preserved or cleared from the forest.

"Where is your vampire boy?" Aunty Clara asked, drawing her from her thoughts.

Faye transferred the cut meat into a bowl and said, "Rune went to check on The Crumbling. He should be here soon with my friend... Sadi."

"That's not what Sparrow calls her," Kimber mumbled under her breath.

Faye kicked the side of her shoe, and the tall brunette winced, mouthing, *Ow.*

The children squealed outside, and Faye glanced through the screen door. The little ones had abandoned Sparrow to run toward the gate.

"Traitors!" her sister yelled.

Faye and Kimber laughed quietly, sharing a look.

Bayle charged up the steps and threw the screen door open. "I'll get the book ready," he called to someone outside.

Faye stepped out of his way before Bayle collided with her, dashing down the hall, running his hand along the wall, his curling black hair bounding with each step.

"Rune is here!" the boy said, running toward his room. "He said he would read to us."

"Hey buddy," Faye called over her shoulder as she washed her hands. "Rune is helping me learn magic today."

"I know. I'm organizing stuff for my team," he answered.

Rune strolled in a moment later, followed by a dozen little ones crowding around him like baby ducklings following their mother.

"Stop bothering the Shadow Prince. He's teaching Faye important magic," Aunty Clara scolded, shooing the children out of her kitchen.

He inclined his head in greeting and said, "Ladies." The children left his side with sour looks on their little faces.

Faye chuckled, watching them slump over in defeat. "Is Sadi here?" Faye asked.

Rune nodded. "She and Damian are in the far end of the yard."

Faye turned toward Aunty Clara and kissed her plump cheek. "I'm going to sight-shield it so we don't scare the kids."

"The kids are fine," the elderly woman said, waving Faye away. "Don't let them touch the swords."

Kimber abandoned the meat she was prepping and rushed out the door.

Aunty Clara used the back of her hand to brush a stray white lock out of her face. "That kid is getting so lazy," she grumbled, pulling Kimber's cutting board closer.

"Did you want me to tell her to come back?" Faye asked, struggling to keep the laughter out of her voice.

"No," Aunty Clara snapped, pushing the chunks of meat around with her cleaver. "They're not even the same size. Always wasting time, this girl."

Rune waved his hand, and the remaining chunks of beef fell into evenly cut cubes.

"I don't need your magic knife," Aunty Clara huffed. "Go teach Faye. Stop touching my kitchen. You think if I wanted to do that, I couldn't?"

"I am s—"

"Noooooo, you made her mad. We need to go," Faye said, pushing Rune out the door. She giggled when the wooden door slammed on her heels.

"I meant no offense," Rune said, glancing behind him.

Faye interlaced her fingers with his. "You can't use her kitchen. You have to ask if she needs help first. Then she'll give you something to do."

"You have strange rituals," Rune muttered.

"The house is full of them," Faye said, now noticing several of the children staring at Sadi. She hoped it was because they could pass as twins, and not the corseted lace and satin she wore.

"Ready?" Sadi asked as Faye crossed into the sectioned-off part of the yard.

Faye nodded, weaving a sight shield over the parameter. A small child's scream broke her concentration. She turned as a young girl with sunset-hued hair lost her tug-a-war with a stuffed bird and fell to the ground. The slightly older boy clutched his prize and turned to leave.

"Hey!" Sadi yelled, stalking in their direction.

The boy paled, fleeing once she opened her mouth wide and hissed.

Faye started after the crazed Familiar, and Damian caught her elbow. She pulled out of his grasp, rounding on him.

"Let her go, dove. Watch," Damian said, pointing at the little girl.

Her sister wandered up beside her as Sadi wiped the girl's tears. She helped her up and held her hand while they talked.

"Your evil twin is being nice to the beasties?" Sparrow asked as the unlikely pair headed for the forest. She turned toward Damian. "She's not going to lead the kid behind the trees and sacrifice her to Chaos, right?"

"If you two would stop hissing at each other, you would see she has more in common with you than just your looks," Damian said.

"I'm team Faye," Kimber said, linking arms with her as she leaned back into a pose with her heel kicked up and hissed.

"That was a good one," Sparrow clapped.

"I learned from the best," she replied, fluffing her dark hair the same way Sparrow did.

Damian leaned his head back, groaning. "The two of you are nauseating," he said, picking at his nails. "Come on, cockatoo. Training."

"Keep fucking up my name and see what I do to you," Sparrow snapped.

Kimber shoved her. "You get so mad over nothing. Mess his name up back. Call him David, or Derrek. Lame-ian."

The Familiar called a sword and pointed it at Kimber. "Didn't you want to train?"

"Yes," the tall brunette squealed before rushing to his side.

Faye found her attention elsewhere as Damian instructed Kimber and Sparrow, keeping tabs on Sadi as she strolled into the forest with the little girl.

Rune's hand smoothed down her back. "Sadi will keep her safe. She is likely crafting her a Familiar toy."

"Out of sticks?" Faye asked.

Her vampire shrugged. "You have been to Chaos. They are typically crafted from bones."

Sadi emerged from the forest with the girl in tow, holding a layer of her lace skirt to cradle sticks and leaves. They wandered to Kimber's garden, and the little girl proceeded to pick three flowers, adding them to the tree clippings.

Her evil twin knelt and sat back on her heels, arranging the twigs and blooms between them. Other children gathered as Sadi moved her hands over the pile. They floated together, gathering into a tight ball.

Faye's lips parted as the sound of songs sung by birds rose in a crescendo from the floating debris. Sadi brought her hands together and balled them into fists, before pulling her hands apart in a sudden motion.

It sprouted wings and a tail, before falling to the ground. The girl giggled as the bird fluttered its wings and hopped into her lap.

The boy who started it all stepped away from the crowd, holding the stuffed animal they fought over. He leaned forward, and she screamed, "No!" The boy threw the stuffed bird at her feet and reached for the magical bird hopping on her lap.

Faye gasped as it exploded into a barrage of sticks and leaves, swarming around the boy. He wailed, holding his hands to his face as he ran.

"Sadi, what are you doing?" Faye yelled as she rushed across the yard.

Her evil twin smiled up at her as the twigs and flowers formed back into a small bird. The enchanted toy hopped back over to the little girl, jumping in her hand when she lowered it.

"You can't make toys attack children," Faye hissed.

"He shouldn't be grabbing things that don't belong to him," Sadi retorted. She turned to the girl and tapped her chin. "Isn't that right, Jamie Lyn."

The girl nodded, cradling her new pet.

Did you hurt that boy? Faye asked directly to Sadi's mind.

"No," the Familiar said as she stood. "It mirrors intent. If anyone is injured by it, know they deserved it."

Faye folded her arms. "And it won't explode on Aunty Clara if Jamie Lyn doesn't want to go to bed?"

Sadi gave her an exhausted stare while she dusted off her belted thigh-high boots. "Mirrors intent," she said, slower.

Jamie Lyn hugged the bird to her chest and gazed up at her. "I love her, Miss Faye. Please don't take her away."

Faye's shoulders sagged in defeat. "Go," she muttered, shooing away the little girl before turning toward Sadi. "I'll need to purchase more of them. She can't be the only one with a toy like that."

Sadi dusted her skirt, picking off the remainder of debris. "I'll make them more, but that one is hers."

Faye watched as Sadi headed back to the sectioned off part of the yard, and reluctantly began to wonder if her evil twin wasn't entirely evil after all.

Thirty-Three

Faye glanced over Sadi's shoulder. Metal gleamed in the sunlight as Sparrow and Kimber swung through drills under Damian's watchful eye. She turned toward the children playing a few yards away, oblivious to their training.

Her vampire stood beside Sadi, straightening his cufflinks. The Familiar finished dusting off her skirts and picked a twig out of the clawed, articulated ring housing her Shard of Darkness. "We'll siphon off Rune today," she said, motioning to Rune before she pulled her hair to one side, checking the ends for debris.

They were starting with siphoning? Faye shrank. "I... I haven't been able to manifest my tendril."

Sadi looked her up and down, exhaling. She closed the distance between them with a small shake of her head. "It's not a manifestation of will. It's an appendage." Sadi's hand shot forward—into the center of her chest.

Faye gasped, staring down at the arm buried in the center of her chest. She expected pain but a chill followed by pins and needles radiated across her ribs.

"Hey, the fuck are you doing?" Sparrow yelled, breaking away from Damian and Kimber.

Sadi ignored her, roughly gripping Faye's bicep. She sucked a sharp breath as the Familiar reached deeper, sinking her arm into Faye to her elbow. Nails scraped against the core housing her magic, and Faye jerked. Her power flared to life, rushing to the surface.

Instinct screamed to annihilate the foreign entity threatening the shards she carried.

"Sadi," Rune warned the same moment. The Familiar curled her lip and withdrew a bloodied hand.

Sadi flexed her fingers as red tracked over her palm and wrist. Faye's lips parted. Were those snake bites?

Sparrow dragged her away from Sadi and flattened her hand between Faye's breasts. "Are you okay?"

Faye was dimly aware of the warmth spreading over her torso as her sister mystically searched for injuries. The deep swollen puncture wounds covering Sadi's hand horrified her. Had she done that? "I'm sorry," Faye breathed.

"Fuck that. She isn't sorry. That's what you get for shoving your hand in her," Sparrow snapped before opening her mouth wide to hiss.

Sadi cradled her hand, responding in kind.

"Ladies, there's no need for such language," Damian crooned, pulling Sadi's back to his chest. He leaned into her, and she snapped her teeth at him. He only grinned. "Don't make me adjust your attitude here. There are cubs present."

Rune strolled past Sadi to Faye. "Are you well?"

She nodded as Sadi slowly wiped her hand over the damage she inflicted. Faye blinked as the Familiar moved higher, revealing clean unbroken skin. Sadi flexed her hand, testing her range of motion before her attention seated squarely on Faye. "We'll do this differently. Look into yourself."

Faye peered down at herself, turning her palms up. She wasn't sure where to begin. The children laughed, racing across the field behind her. She turned and spied Aunty Clara sitting on the porch in a rocking chair. She watched over the children playing, but Faye got the feeling she was examining the space Faye occupied with her court.

She turned back toward Sadi. "I don't know what that means."

Sadi leaned back on her hip, tilting her head as she scratched her brow with the clawed point of her ring. "You feel our depth of power. Focus on it. Familiar who serve Chaos can see the piece of the Darkness anchored in each shard. We call it a core. The housing is located here," she said, tapping the center of her chest.

"Come on, blue jay. Get back to training. My kitten needs to teach her lessons," Damian said, pointing the way with the tip of his sword.

Her sister snorted and jabbed two fingers into the front of her throat in a V, then pointed at Sadi. "I'm watching you."

The Familiar lifted her shoulder and blew Sparrow a kiss. Faye parted her lips to stop the tirade of profanities to follow, but her sister waved it away. She turned on her heel, following Damian.

"I will not be far," Rune said to Faye, sparing Sadi a cutting glance.

Faye rolled her shoulders, clearing her mind. She looked into Alister and his wife after she returned Prinia to her body. She could do this.

A cool breeze slipped past her, carrying the earthy smells of the forest she loved. Faye took a deep breath, letting the stress of her lessons slip away. This was her home. She was surrounded by the people she loved. Faye embraced her sense of calm and focused on Sadi's reservoir of power.

Faye felt it but couldn't quite focus on it. A darker blur rested at the center of the Familiar's chest inside her. She took a step closer, focusing on her core. It snapped into focus and the sunny yard faded to a gray swirling smoke.

Prinia's core was covered with the red spider lilies she loved and Sadi's was no less intricate. A sleek black cat gracefully descended into jagged stones. Curls of embossed, glittering black smoke rose from between the rocks the feline precariously strolled through.

Faye looked down at herself, and her brows crinkled. She saw her body instead of her core. Frowning, she focused on her magic. A large dark blur took shape, and the shift in perspective clicked. It was like looking at the fencepost or the forest behind it. Focusing on one caused the other to blur.

Her body faded as her core came into focus, and her breath caught. "There's something wrong," Faye said. Sharp purple tendrils illuminated the churning black mist as it poured from the top of her core. The overflow obscured her housing, spilling to the floor and pooling a few feet around her.

Movement slithered through the mist at her feet, and Faye's eyes widened. A shadowed snake rose out of the fog, flaring its hood like a cobra.

Faye shrieked, backing away from the serpent—but the churning mist moved with her. She couldn't escape it. Her magic surged to the surface with her pounding heart and more snakes rose.

"Rune!" Faye screamed as power flared between her shoulder blades. Her wings erupted, weighing her down as she scrambled away from the nest of vipers surrounding her.

Hands clapped over either side of her face, and Sadi's dark eyes broke through her vision.

"Are you here? Are you with me?" Sadi asked, searching her face.

Faye panted, her gaze darting over the disintegrating shadows. The curling wisps revealed sunlight and full green grass, returning Faye to her true surroundings.

Sadi stroked her cheek and lightly scratched her nails over Faye's scalp. "Tell me what you see."

Faye couldn't speak. Her court surrounded her—overwhelming her. Worry etched over each of their faces. She curled her wings around her, hiding from their view.

"Do you see sunlight?" Sadi asked gently.

Faye wet her lips and nodded.

"Name things you see. It'll help ground you in the present." Sadi murmured.

She looked past Sadi and breathed, "I see Rune."

He moved closer, taking her from Sadi and encircling her in his arms. "I have you," he whispered against her hair before straightening. "Give her some space."

Faye clung to her mate, enfolding him beneath her iridescent wings. *He has me,* Faye chanted in her mind, breathing in his scent of amber and sandalwood. She held him tighter, focusing on the hard planes of his body. The love she felt for him. She took a deep steadying breath. *I'm safe. He has me,* Faye repeated, amending her mantra.

She listened to the overlapping laugher and squeals from the children behind her. Faye's breathing slowed, the weight at her back lifted as she leaned into Rune. Exhausted.

"You need food and rest," Rune murmured, stroking her back.

Faye nodded, and her surroundings faded as her vampire phased them home.

Thirty-Four

R une tucked Faye into bed and ordered an array of dishes while
the Ra'Voshnik prowled the edges of his mind. *Why did she
scream? If Sadi put something in her head, I'm going to take my time skinning
her.*

Be silent, Rune grated as a pleasant chime sounded. A silver tray
appeared on his desk topped with fresh-cut fruits, steaming bread
rolls, choice cuts, and an assortment of beverages. Rune placed it beside Faye, pouring small glasses of water, tea, and pomegranate juice.

His queen lay on her side, clutching his pillow under her chin,
fighting to keep her eyes open. "You will make a faster recovery if
you eat before you rest. Familiar visions are taxing," Rune said.

Faye pushed herself up with a groan and scooted closer to the
tray. She selected the small plate of choice cuts and a fork. "Don't tell
Sadi I like this. She'll think I'm imitating her," his queen said between

bites of filet mignon. She made quick work of the dish and crossed her legs. "I think there's something wrong with me," Faye said as the saucer clattered against the silver tray.

"There is nothing wrong with you, vsenia. Visions are difficult to navigate," Rune assured her.

Faye lifted the dark sheets over her shoulders and pulled them around her. "This wasn't a vision." Faye raised the small glass of dark red juice. "It's like this is my core, but the pitcher is my power. It overflows and collects at my feet."

Rune stilled, absorbing her words. What she described wasn't possible. The core mirrored the shards. "Call your shards, all of them."

Faye upturned her hand, and a small mass of black churning mist appeared in her hand. Rune collected them, blindly feeling for the individual shards. It was easier to see damage done to a core on the weaker shards since the surrounding mist didn't conceal the crystal at its center.

"What are you doing?" Faye asked as he pinched the dark shards, rolling them between his thumbs and forefinger.

Rune moved to the next and said, "Our shards mirror our core. If you have a crack in your core your shard will be damaged as well." He finished inspecting her free shards and took her hand, feeling her ring. They were all smooth, it was possible the underside of the crystal in her ring was cracked. "I can ask Sadi to look into you to be sure."

Faye shook her head. "I can feel the depth of my power. My reservoir is whole. I know what cracks feel like, I felt them when Sadi healed Prinia and your brother."

"Does it pain you? Is that why you screamed?" Rune asked gently as he returned her shards. His queen's silence intensified his worry as the moments stretched between them. "I need to know what is wrong to help you. I can bring Sadi—or Morbid if you would rather not speak with her."

"There were snakes… in my power," Faye whispered. Rune blinked. He'd never heard of such a thing. It had to be a vision. She nudged the tray and said, "I'm really tired. Can you take this away and sit with me until I fall asleep?"

"Of course, love," Rune answered as his mind raced. Were the snakes an omen? Could she have slipped into a vision instead of the lessons Sadi planned? He exhaled, setting the tray on his nightstand. Pressing his queen while she was exhausted would only frustrate her. He would need to consult with Morbid.

The hellfire illuminating their room from sconces on either side of their bed dwindled to a flicker with a wave of his hand. He sat with his back to the headboard, and Faye rolled onto her side, resting her head on his thigh. He stroked her hair, murmuring, "Rest, vsenia. I will speak with Morbid."

She nodded, drawing the sheets up to her chin. "Wake me up in an hour. We still need to go over the forest I want to keep around my hot spring."

Rune silently cursed in High Tongue. He'd forgotten about their appointment.

I didn't, the Ra'Voshnik growled.

"It is of little concern. We can reschedule when you have recovered fully," Rune promised.

His queen yawned. "No, I don't want to hold up the construction of our court's estate. It's important."

"I will wake you in two," he said.

But his dark queen was fast asleep.

Faye woke slowly, lifting her shoulder to stretch as Rune stroked her arm. She groaned, rubbing her eyes, and was greeted by gray stone walls and dark silken sheets. Rune peered down at her, smoothing away a stray lock of hair.

"You should rest," he said firmly.

"I'm fine," Faye grumbled. The sooner she finished marking off what she wanted the foreman to clear the sooner she could turn in for the night.

Faye got out of bed and opened the drawer in her nightstand, retrieving her brush. She stood in front of the full-length mirror and began combing the tangles from her hair. Rune's reflection passed behind her, and he returned with her fur-lined coat.

She turned toward him. "I've been thinking," she began. Faye wanted her people to have the best chance at success. Her court needed to run efficiently so Anaria could bloom into the realm she'd envisioned. "I want to accept your brother's offer."

"You want to give Alister a position at court?" Rune asked, offering her jacket.

Rune helped her into it as she said, "I want to do what's best for the court. You wanted to hire a hundred clerks to replace him. If it takes a hundred clerks, then he must be good." She looked up behind her. His face remained stoic as he smoothed her back and lifted her hair out. She sighed and said in a smaller voice, "He'll need a space for Prinia. You won't be able to enter."

Rune looked away, slipping his hands into his pockets. A hint of Voshki's shadows stretched from the corners of his eyes, and Faye wished she could hear what they were saying.

Her vampire turned back to her and said, "My brother is perfectly capable of handling court business remotely. I know seeing him distresses you. You do not need to subject yourself to his presence. I am more than happy to be a liaison between the two of you."

He meant well, but Faye didn't want to spend the rest of her life hiding from his brother. He frightened her, but she'd done what Rune and Sadi couldn't. She returned Prinia to him. He wouldn't attack her again.

"You and Alister will never be like Sparrow and me—I know that. I…I only hope you can become brothers and find some civil ground. I want our children to have two uncles on your side. A family."

The tension in his stance was subtle but she saw it. "I am yours to command. However, my brother may not acquiesce to your will," Rune said without meeting her gaze.

"All we can do is try." Faye said gently, while silently hoping their grudge would come to an end during her lifetime.

"I will send word and make arrangements for him," Rune said, upturning his hand. "Shall we?"

Faye stepped closer to him and placed her hand in his. Their surroundings faded and the earthy scent of her forest reached her before the tepid humidity. Excitement filled her. It'd been so long since she'd been here. The small flowering plants bordering her hot spring had grown much larger without her to trim them back. Stray leaves and sticks covered her dusty lounge chairs, but this little space warmed her heart.

And soon it would be part of her estate.

"I want the mountain preserved," Faye said as she walked toward the chairs, gazing up the rocky face.

"This way, vsenia." Rune motioned toward the opposite end. Faye met him at a steep incline into the forest. "Watch your step," he said, offering his hand.

Faye slowly made her way down, losing her footing as dirt and rocks shifted under her weight. She shrieked, grabbing for Rune. He caught her, lifting her into his arms before she fell into the thick brush of tangled roots.

"Thank you," she breathed, circling her arm around his neck. She glared over his shoulder at the uneven terrain, not quite trusting him to carry them through it. He slid and hopped, traversing the incline as Faye's heart leaped into her throat. "Don't drop me," she cried, squeezing him tighter.

Leaves crushed beneath his steps as he chuckled. "I have you," he promised, pressing a light kiss to her hair.

Rune slowed to a stop, and Faye opened her eyes. She'd never come to this side of the forest. The canopy filtered the sun's waning rays as the leaves rustled with the breeze. He gently set her down at the edge of a small clearing.

"Did you want this included with your spring? A tranquil place for a private garden, perhaps?" he asked, strolling into the open space. "We could teach our young about herbs and flowers here."

"Children," Faye corrected, teasingly dragging out the word as she followed him. Her heart filled with love and gratitude until it ached. She couldn't have asked fate for a more loving or devoted man. A smile spread over her lips as she turned. There was enough room for two small gardens. She imagined the twins she'd seen in the Hall of Empty Eyes. They would kneel with her beside the freshly turned earth, their little hands dark with soil. She wondered what herbs and flowers they would purchase.

Blackberries if Sparrow could convince them to grow her favorite fruit. Faye laughed to herself.

A glint of metal caught Faye's eye. A small iron disk hung from a branch by a thin chain. As Faye turned, she noticed more of them, dozens of tiny fixtures hanging throughout the clearing's border.

Blue flames flickered to life in each one, glittering all around her. The soft, blue-tinged glow settled over the forest. Her forest. The climbing vines and arching branches overhead bathed in an effervescent glimmer.

Where only the two of them existed.

Voshki said he would take her on a picnic months ago. Faye giggled, wondering how many times he had badgered Rune before he agreed. The space was beautiful. She beamed, turning toward her vampire. "This is amazing."

Veined misted shadows stretched beneath his gaze, brushing the tops of his cheekbones. He smiled down at her warmly and stepped closer. "You are more than I have ever dreamed of. You have taught me to love and fill our days with joy. My devotion for you is as constant as time. My love is vast and endless as the Darkness. Faye Alexander," Rune confessed, lowering himself onto one knee.

Faye's heart leaped to her throat as he opened his jacket, retrieving a small black box from his inner pocket. Tears gathered on her lashes as he opened it. Her devastatingly handsome vampire gazed up at her. His pale blue eyes meeting hers in a flurry of emotion. The way his lips parted, and his features softened, as though he were utterly captivated by her presence but simultaneously feared she might vanish.

"Tie your soul with mine, and I will walk beside you for all of my days. Will you grant me the honor of being my wife?" Rune solemnly asked.

Her throat constricted as she blinked away the tears. She knew he loved her, but seeing him... kneeling before her. She daydreamed of a family when she was little. The husband she would meet one day. She didn't think it would happen. Never expected Rune or Voshki to come into her life.

They wanted her to be their wife.

"Yes," Faye whispered, nodding her head. "Yes."

Rune took the ring and glided it onto her finger. Faye smiled as more tears came. It wasn't a diamond. The delicate setting was a thin vine opening into two leaves framing opposite corners of the green to violet gem in a basket setting. It shimmered, reflecting the light of the hellfire candelabrums. She tilted her hand, the jewel changing from a deep violet to a forest green and back again. He knew her.

Chose her favorite stone.

Faye wiped her tears. "I love it."

Rune stood and pulled her against him. His lips met hers and Faye closed her eyes.

"And I love you, vsenia. I am yours to command. Now… and always."

Thirty-Five

Faye sat at Rune's desk straightening the stack of petitions. The number of requests for admittance into her court tripled over the past week. She both thanked and dreaded Alister's assistance. A constant stream of paperwork took up most of his time as he prioritized the repairs in each village and assigned guides for the transition of Necromians to Anaria.

He scheduled a meeting with her today. An *in-person* meeting. Faye swallowed her apprehension, but she couldn't help the frown on her lips. Working with him benefitted her people, and all he asked for in return was a Rune-free space for Prinia. Alister had spoken with the foreman and architect, drafting a haven for his wife in the northeast wing of Faye's estate.

Faye had chosen the furthest point from the wing for her family suites.

Faye jogged her knee, concentrating on the crackle of hellfire in the oversized hearth. Its blue flames glittered through the facets of her engagement ring as she tilted her fingers. Sparrow grabbed her wrist and shrieked every time she saw it for the first few days, insisting on shopping trips so Faye could find a wedding gown. There was nothing she wanted more than to kneel with Rune in a blood temple, but she couldn't leave her people to plan a wedding.

She would be Rune and Voshki's wife after their court settled.

Faye dropped her hand, searching for a distraction as she counted the minutes until Alister's arrival.

Her vampire looked out of place at the smaller sitting table, reading a bleached leather-bound book while taking shallow sips from a glass of crimson wine. His stone castle had become her home over the past few months. The bookshelves were filled with ancient tomes, and the simple sconces she once found cold were now a reflection of her solemn vampire. He encouraged her to *mark his space and make it her own.* Faye cut flowers from the gardens and arranged them in the rooms she visited most.

Sparrow, of course, followed her lead and hung a framed imaging crystal next to the door in Rune's study. It was her favorite picture of them. Vash took it a few years ago at her hot spring. Faye sat on a lounge chair, bundled in her fluffy robe with a book clutched to her chest. Sparrow stood behind her, holding lengths of Faye's hair straight out like rabbit ears as they smiled and posed.

Sparrow had gotten her the latest book from her favorite Familiar author for her birthday. Faye hoped Sparrow was exaggerating about kicking over a table to stop another woman from getting the last copy—but with her sister she could never be sure. Faye had no chance of buying a copy for herself when she lived as an Anarian. Shop owners allowed the dark-bloods to make their purchases first. If there was any stock left, day-bloods could pick over what remained.

Her long-standing dream of equality between the castes had become a reality with Rune beside her. It was arbitrary, but knowing she wouldn't have to depend on Sparrow to get her another book or a chocolate orange lifted a thin, constant strain Faye carried through her years. A sense of burden she would be sure no one in Anaria felt.

Under her reign, Anarians and day-bloods would receive the

same dignity dark-bloods were afforded. Faye ran her thumb over the edge of the letters, counting more than a dozen. *They all deserved safety and the simple pleasure of a good book with sweets.*

Rune stood from the square bloodroot table near his bookshelves and moved to her side. "I can see you are not well. You do not have to meet with him."

"I'm fine," Faye breathed. It was a blatant lie, but she wouldn't entertain hiding from Alister for the rest of her life.

The click of a door handle sounded from the hall, much louder than it should have been. Faye turned to Rune as the sound of the door opening and closing echoed down the corridor.

"Alister's way of announcing his arrival," Rune answered her silent question.

Because he knows I'm afraid of him, Faye thought.

Booted footsteps approached the door, and Faye hid her hand beneath the desk, squeezing the edge of the seat cushion. Her body stiffened with tension as she tracked Alister's depth of power through the stone wall. Her mouth went dry, struggling to swallow.

I am here, love. I will keep you safe, Rune's soothing voice whispered through her mind.

Faye gave a small nod, counting her breaths instead of his footsteps. Alister stepped into the doorway, and Faye's airways froze.

"My queen," Alister said with a formal bow. He straightened and turned to Rune. "Brother."

Faye watched him, puzzled. Not because of what he called her but because she felt his reservoir of strength several feet behind him in the hallway. Alister approached them, and Faye observed his footfalls. The soft scrape of his boots matched his steps as he took a seat across from her.

"How did," Faye began, examining the space near the door where his power had stilled. "How did you move your core? I feel you back there."

"My brother favors parlor tricks," Rune grated.

"Some of us need to depend on tactics and cunning rather than brute strength," Alister said, dismissively gesturing to Rune's shard before his image dissolved into shadows and ash. He materialized at the back of the room and strolled to his seat once more.

Rune, Faye said gently to his mind. *Stop. Please.*

He took a subtle step back, placing himself in line with her shoulders—court body language he'd taught her. A Consort's position to his Queen indicated his state of mind. Standing behind her was a place of service, where he obeyed and agreed with her wishes. Standing in front of her was a warning to her enemies. Rune's stance beside her was an unspoken threat, promising death to anyone who aggressed his Queen.

The animosity between them weighed on her, eroding her resolve to move forward with the best interests for her realm. Faye needed this meeting to end without adding to the headache surfacing behind her eyes.

Alister brushed a lock of black hair from his forehead and called three letters. "Your rule shows promise. A handful of dark courts have recognized your reign. They have rallied behind the Court of Shadow and Moonlight," he said, pushing the first letter to the center of Rune's desk.

Faye leaned forward, calming the tremor in her hand as she retrieved the letter. She recognized the harsh script as High Tongue but couldn't read it. A wax seal decorated the bottom of the letter, stamped with an ornate dagger.

"You're going to have to teach me High Tongue," she said, tipping the page toward Rune. She turned back to Alister as Rune took it.

"Is this a good letter or a bad letter?"

"A good letter," Rune answered. "The Court of Shadow and Moonlight is newly formed. Their Queen's name is Moira, and she is relatively young. Her consort, Damien Archonis, comes from an established noble house."

Like her, Faye thought. It would be nice to speak with someone else in her position. "Do you know him? Will they be coming to Anaria?"

"I know of him. He is from one of the oldest turned families. He has always been fair in his court dealings," Rune said, returning the parchment to her.

"They're your allies but will remain in Necromia," Alister added, opening the stack of petitions. He filtered them into two piles and said, "I've distributed the healers and artisans through the villages. You should construct a hall. At the very least a temporary one where you can hold open court."

Faye looked up at Rune expectantly.

"Open court is where your people may voice their issues rather than send a petition," he explained.

Alister paused long enough to glare at his brother, then rolled his eyes before continuing to open the letters. "It *also* serves your disputes." He placed two folded pages on the center of the desk, tapping them with his middle and index finger as he said, "This is a mother petitioning for her daughter's release. She claims her daughter is being held against her will in the Court of the Ageless Sea."

A different kind of tension snaked over Faye's back. Cold and vicious. She'd heard stories of dark courts kidnapping Anarians, but hoped they were just that. Stories. "We need to get her out." Faye's tone was short and clipped as she read the flimsy document. Her mouth went dry as her power skated over her with her growing fury.

The woman, Isobelle, had been held captive for more than five years.

"I'll pen a response," Alister said. "I can have a temporary hall built in a week. They will have until open court to send a response or answer their summons. If your request goes unanswered, you have the grounds to go to their court and meter out retribution."

"This woman has been held for *years,* and I need to wait for her capturers to send a response?" Faye said the remark through her teeth. Every part of her burned. Couldn't they see how backward and archaic their system was?

"It is the way of things, vsenia," Rune said, gently. "Traveling to their court and demanding her release could be construed as an act of war."

"Blood whores are very common," Alister added in an even tone. "She may not have wanted to admit the truth to her family and stopped communicating with them. She could have simply been happy being a pet."

Faye's anger cooled as she considered all the possibilities. She hoped Alister was right, even if it saddened her. It was one she actively avoided, but not everyone shared her sentiments. "Please have the hall built as soon as you can. Would you mind speaking with her mother? Or requesting an audience with Isobelle? If she wants to come home, we can pay out her contract."

Alister nodded and called a roll of parchment, holding it out to

Faye. "These are the plans for Prinia. I will have our home and her flowers transferred to the northern field. When her mind settles, if she wishes, I will have arranged three rooms for her."

"Whatever I can do to make her comfortable," Faye said, taking the bundle of pages.

He straightened his back and tilted his head to examine Rune before his gaze settled back on her. "Do you have sanctuary?"

A growl reverberated from Rune, startling Faye. His eyes found hers, and she mouthed, *stop*. Her attention returned to Alister, and asked, "Is that something else I need to build so Anarians have a place to run to?"

"No, sanctuary from *him*," Alister bit out, pointing at Rune. "The Hunter's Moon will rise tomorrow. He's dangerous."

Faye flushed as Rune stepped forward, grating, "I am no danger to my queen."

Alister stood, flattening his palm on the desk, and leaned toward Rune. "You play a cultured aristocrat, but under it all, you are a monster. I won't stand by and let Faye suffer Prinia's fate," he spat, pointing at her while baring his teeth at Rune.

Faye rushed to her feet, wedging herself in front of Rune. Veined misted shadows stretched to the tops of his cheekbones as his pale blue gaze flooded black before dissipating. His arm circled her waist, and Rune growled at his brother, giving no ground.

Alister taunted him behind her. "You growl like the beast you are, brother."

Darkness, did he have a death wish? Faye ignored Alister, focusing on her enraged vampire. She placed her hand on his chest and sent a thought to his mind, *I need you to stop*. He looked down at her as his eyes flooded black. Faye dug her nails into his chest. *Both of you, please.*

The shadows beneath his eyes receded immediately, and Rune's fingers closed around her palm. He took a step back, lifting her hand to his mouth. "My queen," he whispered before the warmth of his lips touched the back of her fingers.

Faye turned toward Alister and leaned back against Rune. "Court will run smoother if you two would stop bickering."

"It looks like my brother has finally accepted a leash. For your sake, I hope it holds," Alister said calmly; the earlier viciousness in his voice gone. He crossed his arms and lifted a finger to his chin.

A dagger appeared on the desk before her, and Faye nudged the point away. The craftmanship on the embossed leather sheath was beautifully intricate. Windswept stars curved from the scabbard to the handle like smoke.

"Keep it near," Alister said, collecting the documents. "It's like the one you used on me."

Faye recoiled from the weapon. She used a spelled blade on Alister because he was trying to kill her. "I won't need this." Rune would never hurt her.

Alister's movements slowed as he tapped the parchments on their side to straighten them. "I pray you're right, but your rule will end if you die beneath him. I want the new dawn your reign will bring as much as you do."

Faye fell silent, unable to find her words.

"I am not the only day-blood to fall in love with an Anarian. If your court existed when I met her… I would have come to you for sanctuary—from dark-bloods like him," Alister sneered the last, turning on his heel.

Her vampire went rigid behind her, and Faye squeezed his hand, willing him to let Alister go. If the two of them would stop reopening the other's wounds, they might be able to heal and move forward.

Thirty-Six

Rune spent the next hour coaxing the tension from Faye. He'd strolled with her through the gardens after his brother's departure. Their walk inevitably led them to her garden.

He sat in the grass with his queen. The late afternoon sun warmed her, and she sighed, nestling against him. His little queen shared many similarities with the plants she doted over. Sunlight and a soft breeze did more to soothe her than anything he could offer. She entwined her fingers with his and hugged his arm tighter.

"I can have a meal brought here if you wish to soak in the spring," Rune said against her hair.

Faye shook her head, tracing circles over the back of his hand. "I'm still... I can't believe Alister thinks you're going to hurt me. Vampire brothels charge triple that night. Thousands of people wait for the Hunter's Moon specifically. It wouldn't be their most profitable night if it was dangerous."

Alister's barbed words lingered in Rune's mind, echoing until they became deafening. He despised the truth of his brother's words. If Rune allowed his instincts to reign, he would be a creature no better than the Ra'Voshnik.

The creature floated though his mind, amused. *You would be a dull imitation of me.*

Apprehension filled Rune as he surveyed the sky. In little more than a day, the Hunter's Moon would rise, bathing the realms in its eerie glow.

Rune squeezed Faye closer and said, "I am no turned vampire, love. It... may be best if I incapacitate myself tomorrow evening."

"No," Faye said, shoving off his chest.

He met her gaze, silently pleading for her understanding. "Blood and possession drive vampires, vsenia. Our minds are inlaid with rough instincts to dominate prey. It bleeds into every facet of our lives. A turned vampire's previous experiences offer a balance to soften and temper their new... urgings." Rune paused before softly admitting, "I possessed nothing to gentle mine."

Faye wilted. "I don't want you gentle."

"You want me to be rough with you?" Rune asked.

"I want you to stop holding back because *I'm not one of your kind,*" she deepened her voice, mimicking his accent.

Rune looked away, focusing on the willows swaying on either side of the hot spring. Faye didn't understand the dark urges he buried. How he imagined pinning her beneath him. The way she would scream his name while he fucked her with his cock, fangs, and will.

She can't understand if you don't tell her, the Ra'Voshnik growled. *Do you want me to fuck her ass first and get her warmed up to the idea?*

Rune growled at the creature and turned his attention back to Faye. "My instincts are unkind."

"Tell me what you want." Faye crawled over him to straddle his waist. She pulled her bottom lip through her teeth and asked, "Do you want me tied up?"

Rune grew hard beneath her as she rolled her hips. He smoothed his hands over her back. "My nature is to *take* from you. I will possess you and fuck every hole because you are mine." Faye's heart raced. He hoped to frighten her, but when he scented her arousal, he realized he moved in error. His warning enticed his ravenous little mate. "The Hunter's Moon will strip my discipline and self-control. I do not wish to mistreat you."

She leaned up on her knees and wrapped her arms around his neck. "You're not mistreating me," she whispered, touching her forehead to his. "You can have me. I want you to possess me."

Rune's eyes slid closed as he breathed in her subtle scent. His night breeze through plum blossoms. "You will tolerate what I subject you to at best."

"What are you going to do when I like it and want you to possess me more than once a year?" she asked, with a shy smile.

You know she's right, the Ra'Voshnik said in a bored tone.

Be silent, Rune growled.

Take what is offered. Our queen practiced swallowing your cock so you can fuck her pretty throat tomorrow. Scent her. She wants us to fuck all three of her holes, the Ra'Voshnik said, rising closer to the surface. *We could give her a demonstration. Do you want her cunt or her ass first?*

Faye sat back, searching his expression. When he offered no reply, the corners of her mouth dipped. "You're fighting so hard against what you are. Wouldn't it be easier to lean into it so you can steer?"

If you're so worried about the moon, give her to me, the creature grated. *We both know our queen prefers me over you.*

Rune exhaled. She wouldn't if she could hear its thoughts.

The Ra'Voshnik laughed before its voice smoothed into a purr, *Our queen—adores—when I speak filth to her.*

"The moon is going to rise tomorrow whether you want it to or not," Faye said, edging closer to him. "Lean in. Spend it with me."

"You want this, knowing what I will do to you?" Rune asked. She offered him a small smile and nodded.

Rune silently hoped he could hold his mind beneath the Hunter's Moon. His queen was too precious to leave to chance. He formulated a contingency plan to ensure her safety even if the moon stripped him of his self-control.

He unbuttoned his shirt, lacing the beginnings of a spell.

Thirty-Seven

R une shared an evening meal under the stars with his queen.
Faye had asked him to help her prune her garden, and Rune felt
certain he was more of a hinderance than a help as she meticulously checked over each plant. Laughter followed them as they strolled
back to their room with soil on their hands.

They showered before turning in for the night, and Faye slept in,
waking in the early afternoon. He brought her honey-drizzled apples
topped with pomegranate seeds after she slipped into the bath he'd
prepared for her.

He felt Vashien and Sparrow phase out of his realm and remained silent, suspecting Faye requested their absence.

The hours passed without incident until Rune's fangs began to
ache, and his skin became uncomfortably tight. The Hunter's Moon
would rise within the hour, and for the first time in all his centuries,

he felt its pull. The blood-red moon sang to his viciously possessive instincts. It lengthened his fangs and ignited his blood, demanding he pin Faye beneath him.

Rune stood before The Crumbling, hoping the distance from Faye would calm his darker urges. The wall of twisting storm clouds towered above him, rising ominously into Hell's ever-twilight sky. The low constant roar emanating from it coursed over Rune, settling in his bones.

You can always give Faye to me if you're feeling insecure, the creature snickered through his mind.

You will not touch her, Rune bit out, fueled by an unfamiliar possessive rage to protect what was his. He straightened his jacket, fighting the opposing impulses warring through his mind. One demanded the Ra'Voshnik's bloody death, and the other drove him to phase back to Faye. He could hear her breathless whimpers as he imagined taking her throat while he fucked her hard in the bath. Fates, he burned for her touch, the Darkness laced in her blood, the soft feel of her squeezing his cock.

The Ra'Voshnik laughed, and Rune bristled. If his focus was mangled, the creature's undisciplined mind would fare far worse beneath the moon's glow. It would injure Faye, drinking too deeply.

I would never harm our queen, it growled. *Your mind is weak. Sooooo distracted because your cock is hard. The lust you blame on the moon—I've felt it since I caught her scent.*

Impossible. The creature was beneath him, uncivilized and crass.

I've had a year to acclimate my instincts to our sweet mate. Between the two of us, it's you who is a danger to her, Shadow Prince, not me.

Rune's fangs sharpened with aggression. It would not touch her. Rune descended into himself, meeting the creature in his mind. He would bury it until the night was over to safeguard Faye.

"Try it. I'll bury you and make you watch while Faye screams my name," it growled, materializing out of smoke and shadow.

"You will not touch—"

"Save your threats and look into my mind. If you want to fight, you'll lose Shadow Prince," it crooned, leaning closer.

Rune paused, feeling the creature's thoughts, and took a step back. It spoke the truth. The moon held no sway over it. Its mind was clear while Rune's self-control held on by a fraying thread.

It slipped its hands into its pockets and began walking around him in a tight circle. "Might I suggest a bargain?"

Rune watched his eerie-eyed double walk out of view over his left shoulder and circled his right. "A bargain would indicate you possess something I desire."

"I could help you with something you want." It paused in front of him.

Rune waited, annoyed the creature dressed as he did, mimicking him down to its cufflinks.

"You want your fangs in our queen's throat and your cock in her pretty cunt. And if you're honest," it began, spreading its black tipped claws dramatically. "Which you rarely are—you also want to fuck her ass with your will." Rune seized the debased creature's jaw, and it chuckled, stepping into his hold. "What bothers you more?" it sneered. "That I spoke your desires or that you harbor them?"

Rune shoved the Ra'Voshnik away, disgusted by his own thoughts.

He wanted Faye in ways his tangled mind couldn't temper. His craving for her submission bled into his need to eliminate competitors for his queen's affection.

Eviscerating the Ra'Voshnik and fucking Faye while covered in his rival's blood became an appealing solution to all of his problems.

No, Rune thought, shaking his head as though it would order his maddened thoughts. "You have nothing I want. You *are* nothing I want."

It quirked its lip to the side and rubbed its chin. "Is that any way to speak to me when I'm trying to help you?"

He needed to get away from the bothersome creature before he wore its blood like a cologne. "Your taunts are of no assistance."

It canted its head to the side and smiled at him, flashing its fangs. "I could help you. You can fuck our little queen until the moon sets, and I'll make sure Faye is safe."

From him—the unspoken words hung between them.

"She is safe," Rune hissed. He laced a spell to burst his heart if Faye spoke her chosen word. If he was too rough with her, she had only to say *artichoke.*

"And how will she speak with your cock in her mouth?" the creature asked with a cold smile.

Rune cursed in High Tongue. He should have taught her—

"You should… depend on your oldest friend to protect our queen," it said with a smile. "You could taste her while she sucks your cock." Rune's bed appeared beside them. An image of him on his back with his queen straddling his face, followed. She rocked her hips while she leaned over him, sucking the head of his cock as she stroked his shaft.

"Or did you want her to take you into her throat?"

The illusion of Faye leaned forward at its words, taking his entire length past her lips. Rune stifled a groan and banished the fantasy to shadows and ash.

It folded its arms and grinned at Rune. "I've spent lifetimes dreaming of entombing you and taking our body. And while the moon cripples your mind I can."

"What do you want in return?" Rune asked, skeptically. If it expected him to share his body, he was mistaken.

"I want to marry Faye," it said.

"You said as much when I proposed," Rune grated. The creature had bashed itself against Rune's awareness, outraged he'd asked Faye to be *his* rather than their wife.

"I want to be present at *my* wedding. When Faye speaks her vows, she will say them to me. When she gazes at us with adoration, it will be my eyes she stares into."

The Ra'Voshnik expected him to willingly allow it to rise. In public? Allowing the creature to surface privately with Faye was one thing. Now it wanted to stand in a ceremony all the realms would clamor to attend.

Possessive rage and lust collided through Rune. He closed his eyes desperately clinging to reason. He opened them, praying the creature would see logic. "She speaks to both of us, you know this."

Its expression hardened as it took a threatening step forward. "Spoken like a man who has never been forced to live in the shadow of another."

"It is a mortal ceremony—"

"That she cherishes!" the Ra'Voshnik roared.

Rune met the creature's animosity, baring his fangs. Darkness, if Rune had known it would fight him so viciously, he would have considered allowing it to propose to Faye. At least that had been a private affair.

"I deserve to walk through our queen's life as much as you do."

Rune's possessiveness sharpened to a sword's edge, seeking the Ra'Voshnik's throat. He grasped it by the collar, dragging it closer. "You are a vicious creature, ill-equipped for polite society."

"You would be no different if we'd been reversed," it sneered.

Reversed? The parasite living in his mind believed his flesh and bones belonged to it? "The body is mine," Rune hissed.

The creature scoffed. "Because you had it a mere fifteen years before me? I don't mimic you. I *am* you. We *share* the same flesh, existing in tandem or not at all."

"My answer is no."

"Then you'll share our queen tonight."

Rune's temper snapped and he threw the Ra'Voshnik. It flipped to land in a fluid motion, digging its black-tipped claws into the black marble floor with one hand. It slid backward a few feet, leaving deep scrawls in its wake.

"If you won't share her, I'll take her from you. Make your choice Shadow Prince." The creature stood, launching forward in a blur. It sank its black-tipped claws into Rune's awareness and dragged him lower, descending into the recesses of his mind.

Rune had enough of the creature's foolishness. His power surged to him, enveloping the Ra'Voshnik before caging it in his subconscious.

A mental restraint in the form of a chain looped Rune's wrist. He growled, snapping the links as he pulled his arm free. More chains shot from the ground, twisting over his arms. He broke free of the first wave, but for each one he destroyed, three more sprang in its place.

The creature's prison shattered, and Rune struggled harder. He couldn't focus through his frenzied thoughts. This couldn't be happening. The Ra'Voshnik couldn't imprison him. His will was greater than the creature's.

A chain slid up his leg before wrapping around his chest, binding his arms at his side. They tethered him in place, impeding his ability to ascend to his physical body.

The Ra'Voshnik materialized before him and chuckled. "I'm asking for one day, one, and in return I'll help you *safely* enjoy our queen tonight and every Hunter's Moon to follow. Deny me and you'll spend every Hunter's Moon here."

Rune strained toward the creature as the chains cut deeper. "When I am free, I am going to bury you so deep you will perceive nothing but shadows and ash."

"And you'll be here every time the moon makes your dick hard," it said with equal venom.

The two glowered at each other, locked in a deadly stalemate.

The Ra'Voshnik took a step back and stabbed its fingers through its long white hair before scrubbing its hand over its face. "Can't you understand it would be better if we stopped inciting the other's misery and worked together," the creature said as the chains fell to Rune's feet.

He cruelly gripped the creature's throat, dragging it closer. His hand tremored as he fought the urge to tear the Ra'Voshnik's heart from its body. It smiled at him adding, "I won't kill anyone at my wedding, unless Faye allows it."

The hungry desire to eviscerate the creature and the fierce need to have Faye spread beneath him clashed through him, clouding his mind. Rune released the creature and roared, struggling to focus his erratic thoughts.

He was not fit to be in Faye's company, not like this. The erratic needs had only intensified as the Hunter's moon approached the night sky. He could not see his queen tonight.

Not alone.

"You won't be alone. If you offend her, I'll snap your neck, and all will be well," the Ra'Voshnik said, offering his hand in bargain.

Rune scrutinized the creature, deliberating his options to the best of his debilitated mind's ability. "I will allow you to surface for her vows."

"The entire ceremony. I'm not unkind, I'll share the reception with you."

It would trade every Hunter's Moon to kneel beside their queen for a few minutes before a Blood Priestess?

"Yes," it answered viciously. "Do we have a deal?"

Rune studied its outstretched hand, his tumultuous mind shouting the Ra'Voshnik was a rival for his queen's affection.

Faye's affection.

Aligning with the creature would please her and, perhaps, make the Ra'Voshnik more agreeable. Rune blinked as his thoughts frayed. He clasped the creature's hand. "We have a bargain."

Thirty-Eight

F aye adjusted the strap of her lace bra, inspecting her reflection.
Her vampire left to poke around The Crumbling, promising to
return within the hour—*before* the Hunter's Moon rose. Faye spent
her time switching between the two lingerie collars she purchased
with Sparrow. She arranged her hair a dozen different ways, parting
it and testing different styles in the mirror. She settled on wearing it
down. The intricate gray lace she wore displayed her body rather than
covering it. If Rune could see everything, she wouldn't give him a
clear view of her neck too.

Voshki usually made love to her first when the three of them
were together, so she would put Rune first tonight. *Aaaand he would
want lace*, she thought. He'd also want her in the garter belt and stock-
ings, but she'd taken them off. She'd almost fallen, racing across their
bedroom. The grass offered even less traction.

It wouldn't be much of a game if she fell three feet in front of him.

Faye piled her hair on the top of her head, securing it with a teak hair stick. Maybe she should let him peek at her neck. If she could manage to distract him, she might evade him a little longer.

She laid over their dark sheets, posing with pillows as she moved into various positions. Why was it so hard to be sexy? Faye blew out a breath, rolling onto her back and tossing Rune's pillow back to his side of the bed haphazardly. She should have asked Sparrow.

If Rune was going to inspect The Crumbling, maybe she should wait for him on his desk. He'd come back and fill out his report before the moon rose to find her laid out neatly on the bloodroot surface. Satisfied with her new plan, Faye leaped out of bed and went to her closet. She retrieved a long black robe and considered the sheer material. It covered her as well as her bra and panties.

Which meant it was perfect.

Faye swung her hips as the sheer material swept around her silhouette, fanning out at her feet. She turned and leaped back, startled.

Rune stood in their doorway dressed in his black suit. The fine cut of cashmere wool fit perfectly over his chiseled body. Her gaze slipped lower, stopping at his blatant erection through his slacks. She swallowed, losing her bravado as he slowly stalked toward her. This wasn't the plan.

He closed the distance between them, and Faye found herself backed into her closet. Weeks of planning slipped from her mind as he took the ground she gave. Moving in the opposite she met the dresser, and Rune purred, placing his hands on either side of her hip. He leaned forward, inhaling deeply at her throat without touching her.

Faye's heart raced as her breaths grew shallow. Warmth radiated from his body. Amber and sandalwood whispered over her, and she momentarily forgot about the game she planned, wanting him to lift her onto the dresser and take her here.

"Do you accept my advances?" he asked. His accent was as thick as she'd ever heard it.

She leaned in, close enough to share breath. Their quiet intimacy aroused her, making her ache. She was tempted to forego her game, to lean in and kiss him. Ask him to spread her legs and fuck her here.

She was a moment from giving in when wood creaked on either side of her. Faye glanced down. The ash face of her dresser was indented beneath his fingertips, his knuckles white. He wasn't nearly as controlled as he pretended to be.

Faye smiled, turning back to him. She palmed his cock lightly and feathered her nails along his hardened length. "I'll accept your advances," she breathed, nipping at his lower lip. "If you can catch me."

His hand smoothed over hers, caressing her wrist and moving higher. "Do not run from me. It will incite me to do worse."

Heat pooled between her legs as she imagined him catching her in the garden and taking her in a frenzy, face down in the grass. Faye opened her senses, focusing on Rune's depth of power. "Oh, I'm not running big guy," she teased before phasing to her garden to begin the game.

Night fell over her sanctuary. The lanterns bathed the swaying willows on either side of Hell's hot spring in a romantic glow. The moon was low in the sky, its red aura glowing over the towering stone walls.

Rune's strength vanished, and her heart raced. She giggled, phasing and appearing beside the pool as Rune materialized where she stood a moment before. He canted his head at her, phasing again as she did the same.

Faye appeared near her garden, thrilled with herself. She ran to excite him, but the rush of exhilaration racing through her veins each time she evaded him—she relished this.

Her hair shifted with the breeze, surrounding them with the sweet scent of black roses. She beamed. Her eyes glittered with anticipation, tensing to phase again. She evaded him twice more, and on the third he caught the back of her sheer robe. Faye shrieked, twisting out of the garment. She dashed a few steps and phased near the wrought-iron gate, panting.

Rune cast the sheer fabric aside and vanished. Faye did the same, appearing beneath the willow, but he didn't reappear. She took a careful step, scanning the manicured grounds for her vampire.

Then another.

She jumped when a hand slipped over her waist. His reservoir of power surfaced behind her the next instant, and he dragged her backward, lifting her off her feet. He molded her against the hard plains of his body as she squirmed to get free. His cock pressed against her ass, and she stilled.

Faye shuddered, focusing on her Jeweled Thorn, and phased out of his hold. She materialized in front of her garden, and an arm circled her waist before her feet touched the ground. He threw her backward, and Faye sucked a breath as her eyes went wide. She tensed, squeezing her eyes shut—bracing for the ground.

Thirty-Nine

Faye gasped, bouncing over dark silk sheets. She took a moment to right herself, recognizing the gray walls of the room she shared with Rune. Tiny blue embers and ashes plumed around her in wisps of curling smoke. She reached out to touch the sparkling glow, but they faded too quickly and dissipated entirely.

Rune stepped toward her, materializing from shadows and ash. She tensed to phase and managed a flicker. Rune was on her the next instant, caging her throat under his palm as phantom hands roughly spread her legs. He held her down with his will, pinning her arms overhead. Faye's heart raced as her breaths turned shallow. Her vampire glowered above her and angled her head to the side before forcing her chin higher.

Offering her throat to him.

The warmth of his mouth touched her neck, and Faye sighed,

relaxing beneath his hold. Rune bit down hard, sinking his fangs deep, and a shrill cry slipped past her lips. Pleasure shot through her as the feigned sensation of his cock thrusting between her legs seated deep inside her. He withdrew his fangs, and Faye shuddered as the feel of him receded. It returned, thrusting into her hard as Rune drank and receded when he swallowed.

Faye panted beneath him as he drank from her slowly, rocking into her. The seam of his slacks ground over her clit, and Faye moaned, "Rune."

Flickers of blue light drew her attention, and her brow drew together. The same shadow swept embers, and ash glowed at his shoulders, disintegrating his suit as it burned lower. Faye watched as they trailed around him, surrounding them in a beautiful display of smoke lit with tiny embers of hellfire before vanishing completely.

The broad tip of his cock met the lace between her legs, and Rune tensed with a growl. She smiled, wanting to run her hand through his hair to soothe him. She expected him to be rougher tonight but ultimately behaved similarly to Voshki. A misjudgment on her part since Rune had already thrown her on their bed and was seemingly offended she dared to wear panties.

Faye sighed, giving herself over to him. Rune's tongue was bliss, sweeping over his bite as he sucked. He reached between their bodies blindly, grazing the edge of her lace thong. Faye's eyes slid closed. A breathless sigh slipped past her lips as he lifted the intricate lace.

Her breath locked in her throat as he suddenly ripped off her lace thong and cast it aside. With a growl, he thrusted again, forcing several inches into her.

"Rune," she breathed. Faye was wet but Rune always made her come before penetrating her. Gave her time to adjust to his size with gentle strokes.

There was nothing gentle about him tonight. He withdrew and thrusted into her harder. Pleasure laced with a hint of pain ignited Faye's senses as she took more of him. He lifted his head, rasping as he drove his entire length into her, "You cannot escape me, vsenia. I *am* Hell."

She smiled at his words, growing slick under his harsh rhythm. Excitement thrummed in her, vibrating beneath her skin. His thumb left the underside of her jaw and brushed over her lips. She opened her mouth, taking his thumb past her lips, and sucked.

The tension building in her wound tighter with each of his punishing thrusts. Edging her closer to orgasm. Rune took his hand from her mouth, and she whimpered.

He chuckled against her neck before lightly outlining her parted lips with the tip of his finger. "Does my needy queen want something to suck on?" Rune asked.

"Please," Faye breathed, licking the tip of his index.

He purred, sliding two fingers into her mouth, and Faye's lips closed over his offering. She sucked as he thrusted into her mouth, timing them with his harsh rhythm.

She tensed, pulling against the shadowed hands pinning her to their bed. She needed to feel the chiseled planes of his back under her nails. Hear his growl when she dragged them over his spine, marking him as hers.

Faye's lips parted as she came. She moaned breathlessly, squeezing his length as he continued his vicious pace. Rune withdrew his fingers and slanted his mouth over hers. His kiss was as rough and claiming as the rest of him. Opening her wider for him.

She nearly came again when she tasted the tinge of copper in their kiss. He needed her so desperately. Her body. Her blood.

Her.

Faye licked his fang, pressing the tip of her tongue to the point. He groaned, taking her harder. She couldn't breathe as he rolled his hip at the end of each stroke, touching a sensitive spot deep inside her.

Rune, she cried through his mind.

He smiled against her lips and said, "I have better ways to use such an obedient tongue."

Faye pulled against her bonds when he sat back on his heels. His predatorial gaze lowered to where their bodies joined. He watched her there as he slowed his strokes, pulling out until the head of his cock nudged her entrance before pressing into her again.

Faye flushed, squirming under his scrutiny. His pale blue gaze pinned her, and the corner of his mouth lifted. "You are mine, vsenia. To drink," he said, caressing her neck. "Fuck," he rasped, tracing a line between her breasts. "And admire," he purred as his hand swept lower, coming to rest where their bodies joined.

He stroked into her once more and withdrew completely. The phantom hands holding her captive vanished, and Faye sat up to meet him, desperate to have him and Voshki inside her.

"Are you bringing me into your mind?" she asked.

"No," Rune growled. His eyes hardened as he fisted the back of her hair, angling her head up and rising to his knees. Faye's breath hitched. He caged the front of her throat and flicked the tip of his tongue up the center of her lips. "I am not sharing you tonight."

The tension over her scalp increased, and Faye bit the inside of her lip. She expected Rune and Voshki to fuck her under the crimson glow of the Hunter's Moon. Voshki in her mouth while Rune took her roughly from behind. After they came, Rune would press her face down into the grass and cover her body with his, spreading her legs as he slowly worked his cock into her ass, claiming every part—

"Suck my cock while I fuck you with my will," Rune purred, interpreting Faye's thoughts.

Ember lit shadows and ash swirled around them, and Faye found herself on her knees before Rune by their bedside.

Faye smiled at the thick cushion beneath her, sparing her from the bite of the stone floor. Her vampire thought of her comfort even under the Hunter's Moon. She stroked his shaft, looking up at him as she kissed the tip. Tasting herself on him.

She stilled as something wide and blunt slid through her folds. Her breath caught as it roughly thrust into her. She instinctively lifted her hips to escape the invasion, but phantom hands yanked her back down, forcing her legs apart. Rune's eyes lit with possessiveness, and Faye trembled as it stroked into her harder.

This is what he needed. Faye rolled her hips unable to escape or even impede his forceful strokes. Rune had teased her with phantom mouths and hands before, but never replicated his cock. He lifted her chin, and she blinked up at him. The corner of his mouth lifted as she rocked forward with a moan.

"Please me and I might let you come," Rune said, his voice filled with dark promises.

He brought his cock to her mouth and Faye took him past her lips. She'd had Rune and Voshki like this countless times, but it was different knowing Rune was the one fucking her while he stroked into her mouth. The thought of him using his magic on her heightened her arousal, and she greedily hoped he would tease her with his other phantom touches.

Claws gently scraped over her awareness, and Faye moaned confused. She relaxed, opening her mind to let Voshki in. Her beautiful hunter slipped through her senses, blanketing her in his vicious devotion.

The Shadow Prince is neglecting you, Voshki said with a chuckle. *Do you want me to tell him to make you come?*

No, Faye cried as Rune stroked into her throat. He could take her any way he wanted. He'd done so much for her... and she was desperate to please him.

The Shadow Prince is more than pleased, vsenia, Voshki purred.

Rune fisted her hair, holding her still. Faye's eyes slid closed as he fucked her mouth slower. She took his entire length, and he groaned, leaning his head back.

Oiled fingers touched the entrance of her ass, and Faye's eyes snapped open. She knew Rune would fuck her there, but she thought he would take her slowly, using one hole at a time.

Tell me if it's too much, I'll snap his neck, Voshki whispered through her mind.

Don't hurt him, Faye moaned as the tip of an oiled finger pressed into her ass. It withdrew slowly before pushing into her further. The tops of Faye's ears heated as she grew accustomed to being filled so thoroughly. She didn't think she would dislike Rune fucking her ass but expected him to find more pleasure in it than she did.

The foreign pressure gave way to an intoxicating mixture of foreboding delight. Faye dug her nails into Rune's lean waist, arching her back into his illicit touch.

Rune, please, Faye said through his mind in a breathless sigh.

"Is my queen ready for more?" he asked, brushing the back of his fingers over her hollowed cheek. Faye looked up at him and gave a small nod. Rune swept away the moisture collecting on her lashes and rasped, "Come for me, vsenia."

A phantom mouth closed over her clit, sucking and licking as it purred. Faye stiffened, the tension within her coiling tighter.

Rune, please, Faye begged, needing more. He stroked into her ass harder, matching the thrusts of his cock, and the tension building in Faye snapped with a strangled cry. Bliss rained over her as she came hard. Catching her breath, she scarcely realized Rune had withdrawn from her mouth and stopped fucking her with his phantom cock. She lay face-down on their dark sheets as waves of ecstasy crashed over her.

Rune stretched out beside her, snaring both her wrists with one hand and pinning them above her head. The phantom mouth between her legs roughened its purr, forcing Faye to ride her pleasure. She choked on a breath, struggling against Rune's hold as she helplessly rolled her hips. Her face heated as the oiled finger thrusted in and out of her ass, intensifying her orgasm and making her come harder.

Rune brushed his lips over her temple as he palmed the curve of her ass. "I am going to make you come until you are desperate and wanton, begging me to fuck you with my cock and my will."

At his words, a second finger joined the first, stretching her. "Rune," she cried, overwhelmed with the sensation.

A purr sounded behind her, and he replied with a dark whisper, "Take it for me."

Forty

Rune purred, nuzzling his queen's neck as he savored her rich, dark taste. His queen's blood left him euphoric, and she cried so sweetly as he prepared her pretty ass.

"Rune, please," she breathed, tugging against his hold. "I can't come anymore. Please, let me up."

Possessive impulses seized him. If he let her up, she might flee. A dim flicker of realization surfaced in the sane and rational part of his mind. *She could not truly escape him.* But logic and reason were lost, and compulsion ruled him. A sweeping, predatory need to keep her pinned beneath him. He'd captured his prey and would possess her until she understood she belonged to him.

He lovingly brushed her hair behind her ear and whispered, "Perhaps you should not have run, vsenia… A lesson for next year."

He couldn't know for certain if he would have been gentler with her if she'd submitted in the closet. The corner of his mouth lifted into a smirk. Her small act of defiance spurred the vampiric instincts he fought to bury. Urges offering Faye little mercy.

His night breeze tensed as she came again, her sighing pleasure accompanied by unintelligible words. She was flushed and sweat-slick. Her long black hair clung to her now limp body.

Rune glided his hand up the back of her thigh, listening to her heartbeat. Her breathing. The ebb and flow of tension through her lithe body. Silently reading what her body pleaded for as he worked her to orgasm again and again.

Oh, the things he would do to her… and his queen would beg for so much more.

"How long can a trained male hold a woman in her release, love? Do you remember?"

"Thirty… thirty minutes," she said breathlessly.

Rune hummed his agreement, running a finger down her spine. "Yes, we are taught to hold her for thirty minutes. But," Rune paused as Faye tensed again. She strained against his hold, and he kissed her shoulder. Rune gentled the purr on her clit and thrusted into her ass harder. On the third stroke Faye screamed her release and he slowed the oiled fingers, prolonging her pleasure.

"But when we are trained, we only use our mouth." He traced circles over her hip and whispered, "I have so much more than a mouth at my disposal. Shall we find out how long I can hold you here?"

"Please, fuck me," Faye begged.

Rune gripped her hip and licked his bite, slow and deliberate. "Where?" he asked.

"Please," Faye repeated in a broken sigh.

He moved his hand lower, observing her reactions. The way she tremored when he stroked through her folds, arching into his touch. He kissed the back of her neck and pressed a finger into her, curling it the way she favored.

"Here?" he asked quietly.

"Yes," Faye breathed.

Rune smiled, brushing his lips over the shell of her ear. "Yes, what?"

An exasperated sigh slipped past her parted lips, and she weakly pulled against his hold. "Stop teasing me. Rune, please."

"You will take everything I give, until you beg me to fuck you."

"Rune, please fuck me," Faye cried, desperately.

"Where?" he asked again, nipping her earlobe. Faye didn't answer him, closing her eyes tight as another orgasm crashed through her. "Shall I help you?" Rune asked. His night breeze nodded, breathlessly and he couldn't help but grin. "Say, Rune, please."

"Rune, please," she repeated immediately.

Her obedience pleased him. Immensely. He spread her legs, covering her body with his. The tip of his cock teased her opening, and he murmured, "Fuck my pretty cunt and ass."

"Yes."

"Say it," Rune purred, tilting his waist to press the head of his cock into her wet heat. The tops of her ears pinkened but she remained silent. Rune released her wrists and caged her beneath his body. He teased her with the tip of his cock while stroking in and out of her ass. "Let me possess you, vsenia. Say the words."

"Rune, please," Faye begged.

He thrust into her, taking her in a lazy rhythm. "Say it, vsenia. Your silence will only leave you aching for me."

She shuddered a breath, tensing under him. Rune worked her, bringing her a moment from release and stilled.

Everything.

"Rune, please," she cried, rocking her hips. Rune conjured more phantom hands, holding her in place. "Rune, please fuck… fuck my pretty cunt and ass."

Rune purred, thrusting into her. She was his. His to possess and cherish.

And he was hers to command.

Rune bent low and kissed the blood from her neck. She saturated his senses until all he could see was her. The sensual feel of her silken flesh, the intoxicating taste of her blood, and the way she trembled beneath him as she came.

"Hold me," she whispered.

Rune lifted her, turning her to face him as he sat back on his heels. He gazed at her reverently and answered, "Anything, love."

He held her against him, guiding her legs around his waist. She wrapped him in her arms and leaned against him, resting her head on his shoulder. The Ra'Voshnik stirred through his mind and Rune bristled with possessive need. She was his, and he would kill the creature before he allowed it to take Faye from him.

The rational part of his mind was a silenced whisper among the bellowing instincts raging through him. He knew he was no match for the creature under the Hunter's Moon. He recognized his queen's exhaustion and knew a good and kind consort would let her rest.

Rune's vampiric instincts were neither good, nor kind, and he would claim her to his satisfaction.

He lowered her onto his cock, and Faye moaned against his neck. Her nails dug into his shoulders, stinging as she dragged them down his back. Rune's eyes slid closed as he groaned, relishing her marks. He held her closer, pinning her to his waist and thrusting into her in a slow rhythm. Darkness, she felt divine. Sensitive and shaking.

Rune withdrew the phantom hand teasing her ass replacing it with a shadowed replica of his cock. She squeezed him closer as the tip pressed into her ass. "I have you," he murmured before drawing back and pressing a fraction deeper. Rune intensified the purr on her clit, and she whimpered.

"Softer, Rune please," Faye said breathlessly.

He willed the phantom mouth to cease its purr. It sucked and licked instead, teasing her where she was most sensitive.

Faye rolled her hips. "A little more. Purr lightly."

"Lightly?" Rune asked, arching a brow as he gazed down at his night breeze. She nodded and moaned, dragging her teeth over his throat as she took more of his shadowed length.

The mouth he conjured between her legs purred softly and Faye rocked back, panting, "Yes, there."

Rune's will matched his strokes, taking her slowly. He gave her time to acclimate, waiting until his name became a breathless sigh before thrusting deeper. He held her close, murmuring her name until she took his entire length.

He rocked into her, his phantom touch mirroring his flesh. "Come for me, vsenia."

"I can't," Faye cried.

Rune fisted her hair, angling her head back until she offered him her throat. "You can," he rasped, kissing her neck. She swallowed and the corner of Rune's mouth lifted. "You will."

Her breath shook as he fucked her harder. "Rune, please," she begged in a desperate sigh.

He held her with his will, suspended and helpless. Shadowed hands spread her legs wide, and Rune fucked her harder. Her dark hair swayed over their sheets as his harsh thrusts jarred her body. He leaned over her, sinking his fangs into her throat, and Faye screamed with pleasure.

She was close, but he would need to build her release slowly, layering sensations, one after the next. Intensifying their intimacy until she came apart. He drank, finding the rhythm he needed. Phantom hands stroked Faye's back and gripped her hips. Mouths nuzzled the other side of her neck and gently nipped her earlobe. Others alternated pinching and licking Faye's nipples, inching her closer to her pleasure.

"Rune, it's too much," she breathed.

"Take it for me, vsenia," Rune said roughly. "Beg me to come for you."

A shrill cry tore from her as she raked her nails over his shoulder, and Rune smiled. He would never tire of the sounds he elicited from her. She pulsed around him, squeezing him intimately. Faye reached for him again—her nails biting... sharper?

Claws sank into his arm, painting thin trails of crimson over his pale skin. Rune glanced down at his arm and cursed in High Tongue, wishing he could share blood with her. The thought made is cock twitch, and he drove into her harder, desperate to spend within her.

Her iridescent wings flared behind her, scraping over their silk sheets, and Rune purred his satisfaction. He fucked her ruthlessly, needing to possess her completely.

Marking her as his.

His shoulders tensed and Darkness, he was close. He traced little circles on the inside of her wing, where the membrane met her back. She tremored and he thrusted into her a final time. His brow knit together as he closed his eyes, groaning against her throat. Pleasure lashed him each time his cock twitched, emptying more of himself into her. He took a shuddering breath on the fourth and cursed in High Tongue on the fifth.

He released her, vanishing his phantom touch and held her for long moments. Cherishing his dark queen. He languidly rocked into her while he caught his breath.

"This is romantic," she whispered, loosely wrapping her arms around his neck. Warmth bathed Rune as she encircled them with her wings. He opened his eyes and swallowed.

Crystalline vines coiled over their sheets. They climbed the posts like ivy to create a glittering canopy overhead. A host of thin curling vines hung around them and two rose blooms opened near Faye.

She beamed at him, gingerly touching the crystalline flowers.

"This is not my doing," Rune said. He failed to notice how eerily similar Faye's wings and the crystal making up his realm were until now.

"Maybe Hell is celebrating the Hunter's Moon," Faye said, laying her head on his shoulder.

The warmth of her wings faded, becoming darker. The vines mirrored Faye's wings, becoming a swirling black mist edged in bright purple tendrils. Rune stiffened, surrounded by what appeared to be the Darkness itself. It held for the span of a breath before dissipating with Faye's wings.

Rune wasn't sure what unnerved him more, Faye's ability to shape the Darkness or her ability to shape Hell.

Faye pulled away from him, and a possessive frenzy sank its claws through his mind. Rune moved in a blur, pinning her beneath him. He growled, hardening inside her. Faye's hand slid over the side of his throat, brushing lower to his chest. Her heart raced as he leaned over her. He conjured phantom hands to spread her legs, and his attention fell to the thin trickles of crimson lining his bites.

Rune lowered his head and kissed his bite, thrusting into her harder.

You've been fucking her for hours. She needs water and something to eat, the Ra'Voshnik growled through his mind. Rune bared his fangs, and the obsidian talisman appeared next to Faye's shoulder. *If you don't order her refreshments, I'm going to snap your neck and fuck her on your dead body.*

With great effort, Rune reigned in what he knew was irrational anger. The creature was right.

"I am sorry," Rune muttered, kissing the corner of her mouth. "I find myself compelled to give chase when you pull away, and you my love... are very slow."

Faye laughed, curling a length of his white-blonde hair around her finger. "I phase faster than you, but someone's a cheater and had to use his whole realm against me to win."

Rune leaned closer, tasting her lips. "Would you still run knowing what will happen when I catch you?"

Faye's eyes lit with excitement as she smiled, shrugging with one shoulder. "You like to chase. I like to run."

"Do you?" Rune asked. Faye nodded, and he chuckled. "We can revisit your ability to phase after you have something to drink, or perhaps some honeyed fruit."

"And choice cuts," Faye added.

Rune took the talisman, moving it further away from them. He kissed under her jaw, and she giggled. Touching two fingers to the stone, he said, "Water, choice cuts, sliced fruit, and honey."

"And whipped cream," Faye whispered.

He purred, kissing her softly, before adding, "And whipped cream."

Faye ran her finger down the center of his chest. "Are you going to let me up?"

He smiled against her lips. "No."

"You have to let me up when you make your wish to the Darkness," she insisted.

"I will not be participating," Rune said, trailing his lips lower. He licked his bite and Faye shuddered.

"Isn't it a vampire tradition?" she asked, breathlessly.

Rune lifted his head, gazing down at the dark queen fate gifted him. "The Darkness granted my wish. I could ask for nothing more."

Forty-One

Faye blinked at the pre-dawn light coloring the gardens and grumbled. Rune chuckled quietly, and Faye made a mental note to bite him later. He had kept her up the entire night, taking her with his body and will until she was too spent to move.

Rune carried her through the inner gardens, and a breathy sigh slipped past Faye's lips. It was so comfortable being cradled against his chest. His warm scent of amber and sandalwood accompanied the sweet fragrance of the black roses blooming around them. The gentle rock of his silent gait lulled Faye's exhausted body, and her lids grew heavy. She fought to remain awake as streaks of silvery light carved through the soft pink and orange hues lighting the sky.

Dawn marked the end of the Hunter's Moon, and Rune seemed calmer. The willows swayed, rustling with the breeze. Faye tucked closer to Rune, fighting off the early morning chill. He strolled toward the hot spring, completely nude and unbothered by the weather. He'd lifted her into his arms and phased before she could react or think to grab for a sheet. It didn't matter. She was well past caring if Sparrow happened upon them naked.

Rune stepped into the spring, lowering them in. The hot water blanketed around her, sinking into her muscles. He purred as Faye lightly scratched her nails over his back. "I'm tired, big guy. The Hunter's Moon is over. Can we just go to bed?"

"In a few minutes," he said, arranging her on his lap as he leaned back on the stones. "The water is spelled and will heal your... twinges."

"Twinges?" Faye giggled, kissing the side of his neck. "I'm going to be feeling you for a week."

Rune turned toward her and swallowed. "I am sorry, vsenia. I was unkind with you."

"I liked it," Faye breathed, nipping his throat. "*Aaaaand* if this is something you want to repeat... we don't have to wait for the next Hunter's Moon." Her vampire remained silent, and Faye's heart fell.

"I have injured you," Rune whispered.

Faye pitched her head back. "You're so dramatic. I'm not injured." She was well loved with a sprinkling of twinges, as Rune called them, but the hot spring quieted what she overly exerted.

"This is not how a consort should treat his queen."

Faye lifted her hand and splayed her fingers before glancing from her engagement ring to her stubborn vampire. "It's a good thing I'm going to be your wife then." Rune thinned his lips, and Faye flicked water at him. "Do you know how many times Vash has *injured* Sparrow?"

"I would rather not," Rune said quickly.

Faye touched the side of his face, drawing him closer. Her lips met his in an easy, gentle kiss. She pulled back a fraction and said, "I love you, and I enjoyed everything *we* did. Now take me to bed and bring me into your mind so I can sleep between you and Voshki. I'm sure he's given you an earful after stealing my attention all night."

"I will bring you to bed after I have cleansed you and mended my bites," Rune murmured as he smoothed his thumb over the side of her neck. He moved to her shoulders next, pulling her hair to one side than the other. "Lie back," he rasped, growing hard against her thigh.

Faye glanced down momentarily before meeting his gaze. "Your queen needs sleep."

The corner of his mouth lifted into the smirk she adored. "My flesh is weak, but my will has returned."

Faye narrowed her eyes but did as he asked. She leaned back on his arm and Rune held her face above the water. He ran his hand over her body, kneading her tired muscles as he moved lower. Faye didn't argue when he eased her legs apart. He smoothed his palm along her inner thigh, beginning at her knee and stopping before Faye raised her hips.

"Do you want me to tend to you?" Rune asked while he mended his bites on her inner thigh.

"Maybe I can tend to you, after I wake up," Faye said.

She finished cleaning off the remnants of the night, and Rune helped her out of the pool. He phased them to their bedroom and carried her consciousness into his mind. Voshki stepped out from behind Rune, giving him a disapproving look.

"You can change the sheets. I'll see to our queen," he said before draping a warmed black towel around Faye. Voshki dried her off and she leaned on him heavily as he toweled her hair.

Faye drew a sharp breath when Voshki swept her into his arms. Her sharp retort died on her tongue when he tucked her into bed and drew the fresh sheets up her body. The hellfire dimmed in the sconces on either side of their bed and Faye rolled on to her side, pulling the silk to her chin.

The mattress sank beside her, and Faye inched closer, resting her head on Rune's chest. He purred and ran his fingers through her hair. Clawed fingertips gently grazed her scalp, and Faye's brows furrowed. She leaned up to find Voshki on Rune's side of the bed.

"I'm sleeping here today," he said with a smirk.

Rune settled behind her and draped his arm over her waist, positioning himself as Voshki typically would.

"Is this what you get for letting Rune have last night?" Faye asked, settling back on his chest.

"No," Voshki answered. "But the Shadow Prince is finally learning to share."

Faye shifted, finding a more comfortable position. "I'm surprised you didn't make an appearance."

Voshki squeezed her closer and said, "I know you prefer my company to his, but the Shadow Prince was… afflicted."

Not a word Faye would use to describe Rune under the Hunter's Moon. Emboldened might be a better fit. "Weren't you just as afflicted?"

Voshki's dark laughter whispered over her.

"The Shadow Prince is no Pure Blood, vsenia. I am the constant nature he refuses to admit. The moments he suffers—compelled by our true nature—consume my eternity."

Forty-Two

Sparrow swiped a fluffy brush over Faye's cheek. "Sooo, are you going to tell me what happened yet?" Faye rolled her eyes. Her sister pestered her with the same question dozens of times over the past two days.

Faye sat in the den, reluctantly participating in their yearly ritual. An array of cosmetics topped the dining table. Since they moved out on their own, Faye allowed Sparrow to pick her outfit and do her make-up for her birthday *adventures*. They would go to Aunty Clara's house for a birthday lunch, and later her wayward sister would drag her on whatever outing she deemed not boring.

She would trade her evening with Sparrow for lessons with Sadi this year, but she couldn't miss brunch. Aunty Clara always celebrated the day of a birthday. An early gathering was seen as disrespectful, signaling to fate your days were guaranteed but celebrating late was worse, disregarding the time fate gifted you.

Sparrow exchanged her brush for a smaller one and patted a plum-colored gloss over Faye's lips. "Don't be such a prude. Did you tie him up?"

"It's private."

"Darkness, you're so boring," Sparrow whined, stomping her feet. When Faye only stared at her, she took Faye's chin and tilted her face one way, then the other. "Did tall, pale, and scary give you your present yet?"

Rune had wished her happy birthday when she woke and asked her to meet him in the gardens at the end of the evening. Information she wouldn't be sharing with her sister. Sparrow would shift into a cat and hide in an Azalea bush to spy on them.

The gardens were a strange request. A thought bloomed in her mind, and Faye smiled. Maybe he wanted to play tag again.

"He's building my estate," Faye said.

Sparrow fluttered her hand. "That's court stuff. It doesn't count."

"Leave the birthday girl alone," Vash said as he walked in with Rune.

Sparrow snorted, vanishing her assortment of compacts before staring after the two men. "Look at you two, being all chummy and shit."

Faye giggled, getting to her feet. Vash had gotten used to Rune's presence. His wings were relaxed, folded against his back. Faye noticed a long time ago Vash could control his expressions, and if she wanted to see how he was really feeling, she needed to look at his wings.

Sparrow fluffed Faye's blue skirt. "Look what I got her to wear."

The blue dress was strapless and fit tightly over her bust. A wide cream colored leather belt cinched above her waist and the ruffled skirt spilled over her hips. It was too Familiar for Faye's taste. She was grateful the skirt was cut close to her knees in the front and lowered into a full-length skirt in the back. If Sparrow handed her a dress cut as high as Sadi's, she would have outright refused.

Rune stepped closer and Faye smoothed her skirt. "You look beautiful," he said, admiring her.

"Don't encourage her," Faye said softly.

Rune chuckled and helped her into her winter coat. He offered his hand before drawing it back a moment later. "Phase us to your caregiver's home."

Faye frowned. "How do I do that?"

Rune gestured Vashien and Sparrow closer before explaining, "Take hold of our minds and bring us with you."

He made it sound so easy. Faye glanced over her friends. Their reservoirs of power were always present. She concentrated on their strength and pictured the dirt road leading to Aunty Clara's red wooden gate. The image sharpened, and she turned to see if she'd been successful.

Sparrow, Vash, and Rune stood with her, and Faye clapped her hands and smiled brightly. Her sister brushed past her to open the gate. "You're just showing off now."

"If you had half the dedication while training with Damian, you would be phasing right now," Faye said as the small children ran toward her, chirping a chorus of happy birthday. "Thank you, guys," she said, dropping her arm around each child who hugged her waist.

Bayle and his entourage stopped Faye before she reached the porch. "We made this for you," he said, holding a large sheet of black construction paper folded in half.

"Why thank you, sir." Faye took the make-shift card, and her chest tightened as she opened it. Rows of pressed flowers and herbs were glued inside. At the bottom of each little offering was a child's name.

"I did the gluing!" Kimber yelled from the doorway.

"Horse booty helped us. It took a really long time." Bayle squeezed between her and Sparrow and stood on his toes, peering at the card. Faye lowered it slightly, and he pointed at the lavender sprig. "I did this one."

Faye closed the card and hugged Bayle to her side. "It's beautiful, I love it."

"See that, Runey? You better come with your a-game. The beasties are setting the bar high," Sparrow said.

Faye laughed as they climbed the steps and hugged Kimber as the children rushed into the house. Once inside, Faye's mouth watered at the smell of candied bacon and several dishes covered the old dining table. Faye spotted her bacon first. Beside it was potatoes whipped with cheese and a platter of balled fruit. Small jars decorated the space between the dishes, stuffed full of wildflowers and… a few weeds. Faye giggled. She should have come earlier and joined in their flower escapades.

"Well?" Aunty Clara said loudly behind her. Faye turned and was greeted with a hug. "Happy birthday," she said, pressing a red envelope into Faye's hand.

"I don't need this."

"Stop being so silly. It's good luck marks." Aunty Clara patted her cheek and beamed at Rune. "She looks nice," she said, turning back to Faye with a nod. "Your skin is very pretty. Glowing."

"That's because Runey banged the hell out of her," Sparrow muttered under her breath. Faye continued smiling at Aunty Clara and elbowed Sparrow in the ribs. Her sister grunted and said, "Owe, bitch."

Aunty Clara dusted her apron and shook her head at Sparrow, sucking her teeth. She craned her neck up to Vashien, and her look softened. "I hope the bad one isn't causing you too much trouble."

"No ma'am," Vashien answered, and Sparrow glared at him.

"I am the best thing to ever happen to him."

A small boy ran up to Vashien with his arms outstretched. "Can you take us flying?"

"And can Rune read us a story?" Bayle called from the smaller kid's table.

"After lunch," Vashien said. Faye covered her mouth to hide her grin as he opened his wings to usher the children to their table. The same way he escorted people who had a little too much to drink out of his tavern.

Rune lifted his chin toward Bayle. "We will have to reschedule storytime. I have prior obligations to my queen during her lessons. Do you remember how to request an audience with a court member?" Bayle nodded vigorously, and Rune smiled warmly. "Send my Queen a petition and make your request."

"You're going to be fancy by the time you grow up," Kimber said as she helped the little ones get their food before she joined the adult table. They laughed, passing dishes between themselves.

"Are you guys going on a double date tonight?" Kimber asked as she speared a cornish game hen.

"No, Faye's boring and wants to learn magic," Sparrow answered for her.

Aunty Clara tsked. "Everything can't always be fun. You need to work too. It's not good to only play, play, play."

Rune laughed behind his glass of crimson wine, and Sparrow narrowed her eyes. "Keep laughing fang boy, and I'll dress my practice dummies up in your fancy suits."

They finished their meal in quiet conversation and Kimber cleared the table while Aunty Clara retrieved Faye's cake.

Kimber hurried back to her seat and leaned toward Faye. "I taught the little ones some flower petals are edible. So, just smile when you see the cake and choke it down." Faye blinked at her, and Kimber gave an apologetic look. "They know you like flowers so…" She opened both of her hands and twisted her wrists to make a tight circle while mouthing *covered*.

Aunty Clara set the cake in front of Faye, and she fought to hold a polite expression. She didn't dare glance at Kimber out of fear she would burst into laughter. Faye couldn't tell if the frosting was applied by the children or Kimber. The uneven sugary coating was packed with rose petals, pointing up in different directions—as though the children surrounded the cake and squabbled with one another to set their petal.

Aunty Clara wiggled a tall thin candle between the flowers as the children crowded the table. The candle flared to life with a touch of hellfire, and Aunty Clara spoke in a low tone. "We thank the Darkness for granting Faye this year."

"And beseech the fates for another to follow," everyone chorused.

Faye leaned forward and blew out the candle. A thin trail of smoke coiled from the burnt wick before fading away.

"You didn't beseech the fates Runey," Sparrow scolded.

"Apologies. I am not acquainted with this custom," Rune said, gazing at Faye. "I beseech the fates for another to follow."

"You didn't have birthdays, your shadowy highness?" Sparrow asked, then wrinkled her nose at Faye. "Did he celebrate his birthday with you? Because it's been a year."

"Immortals don't have birthdays. They measure their lives in centuries, not years," Aunty Clara said, fanning away the dwindling smoke rising from the candle.

Sparrow recoiled, and Rune chuckled. "We count our years until our immortality seats, and the aging process halts. Once this occurs, we are in our first century." He reached for the candle and asked, "Would you like me to bring you a knife?"

"No," Faye said, grabbing Rune's arm before he reached the cake. "We're waiting for the candle to go out completely. The smoke carries our request to the Darkness, where the fates will hear it."

"I am sorry," Rune said. "I will acquaint myself with your customs."

Aunty Clara removed the candle when its smoke dissipated and cut the cake into pieces, handing everyone a slice. The cake was made of two layers, chocolate, and vanilla, with thinly sliced strawberries and whole rose petals between them. The children beamed, watching Faye. She would ask Vash to show them how to properly serve petals. A cupcake day.

She took a small bite and smiled through the overly sweet taste, cut with the bitterness of too many rose petals. "This is delicious guys, thank you."

Satisfied with their accomplishment the children returned to the kid's table with their sweets. Faye sipped her juice slowly, letting it wash away the taste.

Sparrow used her napkin to discreetly spit out her bite before pushing the plate away. Faye widened her eyes and Sparrow mouthed, *nope.*

"Sorry I'm late, doves," Damian said. "I was helping Alister make the final selections for instructors—"

"Sadi!" Jamie Lyn squealed. She rushed over, pushing past Damian with her twig-bird fluttering after her.

"I can see whose heart this one belongs to," he said as Jamie Lyn threw her arms around Sadi's ruffled skirt.

"Hello, my darling," Sadi said, stroking Jamie Lyn's sunset-hued hair. She pinched the sleeve of Jamie Lyn's boxy shirt between her index and thumb then rubbed her fingers together as though she touched something unpleasant.

Faye's temper spiked as she waited for Sadi to insult the girl's clothing. Her evil twin could be a bitch to the adults, but she wouldn't tolerate her mistreating children.

"I would like to take this one shopping," Sadi said to Aunty Clara. "May I take Jamie Lyn with me tomorrow afternoon?"

Faye blinked, regretting her assumption.

"Oh sure," Aunty Clara said as Jamie Lyn's Familiar totem flew too close to her. She waved a wrinkled hand at the small bird, shooing it away.

Another worry surfaced in Faye's mind. "You can't dress her like a Familiar."

Sadi turned to her, and hurt momentarily crossed her midnight eyes. It vanished as quickly as it came, and Sadi hissed, "Why?"

She couldn't be serious. "That is not appropriate," Faye said, gesturing to Sadi's corseted lace and tulle ensemble.

Her evil twin laughed, and Faye bristled. "I will help her choose her first corseted gown *after* she's invoked her blood, like every other Familiar." Sadi turned back to Jamie Lyn and tapped the girl's chin. "But that is many years away. For now, we can dress in *young* Familiar fashion."

Sadi nudged Jamie Lyn toward the other children, and Damian sat on the ground cross-legged at their table.

"We're going to add one more lesson to your day, but it's more like a game," Damian began. He folded his arms on the table, and the children leaned closer. "You're all part of Faye's court, and it's very rude for strangers to introduce themselves without your Queen. So, if you see strangers—"

"We bite them!" Bayle exclaimed.

Damian laughed. "No, but I like you. Your job is to run away and hide so Faye can introduce you properly, and they don't look silly for being rude."

Faye smiled as Bayle bowed his chest. "We like hide and seek."

"And I'll help you find the best hiding spots." Damian drummed his hands on the table and stood in a fluid motion. "Field. Tomorrow. Eight thirty," he said pointing at Bayle. "I expect you to make sure everyone is on time."

What is this about? Faye asked in Rune's mind.

It is a part of training for the court born. Young are taught to hide from other courts until their queen decides the adults are trustworthy. Warring courts do not typically target them but teaching the little ones to flee is a precaution all courts practice, Rune answered.

Faye picked a strawberry slice out of her cake but found herself suddenly having no taste for it. Dark courts were barbaric, but in this instance she would rather be cautious. The children thought Damian was playing a game with them.

Darkness willing, they would never see it as anything more than an enjoyable memory.

Forty-Three

Faye and Aunty Clara discreetly disposed of the cake while the children were occupied with their slices. Faye began washing the dishes, and the elderly woman quickly shooed her out of the house. The door closed on her heels as she made her way to her court.

They stood in the portion of the front yard Faye claimed as her own. The earthy scents of the surrounding forest were sharper in the cold winter months. A light dusting of snow covered the ground, shining bright in the daylight.

Damian partnered with Vashien as he instructed Kimber and Sparrow through their drills. Faye joined Sadi and Rune away from the clash of swords, bundled in her fur-lined coat to fight off the chill, but Sadi wore so little. Faye wondered how she wasn't shivering.

"We'll work on siphoning again," Sadi said casually.

Faye wasn't sure what to expect but this was an essential skill if she wanted to heal efficiently.

"Are you able to control your tendril?" Sadi asked, holding out her hand palm up. Faye watched as a black shadowy cord lifted out of Sadi's palm and swayed, lifting a foot into the air.

Faye tensed as her nerves returned, decimating the confidence she gained with her phasing. She inhaled deeply and exhaled through pursed lips. This would be easy. Just like phasing. She opened her hand, studying her palm. Visualizing a black cord rising from her hand. Moments ticked by and dread knotted into a pit in her stomach.

Please work, Faye silently begged. She concentrated harder, willing her tendril to lift from her hand.

Nothing happened.

Sadi closed the distance between them. "Your tendril is a part of your core. You guide it through your hand, it doesn't originate there." Her evil twin held her shoulder and stepped behind her. "Your manifestations attacked me when I tried to manually extract your tendril. We'll do it mentally this time."

Sadi touched the edge of her mind, and Faye reluctantly let her in. When Rune or Voshki entered her mind, their emotions saturated her senses, but with Sadi it was the opposite. A foreign presence drifting through her mind.

It shifted deeper, flowing over the core of Faye's power. She tensed as her breaths shortened. Every instinct in her screamed to protect the housing of her magic. To eliminate the threat breaching her mental barriers.

"I know it feels invasive," Sadi said gently. "I won't take longer than I need to extract your tendril and see if you can hold it on your own."

Faye nodded, inhaling deeply through her nose, and exhaling through her mouth.

Sadi pulled, and a cord tugged within her. Far beneath her core, there was a mass of power waiting, disturbed from its slumber. Faint hissing rose, with it as Sadi dragged her sliver of power higher.

"I have it," Sadi said, taking her wrist. She turned Faye's palm up and pinpricks flowed from the center of her chest and drifted down her arm. Sadi lifted her hand past Faye's, and a shadowed black snake rose from the center of her palm. Faye's hand trembled as she outstretched her arm, and Sadi stepped back, and the snake flicked its tongue and flared its hood.

This wasn't a tendril.

Panic fogged her thoughts. They were attached to her. If they attacked the way they did Sadi, she wouldn't be able to get away.

Strong arms enveloped her, and Faye's back met the hard plains of Rune's body. "I have you, love," he murmured. "This is your will. It cannot hurt you." He reached past her, offering his hand to the shadowed serpent.

The cobra reminded Faye of Prinia's wolf. Glowing red eyes left a trail of crimson as it swayed. She feared it would strike Rune, but its flared hood settled as coiled black wisps floated off its form.

Rune's fingers encircled her wrist, and he drew her hand closer. Faye stiffened, unable to breathe as he brushed his lips over her temple and whispered, "Easy. This is your will. Your power. You have nothing to fear."

Faye swallowed hard and weakly nodded. She hated snakes. Now her tendril was close enough to strike her face, and Faye fought to keep her terror at bay.

"What the fuck is that?" Sparrow yelled, jogging over.

Sadi stepped closer, blocking Faye's view of her sister. "Rune, this is wrong." The tendrilled cobra flared its hood, rising higher toward Sadi. A black-light flickered over her as she shielded herself.

"You retrieved it. Is this her tendril?" Rune asked.

"It's a snake Rune. Does it matter if I pulled it off her core?" she snapped.

His arm tightened over Faye's middle. He released her a moment later and whispered, "You possess unique gifts. Do not fear your strength."

"Come on, give her some space to do her lessons," Vashien said as he collected Sparrow and Kimber. He turned them toward their section of the yard and outstretched his wings to hinder their view.

Faye stared at her cobra-tendril. It didn't feel like an appendage. When her wings surfaced, she was clumsy, but she could move them by shifting muscles in her back. There was nothing to help her control the shadowed serpent swaying from her palm.

"Can you tell if this is my tendril and not a manifestation?" Faye asked.

Sadi was silent for a few moments and nodded. "It's constructed like a tendril," she said, turning to Rune. "I've never seen anything like this."

"My queen wears shards we have never seen. Teach her to siphon." Rune stood a few feet from Faye and tapped the center of his chest. "Strike my core, love."

Faye hesitated before meeting his pale blue eyes, and her voice was a trailing whisper. "I'm afraid of hurting you."

"You will not hurt me," Rune said as he closed the distance between them. "Learning to siphon requires a living core. I am best suited for your lessons. The disparity of power would be too great if you used another."

Her insecurities compounded as Sparrow ignored her drills and turned to watch Faye. Kimber linked arms with her and followed suit. Vashien tried to reign them back in, but they wanted to see what she would do.

She had become a spectacle and all of it felt like the first time she invoked her blood—and failed.

Rune gently curled his fingers under her chin and drew her attention back to him. "Ignore them. I can sight shield us if you wish. No one will be watching you." Faye nodded, and his power swept over her. A string of obscenities erupted from her sister, and Rune caught Faye's chin as she turned. "This is a simple skill. You will master this as quickly as you mastered phasing."

Faye took a deep breath as Rune motioned for Sadi to join them. She stopped between them with a sigh and said, "Strike his core."

Faye glanced up at Rune, and the warmth of his smile crinkled the corners of his eyes. *I could do this,* Faye told herself. A simple skill. She lifted her hand toward him, and her tendril didn't respond.

How could she have so much power at her disposal and do so little with it. Faye studied her palm, concentrating on the strange new appendage and nothing happened. She glanced back up at Rune and thrusted her hand at him, but her tendril didn't obey her.

"Perhaps we should make another attempt in a more private setting," Rune offered.

Faye shook her head. "Let me try something else."

Sadi said this tendril was attached to her core. Faye brought her hand closer to the shadow-wisped serpent but couldn't bring herself to grab it. This was her power. It wasn't going to bite her.

Faye clenched her teeth and tapped it on the head before tearing her hand away. The snake didn't respond aggressively. It didn't respond at all. She tapped it again... slower. When it didn't react, she closed her hand over its body.

She pulled, and it took longer than Faye wanted to drag it out a few feet. It coiled above her palm, swaying lightly, but it was easier to control once it extended past her fingertips. Faye swung her tendril like a whip. She flicked her hand at Rune, and her serpent flew, knocking his legs out from under him with the force of the impact.

"Darkness, I'm sorry," Faye said, rushing toward him as Sadi did the same.

"Are you injured?" Sadi asked, opening her hand over Rune's chest.

"I am well," Rune said, getting to his feet.

Sadi swiped her nails at Faye's tendril. When her fingers passed through it, she turned to Faye. "How did you do that?"

"It's easier to control when it's out of my hand."

"No, tendrils are intangible." Sadi extended her hand, and her tendril flew from her palm, striking Faye in the chest.

She didn't feel pain or an impact. She felt it strike her core, and her magic recoiled from the foreign entity.

Faye reached out, touching the black cord sticking out of her chest and it pulsed with power.

"They are only tangible to the person you are siphoning," Sadi explained. The black cord she held lost its substance when Sadi dislodged it from her. She turned to Rune. "I don't like this. Her magic doesn't behave in the natural order of things."

"What's wrong with my magic?"

Sadi turned to her as though she'd grown another head. "The empty-eyed vessels speak to you. You knocked Rune down with an intangible tendril. You wield Familiar magic different than ours, and that's before we get to your shards."

"Enough," Rune said to Sadi. He turned to Faye. "Power is meaningless if you cannot control it."

Faye needed this skill if she wanted to be able to heal past superficial wounds. She glanced at Sadi. "What do I do now?"

Sadi turned to Rune who only nodded at her. She turned back to

Faye and said, "Siphon his magic."

Faye's brow came down. "I don't understand."

Sadi picked at the clawed tip of her gauntleted finger. "He's a cup. Your tendril is the straw. Draw his power into your core."

Faye turned her hand over, and the tendril twisted with her movements. It didn't feel like a straw. She could feel where she was tapped into Rune's reservoir of power, but it remained undisturbed when she concentrated on drawing it to her through the tendril. She tried a second time with no luck and Sadi turned away from her, shaking her head.

Frustrated with the lesson that made no sense, Faye reached forward and wrapped her fingers into a fist. She concentrated on the connection she'd made between Rune and herself.

Her awareness engulfing Rune's strength.

Faye jerked her hand toward herself, and the snow-covered yard was replaced with a luxurious room. Women in splendid, corseted gowns surrounded her, seated in finely crafted chairs and settees. They shared similar facial features and fiery red hair.

What was this?

Faye winced at the rhythmic sound of metal scraping, but a woman with chromatic sage eyes held her attention. She looked like the High Queen's daughter Sparrow sent tumbling into the table at the High Council meeting after she attacked Sadi. Darkness, what was her name? Morgan?

A woman's moan sounded behind her, and Faye's skin crawled as a stark realization struck her. These women weren't looking at her. They intently watched something behind her.

Faye shielded herself and slowly turned. Her eyes widened as bile rose in her throat.

Her mate was stripped and shackled to a modified metal chair. The contraption was bolted to the floor, and Rune's wrists and ankles were affixed to the chair. Trails of blood trickled from a thick metal collar around his neck.

The scraping was the chair shifting against its bolts as a red-haired woman holding her skirts up, rocked over Rune. He glared past the bitch riding him, at the woman who could be Morgan's twin.

Fury burned away Faye's nausea as her power surged to the surface. Her wings flared from her back as black mist pooled at her feet.

Serpents rose from the misted shadows gathering beneath her, and Faye felt each of them. She needed only to name her prey, and her shadowed snakes would strike.

She rounded on the woman riding her vampire.

Her mate.

Before Faye could mark her first target, Rune tore his hand through the shackle trapping him, sheering off his thumb. With pointed fingers, he rammed them through the woman's throat, decapitating her. Black tipped claws sank into the ruined neck as Rune dragged her closer. He savaged her shoulder, drinking greedily as chaos erupted around Faye.

Faye's vision blackened and returned a moment later. Her heart pounded with her outraged fury. They would pay. She would send each of them to the Darkness screaming a symphony of pain.

The room was gone. Faye now stood near the dais of a large throne room. Moss crept up aged stone pillars. The stones making up the building were old and discolored. Hairline cracks forked over the slate gray.

The red headed woman with chromatic sage eyes sat upon a throne as aged and rotted as the rest of the castle. Her court of fiery haired look-a-likes lined the sides of the hall. Faye's stomach twisted as Rune appeared beside her.

He was on his knees. A chain hooked to the thick collar circling his neck, binding him to the stone floor without enough slack for him to sit upright. Manacles clamped over his wrists with spikes driven through them. They were affixed to chains attached to the pillars on either side of the throne room. His arms were stretched outward and up, keeping all three chains tight.

A male with the same crimson hair finished tearing the last of Rune's black tipped claws off with a set of pliers.

"Take his fangs," the Queen of the rotted court said sweetly.

The man fisted Rune's blood-matted hair and brought the iron to his mouth. Rune bit down and sharply twisted his head, snapping off the plier tip. He spat the metal bits at the Queen. "Collect them yourself, Sadira."

The Queen's image flickered, and she materialized before Rune. She stroked his hair lovingly, and Rune didn't move even as the muscles in his back strained. Faye could only stare at her soul shard.

This woman was a day-blood.

"You will learn your place. Bring me a stone chisel and a hammer," she said as she turned to her guard.

Faye's blood ran cold as she caught a glimpse of Rune's ring, his Shard of Darkness, hanging from a necklace around the Queen's throat.

Strong hands roughly grabbed either side of her face and the scene dissipated in an instant, replaced with Damian's face. He was wide eyed and panting as he searched her face.

"Are you here?" He yelled. "You with me, dove?"

Faye blinked, shaking from her vision. "What..." She pulled his hand away looking for Rune. Needing to see he was safe. "I saw—"

She couldn't breathe. Her tendril was gone and Sadi crouched over Rune's still body.

Darkness, what had she done.

Forty-Four

The days bled together as Faye desperately waited for Rune to wake. She'd taken his memories and power, reducing his Shard of Darkness to an empty crystal. Morbid appeared before hysterics consumed her. The Familiar King assured her she'd done no physical damage, and the Shadow Prince would wake when he recovered his strength.

Morbid had phased Rune back to their room and helped her get him into bed. Sadi accompanied them and lingered before asking Faye, "Are you staying with him?" Faye nodded, and she cryptically added, "Shield yourself. He may be disoriented when he wakes."

Faye had left Rune's suit on the first day, hoping he would wake after a few hours. On the second, she asked Vash to hold him up so she could pull his jacket off.

Rune slept, and Faye remained with him, curled into his side as she read books to pass the time. Each morning, she checked his soul shard. It slowly darkened as the days passed. The mist surrounding it returned on the fourth, curling over the points. The sharp edges of his soul shard were clearly visible through the diluted shadows.

A full week passed before the dark mist engulfed his shard completely and she hoped it meant he would wake soon.

"Come on big guy," Faye said, lifting his head and shoulders off the bed to stuff a pillow behind him. She brought a glass of her blood to his lips, carefully pouring its contents into his mouth. He swallowed, and his canines lengthened. *That was new.*

Faye pushed his lip up, inspecting his fangs. They hadn't dropped the other times she fed him. Maybe he *would* wake today. She finished her task and settled Rune back down, making him as comfortable as she could manage. Faye brushed her mind against his, comforted by the mental walls keeping her out.

Rune. Voshki. If you could wake up now, so I can stop worrying. That would be great.

They didn't answer, and Rune didn't stir.

Faye passed the day with a comfort read and settled in for the night. She heeded Sadi's warning and shielded herself before laying her head on Rune's chest.

"Come back to me," she whispered, before drifting to sleep.

Faye woke sometime later. Something sharp dragged over her shield.

"Rune," Faye said, pushing off his chest.

He tossed his head, breathing heavily. Veined misted shadows swayed beneath his closed eyes. Faye glanced down, lighting hellfire to illuminate the room. His shirt clung to him, soaked through. She'd never seen this man sweat.

"Rune," Faye said his name louder, rubbing his chest. "Rune, wake up."

He sat up suddenly, his arms pulled behind him. A violent wave of crackling force surged past her, whipping her hair. Rune snarled and bared his fangs.

The foot of their bed fell as Rune's magic decimated the wooden posts and frame. Faye leaped toward him, wrapping her arms around his neck. A deafening crash sounded behind her as stones and rubble flew forward, pelting their bed. Faye ignored the debris striking her shield. She raised her shoulders to protect Rune from the projectiles. She perceived his heart racing as he welled his magic for another strike.

"It's okay. You're okay," she whispered, holding him tighter. Did she force him to relive the scenes she pried from him the same way she dreamt of drowning under Alister's hand? Her voice cracked as she squeezed him tighter. "You're home. I have you."

Manacles shackled his wrists, held in place with spikes driven through his flesh. He pulled, dismissing the pain as tissue and sinew tore. His fangs sharpened as he studied the faces of every bitch filing into the room, eager for her turn on him. He committed them to memory, promising a slow drawn-out death for each of them.

He lashed a wide band of power meant to reduce the room, and its occupants to scraps of bone and kindling, but his strength did not answer.

Pin them and peel strips of flesh from their bodies, the Ra'Voshnik growled. The corner of Rune's mouth lifted. They could cut him from the Darkness, but they could never take what he was. He didn't need his shards to kill them. Another calculated tug on the shackle.

Rune detested this room. Their unwanted touch. The reek of their scent lingered on him.

He blinked.

Another scent penetrated the hate-filled fog blanketing his mind. It covered him. Softer.

Clean.

He inhaled deeply, recognizing his night breeze.

The opulent room gave way to a clear view of Hell's ever twilight sky—framed in stone rubble. *No.* He turned toward the woman desperately clinging to him.

"Are you injured?" he asked firmly, running his hands down her back. He'd unleashed through her. Scented her blood. He held her at an arm's length, frantically searching for the source of her injury.

Her lightning-streaked midnight eyes gleamed with unshed tears. "Are you okay?"

"Are you injured?" Rune repeated, tilting her head up to inspect her throat. His gaze ran lower, searching the pale fabric of her nightgown for red stains.

Sadira enslaved him for nearly a century and a half. During his imprisonment, she'd encouraged her sisters to breed his dark blood into their lines in hopes of a darker generation. Their attempts had been unsuccessful, and he'd killed dozens from them while they tried. He'd beheaded some and tore limbs off others. Rune grew nauseous as he thought of all the ways he could have unknowingly maimed his queen.

"You were having a nightmare. You didn't hurt me." Faye took his face between her hands, guiding him to look at her.

Faye caressed the side of his neck and Rune flinched as dark recollections cut through his mind. His queen's touch breathed life into memories of other hands gliding over his body. Rune vanished and materialized near their bed. He panted, pulling against the collar of his shirt. Bile rose in his throat. Their scent choked him. Rune stalked to the shower, reducing his clothing to rags as he ripped them away.

The Ra'Voshnik groggily rose as Rune ran his hand over his chest, desperate to banish the feel of those bitches from his flesh. He clawed at the shower levers and a spray of hot water washed over him. *These are memories. This is not real,* he told himself.

But it *felt* real.

Rune reached for the vial of cleansing oil designed to strip scent. His hand shook violently, and it fell through his fingers, shattering on the wet tiles at his feet. A growl rumbled from Rune as his fangs lengthened. He called a small leather case and floated it before him but couldn't recall the order he placed the bottles in.

Rune bared his fangs and crushed the box before throwing it. It crashed into the shower wall, cracking the tiles as slivers of wood and glass spread across the floor.

The Ra'Voshnik growled, scraping its claws over his awareness. *Calm yourself. There is no scent on you.*

He ignored the creature. More than half a dozen scents clung to him—strangling him. He felt their hands. Their mouths. Another layer of feminine musk added to the rest when the next bitch lowered herself over his length and took her pleasure, riding him.

The stone walls closed in. He couldn't breathe.

You're frightening our queen. There is nothing on you. They're all long dead, the Ra'Voshnik grated.

Rune phased to the private gardens and walked into the spelled hot spring, submerging himself. The creature established a mental tether with Faye. His night breeze through plum blossoms whispered through the ghosts of his memories.

Mingling with them.

Rune snapped the mental link, unwilling to integrate his queen into the group of women his court purged.

He exhaled beneath the water. Faye's emotional undercurrents lingered with him. Her worry was a knife against an open wound. Rune stood, rising out of the water and Faye materialized at the edge of the stone border. He stepped back and angled his face away from her. His mind rioted against him, rifling through memories he'd long buried. His queen's beseeching eyes, and parted lips were coarse salt in his wounds. He was her sword, but the blade she'd chosen… was brittle and damaged.

"I am so sorry. I didn't mean to hurt you," Faye whispered. She sat on her knees at the edge of the hot spring, squeezing an oversized black towel.

"I am well," Rune lied, running his hand over his face.

The Ra'Voshnik lingered near the surface and veined misted shadows stretched beneath his pale blue eyes. *Don't push our queen away,* it growled. *She's not one of them.*

Be. Fucking. Silent, Rune hissed. He moved to Faye, resting his palms in the grass on either side of her. Sunlight beamed down on him, and Rune inhaled deeply, concentrating on the sweet scent of the black roses. The frost pink azaleas on either side of the pool.

Anything besides Faye until the memories faded.

His queen shivered and Rune cursed in High Tongue. It was winter and she was kneeling in the grass, wearing a thin nightgown. He called her winter coat and settled it over her shoulders. "How long was I asleep?" he asked. He'd lost weeks while he trained under Saith's tutelage. "Did I miss your first open court?"

Faye slid her arms into the fur-lined coat and shook her head. "It's tomorrow. You've been out for a week."

Rune rolled his shoulders. "What… What happened?"

Faye looked down and smoothed her hands over the towel. "I

tried to siphon your strength but… I think, I saw your memories."

Rune's chest constricted. When her tendril hit his core, the sensation dragged memories of his capture to the front of his mind. His voice hollowed as he asked, "What did you see?"

She wet her lips and couldn't meet his gaze. Hurt sliced through his heart. She'd seen enough to know he'd been tainted and turned from him.

She loves us, you polished fool. The Ra'Voshnik growled, circling his mind, growing more agitated with each passing moment.

"I saw a woman who looked like the High Queen's daughter. She wore your ring around her neck. You called her Sadira," Faye said quietly. She slid her hand beside his without touching him. Rune brushed her pinkie with his index, and a tear slipped down her cheek as she took his hand. "I saw what they did to you."

She met his gaze, and Rune brushed the moisture from her lashes, wondering if he would ever stop being a source of pain for his queen. "It was a long time ago, love."

"They were day-bloods. Even if they took your ring, you don't need it to access your power."

Rune parted his lips and immediately closed them, weighing what to say and what to omit. "Sadira found a way to sever my link to the Darkness."

Faye remained quiet, and after a long moment, she asked, "Was she Familiar?"

"No," Rune answered, before reaching for a kinder subject. "When was your last meal?" Faye searched his eyes, but he held no desire to rehash his enslavement. "You are not dressed for the cold. Shall we?" Rune asked. His queen reluctantly nodded, and Rune phased them back to their bedroom.

He tensed as the stone walls rose around him. This wasn't a dungeon. He stood in his bedchamber.

His queen toed a chuck of stone, framed by Hell's sky. "Do we need to hire someone to fix this?"

It'd been more than a thousand years since he'd woven the spell into the stones to reassemble the destruction his dreams wrought. "Perhaps," Rune said, lending a flicker of his power to the wall.

The rubble at his queen's feet vanished along with the debris covering their bed. The wall slowly rebuilt, appearing stone by stone.

Faye pressed her palm to the reconstructed wall and pushed. She turned toward him and asked, "How did you do that?"

"I grew tired of replacing the wall and modified a spell my brother used on his training dummies," Rune said as he retrieved a robe and pulled it on.

"Can you magic a bigger window?" she asked.

Rune breathed deeply. Faye's subtle scent lingered in the room they shared, calming his mind.

Bring her back to bed and order her a meal, the Ra'Voshnik grated, aggravated Rune had stripped their queen's scent from their body. It urged him to hold her soft curves against him until it returned, sufficiently marking him.

"I can have a larger window installed if you wish," Rune said.

Darkness willing, his unwanted memories would return to the recesses of his mind, and he wouldn't need to repair the wall a second time.

Forty-Five

Faye's heart bled as she watched her vampire. Dark circles marred his eyes when they woke this morning. She was certain he hadn't slept, but the glamour he used concealed any evidence of the contrary. He'd been distant since the garden, and Faye gave him space. She'd even been willing to reschedule her open court by a few days, but Rune refused, saying, "This is the first day of your reign. You cannot afford to show weakness."

His words left her conflicted. She loved her people, and she loved him, but pushing forward with court business felt like she was trading one for the other. Faye lifted her chin as her heart pounded. If Rune was going to sacrifice himself for her court, she would make his discomfort worth the pain.

She would see her realm in practice today. With Rune at her side her dreams were coming to fruition. For the first time in history day-bloods, dark-bloods, and Anarians would join together as equals.

Faye stared at the large double doors of her hall. She'd blended aspects of Artithian and Necromian architecture, creating a space with an open feel with spanning windows and sunlight. Faye had forgone the Artithian's obsession with gold trim and incorporated intricate wrought iron windows and vaulted cathedral ceilings instead.

She was seated on her throne in the center of a raised dais with Rune and Alister flanking her sides.

"Ready?" Alister asked as he glanced back at her over his shoulder.

Faye surveyed the rows of empty seating on the other side of her hall and lifted her gaze to the three rows of balcony seating reserved for the noble houses. Royal blood she didn't possess. Her hall was a miniscule imitation of the grand wedding she and Rune attended for the Artithian Princess.

She swallowed and smoothed her hands over the boning of the turquoise dress she selected. The cut of the gown emphasized her waist, and the long sleeves of raw silk were attached to bracelets adorning her wrists and circling her arm just above her elbows.

Are you well? Rune asked in her mind.

Faye nodded and shielded herself before turning toward Alister. "I'm ready."

She took a calming breath and nodded, folding her hands in her lap. Alister gestured to the footman at the doors and joined the rest of Faye's court to the left of the dais. The two men opened the doors while Faye fought to keep her breath even.

People crowded the pavilion outside. Faye blinked. She'd expected Anarians to join her, but this?

They filed through the doors. Some were dressed in court finery while others wore a more modest dress. Faye smiled as people from Alexander cautiously stepped into her hall. They huddled in a small group, watching the day-bloods with fearful eyes.

Faye's chest tightened as the day-bloods took notice. They watched each other for a heartbeat, then a day-blood woman inclined her head at them in greeting. Faye smiled as her heart swelled. Behind them another group entered. Anarians and day-bloods mingled together, talking among themselves as they took their seats.

This was her court. The realm she wanted to create. Alister's words echoed through her mind.

Do you think I was the only day-blood to love an Anarian? Many will come to your court. You offer safety without ridicule.

This mindset could never flourish under the High Queen. She saw them as less.

The footman's voice carried through the hall startling Faye. "Moira Archonis Queen of the Court of Shadow and Moonlight, accompanied by her consort and executioner Damien Archonis."

The couple walked down the center of her hall. Damien wore a tailored dark suit. His long dark hair was pulled back and tied with a strap of leather. Moira's flowing gray dress swept around her as she walked.

Why are they walking toward me? Faye asked Rune through a mental tether.

They are here to formally recognize your rule, vsenia. Answer with, we thank you.

The pair stood before Faye and inclined their heads. Moira's soft brown curls fell over her shoulder, and Damien smiled at his Queen before turning to Faye. "We honor and recognize your rule."

Faye lowered her head to mirror Rune and answered, "We thank you."

They vanished and materialized in a second-story box seat, and Faye beamed. Dark-bloods agreed with her rule. Noble dark-bloods.

Two other courts were announced, recognizing her rule and Faye looked over her guests. The crowd settled and a final group entered.

"The Court of Ageless Sea answering the petition for Isobelle Rilanash."

A tall handsome man walked toward her, accompanied by two women walking a step behind him on either side. The woman to his left wore a corseted gown. Her silken strawberry-blonde hair strung with diamonds and other precious gems.

Faye's gaze fell to her bare index finger. Rune stepped forward and the trio stopped before her throne. Faye recognized the other woman from the High Council meeting.

Delilah, the Queen of the Court of Lace and Bone.

"It is customary to bow when entering a Queen's hall," Rune said too calmly.

The male shrank at Rune's words, but Delilah stood taller. "We are not part of the realm you stole."

Sparrow snorted, crossing her legs as she propped herself up on the armrest of her chair. "Why are you here? Is he part of your slimy court?"

"He came to me for council," Delilah said, shifting her attention to Faye. Her predatory gaze reminded her of a cat gazing at birds through a window. How much harm she would do if only she could reach them.

Faye glanced to the male. Sweat began to bead over his upper lip. "Will you be freeing your pet?"

"She stays of her own free will, Lady," the man said to Faye before glancing fearfully at Rune.

Isobelle's mother stood from her chair and yelled, "She stays because she's afraid of you."

Isobelle kept her eyes lowered and flushed, standing a full step behind the dark-bloods she accompanied. Faye's stomach knotted. She couldn't be any older than Faye.

Her sister snorted, pulling Faye's attention. "How'd you even meet her?"

The male fidgeted with his cuff. "My court purchased her contract at auction."

"Blood whore auctions. You remember them Shadow Prince, your mother Michelle frequented them," Delilah said sweetly. Her smile turned cruel, and she met Faye's gaze, adding in a lower tone, "She had dozens."

Faye refused to rise to Delilah's goading. "Isobelle," Faye said gently. The woman's gaze lifted. The fear in them made Faye nauseous. "We can pay off your contract if you want to return home."

Isobelle tensed and glanced at the man's back before returning her attention to Faye. "I want to stay."

"Isobelle," her mother cried. The woman lowered her gaze and turned her head to stare at the male's back. "Those monsters are keeping her against her will."

"Isobelle," Faye said gently, willing her to meet her gaze.

Delilah leaned to her side. "The mortal said—"

"Be silent," Rune growled as Delilah continued speaking. Absent of sound.

The Queen of Lace and Bone bared her fangs, and a sword appeared in her hand. After facing Alister's blades, Delilah's looked like a child's toy. The vampire queen stiffened, glancing around the room before vanishing her weapon. She dragged the claw of her articulated Familiar ring under her cheekbone and pointed at Rune. *I'm watching you,* she mouthed.

Faye stood and walked toward Isobelle. To her surprise Rune remained on the dais. The male took a step back as Faye stopped before the woman. She took her hand and gave her a squeeze. Isobelle's gaze lifted to her, still fearful.

"It's your choice if you want to stay. I want to look into your mind to make sure a Familiar isn't influencing you. Is that ok?" Faye's asking was a lie. She wasn't far enough in her training with Sadi to identify if a Familiar twisted this woman's mind and thoughts. But she could feel her emotions and understand why she would want to stay with this court instead of returning to her family.

Isobelle nodded and Faye brushed her awareness over her. Faye hid her shock, there were no barriers around her mind. Nothing to keep her hidden thoughts private. Faye didn't linger or rifle through the woman's thoughts. She concentrated on the emotional undercurrents rushing through the woman's mind.

Shocked, she pulled her mind back. Isobelle wasn't afraid of the male. She was afraid of being taken from him. She loved him.

Isobelle eyes began to water. *Please don't take me away from him.* Faye nodded at her and let her go. She took a step closer to the vampire who held her heart.

"She's not being held against her will," Faye said to the mother, and then turned to the male. "You could reside here with her. You would be safe."

The male glanced to Rune, then returned to her. "I do not wish to leave my court, Lady."

Anger rose within Faye. The vampire was unwilling to leave his comfort for the woman who loved him. Faye clenched her jaw and nodded at him. "Very well." To Isobelle she said, "You will always have sanctuary here."

She nodded, taking the vampire's hand, before the trio vanished.

Faye returned to her throne, running her fingertips over the carved cherry blossom inlay. What had begun with joy and hope was quickly overshadowed with turmoil, and Faye swallowed her guilt.

She failed her.

Forty-Six

Faye gracefully returned to her throne. She appeared serene and calm, but even sleep-deprived, Rune recognized the tension she carried in her slim shoulders. The vampire's rejection cut her far deeper than she was willing to admit.

Perhaps even to herself.

He brushed his mind against hers, offering what comfort he could in this formal environment. Open court proceeded, and Faye kept her composure. She listened to a number of families' concerns and requests.

The first few had shyly approached her but their fear melted away with each new interaction. The crowd warmed to his Queen as Alister handled most of the questions. The Anarians were curious how the village would pay for the repairs being done and if they would be charged for visiting the healers.

A middle-aged woman approached the dais next. She bowed and stopped suddenly to curtsy instead. "My Queen," she began. "I'm from Streck, we're the closest town to The Crumbling. The clouds seem to be getting angrier, ma'am."

"You have nothing to fear," Rune said gently. "You are miles from The Crumbling, and containing it is well within your Queen's capabilities."

The woman's eyes widened as he spoke. She took a step back, glancing between himself and Faye before muttering, "Thank you, my Queen," before retreating with great haste.

I believe I should leave the conversation to you, love, Rune said in her mind.

A ghost of a smile touched her lips, and she listened to a few more families raise concerns about The Crumbling before Alister ended their time, announcing the next open court would take place the following month.

Rune approached Faye's throne and the Ra'Voshnik purred, eager to reunite with their queen.

Faye stood and squeezed his hand, not meeting his gaze. Her voice rang thin in his mind. *Take me home.*

Rune phased and once they were in the privacy of their room Faye threw her arms around him and buried her face on his shoulder.

"Vsenia," Rune said softly as he lifted her in his arms and carried her to the newly-built picture window dominating the stone wall of their room.

The Ra'Voshnik circled his mind relentlessly, wanting to comfort their queen. *Kill the vampire who offended her.*

Calm yourself. Violence brings her no comfort. Rune took a seat in the windows ledge and smoothed Faye's silken black hair.

Then don't tell her, and break every bone in his body, the creature hissed. *He'll agree to live in her realm.*

Rune ignored the Ra'Voshnik and pressed a light kiss to the top of Faye's head.

"She loves him," Faye muttered.

The pain her voice clawed at his temper, and his inability to ease her suffering left him feeling inadequate. "Yes."

Faye wiped her eyes and stared over his crystalline realm. "Why wouldn't he want to live here where she could be his equal."

"It is unlikely he loves her," Rune said softly.

"But he escorted her here," Faye argued. Her expression pleading as unshed tears dotted her lashes.

For all her power his queen was still so young. "His motives were rooted in fear, not love."

"Why would he keep her if some part of him doesn't care for her?"

He wanted to lie and spare her the heartache. "My words will offend you. Please understand I am not saying this to be unkind. Perspective is required to rule efficiently." When Faye nodded, he continued, "Vampires commonly retain blood whores simply because they are fond of their taste. If they are favored enough, they are kept exclusively. I believe that is the reason he keeps her, and he will unfortunately discard her when she ages out of his preference."

Faye hugged his arm to her and lowered her head.

"I understand you desire to be good and kind. I love the passion you carry, but you will not be able to save them all, vsenia. All you can offer is shelter. Accepting it lies solely with them."

"Would you be like him if I was an Anarian?"

Her words cut into his soul, and the Ra'Voshnik surged toward her. *Never! Tell her we are hers to command until the Darkness drags us from her.*

He'd helped carve this injury into her with his early actions. He hoped to mend the wounds she carried through devotion and time. "I was a fool to doubt our tie," Rune whispered, lifting her chin so she met his gaze. His arrogance nearly cost him the Queen he'd spent lifetimes yearning for. "You are my queen. My fate."

Faye blinked and tears fell over her cheeks. She laid her head on his shoulder and whispered, "I thought they would be like you. If I gave them a place to exist, they wouldn't keep people as pets."

What he loved most about her also left her open to so much pain. "You want love to conquer all. It is an admirable trait, but our situation is unique. You were never my pet, vsenia. You will be hard-pressed to find a dark-blood willing to admit they have feelings for one."

Faye remained silent, and Rune wished he could take her anguish. "Focus on the good you have done. There are a number of day-bloods living with Anarians. Couples, like my brother, who found sanctuary in your court. Under your rule."

Faye's voice cracked as she asked, "Why is it so wrong to love an Anarian?"

"Vsenia. These traditions span thousands of years. It will take time."

"Shards shouldn't matter this much," Faye replied on the heels of his words.

"Shards are power, and power is protection. It is the way of things. The hierarchy is a way of preserving the strength of a line and even that fails at times. Lyssa for example,"

Faye groaned against his chest, and Rune chuckled, running his fingers through her hair. "Lyssa," Rune continued, "is a dark-blood, but her parents each carried a Shard of Darkness. My father carried the Darkness, and my mother was dark-blooded. Yet Alister is a day-blood."

"And you have three shards," she said weakly. "No one else in history has carried more than one."

A secret he hid his entire life. "Perhaps it is because I am paired to you."

"Got more than you bargained for when you made that wish."

Rune's tension eased as his queen began to sound like herself. He breathed in her scent. His night breeze through plum blossoms. "You have drastically changed the course of my life."

The Ra'Voshnik purred through his mind, agreeing with his sentiment.

"Is it true what she said?" Rune's brow drew together as Faye pushed off his chest. "Your mother had dozens of blood whores."

"Michelle lived… unapologetically. She had several blood whores both she and my father partook in. They flocked to her because within our court, they were members, not servants. Other dark-blooded queens followed her example. Many of our traditions began with her."

Faye mulled over his words. After a while, she asked, "Did you have blood whores?"

"No," Rune answered. "When I was a young boy, my mother would cut her wrist and fill a cup for me. Pure Bloods eat and consume blood until we mature into our immortality, at which point food becomes unnecessary. As I grew older, your Voshki was too uncivilized to partake in blood whores."

You were too stupid to recognize prey. Always letting it escape, the creature interjected. Rune growled a warning at the Ra'Voshnik and was answered in kind.

"What was it like when you were young? Did you and Voshki get into mischief when you were little?" Faye asked, shifting against him.

"The Ra'Voshnik is not present during early childhood, it manifests during puberty."

She looked thoughtful for a moment then asked, "Did you meet the High Queen's Voshki?"

The creature recoiled, and Rune chuckled low in his throat. *Tell her not to string my name together with Lyssa's.*

"I believe this is the first time I have heard the creature crossed with you," Rune said.

Faye shook her head and exhaled. "Stop calling him a creature."

"Your Voshki is offended you called Lyssa's Ra'Voshnik by its name." Rune smiled to himself as she laughed.

"I'm sorry. I'll call hers Ra'Bitch-nik," Faye managed, wiping the back of her hand over her eyes. "Voshki doesn't play well with other Ra'Voshnik?"

"It held a singular mind of violence before we met you. The cre—Your Voshki is still of a singular mind. His focus is now centered on you."

"Do you think we'll have Pure Bloods, one day?"

Bring her to our bed, and give her the young she desires, the creature purred.

"Perhaps," Rune answered as he dismissed the Ra'Voshnik's urgings. "Or Shadowmen. They may have wings like their mother." The lineage they took mattered little. He would care for them. Teach them. Love his young as much as he loved their mother.

My young, the creature snapped.

"Your mother was a Pure Blood. She didn't encourage you to be friends with Voshki?"

"Saith was my mentor, and your Voshki hindered my lessons. Saith taught me to contain it."

Faye flinched, and the creature brushed the surface of his awareness. *Tell her I got him a few times, and his blood tasted like sewage.*

"I don't want that for them. I want them to be children. I'll teach them to be friends with their Ra'Voshniks. They're going to spend their lives together; they should learn to depend on each other."

Rune reflected on his ancient memories. The initial phrases sounding in his mind had frightened him as they did not originate from him. Snippets of foreign thoughts which formed into another personality in a few short weeks.

Just think of all the fun we could have had if you weren't Saith's bitch, the creature chuckled as it floated through his mind. *We could have ripped his head off and given it to Julian.*

"What's Lyssa's Ra'Voshnik like? I only have Voshki as an example."

"I have not seen her Ra'Voshnik. It is a predator and violent, not something we openly share. We're taught to control it," Rune explained.

"You mean suppress them," Faye muttered as she examined the ends of her hair. She met his gaze and asked, "Have you ever wondered if that's why they're so violent? If you stuffed me away my whole life, I would be angry too."

His queen's intentions were steeped with kind intent, but this was unwise. "A Pure Blood's instincts differ from yours, love. The Ra'Voshnik is volatile. It cannot be allowed to roam free."

"We'll teach them both," Faye insisted. "Voshki can teach the little Ra'Voshniks to behave themselves."

The creature bolstered with pride, and he cursed in high Tongue. "It has hardly behaved itself."

Faye giggled. "Voshki is sweet."

"You do not hear its thoughts."

Says the man who made our queen beg him to fuck her pretty—

Be silent, Rune hissed.

The Ra'Voshnik chuckled. *Under that polished exterior, you're far worse than I could ever dream of being.*

Forty-Seven

Rune refused to admit he wasn't sleeping, and Faye wasn't sure how to broach the subject. She'd hoped after a few days his exhaustion would force him to rest. The deeper rasp of his morning voice gave way to a tired, hollow sound, further confirming her suspicions. The man would say he slept, but the shadows darkening his eyes had nothing to do with Voshki being close to the surface.

It had been four days, and they couldn't go on pretending nothing was wrong. Faye sat up in their bed. "You're not sleeping, are you?"

Rune rubbed his eyes and said, "I am rested."

"No, you're not," Faye pressed. "You can't do this forever. You need sleep."

He sat up, and the dark silk sheets lowered, exposing the waistband of the pajama bottoms he'd begun wearing to bed. "I... I fear hurting you."

"You didn't hurt me," Faye said softly as she leaned closer.

"I could have," Rune answered. He crossed his legs and studied the sheets folded between them. "When I last woke, I did not recognize you were in bed with me until it was too late."

Faye took his hand and said, "They're nightmares, and I shielded myself." His silence answered her and she quietly added, "Tell me how I can help you."

"Vsenia," Rune began.

Faye crawled up the bed to sit at the headboard. She gave Rune an expectant glance and patted her thigh.

"I am sorry I have not been tending to you," Rune said in a soft tone.

"What?" Faye curled her lip as her brows drew together. "I'm not—Darkness, I can't tell if you're joking or not," Faye said, pulling her pillow over her lap. "Lay down."

Rune rolled onto his side and propped his head up on his hand. His pale blue gaze lowered to her lap before lifting to her face. "You want me to lay my head on your lap?"

"It's like you've never been comforted in your life," Faye grumbled, scooting closer to him. His expression fell, and Faye instantly regretted the words. She reached for him and said, "You belong to me, let me take care of you."

"Yes, my queen." He did as she asked and slid his fingers under her calf.

"I can watch over you and shield myself," Faye said gently, smoothing a lock of his hair behind his ear. She ran two fingers along his brow bone, following it to his temple. This always calmed Sparrow after a bad breakup. On her third stroke, Rune closed his eyes.

He looked exhausted, the fatigue shadowing his features, much darker than when he simply pushed too far looking into The Crumbling.

"You're home now," Faye said softly. "I won't let anything like that happen again." She knew the court was long destroyed and a disappointed fury flickered through her. Her power rose with the emotion as pinpricks spread over her nails and along her back where her wings emerged.

The urge to warm her claws in the flesh of each woman she'd

seen in Rune's memories lashed through her mind. Their screams would be a fine symphony to her retribution.

Rune smoothed his thumb over her shin. "What is bothering you, vsenia?"

Faye pushed the thoughts away, gliding her fingers through her mate's hair, comforting herself as much as it comforted him.

"I want to hurt them," she confessed. Saying it aloud tore at her heart, making her darker impulses real. She didn't want them. Her first instinct to anger or pain was to lash out. To make the object of her suffering realize what true agony was.

"They have been dealt with for centuries."

Faye stared out over Hell's crystalline landscape, absently stroking his arm. "I don't know what's more upsetting. That I can't hurt them or that I have the impulse to begin with."

She glanced down at Rune in time to see the corner of his mouth lift. "I have taken my pound of flesh."

"She owes you more than a pound."

Rune chuckled, the corners of his eyes crinkling. "Be that as it may, I cannot sleep with you near."

Hurt stung Faye's heart. "I can go if you want to sleep alone. I can take the room in Sparrow's wing."

"I do not wish to drive you away, vsenia. I have spent these past nights contemplating a solution. I have considered returning to my father's castle, Standing Shadows, and sleeping there every few days."

"I would rather you not wake up alone." He'd been there when she woke screaming from her night terrors. Did he see himself as a burden? She wanted to be there for him.

Rune opened his eyes to gaze up at her. "I cannot risk you. Buildings are easily repaired. If I injured you I would never recover."

Faye grew nauseous when she thought of Rune waking up panicked and alone. "I dreamt of drowning for months. How long did your nightmares last when you first came back."

"Decades," Rune answered, his voice hollow.

Time. Time always stood between them. Decades to him were like months to her. Faye bit the inside of her lip. "What about Voshki?"

The veined misted shadows stretched from beneath his closed eyes. "What about the creature?"

Faye lightly poked the side of his neck. "He's not a creature."

He withdrew his hand from under her leg and asked, "Did you wish to visit with your Voshki?"

"No, but…" After a measure of silence, Rune turned onto his back to stare up at her. "Do you fall asleep together or can you sleep… separately?" Faye asked.

Rune's brow drew down. "We are independent of each other."

"Then let Voshki rise and sleep."

Rune's expression soured. "No."

"I'm sure he would watch you very carefully if I asked him."

"I am sure the creature would agree to anything you request of it," Rune murmured, rolling to his side.

This was a solution. Why was he fighting her so hard? "I'll shield myself. Let Voshki rise and get some rest."

"This is unwise."

Faye wondered if Rune ever relinquished control to Voshki this fully before. It wasn't as though Voshki could trap Rune in his mind. He had much more control than Voshki did. "I don't want to be separated from you a few nights every week."

"As you command, my queen."

"I want you to rest and feel safe. When you wake up, we'll be here waiting for you."

"If the creature becomes a nuisance, burst my heart," Rune said dryly.

Faye glared down at his relaxed expression. "I'm not going to—I don't even know how to do that."

"Remind me to teach you when I wake. Keep your shield on," Rune said, brushing a lick of power over her knee. Her shield blazed to life, crackling against Rune's touch. "And do not let it leave Hell and make a fool of itself, please."

"Yes, my love."

Rune's body relaxed, falling limp for a moment. Then Voshki's shadows stretched beneath the fan of his lashes, and no fatigue hindered his wholly black eyes. He shifted, laying on his stomach, and wrapped his arms loosely around her waist.

"Pet me," he rasped, snuggling closer.

"You're very demanding," Faye said, pulling his long white-blonde hair to one side. "Are you watching Rune?"

A purr rumbled through Voshki. "I have *dreamed* of the day when he would ask me to kick him awake."

"Be nice to him."

"He'll get every kindness he showed me."

"The two of you are impossible," Faye huffed. She ran her fingers over his shoulder, admiring his muscular back. She'd seen the changes in Rune's eyes immediately and how it only grew worse with the passing days, but Voshki's demeanor hadn't changed. He seemed…

Unbothered.

"You've been sleeping just fine, haven't you?"

At her question Voshki lifted himself up, bracing his weight with his arms. He leaned closer, bringing his lips a moment from hers. "I've been sleeping. If you drop your shield I can tend to you," he rasped before his voice deepened. "I've missed tonguing your pretty cunt."

His teasing words heated her blood but this wasn't the time. Faye pushed him away by the base of his throat. "Watch over Rune."

"I am," Voshki said, settling down on her lap once more. "I can see when his nightmares start. It would be my pleasure to wake his royal highness after he locked me away for millennia." He reached blindly for her hand, then placed it on his head. "Touch me. I've missed you."

Faye massaged his shoulder, while he dragged her closer until his arms comfortably encircled her waist. A hint of his claws pricked through her nightgown as he rhythmically flexed the fingers of one hand then the other, like an overgrown cat.

She glanced down at him. "Can I ask you a question?"

"Why yes, I would love to tie you up again and… I might even let you use your riding crop after I've given you a proper demonstration of the Hunter's Moon," Voshki said, the last, flicking a brow up.

Flush burned across Faye's cheeks, and the fucker chuckled. Faye tugged on a length of his hair.

"Ow. If you want to pull my hair, it's back here," Voshki said, fisting his hair at the base of his skull. "Not here." He ran his black-tipped claws through the hair at his temple.

"I'm being serious."

"What do you want to know, my queen?"

Faye hesitated for a moment. "Why don't you have nightmares? You were both captured."

Voshki laughed. A real laugh filled with genuine humor devoid of the turmoil Rune carried. "The Shadow Prince is an aristo raised in a dark court. I am not."

Faye had never thought about it. Sharing a body didn't mean they shared a life.

"It makes me happy you want our young to befriend their Ra'Voshniks. I was caged most of our life. The only time the Shadow Prince truly freed me was when we were enslaved. There was suffering, but we were equals." Voshki grinned, holding her tighter. "We killed so many of them. Before you, it was the best time of my life."

Faye didn't want to dwell on the time haunting Rune or wonder how Voshki could look back on it fondly. "You never told me what it was like for you during the Hunter's Moon last year."

"I was tired of the fighting." Voshki frowned and said, "Well, not the fighting. I was tired of losing. I slept for a long time. Then we caught your scent."

Voshki groaned, posting himself up on one arm while using the other to drag her beneath him. He lowered himself over her, pressing against her shield. Faye giggled as he lowered his head to her neck. His white-blonde hair brushed over her shoulder, and he inhaled deeply, guiding her legs around his waist.

He moved to her ear and purred, "If I was at the fore, I would have pinned you and begged you to offer me your throat."

Faye turned toward him and quirked her lip. "So that was it? I smelled good?"

"Vsenia," Voshki grated, caging her under his perfectly sculpted body. "You smelled like home."

Forty-Eight

R une jerked awake, baring his fangs.

"Easy," the Ra'Voshnik said, shifting its weight to add more pressure to the shoulder he stood on. "I saw the room. Thought it would be best to wake you up before you started destroying things."

"My thanks," Rune grated, shoving Voshki's foot. His head still pounded in time with his heart, but the few hours of sleep helped.

"Our queen says you should sleep again."

Rune's awareness was clumsy and slow to obey him as he reconnected to his physical body. Faye gazed up at him, concern darkening her eyes. The Ra'Voshnik was at the fore, reluctant to return control to him.

"Is he okay?" Faye asked, tucking a strand of white-blonde hair behind his ear. His hair cascaded forward, bright against her black tress spread over his gray sheets.

"Why is she beneath you?" Rune snarled, shifting his attention back to the space within his mind he shared with the Ra'Voshnik. "You should be protecting her, not fucking her."

The creature rolled its neck. "No, what I should have done is kick you awake."

Rune got to his feet with a growl. "I am well. This is sufficient for a few days."

"You're in poor shape. Stop worrying about me stealing our queen's favor. It's not my fault she prefers my cock. I told you I would share her with you," Voshki said, folding his arms. The corner of his mouth lifted into a smirk as he added, "And we already know she prefers me."

The Ra'Voshnik spoke through his physical body. "Your Shadow Prince is stubborn and not listening."

Rune, at most, you slept two hours. Faye's voice carried through his mind, and he glared at the Ra'Voshnik.

The creature shook his head. "Now you're disobeying our queen? And you wonder why I'm her favorite."

"Be silent," Rune said before ascending to his physical body. Faye's face came into sharp focus as his eyes cleared.

"Two hours isn't rest. Go back to sleep."

Rune's brow came down perplexed. He'd expected to return and find himself buried in his mate. The creature wasn't having sex with her. She was still in her nightgown.

She declined my offer, the Ra'Voshnik purred.

"Rune," Faye said gently, cupping the side of his face. His gaze rose to meet hers. "I'm worried about you."

He leaned into her touch and closed his eyes. It was tempting to do as she asked. It would be easy to lie beside her, breathing in her comforting scent. *Until he mistook her for his nightmares and attacked her.*

I've always seen her for what she is. I'll keep her safe, the Ra'Voshnik promised.

Rune opened his eyes. "You have a siphoning lesson with Sadi this afternoon."

"Voshki can take me, it'll be fine," Faye argued.

Rune tensed. She could not be serious. "I do not share the Ra'Voshnik with others. There is little known about our nature, and I prefer it that way."

It would be easy enough to impersonate you, the creature replied.

I'm Rune.

I have no fun.

My perfect evening is burying my nose in a book. In my study. Alone.

Be silent, Rune growled through his mind as the Ra'Voshnik laughed. Faye stared up at him, dissatisfied with his answer. "If you command it, I will sleep again *after* your lesson."

Faye smoothed her hand down the side of his throat and Rune's stomach knotted as he recalled another touch. They had taken so much from him and now, long after their deaths, they threatened the happiness he'd found with his queen.

"I don't want to command you." She lowered her gaze, turning away from him. "I want to help you, but I don't know how."

"You soothe me like nothing else has. It takes time," Rune whispered.

Her lightning-streaked midnight eyes met his, and she gave him a small nod. "Could Sadi help you?"

That bitch is not touching us, the Ra'Voshnik grated.

"You soothe me, Faye, no one else."

Faye scrunched her nose at him. "That's not what I meant. Sadi's Familiar. They can make people have dreams. Can she take them out?"

Rune rolled onto his back, and Faye curled to his chest. He barred his unwanted memories, focusing on his queen's scent as he studied the gray stones making up his ceiling. "Sadi sealed the memories for me after I destroyed half the south wing." He paused, taking a deep breath. "It worked as expected for a week then the memories returned. I was trapped in them and couldn't differentiate memory from reality. I attacked my court while we dined. One of them, my mother most likely, delivered a fatal blow to incapacitate me."

"You're so much stronger than them. How did she land a blow?"

Faye's question was valid. A court secret they'd kept for thousands of years. Rune supposed it mattered not; his mother returned to the Darkness centuries ago.

"Michelle was mortal once. She was a priestess, bred as a Catalyst. When she siphons power, it intensifies through her body threefold. She had the ability to siphon and dispense power at the same time."

"So, she took your three shards and hit you with nine?"

"It does not work in that way exactly, but yes. She used my power against me."

"Is that how she became a Pure Blood?"

"I never asked, but I would imagine so," Rune said as pain lanced his mind, adding to his headache.

The frail-blood isn't a threat anymore. Take your fucking spell off the realm that stabs our brain when anyone enters Hell.

Faye had been placed in harm's way because he was unaware a would-be assassin slipped into his realm undetected. He would never remove the spell. His queen would not fall prey to his enemies a second time.

Rune leaned down to press a kiss to the top of Faye's hair. "Sadi and Damian are waiting to begin your lesson."

She pushed off his chest to look him in the eye. "And you go back to sleep right after?"

"As you command."

Forty-Nine

Faye walked down the hall with Rune, close but not touching.
She'd noticed the way he tensed instead of leaning into her touch
when she slid her hand over his throat. Guilt gnawed at her. She
didn't want to use her tendril again and feared what she would pull
from the next person, but Rune's words filled her mind.

Power is meaningless if you cannot wield it.

So many people were depending on her. She had to wield it to
protect her realm.

Her family.

"I will see you when your lesson is concluded," he said as he
broke away to his study. Faye slowed a half step, watching him silently stroll to his desk.

Faye climbed the ornate staircase in the great room and made
her way to the ballroom. Sadi stood at the center of the unused

dance floor, and Damian lay on his back at her feet with his dark green trench fanned out beneath him. He turned his head as she approached, and a feline smile spread over his lips.

"Why do you look like someone kicked your dog, dove?" Damian asked.

Because I forced my mate to relive his nightmares, Faye thought bitterly. Sadi peered at her, cataloging every movement, and Faye bristled. She held her head high. She didn't shrink from the High Queen, and she wasn't going to balk from her evil twin either.

"I don't want to use my tendril." The words came out much calmer than Faye felt. She'd fractured the bond she shared with Rune, and she didn't know how to fix it.

Sadi raised her brow and tapped the claw of her articulated ring on her full plum colored lip. "You have a realm and court. Do you still want them?"

Darkness, could she not be a bitch. Just once. Whispers of Faye's power reached toward Sadi, vibrating with her coiling anger. She instinctively wanted to hook into Sadi's mind and tear chunks of it out.

Faye looked away studying the arched windows, hating her first instinct was to maim. She would rather kill—there was peace in death. Her blatant desire to cause suffering frightened her. It wasn't who she was.

Sadi leaned on her hip and seductively traced the metal claw of her ring along the plunging neckline of her corseted gown. "You want to hurt me." She tilted her head, looking past her.

"Get out my head," Faye snapped.

Sadi bared her teeth in a short hiss and stepped over Damian. The click of her heeled boots echoed through the empty space. "Then stop fighting it. I oppose you," Sadi seethed, circling her like they were vulture and prey. "Deep down you don't just want to get rid of me..." Sadi stepped closer, her voice turning sweet. "You want my agony."

Faye took a retreating step. "No, I don't. What is wrong with you?"

Sadi blinked twice and met Faye's gaze, smiling wide enough to display her little fangs. "There is nothing wrong with me. I'm honest about my urges. You cower from yours."

Faye's power rose with her outrage. "I'm not like you! I'll never be like you."

"Ladies," Damian said, getting to his feet. He tapped Sadi's chin. "You could stand to be nicer." Then turned to Faye. "And you will be challenged every day of your life if you don't set an example. Your mercy will only encourage your enemies to look for soft spots. When cowards can't hurt you, they will strike at the things you love. They'll target Anarians. An orphanage."

A deathly calm drifted through her, engulfing her mind. Wisps of power fanned away from her. Swaying in a hypnotic rhythm, waiting for her to select a target. She would strip the very being of anyone who threatened her home. Tearing into their minds and ripping away pieces until there was nothing left. Their lifeless shells would serve as a warning to anyone who sought to hurt her family.

"I will protect them," Faye said too calmly.

"How?" Sadi bit out. "My visions show me death is on our horizon. How will you stop it when you can't control your power? And look at what you did to Rune. A man you supposedly love."

Faye's power flared. The wisp arching back, ready to strike. To rend. Darkness, Faye wanted to. She looked away, struggling to reign in her strength.

"Don't fight your instincts," Sadi hissed.

"If I didn't, I'd rip your mind to pieces," Faye snapped.

Sadi's laughter shocked Faye into silence and her magic ebbed away.

"Is that why you're fighting so hard? You don't want to hurt anyone?" Sadi managed as she continued laughing. She exhaled and shook her head. "What did you think Familiar magic was? Glitter and rainbows? My kind are feared. For good reason. Our magic is inherently harmful. We touch the intangible and reach into minds to *break* them. We cripple our enemies, trapping them in their own nightmares."

Faye paled. Like she'd done to Rune. "I'm hurting people I love," Faye said softly.

"Because you need to run toward your instincts instead of away from them."

"If I ran toward them, you'd be dead." Faye's eyes widened as soon as the words left her mouth. "I'm sorry."

A genuine smile reached Sadi's dark eyes. "Acknowledging what you are is the only way to control it. Be honest with your instincts. Accept them. You are so mortal. Hung up on what you view of good and evil, when the only truth is: choice and consequence. Embrace what you are. Make your choice, and live with the consequences."

Faye's shoulders sagged as Sadi's words cooled her anger. She'd been frustrated when she pulled Rune's memories. Careless. She needed to be concise with her magic. Learn to control it, instead of letting her emotions dictate when her power rose.

Faye held up her palm. In her own bitchy way, Sadi was trying to help. Faye sighed. *It's okay if I want to kill everyone. We're not going to,* she directed the thought at the snake-tendril she envisioned lifting from her palm. *But I'm allowed to feel.*

Several moments passed, and nothing happened. She tried lifting her power with the tendril next, but only succeeded in collecting a ball of black misted shadows like her sister did.

Faye shook her hand and the shadows dissipated to nothing. "I don't know how to get my tendril out."

Sadi pursed her lips. "You don't feel it?"

"I don't feel my wings either, when they're not out."

Sadi stepped closer. "Do you feel your core?"

Faye looked down at herself. If she concentrated, her core felt like a cylinder in her chest, connected to a vast reservoir of power far below her. "I feel my core but not my tendril."

"Hold still," Sadi said. Her arm passed through Faye's chest, and she flinched. Sadi's nails slid along her core, unnerving her. She tried to step back, but Sadi gripped her shoulder. "I'll teach you how to do this after you get control of your tendril. This is one of the ways Familiar break shards. We reach into them and destroy their core."

The information her evil twin was volunteering didn't comfort Faye. She sucked a sharp breath when Sadi yanked on a connection to the power dwelling beneath her. Faye stiffened and the cord ripped out of Sadi's grasp.

"That's your tendril, you just pulled it away from me," Sadi said before withdrawing her hand. "Your first lesson is to pull your tendril out yourself. We'll continue with siphoning after you learn to control it."

Faye left her lesson with Sadi, no closer to understanding how to siphon than before. She glared at her ring. The black mist with bright purple tendrils churned with her emotions. How could she be so powerful and so useless at the same time?

She walked further into the south wing, looking for her sister. She found Sparrow at the dining table. Her sword lay over the top, and she casually flipped through a book.

"What are you reading?" Faye asked.

"Accounts of the Hunter's Moon since you won't tell me what Runey did to you," she answered without looking up.

Faye moved her sister's sword aside and took a seat. "Can you pull out your tendril, hooker?"

Sparrow blinked at her and shut the book. "Is this a trick question?"

"How do you…" Faye tapped the center of her palm with her index and lifted it a few inches before looking back at her sister.

"What, this?" Sparrow opened her hand and a thick black cord extended from her palm. It swayed slowly, as small wisps of black smoke swirled around it.

Faye glared at her empty hand. "How do you do that? After your ceremony of blood could you just feel it?"

"Sort of." Sparrow wrinkled her nose. "I guess it would be like your spine. You don't think about it when you're walking around, it's just kind of there. But if you wanted to move it you could," Sparrow said, holding her arms in front of her and arching her back to stick out her chest twice to demonstrate.

Faye dropped her hand and disappointment dug into her chest. "Yeah, well I can't arch my back."

Sparrow snorted. "Well, you're a shit dancer."

"Not helping," Faye dragged out her words as she sank into her chair. "I have all these shards, but I can't do anything."

"Your perfectionist ass needs to calm down. Did you think you would be all magical as soon as you got your shards? I still can't phase and it's been six years. Shit takes time."

Faye didn't have time. She needed to learn how to use her powers to protect her family and people from the death Sadi foresaw.

She closed her eyes concentrating on her core. On the strange connection between her well of power and the housing of her magic.

It was difficult to isolate. She managed to ease it into a rising arch, but it slipped from her control and fell limp once more. After a dozen attempts, Faye fell back in her chair staring upward.

Her sister steepled her fingers and pressed her fingertips to her lips. "Can't move your tendril?"

Faye listened to the hellfire pop and crackle in the fireplace before sighing, "I don't know."

"I can hit you with mine, and you can see if you can siphon through it. Get used to how it feels," Sparrow said, shrugging her shoulders.

Faye leaned forward. "I can siphon through your tendril?"

Sparrow nodded. "Siphoning is supposedly dangerous I think because it's a link between someone else's core and your own. If you hit someone stronger than you, they can reverse the siphoning and break your core."

Shattering your shard, Faye thought dryly. She forced a laugh through her uneasy thoughts and said, "Look at you studying and shit."

Sparrow fluffed her hair and posed with her head turned to the side. "I only make this look effortless."

Faye straightened her back and smoothed the front of her shirt. "Okay, hit me."

Sparrow held her hand up, and her tendril snapped across the table, striking Faye in the chest. Faye didn't feel the impact, but she could feel it embedded in her core. Foreign magic brushing against hers.

Faye glanced up at Sparrow. "I'm afraid to do anything."

Her sister snorted at her. "Come on, stop being a pussy."

Faye wanted to practice, but all she could think of was Sparrow sprawled over the floor with her shard drained and lifeless.

Cold took hold in her chest, like when she drank ice water on a hot summer day. Sparrow's magic streamed into her, mingling with her own. Faye recoiled from the sensation. It stopped immediately, and her sister gave her a toothy smile.

"See, that's good. You stopped my flow of power. Now try to take some. A little bit, don't suck my brain out." Sparrow held her other hand out when the color drained from Faye's face. "No, I didn't mean that. I say stupid shit. I'm sorry. I really didn't mean it like that."

"I'm afraid of hurting you," Faye muttered, unable to meet Sparrow's gaze.

Sparrow tapped the table between them, and Faye looked up at her. "What's the worst thing you can pull out of my head? You'll make me relive the time you rolled over on me and tried to squash me when we were seven?"

Faye laughed in spite of herself. "You're not funny."

"I'm fucking hilarious," Sparrow beamed. "Now, come on. You have a ridiculous amount of power. Just use a tiny bit."

"Maybe something is wrong with my tendril," Faye said absently, concentrating on the small space her magic met her sister's. "Sadi said your tendril is like a straw. I can feel what she's describing through your magic, it connecting to your core. When I did this with Rune, I didn't feel this."

Sparrow shrugged. "Maybe you have a fancy bendy straw. Everything else about you is different, why would your tendril be boring?"

Her sister was entirely too accepting. Faye needed to analyze and make sense of things, but there was so much of herself that remained a mystery. She focused on what she could control and drew on Sparrow's strength through her tendril. A minute rush of cold flitted in her chest, and Faye covered her mouth starting down at the black misted cord. She was doing it. Tears misted her lashes, and Faye blinked them away. Her eyes found her sister's, and she whispered, "I'm doing it."

"See, easy. Now go the other way," Sparrow said before adding, "Gently."

Faye whispered her power through the black cord the same way she would mentally nudge Rune and Sparrow clapped. "I'm a better teacher than your evil twin."

Faye's smile faded as she siphoned and returned power through her sister's tendril, leaving her with a single explanation.

Something was definitely wrong with her tendril.

Fifty

Daylight amplified the whites and golds in the open-air domed building. Faye walked beside Rune as he escorted her to the curved table at the edge of The Eyes. He'd slept for a few hours each day while Voshki watched over him. Over the past two weeks, the dark circles marring his gaze began to fade, but the shadows in his eyes remained.

Rune phased to his box seats, and Faye greeted the other High Council members before exchanging a look of idle courtesy with the High Queen.

Adjusting her skirts, Faye took a seat. She'd purchased this dress in Necromia with Sparrow. Her sister demanded she wear a new gown for every occasion, like the High Queen, but Faye refused to be so wasteful. She would buy a handful of dresses and rotate them throughout her meetings. During their last trip, she selected a beautiful sky-blue silk and had a halter-cut dress made with the material. She'd even ordered the back trimmed low to account for her *accidental* wings, and her sister fawned over the fine boning and laced panel squeezing Faye's waist.

Jha'ant stood and cleared his throat, opening the High Council meeting. A couple stepped into The Eyes while Faye poured her drink. A woman with diamonds woven into her elaborate braids stopped at the center of the raised platform, the male kneeling beside her. She placed her hand on his shoulder and announced him as her consort.

Dark-blood married? Faye straightened the loose pages next to her glass of pomegranate juice. The jewel adorning her ring finger shifted from purple to green in the light, and Faye smiled until she caught sight of Delilah. Seated in the front row, her hateful stare on full display. The dark-haired Queen of Lace and Bone dragged the articulated claw of her ring under her cheekbone and flicked her finger, pointing at Faye.

The gleaming metal glowed red-hot, and Delilah ripped the ring off instantly. It clattered to the marble between her feet, and she bared her fangs, snapping her attention to Rune's balcony seat.

Rune shouldn't have burned her, but it was better than reducing her hand to ash and crushing her spine beneath his shoe. Faye returned to her documents. *Baby steps.*

As she read the requests, Jha'ant called another set of names. Faye flipped through her three petitions: a barn reparation, concerns regarding The Crumbling, and...Her heart sank.

A family claimed their daughter Cleo had been abducted and was being held against her will. Her heart tore as she weighed the outcome of this petition. Cleo was either a woman who'd been kidnapped, or she was like Isobelle and fell in love with a vampire who would only see her as a refreshment. Faye folded the paper in half.

She didn't want to be forced to watch another family collapse because what she offered wasn't enough. Sighing, she focused on what she could control and looked at the first two petitions.

The first could be arranged easily. The second petition asked if the Shadow Prince was closer to ending The Crumbling.

Their concerns were valid. Without magic, they couldn't protect themselves if The Crumbling breached Rune's shields. She would speak with Alister. Rune's monthly reports should put their minds at ease.

She creased the page, setting it below the others. The afternoon dragged on without incident, and Jha'ant closed the meeting. Rune materialized beside her as the audience shuffled out. Faye glanced at where Delilah had been sitting and silently thanked the Darkness she vanished instead of continuing her attempt at intimidation.

"Shall we, love?" Rune asked.

Before she could answer, Sadi appeared on the opposing end of the table with Damian a step behind her. "Would you mind terribly if I borrowed your queen for tea?" she asked Rune sweetly before leaning toward the High Queen. A pointed smile bloomed over Sadi's lips. "Would you like to accompany us to Chaos?"

"No," she answered as the color drained from her face.

"Pity," Sadi replied, turning back to Faye.

Their surroundings changed, slowly blurring to refocus on the darker walls in Rune's great room.

"I'll see if the cardinal wants to train while the ladies are occupied," Damian said, turning toward the stairs.

"Why did the High Queen pale when you asked her if she wanted to join us?" Faye asked. Delicate was a fine meal, maybe tea was Familiar code for murder?

"I didn't ask her to join us. Accompanying a Familiar to Chaos is how you become a fixture in our realm. Bound for eternity and never freed."

The gleeful notes in Sadi's voice were disconcerting, but Faye had more pressing issues on her mind. Rune hid the strain in his eyes, but she recognized it. His few hours of sleep were overdue. "I have a previous appointment, but I can meet you for tea in a few hours."

"We're not going for tea." Sadi laughed. "Did you expect me to announce to all the realms you possess Familiar magic? I'm going to the Hall of Empty Eyes. I can teach you how to read visions while you... manage your unique tendril."

Faye turned toward Rune, and he nodded to her. "A few hours will make no difference, vsenia. Go with her, and I will await your return."

Fifty-One

Thunder crashed overhead as Faye phased to the Hall of Empty Eyes. Sadi started for the temple, completely indifferent to the bones snapping beneath her boots.

Faye glanced down. Curved bones covered the ground this time. She tentatively stepped onto the ribs, and they cracked under her weight. Her stomach turned, and Faye phased to the large double doors.

Sadi gave her a sideward glance. "Bones bothering you?"

Faye chose not to reply and pulled the door open. It creaked loudly, and the hall opened before her. The mirrored corridor extended too far to be contained by this building alone.

"Does anyone else ever come here?" Faye asked.

Sadi stepped over the threshold, continuing into the temple as she said, "Only those who serve Chaos can enter. You've seen what happens to those who hold doubt in their minds."

A few inches of polished dark wood separated safety from danger. Faye steeled herself and stepped over the threshold.

The reflections blurred, growing lighter to reveal rows of naked ashen bodies. They lined the hall standing shoulder to shoulder, silently watching her as they rhythmically swayed.

Faye forced herself to walk toward Sadi. "What do you see? Are they all staring at you?"

"They aren't staring. They're looking for doubt." Sadi paused and leaned toward her. "You don't feel them searching your mind?"

Faye shook her head. She didn't feel anything from them. The hall left a lingering dread in the pit of her soul, and she fought the urge to flee from this unnatural place.

The Familiar assessed her, tapping the clawed point of her ring on her lip. "Your magic is similar to ours, but not entirely. You wield it differently."

Faye stepped away from Sadi to face the mirrors, but the cloudy-eyed vessels were no better than Sadi picking through her mind. Faye pressed her lips together and asked, "You wanted to teach me about Familiar visions?"

"Descend into yourself and step out of the confines of your mind."

Faye's brow lowered as she turned toward the Familiar. "Isn't that just phasing? Where your mind goes, the body follows?"

"Familiar magic is not the same. You feel the depth of other people's strength, their connection to the Darkness."

Faye nodded, attempting to follow Sadi's logic.

Sadi pressed her fingers between her breasts. "That connection is where we descend to gather power quickly. Familiar who serve Chaos are able to step out of that space and into the void. True Familiar magic resides there. It is how we see the past and have visions of the future."

"Where you witness a person's life through their woven cord?" Faye asked.

Sadi nodded. "Don't handle any cords. They snap easily, and the consequences of cutting a life short are far-reaching."

The thought of a life cut short because a Familiar clumsily handled them terrified Faye. "Has anyone warred against Morbid?"

Sadi leaned back on her heels and folded her arms. After a moment she said, "Not to my knowledge, but my father doesn't participate in war."

"Why?" It seemed like the war would be over before it began if all Morbid had to do was snap the life threads of his enemies. Who could stop him?

Sadi shrugged. "Who is he to stand in the way of fate?"

"But your court went to war," Faye said.

A satisfied smile spread over Sadi's lips. "Many times."

"Why wouldn't your father help?"

Sadi's expression pinched as though she asked a simple question she should know the answer to. "Chaos gifts us with Sight because we worship fate and are free of doubt. Morbid allows fate to unfold as it was meant to. Twisting fate stems from fear, and fear breeds doubt. Taking that path will leave you blind. A Familiar without Sight is no Familiar at all."

"But you use your visions to help Rune." If Familiar were supposed to sit back and watch fate unfold without interfering, Sadi should have lost her Sight a dozen times over.

Sadi smiled again, like she was in on a joke Faye didn't understand. "It is my fate to be tied to the Shadow Prince."

To follow him around, more like, Faye thought bitterly. Morbid didn't interfere because he wanted fate to run its course, and all Sadi did was interfere because she believed she was fated to him. Faye wondered if Familiar simply did what they wanted and screamed fate when they were questioned. Sparrow did it often enough.

Faye exhaled a sigh and let the subject drop. She descended into herself, and Sadi slowly faded until Faye was alone in the Hall of Empty Eyes.

"How do I step outside of my mind?" Faye asked.

"Carry your awareness," Sadi said.

Faye glanced up. It was strange hearing Sadi's voice from far above her. Carry her awareness? Sadi might as well tell her to get her wings out. "I don't understand what that means."

Faye felt pressure at the edge of her mind and stiffened.

"Stop fighting me. I'm trying to pull your awareness so you can feel it." Faye didn't answer, and Sadi released an exasperated breath before adding, "I'm not going to rifle through your mind."

"How do you know what I'm thinking if you're not poking around in my head?" Faye snapped.

"Because that's what everyone thinks," Sadi answered with equal venom.

Faye quieted and relaxed her mental barriers, begrudgingly letting Sadi in.

"I can't descend to your depth, so you won't see me," Sadi said, her voice still above Faye but felt closer this time. "You are within your body now. You need to take a step outside of it."

Faye followed the strange tugging sensation and took an imagined step forward. "It feels like pushing my senses past my body."

"You aren't moving. Follow your senses past the bindings of the flesh," Sadi said.

Faye visualized the double doors leading into the hall. *Like phasing but not*, Faye told herself. She moved past her physical body, a force tugging her back like a string until her physical body snapped to meet her.

Faye mouthed a curse, staring at the doors she visualized.

"This is the simplest form of Familiar magic. Why can't you do this?"

Faye didn't care for her accusatory tone, but she had no choice if she wanted to learn. She turned and walked back to Sadi. "I'm trying."

"Try harder."

Faye closed her eyes and descended into herself again. *Just step out of my body*, Faye thought dryly. She envisioned a phantom version of herself stepping out of her flesh. It was endless and spanning. A boundless ocean ready to swallow her, and Faye knew she would never find her way back once she was swallowed by its depths.

"Are you shaking?"

Faye squeezed her hands to her chest, tucking her elbows to her side. She cracked her eyes open, terrified of what she would see. She stood on what felt like solid ground. It was covered with a layer of the Darkness high enough to cover her ankles and obscure her boots.

Faye's eyes lifted to a clicking sound, and Sadi strolled toward her, unbothered by the abyss surrounding them or the Darkness blanketing her feet.

"This feels like the mirrors. When I reached into Prin's mind before she came back."

Sadi nodded. "This is Chaos. You'll get used to it." She took a step back, glancing around at absolutely nothing. "This is where you pull woven cords. You call them the same way you summoned Prinia, but we'll save that lesson for another day. Stay here but ascend back to the physical plane. Don't return to your body."

Faye focused on her position and ascended slowly. Her surroundings slowly took shape, becoming clearer the closer she got to the surface. Faye turned around, startled by her physical body. She looked so much like Sadi. Her eyes were completely dilated, obscuring her golden streaks.

"With practice you won't have to descend first to step outside your body. This is where we have visions and can look into a location's past," Sadi explained.

"How do I have visions?"

"You ask them," Sadi said as she turned and strolled further into the temple with an effortless feline grace. "Chaos clouds the visions each time you ask a question. The first vision will be the clearest. The second will be muddled. I've never asked more than three."

Just ask them, Faye mimicked Sadi in her mind. It sounded so simple. She stared up at the male in front of her and asked, *Hey, why does my evil twin look like me?*

Faye went rigid at the sound of hundreds of feet shifting. Her breaths grew short as the vessels leaned their heads back and opened their mouths wide. The same way they had when they attacked Alister and Prin.

Faye stepped back, waiting for the wet tearing sound and the pain to follow.

The vessels answered as one. Their haunting voice slipped from their unmoving mouths, echoing through the hall.

Flesh made for temptation.

Faye shuddered a breath and snapped her attention to Sadi. "Did you hear them?"

Sadi tensed, stepping closer. She glanced at the mirrors then back to Faye. "They spoke to you?"

Faye watched as the vessels relaxed into their normal state, silently watching her. "How do they show your visions?"

"They *don't* speak," Sadi said quickly. "The vessels part and show me scenes. They impart emotions, and words sometimes appear on the mirrors. The only time they speak is to tear at a mind. Few have heard them and fewer survive the ordeal."

Faye studied the rows of ashen bodies.

"Ask them how to stop The Crumbling," Sadi said. "You may have to rephrase it, wording is important."

"How will The Crumbling be stopped?" Faye asked.

The empty-eyed vessels tipped their heads back and opened their mouths wide. Their single voice sent a chill through Faye.

A choice and a consequence.

Faye repeated the words, and Sadi folded her arms. She tapped the claw of her articulated ring against her bottom lip, and asked, "What was the first question you asked?"

"It's private," Faye said, reluctant to share her thoughts.

She expected Sadi to press, but the Familiar stepped back with a nod. She turned to the mirrors. "Ask your third question. I'll make sure you don't return to Rune an empty shell."

Faye returned her attention to the mirrors. Their eerie unified voice still echoed in her mind. *Who are we meant to tempt?*

The empty-eyed vessels tilted their heads back once more. *The Creator's son.*

Sadi said the answers would become more unclear, but did they lie? The Creator didn't have a son, only a daughter.

The High Queen.

Fifty-Two

Rune returned to his study after Faye and Sadi departed. The rest he found with his queen lessened the constant pounding at his temples, but his concentration remained in shambles. The bone-bleached tomes he'd borrowed from Morbid's library over a month ago sat quietly on the corner of his desk. He should have finished them within a week, but with the current state of his mind, he couldn't bring himself to look over more than a few pages at a time.

Faye's features mirrored a goddess who existed before Saith's reign and The Creator called her a thorn in his side. But for all Rune's efforts and research, he was no closer to uncovering Faye's heredity. Taking his seat, he opened the leather tome and stared at the pages he had no desire to read.

Why does it matter? Our queen has her shards. You waste your time with books when we could be with Faye, the creature grated.

Rune exhaled. For all it claimed to know, the Ra'Voshnik under-stood very little. *Do you honestly believe she carries as much power as she does, without reason?*

Annoyance rippled from the creature. *You don't need to know every-thing. I feel your fears. No one will take her from us. Unraveling her race won't make her any less mortal. We will serve her will and await her return.*

Rune thinned his lips. "We both know magic needs balance. There must be a reason she is this strong."

The Ra'Voshnik idly floated through his mind. *Why do we carry three Shards of Darkness? What reason do we have?*

Carrying his shards was undoubtedly an oddity but one that could occur naturally. Faye's shards were unlike any he'd seen, and she carried ten of them. He needed more information to understand how to best safeguard his queen.

You try so hard to be miserable when happiness is right in front of you. If she's the Elysian Queen, she's a goddess.

Rune glanced at the imaging crystal of Faye framed on his desk. He didn't believe in gods. They were only powerful men and women naming themselves as such. The Creator being one of them, and he would never allow Faye to be used as a pawn in their games.

The Ra'Voshnik growled its agreeance, and Rune resigned himself to his research. After an hour, pain lanced his mind. His night breeze had returned and phased into the great room. She stood quietly for a few moments before her footsteps approached his study. The Ra'Voshnik purred as she turned into the doorway. A hint of a smile crossed her lips, but the sentiment didn't lend to her light-ning-streaked midnight gaze.

The creature's mood soured, and it grated, *If your cat upset our queen, I'm going to take my time making her suffer.*

Rune closed his book and asked, "Are you well, love?" Sadi's absence was certainly disconcerting. But visions were taxing, and his queen would not have looked to Sadi for comfort or support.

Faye remained silent and took the seat across his bloodroot desk. The swing of the grandfather clock's pendulum marked the moments of silence, and Rune phased to materialize beside her. He leaned back on his desk and whispered, "Speak with me, vsenia. What is troubling you?"

Faye gazed up and reached for his hand. Her fingers curled

around his as she breathed, "The visions… they worry me."

"How so?" Rune asked gently, curious as to what she had seen—and why Sadi had not advised him of his queen's distress.

Faye looked away. "I asked them why Sadi and I look the same. They told me we're flesh made for temptation."

The pain laced in her voice twisted Rune's heart. Sadi had been a fixture in his life, but her loyalty and friendship did not compare to his utter devotion to Faye. "Familiar speak in riddles. It is no surprise the visions do as well."

Faye lifted her chin to face him. "They said we were made to tempt The Creator's son."

The Ra'Voshnik bristled. *I told you we should have killed him.*

The creature had resisted Saith from the start. In the awkward years of his youth, when the Ra'Voshnik had initially surfaced, Rune struggled to contain it. The creature's veined misted shadows regularly bled through his gaze.

On one such occasion, Saith had struck him and said, *Silence your creature. If you can't control it, I have no further use for you.* Later during the night Alister had found him and the mark on his face. The creature had slipped Rune's hold and taken control of his body, hissing *frail blood* at his brother.

Rather than admitting the Ra'Voshnik had taken hold, Rune claimed the insult and drove the first wedge between them.

Rune pushed the memories away and answered, "I learned early on not to pain myself over Familiar riddles. Chaos is never orderly and will always be skewed from reason."

Faye shifted in her chair. "They said The Crumbling would end with a choice and a consequence."

"Vsenia, it is like saying the day will begin with a dawn. Our lives are a series of choices and consequences."

She nodded softly. "It's just… I have a bad feeling."

And he was no help. Between her court duties and assisting him with a few hours of sleep, there was little time left for herself. Faye lost track of time often, unknowingly skipping meals. A thing she would remember if she wasn't so preoccupied with his nightmares. Guilt festered in him. He should be caring for his queen, not adding to her list of tasks.

"The Familiar realm is unnerving. It will pass, love. A hot meal and a bath would be good for you," Rune said, lifting her hand.

Faye stood and lightly clasped his fingers. She started toward the door and glanced back at him over her shoulder. "We'll have dinner after you sleep."

Rune followed her to their room, loosening his tie as Faye entered her closet. She slid the hangers aside, and Rune stiffened at the sound of scraping metal. Revulsion curdled in him as memories of Sadira's iron chair echoed through his mind.

Easy, the creature said, replacing his tainted recollections with ones of Faye bathed in sunlight, while she meticulously weeded her garden. *She's looking for a nightgown. Ground yourself in our queen.*

Rune inhaled, focusing on Faye's scent. He was home. He was safe. He was with his night breeze.

Get that look off your face before our queen sees it and worries, the creature grated.

Rune masked his expression and removed his coat as Faye changed into her white nightgown. She crawled into bed and sat against the headboard.

"Sleeping twice a day is no longer necessary. I have sufficiently recovered," Rune said from the edge of their bed.

Faye dragged his pillow onto her lap and patted it. "Quit being so stubborn and let me take care of you."

Watching over you helps alleviate her guilt. Lay. Down, the Ra'Voshnik said through its teeth.

Rune's fangs lengthened. *Be silent.*

He rested his head on Faye's lap. Her fingertips glided along his brow and continued past his temple. The tension in his body began to unravel, and Rune closed his eyes. Exhaustion tugged at his awareness, dragging him into the soothing dark of slumber.

Faye gently stroked Rune's white-blonde hair. She managed to draw up her snake-tendril but hadn't told Sadi. She stared down at her vampire's calm features. If Faye was honest with herself, she feared her magic. Her power was limitless, but it demanded a price each time she called on it. The cost to Rune had been too great, and he continued to suffer for her inexperience.

Veined misted shadows flowed over the tops of his cheekbones, and Voshki opened his eyes. He rose on his arms and purred, leaning into her.

"I need you to watch him for me," Faye whispered.

"You won't wake him. He's not at the fore," Voshki answered.

He smoothed his palm down her arm, leaving a trail of warmth, and Faye sighed. Voshki pulled her under him and rolled onto his back, tucking her to his side. Her men couldn't be more different. Rune avoided physical contact, and Voshki was touch starved, always holding her close.

His scent of amber and sandalwood surrounded her with a hint of… Faye leaned against him, inhaling deeply—an underlining hint of warmth and a scent she didn't recognize.

The backs of Voshki's black-tipped claws glided along her spine as he chuckled beneath her. "Are you sniffing me?"

"You smell really good. Are you using something new?" Faye asked.

Voshki moved in a blur, and Faye's eyes widened as she sucked a breath. She stared up at her beautiful hunter, caged beneath his body. A strand of his long white-blonde hair fell forward, sweeping over her collarbone. His wholly black eyes gleamed with sexual heat, reflecting centuries of longing, need, and desire.

He bent forward, touching his lips to hers in a soft chaste kiss and rasped, "No, but if you like my scent so much, I'll happily cover you in it."

Faye clasped her hand over Voshki's mouth and attempted to maintain a stern look but failed to keep the laughter out of her eyes. "I need you to focus."

He pulled her hand away and smirked. "I'm very focused if that was unclear," Voshki said, rolling his hips.

His hardened length pressed against her thigh, and Faye bit the inside of her lip. She missed his touch and all the pleasure it promised, but she didn't want Rune to wake to find her with Voshki. Or worse, trigger his nightmares.

"Rune isn't in a good place," Faye said quietly. "I don't want to make it worse."

Voshki lowered himself, brushing the side of his face against hers. "The Darkness blessed us with a thoughtful queen."

"I don't think I'm much of a blessing," Faye said, running her fingers over Voshki's shoulder.

He pulled back to gaze down at her. "You are everything we've dreamed and wished for."

But she wasn't. Guilt stung Faye's eyes. "I hurt him."

"Vsenia," Voshki said. He paused, searching her eyes. "The Shadow Prince should have told you why he doesn't allow anyone to siphon from him, and why he hates the scent of others on his body. Don't blame yourself for the hardships we suffered. He wouldn't want that and neither do I."

Faye looked away, staring off at Hell's ever-twilight sky over Voshki's shoulder. He nipped her throat before returning to his side of the bed and dragging her against him. She rested her head on his chest, and Voshki wrapped her in his arms, holding her tight.

"Your Shadow Prince's mind is quiet. He's sleeping soundly. If you promise to stop feeling guilty, I'll promise not to kick him awake."

Faye bit down on his chest with enough force to sting but not cause any real harm.

A purr rumbled from Voshki the same moment he fisted her hair. He pulled it tight for a moment before releasing her. Faye lifted her head and kissed the indents she left on his skin.

"If you want to bite, move a little lower," Voshki rasped, watching her.

Faye's brows pinched. He couldn't mean. "You want me to bite you there?"

"Don't look so squeamish," Voshki teased as the corner of his mouth lifted. "If you were a vampire, I would have had you sink your little fangs into my cock a dozen times by now."

Faye's lips parted. "Doesn't that hurt?"

"Does my bite hurt?"

Faye settled against him, wondering what else Rune and Voshki were missing because she wasn't a vampire. It would be a subject she'd bring up later when Rune was feeling more like himself. She took a deep breath, letting his new scent wash over her. Whatever it was, she loved it.

Voshki slipped his hand behind his head and glanced down at

her. "I'll watch your Shadow Prince, but you need to eat."

"I'll eat after he wakes up."

He raised a brow, and Faye stared up at him. He slipped from bed without a word and bent forward, gathering her in his arms.

"What are you doing?" Faye said, squirming in his hold.

Voshki gently set her on her feet and said, "You've had one meal today. We're going to the kitchen."

Faye sat at the edge of the bed. "I'm in a nightgown."

He canted his head and purred softly. "You're covered." When Faye made no move to stand, he started toward the door.

"Where are you going?" Faye asked. She pulled on her robe and chased after him when he turned down the hall. "Voshki!"

He glanced over his shoulder and said, "To get you something to eat. Your sister always has food in her den."

"You're not supposed to be out," Faye said, grabbing his arm.

Voshki stopped mid-stride and leaned back on his heels. "The Shadow Prince didn't want me leaving Hell, and I've met Vashien."

If he had, Sparrow would have run her mouth, and Faye would have known. Which meant he met Vashien when he was alone. "When did you meet Vash?"

"When we asked your sister what jewel you wanted for an engagement ring." He nudged her forward by the small of her back. "I'll return to our room after you've eaten."

Faye was hungry. This would be a quick ten-minute meal, and they could return to their bedroom. She walked with him into the great room. *Are you watching Rune?* she asked in his mind as they climbed the stairs.

His mind is easy. I'm getting better at keeping the nightmares away, Voshki answered. He glanced down at her and caught her hand, intertwining his fingers with hers. "It's nice," he said, lifting their hands as the corner of his mouth tilted upward, "holding you in the flesh."

A pang of guilt stung Faye. It was unfair to hide Voshki. He was a person. The scent of roasted meat pulled Faye from her thoughts. Her mouth watered, and Faye's stomach knotted. A platter of cubed meats and cheeses were arranged with slices of fruit.

Faye took an apple slice as she sat down. She took a bite, and Voshki picked up a plate, piling it high with a variety of snacks before setting it in front of her.

"Eat, vsenia," he said as he poured her tea.

Faye moved the dish closer and Voshki pulled his chair up beside her, sitting so close their legs touched. He leaned back in his seat and rested his arm on the back of hers as she ate. She cast him an amused glance. He was so unlike Rune.

"I almost had him," Sparrow's voice carried through the corridor.

Vashien's wing shadowed crossed the doorway. "He disarmed you and knocked you on your ass."

Her sister snorted. "If I had a better sword—"

She stopped in the hall, staring, and Vashien flared his wings to stop himself from running into her. "Darkness, Runey. Fucking, scared me," Sparrow said, rubbing her fingers over her heart. To Faye, she said, "Those are the eyes you like? I couldn't perform under those conditions."

Before Faye could speak, her vampire leaned forward. "I'm not the Shadow Prince." The color drained from Vashien's face as Voshki said, "Ra'Voshnik."

Sparrow's face lit, and Vashien caught her by the arm. "Oh! You're her Yoshi. Voshi? What the fuck does she call you?"

"Voshki," Faye answered, slipping her hand through the crook in his arm and giving him a small tug. She couldn't hope to overpower him, but this small gesture would let him know she wanted him to remain seated.

She hoped.

He leaned up, pulling against Faye's hold as Sparrow, and Vash took their seats. Voshki inhaled deeply and exhaled, baring his fangs. "You. Keep your scent off my mate, or I'll tear your wings from your ba—"

Faye clamped her hand over Voshki's mouth. "You can't say that!" She turned toward Vash. "I'm so sorry."

Voshki shook free of Faye's hold. "She's not sorry, and I don't make idle threats."

Faye giggled, taking Voshki's face between her hands. She turned him toward her and struggled to keep a straight face. "You can't just say whatever pops into your head—"

"Why? She does," Voshki said, lifting his chin at Sparrow.

Faye smoothed her hand over his cheek. "It's not appropriate. Be nice." A low growl rumbled past his lips, and she added, "Please."

"As you command," he said begrudgingly before turning his attention to Vashien. "If I catch your scent on my queen, I'll *break* your wings." Faye jabbed him in the ribs, and he smiled down at her. "Yes, love."

"Nice," she hissed.

"Fuck nice. Tell me what you did to her on the Hunter's Moon," Sparrow said through a wide toothy grin.

Voshki smiled at her sister. "I didn't do a thing to her."

Fifty-Three

Rune snapped awake as the Ra'Voshnik backhanded the side of his foot. The mindscape he shaped into a replica of his bedroom rippled as tension and anger gnawed at him. He slept on his side of the bed as he did in their physical bedroom. The creature meandered closer, running its blacked-tipped claws over the dark silk sheets.

It leaned over him, ignoring the growing strain between them. "You're starting to look better. Another week and you might make a full recovery," it said, offering Rune a hand.

He hesitated, contemplating its behavior. The creature fought him incessantly during his first century and now watched over him while he slept, by his queen's command. Rune silently wondered if he would have watched over the creature if their circumstances had been reversed. He didn't have to dwell long to know the answer.

The creature dropped its hand. "I'm not helping you out of the goodness of my heart. Seeing you wounded upsets our queen."

Rune bared his fangs as he got out of bed. "I am not wounded."

The creature idly studied his nightstand and opened the top drawer. "Your mind bleeds memories you don't want," it said, rifling through the neatly arranged stationery. It closed the drawer and glanced back at him. "What would you call it?"

Rune's weakness frayed his patience, and worse, the creature knew his thoughts—His turmoil. "Be silent," he grated.

"No," it said, stepping closer to him. "You can't dismiss me. Not anymore. Our queen favors my company over yours."

"It is easy to be favored when you lack will and conviction. You tread through fair weather. You have never faced choices or lived with their consequences."

"And what choices have you made?" the Ra'Voshnik asked. Its voice was laced with sweet venom. "You told the frail blood she was your whore."

Rune tensed as memories of Faye's tear-stained eyes rekindled in vivid detail. The sound of her footfalls when she ran from him.

"I saved her," Rune bit out, unconvinced of the truth in his words.

The Ra'Voshnik scoffed. "I would have eliminated the threat."

"You risk too much," Rune shouted. "Alister would have slit her throat. If you possessed the capacity to think beyond your cock, you would understand this."

The creature clenched its jaw and growled, "I love her."

"You love fucking her," Rune answered in equal venom.

"I should be inciting your nightmares and driving you to madness," the creature hissed. "Do you know why I don't? The only reason I've spared you." It jabbed him in the chest with two fingers, punctuating the last. "I love her more than I hate you!"

Rune growled, leaning closer, until his lips were at the creature's ear. "The feeling is mutual."

The Ra'Voshnik shoved him away and ran a hand through its hair. "At least tell Faye I can tend to her while you're sleeping. You may not have the appetite to have her beneath you, but I can assure you, I still hunger for our queen."

Rune dismissed the creature and ascended to his physical body.

Faye slept, snoring softly on his chest with her arm thrown over his torso, and her legs tangled around his. The soft curves of her body molded against his side, and their sheets bunched low on her waist.

Do you need my blessing when you have already tended to her? Rune asked the Ra'Voshnik.

Do you even look at my memories before you open your mouth? the creature snapped, prowling the edges of his mind as it watched their queen.

He had not. He'd assumed the creature would spend its time fucking Faye, and Rune wasn't in the frame of mind to witness its debauchery.

I've tried, but she declines my offers. She said she was hot and stripped a few hours ago. I tried to pull the blanket over so she wouldn't catch a chill, and she bit me, the creature chuckled.

Rune thanked the Darkness the Ra'Voshnik left him clothed, and it growled through his mind. *Don't reject her affection. You'll turn her from us.*

Be silent, Rune snapped, agitated by the creature's incessant prattle. He pulled the sheets over Faye, and her expression soured before she kicked them away. *Minx,* he thought while weaving a warming spell around her. He stroked her hair, listening to the quiet cadence of her heart. A faint, rapid whooshing sound overlapped with... another? Rune tuned his ear, straining to isolate the sounds. His breath left him as he stared down at Faye. Her dark hair gleamed in the soft light of Hell's ever-twilight sky.

His queen was pregnant... with twins.

Tell her. It will make her happy, the creature purred.

No, Rune answered. Several races possessed heightened hearing, and it was not socially acceptable to reveal certain conditions their senses uncovered. *She will discover them on her own soon. Let her come to us.*

I'm the father of our queen's young. Those two are mine, the Ra'Voshnik said entirely too pleased with itself.

Possessive aggression steeped his mind. His body begot his young onto his queen, not the parasite he shared his queen's affection with.

The Ra'Voshnik chuckled. *I can share. If they take your lineage as a Shadowman, they're yours, but we both know my twins will be Pure Bloods. So they're mine.*

Rune growled through his mind without realizing he'd done so aloud. Faye's nails dug into his side. She grumbled, rubbing her face on his chest. "I'm tired, Voshki."

The Ra'Voshnik laughed itself hoarse as he said, "Rune, vsenia."

Faye lifted her head immediately, blinking several times. Her tone was much softer as she asked, "How did you sleep?"

"Apparently better than you. Is the Ra'Voshnik not allowing you to rest?" Rune asked, and the creature dragged its claws over his awareness.

"Voshki has been sweet." She paused and added, "He met Sparrow and Vash last night."

"What?"

I didn't leave Hell, the creature argued as it calmly drifted through his mind.

"Please don't be upset with him. He's a person. When we have children, I want them to be friends with their Ra'Voshniks."

Tell her! the creature roared.

Be. Silent. Rune tucked a strand of hair behind Faye's ear. "We will have years to discuss your wishes. The Ra'Voshnik manifests as the body matures into adulthood." Faye nodded and curled up beside him. "Are you well, vsenia?"

"I'm just tired and hungry," Faye said, pulling the dark silk sheets around her to create a barrier between their bodies.

Rune was grateful for her care, but knew she blamed herself for his memories. He turned to his side, offering her the quiet intimacy he was capable of. "What would you like to eat?"

Faye scratched her nose and stretched her back. "Chicken fingers and clam chowder from Lost and Found," she mumbled through a yawn.

An odd combination, but Rune was certainly not going to point it out.

You're smarter than you look, the Ra'Voshnik snickered.

Rune ignored it and called his obsidian talisman, stretching his arm over Faye to the side of the bed she abandoned in favor of his. He set the black stone on the bed and touched his finger to it.

"Go to a tavern called Lost and Found in the merchant district and bring me an order of their chicken fingers and a bowl of clam chow—"

Faye tapped his arm and held up two fingers.

"Two bowls of clam chowder," Rune corrected.

The creature brushed the surface and growled, *She's going to get sick if she eats all of that.*

Did you want to advise her on what she should be eating?

It bristled at his question, and without a word sank deep into his mind.

Faye's silky hair slid over his side as she sat up. His queen leaned forward to retrieve her discarded nightgown, and he admired the elegant curve of her back. She was so beautiful. Rune ran the backs of his fingers down her spine as she pulled the simple blue gown over her head.

"Is a waiter from Obsidian going to order my food from Vash's place?" Faye asked, adjusting the sheets at her waist as she crossed her legs.

"I am not sure. I imagine they have a runner collecting your breakfast."

Faye folded her hands in her lap and studied her nails. "I'll need to check with Alister today. There's another woman being held by a dark court. I'm worried she's like Isabelle, and their parents think they've been kidnapped when they're actually in love with an asshole incapable of loving them back."

His queen's unspoken wounds cut him as deeply as they injured her. "I know this is difficult for you. I can check on her if you wish."

Faye shook her head. "This is the realm I wanted to create. I need to be present."

Rune schooled his expression. Her people would never know how she suffered so they might have the life she dreamed of. "I will speak with Alister."

A pleasant chime sounded a few moments later, and a silver tray appeared on Faye's side of the bed. She scooted back and placed the tray between them, laughing. "I forget you don't eat sometimes," she said, dunking a strip of breaded chicken into the bowl of clam chowder and taking a bite.

Rune made idle conversation as she ate, silently adjusting the spells maintaining his estate. He cooled the hot spring and the water throughout his home to a safe temperature for his queen and young.

We need to tell her. What will you do when she uses magic to heat her bath?

the creature snapped.

His lessons had not included heating water, and there would be little need for it. He drew her bath each morning and washed her hair. *She will discover her pregnancy in less than a week. Leave her be.*

Rune reached for Alister's mind as Faye finished her last piece of chicken. *Brother.*

Alister's gravelly voice rang through his mind. *What?*

Rune leashed his anger. His brother's wrath was justified. *Apologies for disturbing you. Faye received a petition from a mother claiming her daughter is being held against her will.*

Alister remained silent for a time. *I will look into it after lunch. I received a copy of her correspondence. My wife is particularly lucid today. You are not welcome here.*

Rune was a moment from snapping the tie between them and paused. His queen sought peace between himself and his brother. *I am glad Prinia—*

Do. Not. Speak my wife's name, Alister hissed before severing the mental link.

Rune smiled to mask his aggravation as Faye finished her second bowl of soup and pushed the tray away. "I think I ate too much. I might need a nap," Faye said as she curled on her side and clutched his pillow to her.

The creature chuckled. *You wouldn't be so feared if they could see the way you fawn over our queen hugging your bedding.*

Rune didn't reply and vanished the tray. He smoothed his hand over Faye's thigh, straightening the hem of her nightgown. "Can I draw you a bath, love?"

Faye nodded. "That would be nice. Thank you."

Rune went to the soaking tub and opened the faucet. He selected a floral oil Faye favored and a milky white vial used to soften skin. The water clouded after he added the vials and set the short bamboo stool at the head of the tub.

He leaned in the doorway, gazing at his queen. In a matter of months, she would be heavy with his young. The corner of Rune's mouth lifted. Undeniably his.

Ours, the Ra'Voshnik interjected. *And they're my young.*

Faye rolled over to face him, and Rune unfasted his cuffs. He began meticulously rolling up his sleeves as he imagined twin boys with his pale coloring. The creature quickly replaced one of the males with a girl. Her dark hair and lightning-streaked midnight eyes matched their mothers.

Faye wants a son and a daughter, it said.

Worry soured his mood. What kind of father would he be? He had so little to offer. Saith was no example to follow, and his own father Julian, while devoted to his mother, was woefully uninvolved in his upbringing.

We're not them. You'll be a good father. We'll offer them the same devotion we freely give their mother.

He would be present in his offspring's early years and immerse himself in their lives. Reading them stories in the mornings and teaching them to speak High Tongue at night. Rune hid the smile tugging at the corners of his mouth. Perhaps he could teach Faye and their young together.

Rune hesitated before speaking into his mind, *Thank you.*

Fifty-Four

Faye smiled as her vampire leaned in their bathroom doorframe. The tendons and muscles in his forearm flexed as Rune finished rolling his sleeve into a neat cuff above his elbow. A few months ago, she would have been laughing with him as she dragged him back to bed.

But she'd hurt him.

Her vampire needed time to regain the balance she stripped from him, and she was reluctant to use her magic.

"Your bath is ready, love," he said quietly. "I am sorry. The temperature is a little cooler than you favor. I had not considered the additional court members in resident and the water reserves we would need. It will be a few days before it returns to normal."

Faye smiled, getting out of bed. "I'm sure it's fine," she said, slipping past him. Blue clouded her vision as she pulled her nightgown over her head. She discarded the cotton slip on the counter and stepped into the bath. The milky water was warm enough. Faye sank into the heat and leaned back on the lip of the tub.

She glanced at her vampire and giggled. He folded her night-gown and placed it near the dark wood tray holding his toiletries. She leaned up to see if her garment was equally spaced between the tray and the marble edge and laughed when she saw it was.

"You're so tidy," Faye teased.

Rune arched a brow at her as he sat at the head of the tub. He placed his hand behind her neck, and Faye relaxed, letting him guide her down.

"And you, my queen, have not made your bed once."

Rune held her face above the water, and Faye cracked her lids to find him smiling down at her. She stuck the tip of her tongue out at him, and to her surprise, her solemn vampire responded in kind. She laughed while he lifted her head out of the water.

Faye sighed as he worked the cleaning oils over her scalp. Tingles spread down her neck and over her shoulders. His touch was bliss.

He rinsed her hair, and she sat up so he could smooth the con-ditioning balm into her hair. Faye stared down at her hand under the white cloudy water. She drew up her tendril, and the shadowed snake rose from her palm. Her serpent lifted out of the water, and Rune's stroking fingers stopped.

"You have been practicing," he said.

The smile in his voice stung her heart. Faye closed her hand, and her tendril faded. "Can I ask you something?"

"You can ask me anything, vsenia."

"You don't have to answer. I'm… I'm trying to understand how this thing works," Faye said, lifting her hand above her shoul-der. "Were you… thinking about those memories, or does my snake friend just find everything awful and drag them to the surface?"

Rune's silence intensified her apprehension. Faye shrank into herself. She shouldn't have said anything. How could she be so in-sensitive? "I'm sorry. I've been able to draw out my tendril, but I'm afraid to use it. Sadi said Familiar magic is inherently destructive. I don't want it if all it does is hurt people."

"Be easy," Rune murmured as he stroked her with the back of his fingers. "Your tendril did not seek out my memories. I was thinking of them."

Faye curled forward and hugged her knees. "I don't know if that makes me feel better or worse." She failed him in so many ways. He physically distanced himself from her. She wasn't enough to keep his nightmares at bay.

He'd been so good to her, and she repaid his kindness and understanding with pain.

Rune began smoothing the balm through her hair again. His voice was hollow as he spoke. "You saw the Queen?" Faye blinked and slowly nodded. "She resembles Lyssa's daughter, Morgan, because she's her grandmother."

Faye's stomach knotted. She glanced over her shoulder in his direction. She couldn't see him, but at least it felt more like a conversation than him speaking to her back. "Did they capture the High Queen too?"

Another bout of silence rang between them. He finished her hair and said, "Lyssa freely became involved with the Queen's son, and his court took her. He was killed freeing her, and I departed to purge their court."

Faye turned to face him, taking his hand. "You don't have to talk about it."

He stared into her bathwater, strain tightening the corner of his pale blue eyes. "I do not wish to keep secrets from you. Vague accounts were reported to conceal the type of magic their court possessed."

Faye saw the bitch wearing Rune's ring around her neck. What kind of magic was strong enough to stop him? He wore three Shards of Darkness.

Her vampire took a deep breath and spoke quietly, "The Queen's name was Sadira. She was a girl when the Great War occurred. Her people sided with Saith. When my father won, he killed his brethren and slaughtered the races who fought against him. Julian acquired a dagger with the ability to sever your tie to the Darkness. He used it to slit Sadira's throat, but she survived. She aged into her power and invoked her blood, reconnecting to the Darkness."

Faye's mouth went dry. His father murdered children? She silently wondered how Rune managed to have any moral standing raised by men like Saith and his father.

His deep, accented voice drew her back to the present. "Her blood retained the ability to sever you from the Darkness."

"She made you drink her blood?" Faye asked quietly.

"No," Rune said with a humorless chuckle. "I would have chosen to starve. She forged metal collars made with inward facing barbs. They poured vials of her blood over the spikes and closed the collars over our necks."

Anger crackled through Faye's power, rousing it from its deep slumber. She wanted to hurt them. To choir their screams in a symphony of agony. She pushed aside the vicious urges and whispered, "I'm sorry I made you relive those memories."

He met her gaze then, heart sore and pained. "You did not do this to me, vsenia. The reason I thought of those memories is because she used tendrils to subdue me. They spelled women to strike my shields and draw unchecked amounts of power. The backlash destroyed them. I had never experienced warfare like it, and I hesitated. One moment cost me a hundred and thirty-seven years. They broke my shield and drained my core. Sadira depleted her arsenal capturing me."

"This is the reason I am not used as a well when Sadi needs power. Why I have no tolerance for the scent of women on me." Faye pulled her hand away, and Rune caught her wrist. "Except you, vsenia," he said, bringing her hand to his lips. "It is not my intention to push you away."

Tears stung her eyes. "But I hurt you."

Rune went to his knees and drew her closer until her head rested on his shoulder. "You have done nothing but be patient while I sort through my memories."

Faye tried to pull back, but Rune held her close. "I'm getting you wet."

"It matters not."

She blinked, leaning into him. "How… How long did the nightmares last when you came home the first time?"

"Decades," Rune answered.

Faye stiffened, calculating the years. She would be thirty-six—forty-six before he could sleep comfortably again.

Rune murmured comforting sounds and said, "I was alone, vsenia. I have you, love, to ground me and calm my mind."

"And Voshki watches you while you sleep," Faye added.

A puff of breath tickled her ear. "I am still debating if that is a boon or a curse." Rune paused. "I am not able to suitably tend to you, but your Voshki can."

"I don't want—"

"I am able to disengage from my physical body. It will not disturb me. The creature misses you."

"No." She wasn't going to discard him and use his body. "We're in this together, and when you are ready, we can all be affectionate."

Rune chuckled, and Faye looked up in time to see the veined, misted shadows stretch from beneath his eyes, swaying over his cheekbones.

"As you command, vsenia."

Fifty-Five

D uring Alister's research over the past week, he concluded the Court of Whispering Dusk didn't have a single vampire within their ranks. The news should have lightened Faye's heart. No vampires meant no blood whores. But why else would an Anarian woman be in a dark court? She needed to address Cleo's mother's claim during her open court—If they had shown up.

Her realm's monthly meeting went smoothly and concluded in a few hours. However, the court in question didn't make an appearance. They ignored the requests Alister penned on her behalf, and now she was free to bring her court to their doorstep.

Rune had contacted a coach station. He'd explained this was the easiest way to travel to the lesser-known courts. A woman appeared moments later and phased them to the Court of Whispered Dusk's landing.

A warm breeze tossed Faye's hair. Rune stepped off the platform, followed by Sparrow. A large, manicured yard stretched before them. The home, however, was smaller than Faye expected. She expected a rich Necromian to live here. While the building itself was still impressive, this was nothing more than a country manor. Its multi-story home consisted of elegant peaks and large bay windows covered in vines. Horses neighed from an oversized well-kept stable beside it. Faye stood on her toes, looking over the stalls as they walked toward the doors; a few of the steeds hung their heads out, flicking their ears. They were sweet looking animals instead of the fanged, fire-breathing brutes Rune called nightmares.

Rune knocked on the heavy door, and Sparrow linked arms with Faye, leaning closer and whispering, "I'll bet you a gold mark one of them faints when they see Runey here."

Faye elbowed Sparrow, shaking her off as she hissed, "We're here on business."

The door opened, and a brunette woman looked up at Rune and paled, stammering out his title. Sparrow giggled quietly, and Faye discreetly elbowed her a second time.

"I've come for a word with your Queen," Faye said.

The woman nodded, opening the door wider. "If you could wait here, please," she said. Another woman in a long, plain dress, wearing a day-blood shard, dusted a vase in the foyer. She froze, glancing in Faye's direction, but she didn't sense her reservoir of power.

"Tell the other servants to return to their quarters," the brunette said, shooing her away.

They swiftly disappeared though the doors out of sight. Whispers of power streamed back and forth, and Faye turned to Rune. *They aren't happy we're here.* She felt several sources of power, flickering in a room a few feet behind the foyer.

They are afraid, but the maid tasted of relief.

Maybe the maid didn't like seeing Cleo kept here against her will. Faye didn't have time to think on the matter. A darker presence joined the others, and Faye narrowed her eyes at the wall separating her from the room they gathered in.

Faye tracked one of them as they returned. The door clicked open, and the same brunette she'd seen earlier bowed her head and held her hand out. "Our Queen will see you now."

Faye took a calming breath as she shielded the three of them and followed the young woman down the hallway. She turned the corner and couldn't help but feel like she was walking into a trap. They wouldn't attack her like this. Rune would decimate their court. *This would be an uncomfortable meeting like Isobelle's.*

They entered a large sitting room, and Faye realized how wrong she had been. Delilah sat beside a dark-haired woman in an elaborate corseted gown with jewels strung through her hair. The rest of her court stood or seated behind her.

This wasn't a typical trap one would expect from a dark-blood court, but a trap all the same.

The Queen picked up a cup and saucer, stirring it as she looked over Faye. "What can I do for you, Queen of Anaria?"

Faye bristled and took a step toward the Queen and her entourage. "You failed to answer the petition for an Anarian being held here. Her name is Cleo."

The Queen hummed as though she were hearing this for the first time and sipped her tea. Delilah crossed her legs, her gaze raking over Rune with a blatant sexual heat Faye didn't appreciate. The Queen of Lace and Bone turned to Faye and said, "You're not our Queen, and we're not in Anaria. Your word is meaningless here."

"Why are you here?" Sparrow blurted out.

Delilah called a stiletto dagger and used it to clean her nails. "Emily called on me for council. I'm doing what Lyssa cannot."

Faye refused to acknowledge Delilah and focused her attention solely on the Queen. "Bring me Cleo. If she wants to remain here, we will leave."

The Queen of Whispered Dusk's lips quirked up into a lopsided smile. "No."

Anger flared in Faye, surging with the impulse to crush this court. Viciousness swept through her mind in a seductive caress. Her senses guided her, willing her to break each of their cores, leaving them powerless. To shatter their minds and watch them splinter. Faye's power rose like serpents around her ready to strike, and Faye tensed. She drove it down, channeling her excess power into her shield instead.

Faye gazed past them. She could sense one other presence further in the house. The lone dark-blood would be guarding the servants, and they would know where Cleo was.

"I'll find her myself," Faye said, starting toward the door behind the Queen's men.

One of the males reached for her as she passed. A sizzling crack sounded when he met her shields. The backlash threw him back, and he toppled over a chair before crashing to the ground. Tendrils of smoke rising from his still body.

"If any of you attempt to touch my Queen, I will remove your arms," Rune's threat followed her into the hallway.

Faye deftly moved through rooms and halls with Rune and Sparrow trailing behind her. "This is an act of war," Delilah snapped, following them as she picked up her black and gray skirts.

"Touch my Queen, and your life is forfeit," Rune growled.

Faye followed the presence, doubting Delilah would attack. She glanced at her mate. Tension lined his shoulders, and she caught a glimpse of his lengthened fangs. Challenging Rune now would be suicide.

Faye turned the corner and found a male guarding a door at the end of the hall. He looked past her, and the color drained from his face. "I want to see the servants," Faye said, surprised the man didn't try to stop her as she reached past him for the door.

"Raphael," Emily snapped from behind her.

"I'm sorry, my Queen," he said, pressing his back to the wall as he fled.

Faye opened the door, and a dozen men and women dressed simply were huddled in the back of the room. They stared at her wide-eyed as she looked from her to the Queen in the hall.

Faye bit the inside of her lip. They all wore day-blood rings, but she didn't feel a depth of power connected to any of them. She stepped into the room. "Do any of you know where Cleo is?"

"I'm Cleo," the woman who had been dusting the vase in the first room answered.

Faye took another step and froze when the group collectively squeezed tighter against the wall. Their actions stung her heart. They were afraid—of her. Faye struggled to keep the hurt from her voice. "Are you a servant here?"

Cloe didn't answer, looking toward the Queen.

Faye took a half step closer, holding out her hands in a peaceful gesture. "My name is Faye. Your parents sent me a petition saying you were kidnapped and being held against your will. I came to see if you want to be here."

She couldn't be much older than Kimber. Sunkissed freckles sprinkled over her cheeks and the bridge of her nose. Her dark eyes turned glassy as tears rimmed her dark lashes. She took a shuddering breath and shook her head no.

A protectiveness took root in Faye's heart, and with it, a deafening rage. She took another step toward Cleo, holding out her hand. "We'll take you home."

The woman flung herself at Faye, hugging her tight as a sob broke from her. "None of us want to be here," she whispered.

How long had they been here? "All of you are being held?"

A male who looked to be in his forties stepped forward. "We're not servants. We're slaves."

Faye's breaths turned cold as her power and instincts seduced her senses. She'd been too late to draw a cacophony of screams from the Queen who enslaved Rune, but she could liberate her people with the singed marrow of their slavers.

"Is there anyone else?" Faye asked too calmly.

"Christine," a young woman said.

An older woman answered, "Christine is a pet. She wants to be here."

"I'll ask her myself," Faye said, untangling herself from Cleo. She stroked the woman's cheek. "Sparrow will stay with you." Cleo nodded, and Faye looked over the crowd, nodding in her direction. She touched Rune's arm as she passed. "Phase them to Anaria. We need to find one more."

Faye refused to allow her people to suffer under dark-blooded rule. She would bring them home. Even if she had to visit every court in Necromia. Every Anarian was under her protection. It didn't matter what realm they were stolen to. They were hers. Every. Last. One.

Emily tapped her fan against her palm. "Are you going to free my horses, too, when you leave?"

Faye's rage spiked, scorching the walls as she hissed, "They are not animals!"

The Queen took a step back, and her shield flickered with a false sense of protection. Her gaze passed back and forth between the blackened marks, crawling up the walls, and Faye.

Delilah stepped in front of the Queen, unbothered by Faye's display. "You have what you came for. Leave."

Faye shifted past Delilah, turning her attention to Emily. "Bring me Christine, or I will tear your home down looking for her." Her serpents rose behind her, unseen. Hungry to strike. Awaiting targets.

"She's my pet," a male said toward the back.

"Bring her forward," Rune crooned.

"She's in my room," the man said, walking back down the hall. Faye and Rune followed him down a few halls, and he opened a door, motioning for them to step in.

A blonde woman sat on a bed, holding the sheets up to her chest. Her gaze swept from the man to Rune and back again as her breathing quickened. With the lacey straps over her shoulder Faye could only imagine what she was wearing.

Faye swallowed. She couldn't tell if her fear stemmed from being given away or because of the man himself. "I'm freeing the servants. You can come with us, or you can stay if you want."

Her gaze shot to the male, and Faye's stomach dropped.

"Please take me away from him," Christine said, never taking her eyes off the male.

Veined misted shadows stretched beneath Rune's gaze, and Faye seethed, turning on the male. "Did you force her into your bed?"

He took a step back, holding his hands up and exhaling sharply through his nose. "I didn't force her to spread her legs if that's what you're asking."

Faye's power reared too quickly, snaking around her. A shadowed serpent shot from the center of her chest as instinct washed through her. *Prey.* It struck the male slamming him into the wall behind him. She'd pierced his core, pinning him to the wall like the insect he was.

Insignificant.

Her shadowed serpent sank its fangs deeper.

Pitiful.

His core cracked beneath her tendril's bite.

Scream for me.

The man wailed, and the vicious haze clouding her mind receded. Faye gasped, taking a step back, and her tendril retracted, disappearing within her. The male fell in a heap on the floor. Screaming broke out in the hallway, and Faye snapped from her violent trance.

What had she done?

She cracked his core, fracturing it. Reveled in his agony and fear. His core, a broken glass with its contents pooling out.

Delilah pushed past her, rushing to the man's side. She held her hand over his chest, her head whipping up to Faye. "What did you do?"

"The coward deserved worse," Rune growled.

Faye stepped back into Rune and turned toward Christine. She pulled the sheet securely around the woman and helped her to her feet.

"Take us home."

Fifty-Six

Few deeds truly courted Rune's temper. Rape was one. Enslavement the other. Vicious hatred seeped through him, and his magic answered his will, crackling beneath his skin.

Rune extended his awareness beyond his body, encompassing every soul within the building. A quiet lick of power would destroy this court. The dark-bloods would be driven to their knees while he reduced their organs to shadows and ash.

Kill them, the Ra'Voshnik purred, hungry for the spray of blood and the snap of bones.

Rune reigned in his visceral reaction and isolated the blonde harpy, his queen, and her Anarians. Faye would deny his request to purge Whispering Dusk, but he would make his request all the same.

He glowered at Emily and Delilah. The weaker woman cowered behind the Queen of Lace and Bone. Delilah wet her lips, and Rune taxed every shred of self-control he possessed, quelling the unrelenting desire to liberate her head from her shoulders.

Rune phased his queen and her people into a large sitting room within her estate. Faye vanished with Christine, and her sister offered seats to those who remained. Rune approached a middle-aged male, and he shrank in his seat. He stilled. The Anarians eyed him warily, his proximity causing more harm than good. Rune walked to stand near the doorway, and they calmed with his distance. He spelled the room to be a few degrees warmer, unable to assist them in any other way.

Vashien appeared a short time later, holding a tray of warm cider, meats, and bread. He placed it on the large rectangular ash table in the center of the room and began distributing food and drink. The Ra'Voshnik skimmed the surface of his awareness. *Phase back. We can purge them before our queen returns.*

Rune exhaled as Alister stepped into the room and came to a stop behind him. "What happened?" his brother asked.

"A minor court kept Anarians as slaves," Rune answered plainly.

Alister moved through the group, and Rune thinned his lips. They didn't fear him. His brother quietly collected names and villages. Faye reappeared with Christine. The woman was dressed in his queen's clothing. Faye poured her a cup of warm cider and coaxed her into a leather chair. After Christine calmed, Faye circled the room and spoke to each of her people, reassuring them they were safe.

Alister sectioned the group into their villages. He and Vashien phased out with Anarians, returning them to their families.

Our queen is troubled, the Ra'Voshnik growled through Rune's mind.

Rune agreed with the creature's notion. His dark queen used her tendril in a way he had never seen. Suspending a male who was considerably heavier than her.

It was beautiful, the Ra'Voshnik purred, aroused by the violence.

Her magic was neither Familiar nor what he wielded. Faye would need to come to terms with her abilities, but for now, assisting her people would soothe her more than he could.

Rune approached Faye after the last Anarian was returned to their village. She leaned back on her desk and glanced at Alister. "We need to change the timeframe these courts are allowed to respond in."

Alister frowned. "Protocol gives them four weeks or until the next open court. Whichever is sooner."

"No," Faye said with a shake of her head. "It's too long. I left them there for weeks."

She could not blame herself for this. Rune stepped between her and Alister. "Vsenia, you did not do this."

"I did," Faye said, pushing away from the desk. "I left them there."

"Vsenia—"

"I want the petitions changed," Faye said, determination lacing her words. "They have a day to respond."

"And if they don't," Alister asked curtly.

"Then the Court of Chaos and Darkness will pay them a visit," Faye answered.

Rune poured his queen a glass of pomegranate juice from her personal stock and handed it to her. Faye's actions were a declaration of war, but he had always known her heart held no limits when it came to her people. After seeing her reaction to Christine, Rune knew she wouldn't be swayed. He would never oppose his queen publicly. They would speak at a later time, privately.

Alister exchanged a glance with Rune. He subtly narrowed his eyes and momentarily lifted the tail of his brow. His brother's expression fell away as quickly as it had come and he said, "I'll have a list of pending petitions each morning. If there are several, we can split them among ourselves. Sparrow is proving to be surprisingly capable."

"Don't fucking say my name, coffin water." The blonde harpy snapped.

"Sparrow!" Faye hissed.

"No. Fuck this day-blood," she said to his queen while aggressively pointing at Alister with a hateful finger. She squared her small shoulders, turning on his brother. "If you touch her—you so much as give her a headache—I'm going to put your head on a spike."

Rune immediately shielded the harpy, but to his surprise his brother didn't call in his blades.

"Your anger is justified, but it makes you sloppy," Alister said calmly. He lifted his chin at Faye. "You would be an asset to your sister if you reigned in your emotions and focused on her true enemies with calculated efficiency."

The harpy pulled her shoulders back and opened her mouth wide, hissing at Alister. His brother gave her an unimpressed look and looked over her head at Faye. "Prin asked for you this morning. She wanted to invite you for tea."

Faye linked arms with Sparrow and pulled her away from his brother. "I would love that—"

"No!" Sparrow snapped. "She can come here."

"Hooker stop," Faye said through her teeth.

"You can't be alone with this asshole," Sparrow snapped, then forcibly moved Faye to meet his gaze. "Protect your queen, fangs."

"Sparrow," Vash said sternly. She snorted at him but held her tongue.

Faye smiled at Alister. "Can I see Prinia in an hour or two? I'm tired, but I think it's because I'm hungry."

Sparrow abandoned Faye's side and shifted into a fluffy white cat, leaping for Vashien's lap. He scratched her neck and Sparrow purred loudly. The winged male glanced his way. "You don't need to send people from Obsidian to pick up chicken fingers for Faye. You could have just told me."

Tear his wings off his back, the Ra'Voshnik grated. Irritation vibrated off him at the thought of another male providing for his mate, carrying his young.

The creature wasn't close enough to the surface for its presence to bleed through his eyes, but the notch in Vashien's throat bobbed. "I'll have a platter of them made and delivered to the kitchen here."

"That would be nice. Can you add your clam chowder?" Faye asked before draining her glass. She hummed, pointing at the winged male, holding her glass as she swallowed the remainder of her drink. "And fries with your cheese sauce."

The next time you go to sleep I'm going to take his wings and shove them up his—

Rune cleared his throat, and Vashien paled, swallowing the contents of his glass in one gulp.

A brilliant light engulfed Sparrow, reforming larger. She sat on Vashien's lap as a woman and wrinkled her nose at Faye. "Tell me you're not mixing it all together."

Faye rolled her eyes and waved her hand at Sparrow. A strange gesture they did to end disagreements among themselves.

"Shall we?" Rune asked, smoothing his hand down Faye's back. He phased them to their bedroom in Hell when she nodded.

Do not offend her, the Ra'Voshnik growled.

The creature's constant desire to please Faye was misguided. Allowing courts to align with Delilah would cause far more death than simply purging one court as an example. Rune hesitated and spoke quietly, "Vsenia, we must strike at Delilah, courts are gathering to her. Your new decree will drive countless more to her."

Faye sat at the edge of their bed. Her slumped shoulders muted her slight frame. She studied her hands silently and after a while said, "If we make an example of her, we're no better than she is."

Rune knelt before her, placing his hands on her knees. "I understand you wish to proceed in a way you believe to be correct and just. Every act you allow Delilah to commit without repercussion paints a brighter target on you and your court."

Faye's lightning-streaked midnight eyes bore into his soul, and he silently begged her to see the situation for what it was.

"We could hurt her, even kill her, and it wouldn't matter," Faye began, cupping his cheek. "Another dark-blood would take her place. Anaria is my garden. We've cultivated the soil, and Delilah is a weed trying to sprout. If I dig her out, it will only bring other seeds to the surface who will germinate like she did. She's exposed on the surface. Let her wither and die."

If we massacre the weed, the others will be too afraid to grow in her garden, the Ra'Voshnik purred, prowling his mind.

Faye's hand dropped, and she looked away.

"Is something else bothering you, love?" Rune asked.

Her expression pinched, but she didn't look at him. "I'm too strong, and I can't control it. I fractured that man's core." She turned toward him, her lashes glittering with unshed tears. "I could have done that to you."

Rune shook his head once. "You would not harm me."

"But I did," Faye's voice broke. "All I do is hurt people."

Faye's pain was a knife in his chest, and each tear she spilled only twisted the blade further.

"You are a good queen who cares for her people. Magic takes time to master. You should eat and rest. I can take you to the outskirts of my realm where you can draw on your power without the worry of hurting anyone."

Faye pulled back, wiping her eyes with the back of her hand. "Sadi said I should embrace my instincts."

The corner of his mouth lifted at her begrudging tone. While he appreciated his dark and glorious queen's base urges, he knew these feelings ran contrary to her heart. Silencing instincts was an impossible task, but they could be controlled.

"Fighting yourself serves no one," Rune said gently.

Faye adjusted the lapel of his jacket. "I want to hurt people," she whispered. "That's not who I am."

Tell her I can hurt them, the Ra'Voshnik said, pleased with itself.

The creature had a singular mind, hyper focusing on sex or violence, both of which hinged on Faye's mood.

Rune slipped two fingers under her chin and lifted until she met his gaze.

"Accepting the instinct does not mean it needs to be acted upon. It is merely acknowledging a desire and making a choice."

His mate's brow pinched slightly, and she blinked. Her lips met his palm a moment later. "Thank you."

Fifty-Seven

Faye had a bowl of Vash's chowder and spent the next hour curled up beside Rune. Her vampire read while she slipped in and out of sleep. The rustle of pages roused her mind. He wasn't reading the aged, bleached tomes she usually saw him with. This was bound in a supple leather and looked new.

"What book is this?" Faye asked. He closed it on his index finger and tilted the cover toward her. Faye quirked her lip, squeezing her pillow tighter. "I can't read High Tongue."

Rune chuckled, returning to his book. "Since we are in this together, I am learning how to properly rub your back." He glanced down at her as his elegant fingers slid down the edge of the page, turning it. "I could skip a few chapters if you would rather, I rub your feet."

"Don't say that in front of Sparrow. Vash will never hear the end of it." Faye laughed as she got out of bed. She pulled on her winter coat and turned, sucking a sharp breath.

Rune stood near her closet door, and the corner of his mouth lifted into a smirk. "Apologies."

"I'm going to tie bells to your shoes," Faye said as she secured the belt over her waist.

Rune chuckled and said, "I would prefer if you did not." Faye smiled up at him, and for the first time since his nightmares began, his eyes lit with humor. The glow faded as his gaze drifted over her coat and briefly stopped at the leather belt before he met her eyes. "Keep your shields about you. I will await your return."

"Yes, dear," she said. He vanished a moment later, and Faye phased beside the road leading to Alister's home.

The afternoon sun offered little warmth, but the sweet scent of the surrounding spider lily fields drifted through the air. A sea of crimson flowers swayed with the chilled breeze beneath the expansive greenhouse of intricate ironwork Alister commissioned for his wife. Faye brushed the petals. Alister must have the fields spelled to bloom all year long, like Rune's gardens in Hell.

Prinia crouched on the other side of the field, in front of her home. Her fawn waves peeked over the flowers, gleaming in the sunlight. Alister stood beside her, holding a shallow woven basket with a braided handle. The red whiskers of the flowers pointed in all directions as Prinia handed three stalks to Alister. He collected the blooms, and the bursts of petals beside Prinia shook and fell as she clipped her next bunch.

Alister's pale blue eyes found Faye first, and she froze. He dipped his chin a fraction and averted his attention to his wife. He smiled and spoke a few words Faye couldn't hear. Prinia stood quickly, excitedly waving at Faye with her sheers. Her wide grin faltered when she realized what she'd done. She stuffed it in the basket Alister held and waved again with a shy smile.

Faye's apprehension thawed with each step. Alister was relaxed. The cold set of his jaw and aggressive posture no longer painted his body. Faye wasn't sure if it was because of Rune's absence or Prinia's company.

"Allie told me you would visit today. Would you like some tea?" Prinia asked.

"That sounds wonderful." She followed Prinia as she started up the stairs. Faye glanced down either side of the wrap-around porch. She was expecting to find the shadowed hellhound dozing in front of the three rocking chairs like a normal dog.

Prinia opened the door, and Faye asked, "Are you harvesting the flowers for anything or are you making a bouquet?"

She smiled, turning to look past her to the crimson blossoms Alister carried. The joyful glow lighting her dark eyes faded as her lips slowly downturned. She blinked, staring at the flowers as her brow pinched.

Alister stepped past her fishing a stem free. "I brought you some of your ugly flowers," he said with a kind chuckle.

The light returned to Prinia's dark eyes. Her slim fingers brushed Alister's as she took his gift. She brought the flowers to her nose and breathed in deeply. "I think they're beautiful," she said quietly. She stepped into their home followed by Alister, and Faye's heart squeezed.

Alister cared for Prinia's body for centuries when she'd been lost to Chaos. Faye managed to coax her back to her body, but after eight centuries, she wasn't the same. Alister didn't abandon her or curse her difference. This was love. Real love. Not the devotion and ownership dark-bloods claimed. She stepped into their home, glad Prinia had Alister to share her life with.

Her eternal life. A pang of sorrow cut into her heart and fear slipped in. She wasn't immortal. Rune wouldn't have an eternity with her.

Faye brushed the thoughts aside as she unbuckled her coat. Alister pulled a chair out of his dining table. After Prinia took her seat, he called a vase. Faye approached them slowly. He wasn't so terrifying when he organized flowers for his wife. His short black hair was neatly arranged, the slightest hint of his white hair beginning to show at the roots.

A quiet smile tugged at the corners of her mouth as she silently wondered if Alister went to the salon more often than Rune. She hung her winter coat on the back of her chair, and Alister's gravel filled voice sounded through her mind. *Prinia is more lucid after she drinks. Letting her lead the conversation helps her confusion.*

"The flowers are so pretty but be careful with them. Allie shields his hands and picks them for me," Prinia said brightly.

Faye studied the strange red flowers. She didn't know much about this flower. She hadn't seen them before Rune brought her to these fields. "Are they poisonous?" Red was usually a warning sign in nature.

Alister lined three teacups in a neat row. He poured his wife's tea first and set it beside her, then filled the remaining two. "Steeping her flowers in tea will make you ill," he said, placing her tea in front of her.

Faye pulled it closer. The warmth seeped into her fingertips, reminding Faye of the countless home cooked meals she enjoyed at Aunty Clara's house as a little girl. When she grew older, she poured the cups of tea for Aunty Clara and the other children.

The steaming liquid was golden brown. She inhaled and was greeted by bright notes of floral with a touch of woody bitterness.

"It's young oolong," Prinia said as she brought the tea to her lips. She smiled against the cup's edge and cut a playful glance at her husband. "Allie is really picky with his tea."

Faye took a sip. The mild sweet flavor balanced the woody taste. It was perfection. "It's really good," Faye said. It was tempting to ask for the blend, but she remained silent.

Prinia held her tea and breathed in deeply. Her expression pinched, and she lowered the cup. "You smell different," she said, leaning forward slightly and inhaling again.

Did she smell bad? Faye touched the collar of her shirt. "I soaked in a bath this morning. Is the rose scent too strong?"

"You're different," Prinia whispered as her gaze lowered over Faye's body.

Alister gently brushed Prinia's arm. "She changed her clothes, sweetheart."

"No. I hear…" Prinia's deep brown eyes momentarily flooded black. "You have many heartbeats."

Alister's lips parted. "Are you pregnant?"

Faye blinked. His words were kind, but she couldn't form the words to answer. She'd been late before, but the disappointment of her cycle cut her deeper than she would ever admit. She hadn't told anyone, wanting to wait another week before visiting a healer to know for sure. Prinia was sweet, but Faye had no way of knowing if she was truly pregnant or if Prinia was hearing things she wanted for herself.

Prinia giggled, and a purr rumbled through her. She leaned into Alister and said, "Will we have heartbeats, Allie?"

He took her in his arms, and the harsh edges around his eyes softened. "We will have whatever you want." His attention shifted to Faye as he stroked Prinia's back. "Shhh, love," Alister whispered.

Prinia quieted, and Alister turned his head, closing his eyes. She brought her lips to the shell of his ear and whispered, "Do you hear them?" Prinia made a series of rapid whooshing sounds and wrapped her arms around his neck.

Faye stiffened, desperate to know if this was real, terrified it wouldn't be.

Alister nodded. "You're carrying my brother's young."

The statement was neither a statement nor a question. Faye's chest constricted as her heart raced. "Am I?"

"I'm not a healer, but I can hear two of them."

Unshed tears wet Faye's lashes as realization strangled her elation. "If you can hear them, he could too." Why wouldn't he tell her? How could he keep this from her?

"Don't... don't be too harsh with my brother. Vampires have sharp senses. It's customary to allow women to discover pregnancies."

Faye wiped her eyes and grumbled, "It's a stupid custom."

"I'm sorry you found out this way," Alister began. "Prinia is still learning herself."

"It's not her fault," Faye said. She finished her tea, and Alister carefully held Prinia against him as he reached for the tea pot. "Thank you, I've had enough."

Prinia was perfectly content on Alister's lap, nuzzling his throat. They looked happy, and Faye didn't want to intrude on their time while Prinia was lucid.

"We should meet for tea again. You could visit my home," Faye said.

Prinia straightened, and Faye caught sight of her canines lengthening. "That would be lovely. Allie and I can bring cookies."

"See you soon," she said, attempting to hide the grating tone of her voice. After she phased to Hell, Faye planned on having a long conversation with her vampire about his archaic principles.

Fifty-Eight

Faye tapped her nails on the door frame before entering Rune's study. Her vampire sat behind his desk, reading the same leather-bound book. "Do you have something to tell me?" she asked, approaching him. She stopped beside him and pushed up to sit between his books. When he leaned back in his chair and canted his head, Faye fought the urge to bludgeon him with the spine of the book he held.

She scooted, sitting in front of him, and placed the balls of her feet on his chair between his legs. She curled forward and wrapped her arms over her knees before setting her chin on her forearms. "Something you hear?"

His smile broadened, and he cursed in High Tongue. Rune leaned forward, abandoning his reading. He brushed his lips over hers in a soft kiss as he encircled her in his arms, palming her ass. He pulled back and whispered at her lips. "I heard our young this past week."

Faye wrapped her arms around his neck, and Rune drew her closer. She straddled his waist, and he held her loosely. "Why didn't you tell me?" Faye asked quietly.

Rune flattened his hand below her navel, and Faye's heart tightened. She would have a family with the man she loved.

"It is for you to discover," Rune replied as he gazed up at her. "Not for me to inform."

Longing and hope lingered in his pale stare. Her smile widened as veined misted shadows stretched beneath his eyes. Faye cupped the side of his face and brushed her thumb through Voshki's shadows. They swirled in different directions before fading completely. "You hear two of them?"

Rune nodded as a purr rumbled from him. "You carry twins."

Faye looked down and smoothed her hand over Rune's. Over their children. Her family. The little boy and girl she dreamed of. The two she saw in the Hall of Empty Eyes.

Tears wet her lashes and spilled down her cheeks, and Rune stiffened. "I am sorry, vsenia," he murmured. "It was not my intention to hurt you."

"I'm happy." Faye smiled. "But we need to talk about your dark court garbage." Rune chuckled, and Faye pressed her hand over his mouth. "No. We're a team. You tell me everything. Especially this," Faye said. She looked down and dropped her hand from his mouth to poke her middle. "You really hear them?"

"I do, vsenia."

Twins. There were so many things she needed, cribs, bedding, mittens. Motherhood was as daunting as ruling a realm. "We'll have to settle on names," Faye said absently. The corner of Rune's mouth lifted into a smirk, and Faye glared at him. "You're going to help me name them."

Her vampire brought her hand to his mouth, and a feather-soft brush of his lips warmed her fingers. "My kind are not named in such a manner. The stones bear our name when we are born."

Faye parted her lips, giving Rune a quizzical look.

"Come, it will be easier to show you," Rune said, guiding Faye to stand.

He stood beside her, and her surroundings faded to refocus outside. Loose crystals shifted underneath her shoes as she adjusted her stance. They stood in the middle of large stone slabs arranged in a circle.

Faye glanced around and looked up at the structure towering behind them. She recognized the floor to ceiling, intricately designed window to Rune's study above them.

Rune took her hand and led her to the large slab furthest from his estate. Faye sensed she'd been here before as dread weighed her down, suffocating her.

She pressed closer to Rune as they approached the slab. A glimmer caught her eye. Shining against the flat gray stone as they moved closer.

It was writing.

"This is where you will have our young. The stones name us and bind us to Hell," Rune said.

Faye peered at the slab. Names were carved into the foot of it, and a liquid pulsed through the grooves, mimicking a heartbeat. She reached forward, gingerly touching the rough edge of Rune's name, careful not to touch the molten diamond fluid flowing within it.

Sacarlay was etched at the top in large letters. Beneath it read: *Julian, Alister, Rune,* and *Jareth.*

"Looks uncomfortable," Faye said.

Rune glanced down at her. "It will not be bare when the time comes." He smoothed his hand over the engravings. "Our house name. My father and brothers."

The next stone also had names carved into it, but they were lifeless. The diamond blood pulsing in them, absent. "Why are their names empty?"

"My father purged their lines after the Great War," Rune said.

Purged. "As in murdered?" Faye asked.

Rune thinned his lips and smoothed his hand over Julian's name. "My father was a flawed, untrusting man, but he was loyal to my mother."

Faye peered at the other dull, carved stones. "If they stop shining after they were killed, why is your father's name still lit up?"

"I am not sure. Julian purged the other lines long before we were born. I did not see the stones while his brethren and their heirs were still among the living," Rune said, stepping away from the stone slab. "Perhaps his name is kept since his line still survives."

"What if I don't like the names *your* rock choses?" Faye teased.

The corners of Rune's eyes crinkled. "We will choose nicknames you find suitable."

Rune wrapped her in his arms as she gazed off into the glittering horizon. Faye adjusted her engagement ring. "Our wedding will have to wait." She refused to rush it or be severely pregnant when they stood before the blood priestess.

"I am yours to command," Rune said against her hair. "When were you planning to inform your sister?"

Telling other people hadn't crossed her mind. She had to inform her sister, Aunty Clara, Kimber. She lifted her face and leaned into her vampire. "We can tell her together. She's probably eating in the den."

"Likely," Rune chuckled. "You will need a healer. I understand you and Sadi do not see eye to eye, but she is gifted in her craft."

Sadi carried a Shard of Darkness like Rune, and she would be motivated to protect Rune's children, ensuring they were delivered safely.

"Will she want to help me?" Faye asked.

Rune nodded. "She will. We are of the same court."

"Keep an eye on her and make sure she doesn't try to kill me," Faye teased, though she was only half joking.

Her vampire grew solemn. "She would never harm you, love."

Faye understood Rune trusted his Familiar bestie, but she didn't. He took her hand and pulled her toward him, setting his arm around her as she leaned into him. She brought her nose to the base of his throat and inhaled. Darkness, his scent was divine.

"You have to be using another soap or something," Faye said, glancing up at him.

Rune's brow came down. "Pardon?"

"You smell nice," Faye said, remembering when she first noticed it. Rune had begun sleeping in shifts. "Does Voshki wear cologne?" Rune chuckled, and Faye jabbed him with a nail. "I'm being serious."

"You are likely smelling my blood." Faye wrinkled her nose, disgusted with his answer, and his broad grin widened. "Did you truly think you would carry my young and not drink blood?"

"It doesn't smell like blood. You smell good," Faye insisted.

Rune hummed, sensually stroking the back of his index over the side of her neck. "And how do you think blood smells to a vampire?" Rune purred.

Faye quirked her lip at the thought. "I eat food. I don't drink blood."

"You will drink when you are thirsty enough," Rune whispered.

Faye pulled away from him, muttering her displeasure. She turned her attention to his stone slab. "Can we bring your rock inside?" She could deal with the rock situation if she could add cushions to it, but did it really need to be outside.

"The stones are fixtures to the realm," Rune said, glancing behind him at the large stone structure. "The estate was moved to the stones, so my mother did not have to travel far. It may rain when your time comes." Faye faced her vampire. She'd been here for more than a year and never saw the sky change. "Morbid said the rain is Hell welcoming power. It rained when I was born and when I invoked my blood." Rune explained.

Faye stared at the waning streaks of sunlight as they warmed the night sky, ushering in the stars twinkling behind them. Would the sky mirror Chaos since they were sister realms? Faye stepped away from Rune and straightened her coat. "Meet you in the den?" she asked over her shoulder.

"Phase us both," Rune said, watching her with a predator's gaze.

Faye glared at him. "You can phase yourself."

Rune shrugged. "You need the practice."

"You're supposed to be nicer to me," Faye said, crossing her arms. "I'm pregnant."

The corner of his mouth lifted. "I am the picture of devotion."

Faye hummed her disagreement. "How do I take you with me?"

"Similar to holding a shield over a space. Push your awareness over me and take my mind with you when you phase. My body will follow. A physical connection helps at first, but it can be done without one."

Faye narrowed her eyes, pushing her senses beyond herself. The feel of Rune's mind was a familiar comfort. Her power flowed past her, encompassing him. Faye took a steadying breath and phased to the den. Rune stayed in focus as her surroundings slipped into darkness and returned before the large fireplace.

Rune smiled. "A simple task."

"Stop showing off, bitch." Sparrow yelled. Faye turned in time to see her sister throw a cubed piece of cheese toward her. Faye leaned away, but Rune caught Sparrow's projectile.

"We do not throw food," Rune lectured. He tossed the cheese back on the platter when they reached the table.

Faye took a seat across from her sister and pulled the tray of fruits closer. "We have something to tell you."

Sparrow nodded, and immediately froze. "Are we talking about the *something*, something?"

Faye beamed, nodding.

Sparrow shrieked and rushed to hug Faye. "I'm so happy for you. I already have the *perrrrfect* name for you. If it's a boy... Sparrow, and if it's a girl... Sparrow is the obvious choice as well. I know what you're thinking—It's perfect. No need to thank me."

Rune took a seat beside Faye as her sister pulled the other plates closer to her. "You need to eat more, scrawny ass," Sparrow said, turning to Rune. "You won't object to a bachelorette party at a brothel would you. I mean, you took her to training on your first date."

"I'm not having a bachelorette party," Faye said as she picked over the sliced melons.

Sparrow rolled her eyes. "Everyone knows you love your tall, pale, and scary, but I've been planning this for years. It's happening."

"The wedding will wait until after our court is settled," Faye said, pulling the plate of fruit in front of her.

Sparrow snorted and eyed Rune. "Didn't want a fancy wedding so bad, you had to go and knock her up."

Fifty-Nine

Days passed, and Faye's estate neared completion. Sparrow had begun sparring with Damian in the private courtyard each morning. Her wayward sister found her passion in steel and grit while Faye hid from her powers. She'd spent several days turning over Rune's words.

Accepting the instinct does not mean it needs to be acted upon. It is merely acknowledging a desire and making a choice.

She was desperate to believe in his words, but how true did they ring when she couldn't stop her shadowed serpents from striking? When at the end of each evening, instead of going to bed nude, Rune wore pajama bottoms. A constant reminder of how badly she'd wounded him and the chasm she'd unearthed between them.

Intent was meaningless when all she caused was harm.

Faye curled up to him and rested her head on his chest, careful not to touch anything he left clothed and drifted to sleep.

Her brows drew together at the knot of hunger pains waking her sometime later. She shouldn't be hungry. She'd been famished at dinner and had eaten twice as much as Vashien did. She shifted against Rune taking a deep breath. His scent of amber and sandalwood, laced with a warmth she couldn't place, filling her senses, and she leaned her head back to gaze up at him.

He slept with his head turned away from her, emphasizing the sharp cut of his jaw and the strong lines of his throat. She stared at the flutter of his pulse as her breaths grew short. Her nails dug into his chest, and she lunged forward. Rune stirred as her heart pounded. She panted against his throat, leaning closer… her lips parting and preparing to bite.

Horrified, she snapped her mouth shut and shoved him away, catching her lip in the process.

A torrent of emotions crashed down on her. She ached for him, needing his hot flesh under her teeth. Darkness, why did he smell so good. His scent left her dizzy and euphoric. Begging her to crawl over him and feel the hot rush of blood over her tongue. Her emotions overwhelmed her. She felt too much, too deeply. Unable to control any of it.

Rune sat up, and the sheets bunched low on his waist. His long white-blonde hair fell over the hard planes of his chest as he reached for her. "Are you well?"

Faye panicked, not wanting him to see her like this. "No," she said weakly. Her frustration and shame mounted as tears pricked her eyes. Faye furiously wiped them away, crying, "What's wrong with me? I don't even know why I'm crying."

"Come here," Rune said, scooping her into his arms. He placed her beside him and smoothed her hair behind her ear. He wiped her tears and murmured, "I would like you to show yourself the same kindness you freely give to others. You are under strain. Carrying young."

"I'm pregnant. Stop calling our children 'young,'" Faye halfheartedly threatened.

"You are carrying our *children*," Rune corrected as he brushed her cheek. "What has driven my beautiful queen to tears?"

Faye remained silent, unable to trust herself. "You smell like you taste good," she finally said, feeling foolish. Her mind raced. They had so many other things to worry about—Rune's nightmares, Delilah, Lyssa.

Faye blinked through the fresh set of tears. She could only imagine what Lyssa would say at their next High Council meeting. Faye sniffled. If she was lucky, the High Queen would just ignore her. It suited her since she could ignore Lyssa too.

"Is that all?" Rune's deep accented voice called her racing thoughts back to the present.

Is that all? Faye pulled back to meet his gaze. "I'm not supposed to want to eat you." When she imagined having a family, her fantasies never included drinking her husband's blood.

But he wasn't her husband. She'd pushed off their wedding to establish her court and safeguard her people. The thought smothered her. She couldn't breathe.

"Shh," Rune crooned as he pressed his lips to her forehead. "You are allowed to feel whatever you wish, but you are upsetting yourself over nominal details, love." He smiled, the corners of his eyes crinkling.

Faye's gaze lowered to the pulse point in Rune's throat, and she looked away.

"You will feel better after you have fed."

"Or I'll throw up on you," Faye said.

Rune pushed his hair behind his shoulder and veined misted shadows poured from beneath his pale blue eyes. He raised a black-tipped claw to the base of this throat and nicked himself.

"Humor me," he said, lifting his chin the same way she did when she offered him her throat.

Faye shifted position to face him, sitting on her knees. He watched her quietly, the slightest smile angling the corner of his mouth. The thin trail of red was a stark contrast to his pale skin. It slipped down his throat, collecting at the hollow of his collarbone.

She leaned closer, and Rune remained perfectly still. Darkness, she thought he smelled good before. She recognized the scent now; the rich warmth reminded her of the spiced honey she drizzled over apples during the cold winter months.

Faye used his shoulder to brace herself and leaned in. She parted her lips and dabbed the tip of her tongue over Rune's blood. Faye blinked, running her tongue over the roof of her mouth. She expected a metallic taste, like the kisses she shared with Rune after he'd bitten her or when she licked his fangs. His blood tasted like her favorite spiced honey flavored with lemon, cloves, and a cinnamon stick.

Faye dug her nails into his shoulder and licked where his blood had gathered at his collarbone. His scent and taste intoxicated her. Faye sighed, swirling her tongue over the small nick on his throat.

She swallowed, and Faye's breaths came faster. His blood made her skin tingle. She wanted his hands on her. Heat pooled between her legs as she grew slick for him.

Her heartbeat drummed in her ears, and Faye's hand slid up Rune's chest. She bit down and drew against him. Her hand tangled in his hair as possessiveness slipped up her spine. Her muscles tensed. She needed more—more blood, more of him. She needed to lose herself in the feel of him.

Faye moaned, straddling his waist and sucking harder. She clung to him, rolling her hips and grinding her clit on his hard length.

Then the euphoria stopped. It took Faye a moment to realize Rune had shoved her off his lap and another to realize what she'd done.

Faye squeezed her arms to her sides, unable to meet his pale blue eyes. "I'm so sorry." She shrank from him, retreating to her side of the bed, but Rune caught her wrist.

"Vsenia."

Faye didn't answer, weakly pulling against his hold as the tears came.

"Faye," he said in a firmer tone.

She couldn't face him. She wanted to run and hide. A wave of nausea rolled through her. She was a bad person. All she did was hurt the people she loved.

Faye gasped, weightless for one moment, and the next her back was pressed to Rune's chest. He was seated on his heels with her tucked between his legs. His strong arms banded around her. "This is not your fault," he whispered. "I did not anticipate you reacting as a vampire would."

Faye tried to curl forward, attempting to make herself smaller, but Rune held her fast.

"I'm sorry," she sobbed.

Rune held her as she cried, reassuring her she'd done nothing wrong, telling her he loved her. He held her until the tears slowed and laid her on her side. Faye was grateful to have her back to him. Her eyes felt swollen, and she was sure her cheeks were blotchy.

He exhaled, rubbing the side of his face between her shoulder blades, and said, "Blood and sex go hand in hand with vampires. Your reaction is normal." Rune squeezed her closer as he lifted the arm she lay on across her throat and bit his wrist. He eased down behind her, bringing his wrist closer to her face.

Faye's mouth watered, but she made no move to take what he offered.

"You cannot starve our children, love." After another beat of silence, he said, "I am sorry I cannot give you what you need. I can let Voshki rise. He is more than—"

"No," Faye said, entwining her fingers with his at her hip. "He'll have to wait."

Rune chuckled, his breath tickling her back. "The Ra'Voshnik crossed with you."

Faye giggled. "What did he say?"

"Nothing worth repeating to a lady."

"I'm sure he'll tell me later."

"I am quite certain it will have many things to say," Rune said before nipping the ledge of her shoulder blade. "Now drink."

Faye took his hand, angling his wrist toward her mouth. She glanced back and asked, "Can you hold me?"

"Of course, vsenia," he said, flattening his hand beneath her navel. "I had planned to take you to the outskirts of Hell this afternoon, but if sleep escapes you, I would happily escort you after you have taken your fill. My realm is barren. You could call on your powers without consequence." Faye stilled, positive her vampire observed far more than he let on. "Take from me," he purred, tracing small circles over her flat belly.

Faye breathed in the alluring scent of his blood and shifted into a more comfortable position. Her eyes slid closed as she lifted her chin, parting her lips to drink.

Sixty

Loose crystals ground under Faye's shoes. She adjusted her stance for the third time while quietly wishing she was still in bed with her vampire. She'd drank from him for several minutes, pressing her legs together and fighting the urge to roll her hips. She could have asked Rune to allow Voshki to rise, but she couldn't discard him. Not when she'd been responsible for the turmoil congealing around them.

Faye had taken enough blood to satisfy her, and then she dressed. She took Rune's hand, and he phased them to the outer edge of his realm. They stood before a towering wall of storm clouds. Lightning crashed within it, illuminating its depths of grays and purples.

The sight clawed at Faye's heart, filling her with dread. It was more than the fear of being in The Crumbling's proximity, or the fact that it disintegrated everything it touched, consuming it utterly.

The wrongness of its existence burrowed under Faye's skin until she feared it would somehow infect her.

"I don't like this," Faye said as she backed away from the ominous clouds.

"The Crumbling is held back by my shield. We are perfectly safe." Rune's deep accented voice did nothing to calm her nerves. Overhead the clouds churned, grinding against glimmering flashes of black light. They sparked occasionally, shoving the rolling storm back, but they returned with ferocity, endlessly battling the magical shield holding it at bay.

Faye took another step back, staring as the clouds sparked against the shields once more. "Can we go somewhere else, please?"

Her surroundings dissipated into shadow and ash, revealing another crystalline field beneath it. This one without The Crumbling looming above them.

Faye rubbed her forearm, glancing over the glittering landscape soothed by The Crumbling's absence. "Is there a name for what you did? Hell phasing?"

Rune chuckled. "No, but what good is being tied to a realm if I do not use it from time to time."

Faye smiled and shook out her wrists, as she took a deep breath. The expansive space was perfect. Miles of isolation surrounded them. No buildings to damage with her uncontrolled magic. No one she might unintentionally hurt... except.

She turned toward her vampire.

No one except the man she loved... The father of her children... Her kind and loving consort. Her guilt gnawed at her. She'd done enough to him. "I can phase back home after I'm done."

Rune thinned his lips and spoke plainly. "I am not leaving."

"I might hurt you." Again. The words hung between them as Faye silently begged him to go.

The corner of Rune's mouth lifted, and he stepped closer, brushing her hip. "You are the dark queen I have wished for my entire life," Rune said as he slowly circled her. His hand smoothed over waist, skimming over her belly when he stepped behind her. Possessive fingers splayed over their twins, and he leaned down. His chest pressed against her back until his lips touched the curve of her ear. "I will never run from you, vsenia."

His closeness, the heat of his body, only added to her pent-up frustration. She sighed, wondering if it was Voshki or Rune who rasped at her ear.

Faye turned, met with veined, misted shadows beneath Rune's pale blue eyes. Voshki was close to the surface, probably arguing with Rune right now.

She wanted to touch him, to run her hands down the hard plains of his body. Tantalized by the memory of the cut of his sculpted muscles, each ridge defined under her touch.

Faye inwardly shook herself and said, "I need some room unless you want to get hit with my wings."

"Yes, my queen." Rune pressed a kiss to her hair and stepped away.

Faye closed her eyes and tipped her chin up, opening her hands. She drew her power up from far below her. It sluggishly obeyed her, climbing little by little. Faye dropped her hold. If this were a real fight, she'd be dead.

Her strength was vast, but it moved like a slumbering beast on the first day of spring after months of hibernation.

Faye thought of Sadi to provoke her anger. The bitch's condescending looks. How she'd been certain she was fated to stand at Rune's side. Arrogant and proud, looking down at her.

The anger Faye needed to summon wouldn't come. Sadi was far from perfect, but for all her faults, she was loyal. Faye couldn't say she wouldn't behave the same way if their roles were reversed.

Faye's mind flitted to Lyssa momentarily, and dark-bloods generally, before she thought of the man who intimidated Christine into his bed. A hot spike of rage flared in Faye. Her initial reaction was to push it down. Faye's hands closed into fists. She reached for her rage, envisioning his smug face as he said, *I didn't force her to spread her legs if that's what you're asking.*

He was so sure of himself, because she was an Anarian. No one would come looking for her, because she was a powerless mortal. Unworthy of respect or decency. Overlooked as she had been before her shard decorated her index.

Faye lifted off the ground as her magic surged forward in a cresting wave of fury. It crashed over her, spilling from her back as she adjusted to the familiar weight of her wings. Dark power sparked through her, pooling around her as her serpents rose. They swayed hypnotically, fanning their hoods wide.

I could hurt them, Faye thought bitterly. Their cores would crack and splinter between the jaws of her shadowed snakes. A smile played on her lips. She could make them into the prey they hunted, and she would offer no sanctuary when they were broken. Not for them. She would exile them to live in the constant fear they inflicted.

She reached forward as her surroundings took on a gray haze. She felt for the minds of her prey and paused. She curled her fingers, gazing at her dainty claws. The way her misted shard churned in on itself, raging in time to her emotions.

Power is meaningless if you cannot control it.

Rune was right. She needed to master the fury sleeping within her. Faye rolled her neck as her cobras slithered higher, stretching all around her. Her power was a living, breathing entity, desperate to execute her will. Faye opened her hands, and the jagged spikes and mountains of crystal exploded as her power lashed from within her to her targets.

The ground shook and groaned as new spikes rose for her. Faye smiled, letting her power tighten her, dressing her as she was meant to be. Layers of ethereal fabric and lace floated around her. The pinks, blues, and grays glittered against her skin. Perfectly matching her mate's realm.

It hung low off her shoulders and back, away from her wings. The panels of the skirt pooled below her, exposing the length of her leg as it swayed with an unseen current.

Screams and agony would be the currency she extracted to repay the debt owed to her people.

I am the Darkness embodied, and the realms would tremble at my feet.

The flood of power intoxicated her senses. Faye destroyed the crystalline spikes faster than Rune could raise them. She flickered, nearly phasing to the Court of Whisper Dusk. She wanted to break them, shattering their cores beneath her serpent's fangs. A symphony of agony the entire realm would hear.

No. Faye grit her teeth. "I want to," she whispered. Darkness, she wanted to. A shuddering breath tremored past her lips. "I'm choosing to spare them," Faye muttered to herself.

These are my instincts, and I don't have to act on them.

Faye took a steadying breath, and Rune's scent of amber and sandalwood came to her as though she were curled up on his chest. Possessiveness colored her mind in shades of crimson. She sighed, the memory of his blood, hot and sweet on her tongue. She wanted his hands on her... needed his cock stroking into her wet heat. Stretching her, claiming her—because she belonged to him.

And he belonged to her, she thought viciously, fantasizing the hard plains of his chest were clutched under the curve of her claws.

She panted, opening her hands. What was wrong with her? She didn't want to own Rune. She didn't want to own anyone.

No, Faye thought sharply. Fighting her instincts served no one. Wouldn't protect her family. Her breaths shortened. Rune and Voshki *were* hers. Her nails began to tingle and something in her clicked into place. Pieces she fought so viciously to keep separated fit together seamlessly.

The possessive feel of owning him didn't mean she saw him as less. He was her equal, her lover, her master, and her slave. Love and possession were not mutually exclusive, and one did not negate the other.

Power flared from her back, and Faye laughed as she lowered to the ground. Her wings felt different—more stable. When her wings spontaneously appeared with an outburst of emotion they felt tied to her magic, slowly ticking away as her power slipped like grains of sand through an hourglass.

This. This felt... secure. Her power obeyed her will, rising as she outstretched her hand. A crystalline cliffside detonated as glimmering slivers rained to the ground. Faye smiled, exhilaration thrumming beneath her skin. She was done running from her urges. It was time she made a choice and lived with the consequences. *Her instincts would not cripple her.* Her dark power lashed another monolith. Rubble scattered over Hell's glittering floor, and she smiled.

She would rule them.

Sixty-One

Rune admired the beautiful destruction Faye wrought over his realm. His night breeze floated a foot off the ground. Her shadowed iridescent skirts swayed with the Darkness pouring from her wings to pool beneath her feet. Dozens of serpents rose from the churning mist, swaying around her as they lifted higher, forming a dark halo of power.

Tell her she is breathtaking, the Ra'Voshnik purred.

Faye glanced back at him as though she'd heard the creature and began gracefully lowering to the ground. "I think…" She squeezed her hands to her chest and outstretched her glimmering wings. They snapped shut and lifted higher the next instant. Faye beamed. "I think I can keep them out."

His chest tightened at the excitement reflecting in her light-ning-streaked midnight gaze. The creature chuckled. *You're feeling happiness. Don't look so perplexed.*

Be silent, Rune replied, but his words lacked their usual bite. He raised his palm and curled his fingers, twisting his realm to his will. The ground shook, and rows of crystalline spikes erupted against the ever-twilight sky.

Faye turned, and the jagged crystals shattered two at a time. An easy task with the way he clustered them. Rune spent the next hour distributing pillars in different locations, testing her ability to manifest her will and asking her to destroy specific monoliths or sever the tops.

Rune chuckled when she missed sheering a crystal tower and toppled over the next. She stuck her tongue out and countered, "My aim is better when I'm not tired." The Ra'Voshnik agreed while Rune hummed his disagreement, holding his tongue.

Faye splayed her fingers and flexed her claws. "How do I change back?" she asked, looking up at him. "Is it like a shield, and I let it fall away?"

Rune blinked, puzzled. He didn't know. The Ra'Voshnik's characteristics surfaced when the creature was close to the surface of his awareness. Rune considered the Darkness flowing past his queen. Perhaps hers would behave similarly to a shield.

"I am not sure, vsenia. You may be sleeping in your wings tonight." He stifled a laugh when his night breeze bounced in place, shaking her wrists.

"This is fine. I'm just going to put it all back," she said, tossing her hair as she looked to the sky.

Rune waited patiently as the creature prowled his mind, certain Faye lifting her chin and closing her eyes meant she wanted to be kissed. He'd been a moment from silencing the creature when her serpents lowered and slipped beneath the churning mist at her feet. Her elegant wings darkened into swirling shadows, and finally, the Darkness itself. They dissipated, and she stared at the pink nails that replaced her claws.

She stifled a yawn, and Rune outstretched his hand. "You have done more than enough for one evening, vsenia. We should return to bed. I will shield our wing so you can sleep in," he said warmly, giving her a small smile.

Her hand smoothed over his palm, and he phased them to their room. They turned in for the night, and Rune idly stroked Faye's dark silken hair.

Her soft snore amused him, and his mind drifted to the moments after Faye drank from his throat. The humor fell from his lips. He'd rejected her. Basic, fundamental needs his queen, and future wife deserved—things he was unable to provide.

We can visit Sadira in Julian's palace if you want to work off some turmoil, the Ra'Voshnik purred.

During the first century after his liberation, Sadi wove a beacon through Sadira's mind, snaring her consciousness in a pristine fantasy of Sadi's creation.

One where she was on fire.

Sadi invited him to witness the torment of the Queen who enslaved him, but Rune declined. The bitch had taken enough from him. He would not gift her with his presence. Taking a deep breath, he exhaled slowly. How low had he sunk that the Ra'Voshnik sought to comfort him?

The creature bristled as its annoyance reverberated through his mind. *We will have a Pure Blood son and daughter. How do you expect to teach them to befriend their Ra'Voshniks if we're at each other's throats?*

Rune stared down at his peaceable queen. The low glow of hellfire outlined the curve of her shoulder, flickering shades of blue. *When did you become sensible?* Rune asked.

The Ra'Voshnik's laughter drifted through his mind. *Being caged rankles my temper,* it said, quietly floating through his mind. The creature went still when Faye shifted beside him, sinking her nails into his side as she pulled herself closer.

Rune's mind was tangled. His desire snagged on commonalities between the touch of two very different situations. It twisted with the feel of his queen, with the desecration he'd been subjected to under Sadira's court until he could not discern one from the other.

The creature disbursed the unkind memories, replacing them with a day he'd spent with Faye in her gardens. *You've been sleeping better. Why don't you apply your methods to our queen as well? You can't lie to me. I know you miss touching her.*

The Ra'Voshnik rose to the surface, and Rune conceded his arm. *Feel her.* It glided his fingertips over Faye's side, adjusting itself to her hip. *Remind yourself you are with our queen. That you are safe. You cannot sleep through the night, but you have salvaged hours of rest. You could regain those same hours with our queen.*

The Ra'Voshnik slipped back into his mind, returning control to Rune. *I will tend to her when you need to step back.*

It was strange speaking with it instead of arguing. *Him*, Rune thought to himself. *Thank you.*

Voshki didn't answer, settling deep within his mind.

Rune stoked Faye's back, outlining the place beside her shoulder blades where her wings extended. He'd been slowly moving through Morbid's library, searching for any information on the fabled Elysian Queen.

He stared out the expansive window and while Hell's sky remained unchanged, Rune could feel the passage of time on his realm. Dawn had risen, marking a new day. Damian and Sparrow would be sparring at this time in Faye's private courtyard in Anaria. Rune shifted his attention, reaching for Sadi's mind. *I require your assistance on a matter.*

Are we hunting Whispered Dusk?

Excitement thrummed over Sadi's mental tether, and Rune smiled softly. *Leave them until Faye commands otherwise. I would like to witness my father's creation.*

Saith had used the Elysian Queen to ground his magic, trading her life to create his own. Perhaps if he could see Faye's ancestor, he could find something useful. Maybe a piece of jewelry that had become an heirloom over the generations. A crest, anything that might point him closer to his queen's race.

Is this a lesson? Sadi asked.

His night breeze dozed off, lying on his shoulder. What he wished to see would be brutal and likely upset his queen.

I will ask her when she wakes, Rune replied. It was not his place to make decisions on her behalf. Faye should decide for herself.

She hasn't returned with me to the Hall of Empty Eyes, Sadi said coolly.

Rune remained silent and then admitted, *I have been accompanying her.*

And what good will that do? You are not Familiar. Your magic is useless in the temple.

Rune exhaled. *I am aware. Morbid is never far.*

Sadi hissed. *She'll be your downfall, and it will be the realms who pay when it happens.* She snapped the link between them before he could respond.

Sixty-Two

Faye woke curled up to her vampire, warm and comfortable. She breathed in, savoring his scent of amber and sandalwood, but the undertones of warmth were absent. Faye shifted against him, sliding her hand over her middle. If she paid attention and drank often, maybe her reaction wouldn't be as intense.

"Did you sleep well?"

Faye smiled at the deeper timbre his voice took when he first woke. "You sound like you did."

"Voshki woke me," Rune said as he lifted the sheets over her shoulder.

Faye propped her chin on his chest, and her vampire lifted a brow. "He should be letting you sleep."

Rune chuckled. "We are working through a system. I requested he wake me when you roused."

She quirked her lip and laid back down on the hard plains of his chest. "I don't think I've ever heard you say his name. It's always '*the creature*' or '*your Voshki*.'" Silence answered her, and Faye traced the chiseled line of muscle over his ribs.

"I am attempting to embrace the life you wish for our young," Rune said finally.

The quiet happiness of peace and contentment blanketed her. She'd asked him to join her circles when he began courting her, refusing to trade her values for wealth and power. He'd initially recoiled vehemently, but he loved her and respected her core beliefs even when he didn't agree with them.

Faye pressed a kiss to his chest before muttering, "Stop calling my babies young."

"Yes, my queen," Rune said, tapping her back twice.

Faye rolled onto her side, and Rune got out of bed. She clutched his pillow as he silently walked toward his closet. Faye admired her consort, the way his muscles shifted and flexed with each step. He stepped into his closet. Faye followed him and leaned against the doorway. Her sweet vampire sorted through his tailored garments before settling on which of his multitude of black suits to wear. He hooked his thumb in the waistband of his pajama bottoms, and Faye retreated to her own.

"I am having trouble isolating information on your race," he called to her. "The Elysian Queen is usually depicted with your wings and claws. She was a goddess worshipped for good harvest before Saith came to power. The text on her is limited. Saith used her to create my father."

Rune phrased it so calmly. "Used to create." The woman was an ingredient in one of The Creator's spells. Faye pulled a shirt over her head, and it squeezed tightly over her breasts. She frowned, tugging the hem down, and sighed. Maybe Sparrow was right, and her chest was getting bigger.

Her vampire knocked on her doorframe before stepping into her closet. "Sadi will allow me to witness Julian's creation and possibly shed some light on the Elysian Queen. She can teach you this type of Familiar magic if you wish. What I need to view will be unpleasant. The women Saith used to create my father, and the other Shadowmen did not survive his magic. I could ask Sadi to teach you a kinder event."

"No, I want to go with you," Faye said, hoping she would feel a connection to this woman. A distant ancestor she shared the same wings with, even if she died at Saith's hands.

"I will have it arranged when you are ready."

"After we eat?" Faye asked with a smile. She expected to have cravings. Faye pulled off the shirt she'd outgrown. *Rune's blood was technically a craving*, she supposed, but she thought she would want chocolate or a specific fruit. Faye craved food in general, always in a constant state of hunger.

She pulled a simple cotton dress off its hanger. It was a little tight in her bust but fell over her hips comfortably. "I think I'm going to need new clothes soon. Your twins are making me gain weight."

"Oh, now they are mine?" Rune chuckled, sliding his jacket on.

"Yes," Faye said, stroking his arm as she passed him. "While we're out, we can get you some normal clothes."

"Perhaps," Rune said. "Did you wish to dine with the others, or shall I bring you a meal?"

"We should be social."

"I care not for appearances."

Faye laughed. "Says the man who gets his eyebrows done every month."

Faye placed her hand in the crook of his elbow, walking beside him. They entered the great room, and Rune continued instead of turning left up the stairs. Faye leaned closer and asked, "Where are we going?" She wanted to eat with Sparrow, not her evil twin.

"I hear them in the kitchen," Rune answered.

Rune was right. Sparrow and Sadi sat at opposite ends of the island counter while Vash and Damian sat beside each other between their women.

Her sister slouched, looking over her shoulder as Faye and Rune entered the kitchen. "Bitch, eat some of this so Vash will let me eat it too."

A wide smile spread over Faye's lips. A pan of crispy golden chicken fingers was plated next to Sparrow, paired with a side of crinkly fries. Sadi peered over the steam-covered pot, the ladle and soup bowls piled beside it.

Faye broke away from Rune, taking a seat beside her sister. "Thank you, Vash."

Damian chuckled, leaning toward Vashien. "She's trying to get you killed, friend."

"No, I'm not," Faye said, filling a plate with chicken strips.

"You're letting another male provide for you while you're pregnant." Damien said, sipping his coffee before nodding toward Vashien. "I'm honestly surprised you still have wings."

Faye flushed, eyeing Rune. She thought they would tell people together. "Word travels fast, or could you hear their heartbeats too?"

"Our hearing isn't as sharp, but I can smell it on you now, dove," Damian said, lifting his chin and lowering his lashes.

Sparrow's fork clattered on her plate, and she shrieked. "Darkness, I want to see the High Queen's face when she smells you're knocked up."

Rune poured a cup of tea and placed it in front of Faye. "Lyssa is aware."

The High Queen knew?

"Who else did you tell?" Faye asked.

Rune canted his head. "It is customary to inform the Queen's Circle, and I sent word to my previous court."

Faye's heart raced as her sister asked, "The Queen's what?"

"The Queen's Circle are the members who initiated the court with said queen, dove," Damian said, twirling his finger.

"When did you send those out?" Faye asked.

Sparrow stared at her wide-eyed. "You didn't tell Aunty Clara yet, did you? Oh, you're in *soooo* much trouble."

She thought she would tell people in their own time, but fate tied her to an archaic dark-blood. Faye took a bite out of her chicken and pushed herself away from the table. She grabbed Rune's wrist and said, "We need to tell Aunty Clara now."

"I am sorry, love. I did not mean to upset you," Rune murmured.

"You better hope Lyssa kept her face shut about it, Runey. Aunty Clara is the biggest gossip in Anaria. If any of her servants heard her meltdown—"

"You're not helping," Faye snapped.

Sparrow saluted and dumped Faye's plate onto her own. "May the Darkness carry you."

Faye phased to Aunty Clara's house, and the children squealed, running toward her while Rune opened the gate. "I'll get some snacks after I talk to Aunty Clara," Faye said, dropping her arm around the little ones, who ran up to hug her at the waist.

Several of the children had twig-birds or twig-cats running on their heels. She didn't remember Sadi making this many. The screen door crashed open, and Jamie Lyn ran down the stairs.

Faye wouldn't have recognized her if it wasn't for her sun-set-hued hair. The girl was dressed in layers of ruffles, black lace covering her from chin to ankle. Her hair was combed into two pig-tails with matching black satin ribbons and lace accents, her Familiar totem perched on her shoulder.

Jamie Lyn stopped before leaning to one side to look at the gate. "Is Sadi coming today?"

"I'm not sure sweetie," Faye said, smoothing the puffed tulle. "Aren't you hot in this?" Winter quieted for Spring, but the girl had to be uncomfortable under so many layers.

She drew up the hem of her skirt halfway up her shin, showing off her polished black boots and black tights. "They're magic clothes. It's *really* comfortable," she said, dropping her flowing shirt and giving a little twirl.

Faye glanced up at Rune, and he shook his head once. "I have never seen Familiar young or their typical dress."

"I did!" Jamie Lyn beamed. "They have whole cities. Sadi said I can live there when I'm big enough."

Faye stroked the girl's cheek with her thumb. "That's wonderful. I'm glad you have each other." Jamie Lyn nodded and raced off to join the other children.

Sadi better take care of her and keep her promises, Faye said directly into Rune's mind as they climbed the steps.

Rune opened the screen door, replying, *I am sure she does not engage the girl idly.*

Faye cast him a sidelong glance as she walked past him. He always saw the good in his Familiar 'bestie,' and Faye ground her teeth. Orphans craved belonging and family. Faye didn't care how much of a bitch her evil twin was to her. If she got bored and discarded Jamie Lyn like an accessory she tired of, Faye would *idly* pull off her tail and skin her alive.

Bayle, Kimber, and Aunty Clara sat at the table with a mound of ground meat between them. They each had thin wooden spatulas and scooped a small amount into a dough wrapper before pinching the dumplings closed. Trays were next to each of them. Aunty Clara's was filled with rows of pristine dumplings. Kimber could never scoop the same amount of filling. Hers were either too skinny or overly stuffed. Faye smiled at Bayle's misshapen dumplings, remembering her own when she first started.

"Zou san, Aunty Clara," Faye said as she took a seat beside Bayle.

"Zou san," Aunty Clara huffed. "It's halfway to dinner time. Why are you sleeping so late?"

"Help me," Kimber pleaded as she slid a bamboo scoop across the table. "The trays are behind you."

Faye laughed, correcting one of Bayle's dumplings. Kimber hated prepping these since she was his age. Rune sat down, holding two trays, and Faye smiled at her vampire. "Are you helping too, big guy?"

"It does not appear significantly difficult," he said as he called the last bamboo tool.

Bayle pinched his dumpling shut with a sigh. "It's really hard, but the ugly ones still taste good."

"It's easy if you pay attention," Aunty Clara scolded, then pointed her stick at Kimber. "Get the red wine for Faye's husband."

"I am well, thank you," Rune said quickly.

Aunty Clara eyed him while pleating a dumpling, then shifted her attention to Faye. "You let him bite-bite too much. He can drink the crimson wine."

Faye's face heated, and her mind blanked. "He doesn't—he's old. He doesn't need to drink all the time." And why was she bringing up vampire bites in front of Bayle.

"Old," she grumbled. "His body is not old. You better watch out before you have all kinds running around."

Faye didn't respond, walking through the steps slowly as Rune watched. She finished the first and folded the second, pausing while Rune copied her steps. She supposed she should be thanking the Darkness as she started the third. If Aunty Clara knew she was pregnant, she would have said so by now.

The plump old woman pointed at Kimber. "Look. His looks better than yours because he pays attention."

Kimber squeezed her miss-pleated dough ball and plopped it on

371

her tray. "Tell your man to stop making me look bad."

"You make you look bad," Aunty Clara interrupted, and Faye giggled.

Faye cleared her throat, meticulously folding her wrapper. "I came by because I had something to tell you."

Aunty Clara hummed, correcting more of Bayle's misshapen dumplings. "Are you in a family way?"

Faye's hands froze. Did she know? She panicked, afraid she'd upset the person who always supported her, who taught her kindness and compassion. She glanced up, and Aunty Clara watched her, neither condemning nor angry. A burden lifted from Faye's heart. She'd been so afraid she let her down by not doing things traditionally. By not telling her sooner.

She answered with a small nod, and Kimber shrieked, clapping her hands. "I'm going to be an aunt! Did you tell Sparrow? Please tell me you didn't tell Sparrow yet, and I know before her."

"Of course, the lazy one knows. How long have you known them? Those two cannot keep secrets from each other." Aunty Clara went back to her dumplings. "It's good. You're finally settling down with a good boy."

"Did she just call the Shadow Prince a *boy*?" Kimber whispered.

"Well, sure," Aunty Clara answered. "Sparrow has the wing boy, and Faye has the vampire boy."

Faye watched the feared Shadow Prince prepare dumplings in her childhood home. She'd found the man she would spend the rest of her life with.

Sixty-Three

Faye conjured a lick of hellfire in the iron sconces of her room. She stepped in front of the full-length mirror, envisioning the changes her body would undergo in the next few months. Her visit with Aunty Clara had gone smoother than she expected. Aunty Clara probably knew. The plump old woman scoured every bit of scandal whispered through the village and traveled to Necromia each week to purchase her gossip articles. Faye couldn't imagine the High Queen reacting calmly. It must have been mentioned, and Aunty Clara didn't scold her because she was the "favorite" as her sister would say.

She smiled, missing Aunty Clara even though she'd visited days earlier. Everything she'd wanted was at her fingertips—equality for her people, safety for her realm, and her budding family.

Faye's dreams were unfolding before her, and she finally got a handle on her powers, even if the Familiar elements of her power were frightening. Sadi would arrive in the late afternoon and show her how to *witness*, a Familiar skill used to replay the past in a person's mind or location.

Between witnessing and harnessing the ability to peer into a person's mind, Faye wasn't sure which was more terrifying. If it wasn't enough, Sadi's visions cast a shadow over her for months since their first dinner as a court. Her evil twin felt death looming on their horizon. Faye slipped a hand over her middle. She and Sadi were made to tempt The Creator's son. Her heart raced. If he was a danger to her twins?

Faye shook herself. Whomever this man was, Rune wouldn't let him near their family.

She walked the short distance to Rune's study, and he removed himself from a dark leather-bound book. The stack of bone-bleached leather tomes had become a fixture on his desk but were soon replaced with dark books.

"Did you read all the white ones?" Faye asked as she examined the stack of books aligned perfectly with the edge of his desk. It looked common and felt new. Faye turned it over. *Keeping Your Wife Happy While She's Pregnant*. Faye giggled and tilted the cover.

"I am a devoted consort," he crooned, showing her the cover of his current read. *Foods Proven to Reduce Morning Sickness*.

"Are you reading in common tongue *to curry my favor?*" she asked, mimicking his rough accent.

The corners of Rune's mouth rose into a warm smile. "I spelled them into High Tongue so I could research without drawing your suspicion, minx."

Faye leaned back on his desk, admiring the crystalline landscape. "Do you have time to come with me to the Hall of Empty Eyes?"

Rune closed his book and gave his undivided attention. "Is something bothering you, love?"

Faye didn't answer. She knew her apprehension regarding Sadi's visions weren't rooted in logic. Wanting to go to the Familiar temple and rationalizing her trip were two entirely different things. *I need to make sure The Creator's son isn't going to hurt my babies*, sounded perfectly reasonable moments ago, but now she felt foolish and paranoid.

"I will escort you anywhere you wish to go. You do not need to explain yourself," Rune said gently.

Faye smiled weakly. "Thank you."

Rune stood and straightened the neat stack of loose pages on his desk. He extended his hand and said, "Shall we?"

Her fingers slid over his palm, and their surroundings changed. They stood on the landing before the Hall of Empty Eyes. Faye phased to the heavy bloodroot doors, avoiding the bones littering the ground. Lightning flashed, harshly illuminating rows of teeth and eye sockets beneath the ominous sky. *Skulls today*, Faye thought as she quietly wondered if there was a pattern the bones followed and when they changed.

If the bones bothered Rune, he didn't let on. Her vampire strolled toward her. His usually silent steps were punctuated with the snap of bones. The tall black wood door creaked, startling Faye as it eerily swung open under its own power.

Rune stood beside her, peering into the mirrored hall. "I would prefer it if you had a Familiar with you. Morbid, if you wish to distance yourself from Sadi."

Faye stepped closer to the threshold. "Sadi comes here all the time, and you don't bat an eye."

"Sadi is a trained Familiar, and you are carrying my young."

"I'm going to bite you every time you call them young," Faye said, crossing the threshold. Rune's purr followed her into the temple, and she turned to glance at her mate.

Black flooded his gaze as misted veined shadows stretched beneath his eyes. "Is that a promise, love?" Voshki asked with a smirk.

"Behave," Faye said, walking deeper into the temple.

"Yes, my queen," Voshki muttered as the shadows receded, and Rune's clear blue eyes returned.

Faye stopped in front of the mirrors. Instead of her reflection, rows of naked ashen bodies watched her. They swayed back and forth in a haunting rhythm. She couldn't get the answers she needed from something nice, like fluffy rabbits. No, this was Chaos, where the ground was covered in bones, and everything was terrifying.

Faye took a deep breath and stared at the woman's collarbone before her. It was easier to stare at a point on their sickly bodies than their clouded, unseeing eyes. The sooner she asked her questions, the sooner she could go.

Sadi told her wording was important, and she had spent the past few weeks dissecting her questions.

She and Sadi were flesh made for temptation. Faye bit the inside of her lip, going over her questions again. *What will happen when the flesh made for temptation is succumbed to?*

The vessels shifted, tilting their heads back.

Choices and consequences.

Faye tapped the nail of her index finger against her thumbnail. They'd given her the same answer when she asked how The Crumbling would be stopped. Were they connected or was Rune right to say they spoke in half-truths, and she was better off not dwelling on their words. Faye bit the inside of her lip. She needed better wording, a phrase that left nothing to interpretation. *Who were we made to tempt?*

The Creator's son, the vessels answered in their eerie singular voice.

The High Queen was The Creator's only legitimate child, but with the dark courts and their escapades, Saith could have fathered other children. He may not have even known he did.

Faye debated on her third question. The vessels would give her nothing worthwhile, but if she was going to ask again when she returned, what difference did it make? She would keep the question simple, give them less room to butcher her request.

Show me The Creator's son.

The vessels shuffled, clearing a space before Faye, and then the mirror changed, showing her a reflection. Faye turned back to look at Rune, standing at the doorway, still watching her.

Faye's attention returned to the mirror where Rune's reflection appeared as though it were placed in front of him. Rune and his brothers were the very image of their father. He couldn't be The Creator's son.

Sixty-Four

Faye didn't mention her visions to Rune. The third question could have been skewed as Chaos twisted her questions. She would need to return in a few days to confirm Rune was supposedly The Creator's son.

When Sadi arrived a few hours later, she and Rune phased to the stone slabs outside his study. The same suffocating dread clawed at her neck, and Faye stepped back. Maneuvering herself between herself, Rune, and the slab she would have their children on. She was certain something terrible happened here, and Rune confirmed it. The lives lost somehow sank their essence into the very stones she was now surrounded by, warning her away.

Almost sensing her discomfort, Rune stepped into her, stroking the back of her neck as he pulled his fingers gently through her hair. "Are you well?" he asked.

Faye nodded, turning toward Sadi.

"It would be better to be further away. Less chance of being walked through," Sadi said as she strolled out of the circle of stones. Her lace train swept over the crystalized ground.

Faye followed immediately, eager to get away from Rune's family altar. Faye expected the apprehension to grow as she approached the other ancient, moss covered, carved boulders, but her nerves calmed the further she got from the stone tying her mate to Hell.

"Witnessing is similar in skill to asking questions in the temple. Descend into yourself, and step out of your body. I'll be waiting," Sadi said, gazing into the unseen.

Faye did as Sadi said, withdrawing herself and subtly stepping out of her body and into the endless void. She glanced at the dark expanse, the rolling black mist clouding at their feet. Sadi materialized from the shadows and sashayed toward her. The mist drifted with her steps, and the sweeping train of her dress revealed a gleaming black marble floor.

"Where's Rune?" Faye asked, glancing at the place he'd stood in the physical realm.

"I have his consciousness," Sadi said. She held her hand out and waved her fingers in a tight roll, making a loose fist as she lifted it slightly. A shimmering silver strand rose from the mist at their feet and hovered in line with Sadi's waist.

It stretched past her sight's ability to follow, the strands varying in thickness. A few larger cocoons were braided in between the thin silver thread. "What is this?"

"Rune's woven cord. This is his life," Sadi answered.

Faye studied the end in front of them, recognizing her cord immediately. It resonated with her, embedded in her very being. Three threads constricted as if being woven by an unseen force, feeding the line as it slowly lengthened. When she concentrated on the center strand, Rune's scent enveloped her, comforting her with the presence of his mind. She reached forward, desperate to touch the cord bound to hers.

Sadi snatched her wrist before she made contact. "Do not touch the strands. Snapping threads end lives."

Faye's gaze shot up to Sadi, "Breaking this will kill him?"

Sadi released her and admired the silver thread, remaining silent momentarily. "Rune would be difficult to snap. His thread is at the center of fate's woven cord. Every life he is connected to intertwines with his." Sadi pinched her fingers near Rune's thread and pulled her hands apart. Two threads broke apart. "Rune, you, and I," Sadi said before allowing the threads to rest together once more.

Familiar were feared, and the more Faye learned of their magic, the more she realized how terrifying their power truly was.

"Familiar can kill without touching you," Faye said absently.

A smile played over Sadi's lips. "Those who cross Familiar wish they were dead."

Faye quieted at Sadi's smile. "How do we witness?" Faye asked, luring the conversation from what she was sure were murderous thoughts.

"There is an imprint of awareness," Sadi said. She hovered her hand over Rune's thread, curling two fingers as she flicked her wrist. The silver cord whipped past them in a blur. "Seize it and draw it out of the thread."

Their surroundings shifted, reshaping itself into gray stone walls, similar to the room she kept when first arriving in Hell, but the furnishings were different. Rune materialized from the shadows, straightening his jacket as he silently strolled toward his room.

There was no reservoir of power attached to her mate. Faye swallowed when his hand closed over the doorknob. "This isn't Rune. You're showing me his past."

"Witnessing a portion of his life," Sadi said from behind her.

Anger coiled inside her, snaking through her chest. She bit the urge to lash out at Sadi, knowing the High Queen would be in her bed waiting for the man they both called consort.

Rune opened the door, and Faye glimpsed gauzy pale blue material draped over an ornate canopy bed. The High Queen sat perfectly poised and bound in corseted lace.

Faye turned to Sadi. "You're a bitch."

The room blurred, dissolving away until they were in the strange void outside their bodies. Sadi cleaned her nail with the articulated claw of her ring. "If I wanted to be a bitch, I would have put us in the other room," Sadi said with a shrug. "Or brought us to Lyssa's Ceremony of Blood."

The only thing she wanted to see less than Rune with the High

Queen was her consort with her evil twin. Her serpents rose as her self-control deteriorated, begging to strike at the source of her ire.

Faye fought for patience as Sadi smiled. "Bearing witness can be unpleasant. Remain focused and hold your presence of mind. You did well."

Her shadowed snakes rose higher, flaring their hoods. This bitch was testing her? "What happens if you lose focus?"

Sadi waved her hand, and Rune's woven cord fell to the floor, vanishing into the rolling mist. "Never leave the thread you're using to connect to the past, and do not reach for minds. We pull memories from present minds, and we bear witness to the past."

Faye struggled to take the lesson, as unorthodox as it was. "What would have happened if I followed Rune?"

"Holding the thread becomes harder the further you travel from it. If you lose the thread connecting you to the present, you will be trapped within the memories you pulled forth."

The thought chilled Faye, dousing her fury. Was this one of the ways Familiar imprisoned people within their own bodies?

"What happens to them?" Faye asked.

"Chaos claims them, or they are rescued by a skilled Familiar."

And brought back to their bodies. If she lost herself here, would her body be a vacant-eyed shell? Her hand lowered to her twins, and a feral possessiveness tore through her.

She would never allow it.

"How did you call Rune's cord?" Faye asked.

Sadi arched a brow. "The same way you call a person in the Hall of Empty-Eyes."

Faye welled her power and held her hand over the rolling black mist. She summoned Prinia from Chaos's Heart. She could call Rune's fated cord. She thought of her mate, her most potent memory of him was when he held her close, the taste of his blood sweet on her tongue. She reached for his mind. His scent reached her first, amber and sandalwood calming her senses. His silver thread rose from the misted ground, lifting to her hand.

Faye smiled. It felt like a mental tether she used to speak to Rune telepathically. She let the connection snap, and the thread vanished beneath the floor.

"Good," Sadi said as her body evaporated into mist and shadow.

Her disembodied voice filled the space she stood. "Now rise to the physical plane."

Faye met Sadi and Rune in the strange mental space beyond the flesh.

"Places can also be witnessed. They don't have life threads, but time leaves an impression, embedding memories within the land. Your will calls upon the past," Sadi said as the stars in Hell's ever-twilight sky twinkled and moved rapidly across the sky.

Flickers of people appeared and vanished before Faye could identify them. Storm clouds flashed above them only to reappear a short time later. A dark-haired woman lied on plush red bedding over Rune's stone. She stood on her knees, baring down and fisting the shirt of a man who looked to have been Rune as she screamed.

They vanished with time before Faye could get a closer look. It continued for long moments, then…

Time froze.

Faye couldn't breathe.

Winged women were tightly bound to the stones, circling all around them. The cruel image faded as a prickling sensation snaked up her spine.

Another woman was here. Her body was dragged by her wrist, wings scraping against the unforgiving edge of the rocks.

This was punishment.

It felt too familiar, slashing at the back of her mind until she felt the biting grip of her own wrist—the sting of her phantom wings. The loose crystals ground under her feet as she planted her heels. Faye began to hyperventilate. Feeling every sensation as if it had happened to her.

The scene played in Faye's mind even as their surroundings remained frozen.

You can't do this! The realms must be balanced! Faye screamed as The Creator dragged her.

Faye fought, desperate to get away. Her fear saturated her senses, but it wasn't her life the woman's terror dug its claws into. She feared for her village and lands, of the lives who would perish during the next winter without the Elysian Queen's blessing.

The Creator bound her to the stone slab with a flicker of power. She fought frantically, but his magic was too strong, holding her in place.

I must complete the ritual, the woman cried.

The Creator's black hair fell over an eye as he glared down at his prey. Hell's twilight accentuated his high cheek bones. His full lips and chiseled features would have been handsome if not for his cruel yellow eyes.

Be silent, The Creator rasped.

Faye's voice was locked in her throat. Thousands would die, and she was helpless to save them.

Saith's magic crept up the stone, touching her feet and slithering up her legs. It gathered between her breasts and sank into her ribcage. Bile rose in Faye's throat. His magic felt tainted and wrong. Twisted.

A searing pain came next, and Faye's legs gave out. A scream tore past her lips as the magic The Creator laced into her body ripped free.

Sixty-Five

Rune caught Faye, her legs buckling as their surroundings returned to the present. Her desperate shriek lanced his ears, and she clawed at the center of her chest.

"Faye!" Rune yelled. Wild aggression lengthened his fangs as his gaze shot to Sadi. "What happened?" he demanded.

Sadi phased closer, pressing one hand to the side of Faye's face and the other to her belly.

"We didn't begin," Sadi said, assessing Faye.

The Ra'Voshnik roared as a second deafening scream lanced the sky. His queen shook in his arms, panting as her heart raced.

"How badly is she injured?" Rune snapped. He scented no blood and struggled to isolate the quiet heartbeats of their young.

Disembowel the fool who attacked our queen, Voshki demanded.

Be silent, Rune grated. Witnessing events never touched those watching, but his queen defied all rules of magic. Rune thanked the Darkness Sadi was close. She could heal any injuries Faye sustained.

Sadi pulled away, shaking her head. "I don't feel any damage."

Faye blinked, searching the stones as her lightning-streaked midnight eyes turned glassy with tears. She clutched her belly and sobbed. "Did he hurt my babies?"

He? Voshki fixated on the word as a cold, precise rage rolled through his mind. *Find him and strangle him with his spine.* A growl rumbled deep in Rune's chest. If anything befell his queen or their young, the realms would pay.

"No, your twins are fine." Sadi covered Faye's hand with hers. "Push your senses past your hand. You'll feel them. They're strong." She nodded and after Faye answered in kind, Sadi wiped the tears from her cheeks.

The intensity of Rune's rage leveled off as some of the tension in Faye's body left. He held her tighter, purring as she attempted to take deeper breaths. Her heart calmed as she softly ran her hand over her belly. "They're safe. They're okay," she chanted breathlessly.

His queen turned toward the stones and shrank against him. "Take me back to Anaria. I don't want to be here."

Rune nodded to Sadi before phasing into Faye's estate. Most of the rooms were furnished and ready for inhabitants.

The door opened and closed with a flicker of his mind. Rune shielded the room to afford his queen some privacy. A set of sheets were folded at the foot of the bare mattress.

"Speak to me," Rune said softly. He adjusted her in his arms and took a seat on the bed. Her shuddering breaths twisted his heart. He shifted his back and rested against the ornately carved headboard, collecting her on his lap. He flattened his hand over hers, still pressed to her stomach. "Our young are well, vsenia. Sadi assessed them. I hear their heartbeats."

He held her in silence and pressed a kiss to her hair. "Speak with me, love. Tell me what happened."

Bring her into our mind, Voshki growled. He prowled the edges of his mind, searching for an imaginary opponent to eviscerate. Viciousness and temper rolled off him in scorching waves.

Calm yourself. She needs comfort not violence, Rune grated.

The Ra'Voshnik growled but contained his rancor. *Bring her into our mind or get out of the way.*

"May I bring you into our mind. Voshki is growing increasingly concerned," Rune spoke softly, running his thumb over her back in small circles.

Faye nodded, leaning against him. Rune held her close, stroking her hair. He carried her awareness with him as he descended into himself.

Voshki sat beside him with Faye's legs in his lap. He unlaced her boots, tossing them to the ground. He rubbed her feet and a soft growl rumbled from him. "Who hurt you?" Voshki asked softly, masking the vicious need to massacre whoever attacked their queen.

"I saw…" Faye swallowed and wet her lips. "The Creator and a woman with wings. I remember it, felt it… like it was happening to me."

We should have killed Saith, Voshki growled.

Voshki's incessant focus led him in the wrong direction. The Creator returned to the Darkness centuries ago. Rune was more concerned with why Faye would recall the memory as though it were her own.

"We have you," Rune murmured, running his hands through her hair. "Are you in pain?"

Faye hugged his arm, pulling him closer. "No, it's the feelings."

"How do you mean?" Rune asked.

"It's fuzzy," Faye said, rubbing her collarbone. "I had to do something." She exhaled through her nose, seemingly frustrated. "The Creator stopped me, but there are gaps in the memory. I don't remember what I was supposed to do. People were going to die. I could feel it."

The Ra'Voshnik stroked her leg and said, "Familiar magic might affect you differently. We witness events. You might live them."

Faye ran her foot over Voshki's thigh. "You sound like Rune."

"I know everything he does," the Ra'Voshnik said. He smoothed his palm over Faye's calf and peered up at her. "You're still tense."

Faye shook her head. "It's nothing."

"Speak with us," Rune crooned. When she didn't respond, he added, "We are a team, vsenia."

She sighed and relaxed in his arms. "You can't use my own words against me."

"I most certainly can," Rune countered.

She fiddled with the cuff of his sleeve and said, "Sadi was being a bitch and showed a memory of you with the High Queen."

"I'm killing her," Voshki announced.

"Not *with her*, with her." Faye quieted. "You were going to her room from the consort's room."

Rune's face heated. His queen should never have borne witness to his past with Lyssa. "I am sorry," he said. "I will exchange words with her."

"I'm going to exchange the position of her organs," Voshki growled.

Rune glared at the Ra'Voshnik, and he winked in response. He inhaled for patience and buried the urge to drag him into the recesses of his mind. Voshki served their queen in his own way but obeyed her will without question.

"Can I do anything for you? Run you a bath?" Rune asked.

"Sit with you while you visit your garden," the Ra'Voshnik added.

"I'm tired," Faye sighed.

"Shall I make the bed here, or did you want to return to our room?" Rune asked.

Faye took a deep breath. Rune was a moment from lifting her to arrange the bed when she answered, "Our bed. I can't be around the stones for a little while."

"Yes, my queen." Rune stood, ascending to his physical body.

She stays with us. Take her from me, and I'll open your throat, the Ra'Voshnik grated.

Uncivilized as ever, Rune muttered.

You could remain here and give me our body. Apprehension filled Rune, and the Voshki laughed, before adding, *Share her, or I'll take her from you.*

Rune refused to rise to Voshki's bait. He divided his attention between his mind and his physical body and phased them to their room. The Ra'Voshnik waited for them in bed. At the very least, he had the decency to partially cover himself at the waist.

We won't be fucking her until you feel more like yourself, the Ra'Voshnik said as Rune leaned over their bed to place Faye between them.

Rune slipped out of his jacket and removed his cufflinks. Faye rolled on her side, clutching his pillow. Rune smiled softly.

It would appear she prefers me, Rune said to the Ra'Voshnik's mind.

Voshki purred, curling up to Faye's back. His arm draped over her, laying a possessive hand over Faye's abdomen. *She's taking pity on you since I fathered her young.*

Rune's smile widened as he removed his shirt. Faye's children were his. Voshki hadn't been present during the Hunter's Moon. Rune tugged on the corner of his pillow, and Faye grumbled as he pulled it away.

Faye rested her head on his chest when he joined her. Her legs tangled with Voshki's as he brushed the back of his claws over her belly.

"If the realms were wise, they would protect you," Rune said.

Faye slid her hand down the Ra'Voshnik's forearm, taking his hand. "I think Necromia is doing the opposite."

Voshki closed his eyes, settling behind her. "The realms will burn if anything happens to you."

"We don't burn realms," Faye said sternly. The Ra'Voshnik didn't reply, and Faye snuggled closer. She inhaled, her nails scraping over his ribs. "You're starting to smell really good again."

Faye breathed deeply even as her remaining tension slipped from her body. He spoke quietly, running his fingers through her hair.

"You can feed when you wake."

Sixty-Six

Rune lay awake, listening to the steady beat of Faye's heart. Voshki mentally nudged him, and he turned the Ra'Voshnik's way.

Sleep. I can watch your dreams.

No, but thank you, Rune replied to Voshki's mind. His queen had been through enough. The last thing she needed was for him to wake from a nightmare disorientated and attack her.

Rune watched over his ever-twilight sky for a handful of hours while his night breeze and the Ra'Voshnik dozed beside him. Faye slept often, but Sadi assured him fatigue was common during pregnancy.

He would need to speak with her. Rune exhaled. He was certain Sadi's intention aligned with his own, but it did not afford her liberties to disrespect his queen. *Their queen,* Rune thought. Sadi served in Faye's court. It was time she was reminded of the fact.

Faye shifted beside him, groaning as she stretched her arm out and yawned. A low rumble sounded from the Ra'Voshnik, part growl, part purr, as he tightened his hold on her.

"I'm so tired of being exhausted or hungry," Faye said with a groan.

"You have a few more months of it, love." Voshki pressed a kiss between her shoulder blades and returned Faye's awareness to her physical body.

Rune ascended, glancing down at his night breeze.

Let her drink. I'll tend to her when you need to step back, the Ra'Voshnik's voice floated through his mind.

"Do you want blood, or shall I bring you a plate of chicken fingers?" Rune asked.

Faye was quiet, tracing shapes on the center of his chest. "I can drink from Voshki," she said, her voice scarcely over a whisper.

It warmed his heart how much she cared for him. "He will rise when I need to take a step back," Rune said, placing his hand over hers, stilling her movements. "Your presence calms me. You allow me to work through the memories."

Faye glanced up at him. Hurt tinged her smile and it uncoiled a knot deep in his chest. His queen beheld every part of him, and fear never stained her. She would share in his victories and his pain. A partner and equal he would serve until the Darkness dragged him from her.

She took his hand and lightly nipped his wrist before pressing her lips over her bite. "Do I drink from here again?"

"For now," Rune said, lifting his chin to motion behind her.

Faye rolled over and Rune positioned himself lower. He breathed in her delicate scent. The night breeze through plum blossoms he would follow for eternity. He clenched his jaw as his fangs lengthened.

He leaned up squeezing her close as he bit into his wrist. Rune lowered himself behind her. One arm around her waist, pinning her ass to his ribs and the other beneath her with his wrist near her face.

Her mouth closed over his bite, and Rune closed his eyes. The feel of her lips and tongue stirred his body, immediately taking his mind to the metal chair Sadira and her court strapped him to.

Scent her. You're with our queen. Open your eyes. The Ra'Voshnik replaced his mental image with one of death and carnage. The massacre his court wrought when they freed him.

Rune opened his eyes, pulling Faye tighter to him. She was his anchor and tether to the present.

He was home. In his bed. With his queen.

Rune slipped his hand under Faye's shirt, feeling the softness of her skin. Her muscles were tense, but she didn't move. Didn't make a sound. Drinking from him as her breaths became labored.

He scented her arousal, and a pang of guilt stabbed him. Perhaps she was too perfectly suited for him. She wasn't one of his kind, but she behaved as one. He should have her pinned beneath him and let her drink from his throat. Fucking her until she screamed his name with her teeth still holding her bite.

Touch her. She misses you. The Ra'Voshnik urged his hand lower, wanting him to press his fingers into her slick heat until she came on his hand.

He couldn't, afraid to mix Faye into his haunted memories. He closed his eyes, rubbing the side of his face to the middle of her back. A soft purr slipped from him, and he lifted his hand higher. His fingertips stroking in a feather light caress.

A breathy sigh sounded above him as he found the space between her breasts and traced the swell of the underside in lazy strokes. Moving from one side to the other.

I am home, in my bed, with my queen.

Rune repeated the words thinking only of the woman in his arms.

Faye's blood heated with Rune's touch. Her toes curled as she struggled to remain still. The rich taste of his blood made her skin tingle. Increasing her sensitivity. The slow stroke of his hand pulled at her shirt, shifting the material across her nipples, driving her mad.

She squeezed her thighs together, fighting the urge to roll her hips. Darkness, she was wet and aching for him. Desperate for him to fill her.

Faye squeezed his hand, holding his wrist while she drank. Rune needed time, and she would give it to him.

His hand suddenly left her shirt, and Faye opened her eyes. Disappointment bloomed in her at the loss of his touch. Rune pulled away from her, rolling her onto her back as he rose above her.

Veined misted shadows stretched beneath Voshki's dark gaze. "Rough or gentle?" he asked with a smirk.

Faye cupped the side of his face, and Voshki's lids slid closed as he purred, leaning into her touch.

"Where's Rune?" Faye asked.

He inhaled deeply and nipped her palm. "He needed to step back. He's fine, vsenia." Voshki lowered his head, trailing kisses along the side of her neck, stopping at her ear. "Do you want to be tended to or fucked?"

Faye turned toward him, flicking her tongue over his bottom lip. "I'm still hungry, and I want this," Faye said, stroking his hard length through his slacks.

"Thirsty," Voshki corrected, sitting back. He pinned her hip to the bed and gripped the front of her pants.

Faye gasped when he tore the fabric, tossing the shredded remains to the floor. He ripped her shirt open next and left the tattered material on. He canted his head as the corner of his mouth lifted into a smirk.

"You are most beautiful naked and spread beneath me," Voshki growled.

Faye smiled up at her beautiful hunter. "You talk too much," she teased.

A wide grin spread over his mouth, revealing his lengthening fangs. "If you wanted me silent, you should have asked me to tend to you."

Faye giggled as he lifted her against him. His black tipped claws carefully dragged over her ass while he unfastened his pants, pulling himself free.

"Drink and writhe on my cock," Voshki said, running his claw over the side of his neck.

Crimson pooled at the base of his collar bone, begging to be tasted, trickling over his chest. Faye pressed her mouth to his throat, sweeping her tongue over what he offered. Spiced honey coated her tongue. She swallowed and as his delicious warmth spread through her, settling between her legs.

Faye wrapped her arms around him, molding her breasts to the hard planes of his body. She moaned at the feel of Voshki's cock. The broad head pressed through her desire slick folds, teasing her entrance. Stretching her to take the very tip of him but going no further.

Faye moaned, sucking harder. She wiggled her hips, attempting to lower herself on his thick length. Needing him inside her.

Voshki chuckled and held her up. His fingertips digging into her hips as he teased her with shallow strokes.

Frustrated, Faye raked her nails over his back.

Voshki groaned, leaning his head back but continued his slow torture. "You're getting warmer, vsenia."

Faye took another greedy swallow, scratching his back again. Warmer? He wanted her to do something before he would fuck her. Faye smoothed her hand up the back of his neck, tangling her fingers through his hair before fisting it.

Voshki growled, and Faye released him.

"I'll be sure to fist your hair when I fuck your throat," Voshki said, his tone teasing.

Faye bit him playfully and Voshki groaned, thrusting a few inches into her. She moaned, easing her bite and he withdrew.

She glanced up at him, knowing he couldn't see her, but she hoped he felt her annoyance. Faye bit down hard and was rewarded with his brutal rhythm. She came around his cock as bliss rained down through her body. Each note intensified with the taste of his blood.

Faye's eyes fluttered shut. She was dimly aware of the bed meeting her back, and Voshki hooked her knee with his elbow, holding her legs open as he drove into her.

A breathy cry escaped Faye's parted lips as she wrapped her arms around his neck. "I will never get tired of the little whimper you make when I stretch you around my cock," Voshki murmured, pinching, and plucking her nipples.

Faye's breathing became frantic, and she bit down, needing him rougher. A purr or growl rumbled beneath her teeth, and Faye smiled before biting harder.

He mercilessly fucked her, and Faye cried, "Voshki!"

He growled and angled her head to the side. Faye panted, taking his harsh cadence, helpless to do anything else as she writhed beneath him. His rough pleasure overwhelmed her senses, and she needed more. Wanted everything. Needed him.

Faye dropped her shoulder and leaned into Voshki's hold, offering her throat.

The cool brush of his hair skimmed over her breasts. Tension coiled in Faye as his lips brushed her throat. A touch of warmth. The kiss of fangs.

Faye screamed, coming with his bite. Voshki gentled his strokes, drawing out her pleasure until she clawed at his back and wantonly rocked her hips.

"Harder," she breathed. She wanted him rough and claiming.

He filled her, stretched her, and drank her. The tension in her rose too quickly. She shook violently, screaming his name as she shattered. Pleasure cascaded through her, pin pricks along her nerve endings as she stared, limp and euphoric.

Voshki tightened his embrace, groaning against her as he thrust into her a final time. His cock twitched and a lazy grin spread over her parted lips. He poured himself into her, squeezing her close each time his cock pulsed inside her.

Short of breath and covered in a thin sheen of perspiration, Faye tucked a length of white-blonde hair behind Voshki's ear. He purred, nuzzling his bite as he whispered to her.

"I love you, vsenia. Now and always. I'm yours to command."

Sixty-Seven

Rune sat at the head of the tub while Faye soaked. Her shoulders sunk beneath the warm water as he rinsed the sparkling nectar shampoo coating her hair. The steam lifted through the air, causing his back to burn further. Not from the memory of being whipped at Sadira's court, but from scratches Faye left over his back.

Faye's lightning-streaked midnight eyes met his and moved lower. A frown formed on her dark lips.

"I think I bit you too hard," she said, lifting her hand out of the water.

Her fingers grazed over the side of his throat, the touch soft and gentle, opposite of the sensations plaguing his dreams. Rune smiled. He missed his queen even though she'd never left. "I assure you, you did not."

The tender bite would be healed by morning. He rather enjoyed the marks she left on his skin.

There is a method to my madness, the Ra'Voshnik's voice sounded. Voshki rested in the recesses of his mind, on the verge of slumber. *Her claws replaced their whip. Her teeth replaced their touch. It will help ground your mind,* Voshki yawned the last before falling silent.

Perhaps the Ra'Voshnik had a point. Rune gazed down at his queen. The woman he wished for his entire life.

"If only you had fangs," Rune teased, brushing the pad of his thumb over her bottom lip.

She nipped him and sat up. "You've pampered me enough. I need real food now."

"Still craving Vashien's cooking?" Rune asked as he retrieved a towel for her.

Faye gave him an apologetic look as she dried off. "It's comfort food."

Rune arched a brow, and Faye laughed, throwing the towel at him. He hung it on a bar as she walked past him. Her body hadn't changed much. She'd grown fuller through her torso. A change Rune already liked.

She disappeared into her closet, and Rune heard fabric rustling. Rune leaned in the doorway as Faye pulled her shirt off. "We're going clothes shopping today," she demanded.

Rune swallowed the chuckle in his throat when she glared his way. "Yes, my queen."

"These clothes make me feel like a sausage," Faye said, throwing the shirt on her dresser.

Tell her she's a very cute sausage, Voshki said groggily.

Have you gone mad? Rune growled. The Ra'Voshnik muttered to himself before dozing off again.

"Voshki is sleeping. I believe we can have an uneventful trip to The Square," Rune said, sifting through a few of her dresses until he found the flowing blue material least likely to offend his queen. He pulled the dress free and held out his peace offering. "You and the blonde harpy haven't been to Necromia in some time."

"I'll bribe her with food," Faye said, pulling the long dress over her head. "And you need new clothes."

"I could adopt Familiar dress and wear a scarf."

"No, you're getting some normal clothes. Go get dressed. I'm hungry," Faye said, shooing him out of her closet.

Rune stripped out of the slacks he'd worn all night and dressed in a fresh tailored black suit. He turned his head to the side, inspecting the edge of Faye's bite peeking over the collar of his shirt.

"Bitch," Sparrow yelled, followed by a pair of footsteps running down the hall. Vashien no doubt attempted to bring Sparrow to heel. "I'm starving. Let's go!"

Vashien caught Sparrow's arm as she stepped into their room and pulled her back into the hall. "You don't need to be in their room, woman."

Sparrow brushed him off dramatically. "This is Faye's room, and I'm always allowed in her room..." The harpy's gaze fell to his rumpled sheets. "At least make the bed, so it doesn't look like you just fucked her. She's pregnant. You did your job. You can get off her now—"

Rune didn't have the chance to cover his ears before Vashien threw her over his shoulder. "We'll be out front," Vashien said, mouthing *sorry* and vanishing.

Rune arched a brow, and she shrugged with a lopsided smile. He offered his arm and said, "Shall we."

They strolled to the great room, and Faye leaned closer to him. "I thought I would be walking in on an earful."

Sparrow snorted. "He might find himself tied up tomorrow morning after he goes to sleep."

"No," Vashien said.

Sparrow's arms fell to her side, and she dropped her head back dramatically. "Don't be a pussy. Faye ties Runey up all the time." The petite blonde pouted when her male didn't respond. "Faye showed me how to tie a cute star on your chest."

Rune lifted his chin toward Sparrow. "She will lie and say your arms need to be behind you to achieve the effect. They do not."

Sparrow bounced up on her toes and gave Vashien a toothy grin. "I'll leave your arms out."

Vash curled his wing around her, tucking her to his side. "No."

Sparrow transformed with a flash of light, illuminating Vashien's wing for a moment into oranges and pinks. His darker veins forked through his membranous wings before fading to their normal dark green. A small white cat climbed up his sleeve to perch on his shoulder.

"Don't fall and break your kitty nose," Faye laughed.

Sparrow pinned her ears back and bared her little fangs.

"Shield yourself, please," Rune said, running the backs of his fingers along Faye's arm, prompting her to take his hand. "Shall we."

Rune phased the four of them to the landing pad in Necromia. Sparrow leaped down from Vashien's shoulder and rose a woman.

"This is The Square," she said, gawking at the brightly lit signs. Ignoring or oblivious of the crowd that drew away from them.

"It is," Rune answered as he strolled forward with Faye. The Square was a collection of fine shops with a sprinkling of eateries and a few fine restaurants. Where the darker more established courts came to shop.

An array of scents assaulted Rune and he recalled why he avoided this place, preferring vendors to bring their wares to his home instead. The smell of grilled meats with hints of onion, garlic, and rosemary drifted from blocks away, mingling with a wide variety of sweets. Layered with the food where the people and the perfumes pretentious nobles deemed popular for the time being.

"Can we go to Obsidian, Runey?" Sparrow beamed.

"Sparrow," Faye said, widening her eyes at her sister.

"What? You have to be royalty to get in there. This…" Sparrow waved her hand at Rune. "…is royalty." Sparrow clamped her mouth shut, then whispered, "Bitch, *you* are royalty." She snorted. "We don't need you anymore, your shadowy highness."

"Don't make me throw you over my shoulder in public," Vashien said.

Sparrow wedged herself between himself and Faye, then pulled her hand from the bend of his arm.

"Ow, hooker, that was my foot," Faye said.

Sparrow linked arms with Faye and sniffed loudly. "That bakery smells amazing," the blonde harpy said dreamily. Without another word, the pair hurried across the street.

Vashien fell into step beside him as they followed their women. "I'll try to minimize her influence over the twins."

Rune chuckled. "It is appreciated."

"I don't think they notice the crowd parting for them," Vashien said quietly as the patrons exited the bakery.

The corner of Rune's mouth lifted. "Sparrow has a way of

drawing and keeping attention, does she not?"

"That's a nice way of putting it," Vashien laughed.

Rune entered the colorful shop. Faye laughed with Sparrow, eating what looked like cut apples, nuts, and honey out of a small cup. The shopkeeper met his gaze and her eyes widened. Rune tensed, ready to restrain the Ra'Voshnik but the charge of violence never came.

He reached for Voshki and found him sleeping peacefully, in the deep recesses of his mind that once imprisoned him. Perhaps Faye had been correct. Life was far more manageable cooperating with the Ra'Voshnik instead of fighting it every moment of his life.

The shopkeeper averted her gaze and smiled at Faye and Sparrow holding a tray of small cakes. Faye picked one with ripe berries, a whipped layer of cream, and a golden yellow pastry peaked over the rim. They selected half a dozen sweets, and the shop keeper packed each sister a flashy box topped with glittering ribbons.

Faye and Sparrow handed their boxes to their respective men and walked past them into the street, enjoying their treats. Rune glanced down at the flamboyant box and arched a brow at Vashien.

"You knew what you were signing up for," Vashien said, following Sparrow and Faye.

"And I still only have her out of proxy," Rune answered with a chuckle.

They followed the sisters, weaving into one shop after the other. Sparrow stopped in front of a two-story clothing store, Verity Gordon Couture.

"Hooker, you need a dress by Verity. Her designs are amazing aaaaand she's Familiar," Sparrow said, fluffing her hair as she led Faye through the revolving glass doors.

Rune sat with Vashien in high-backed leather chairs as Faye and Sparrow searched through racks of clothing. Verity laid out several clothing articles and brought fabric bolts when she learned of Faye's pregnancy. His queen would need three wardrobes to suit her phases of pregnancy, and she was nearly done with the first.

Rune acclimated himself with what to expect the very day their beating hearts woke him. Sadi was a gifted healer and checked the development of their young routinely. He exhaled, thinking of the Familiar princess.

He reached for her mind, sipping his glass of crimson wine. *We must have words.*

How is she? Sadi asked.

The Ra'Voshnik roused at the sound of Sadi's voice, rising through his mind.

She is well. What possessed you to bring her to witness my time with Lyssa? Rune asked, attempting to keep the growl out of his voice.

She needs to be tested, Sadi hissed.

She does not—

She has no hold on her power. Rune, she is too strong to allow her magic to be at the whim of her emotions.

Sadi's words riled the Ra'Voshnik. *Let me kill her,* he growled to Rune.

Faye held up a pink blouse and a gray dress, smiling at him. Rune motioned to the dress, and she went back to speaking with Verity.

She is gaining control. Do not disrespect my Queen. Your Queen, Rune bit out. He smiled at Faye and lifted his chin, allowing her to hold a sweater to his chest. She quirked her mouth to one side and exchanged the sweater with a turtleneck.

Faye walked off and Rune silently prayed she would not make him wear either but knew she would purchase at least one of them.

She is not my Queen. I serve your interests not hers, Sadi said with a deathly calm.

My interests are only of my Queen. Do not disrespect her a second time. You are too clo—

Rune snapped the mental tether and relished the quiet evening of his queen shopping with her sister.

Sixty-Eight

Faye watered her garden, enjoying the sun on her back. One week passed since she decreed for her petitions to be answered in a day. She'd hardly slept the first few nights, expecting the dark-bloods to ignore her requests. To her surprise, they hastily replied, communicating directly with Alister.

She set her oversized watering can beside the half-moon fountain and pushed up the sleeves of her new maroon dress. It had simple lines but fit over her new curves. Faye banished her original wardrobe. She wouldn't be able to squeeze into them until after the twins were born.

Faye. Alister's voice ricocheted through her mind, and she tensed. *We have an issue at your estate. Hurry. I'm calling the others.*

He snapped the communication tether before Faye could reply. She phased into Rune's study.

"Did Alister tell you what's happening?" she asked.

He silently strolled toward her from behind his desk and offered his hand. "The court is gathering. We will know shortly."

Faye nodded and slid her fingers over his palm. Their surroundings faded, and they reappeared in her study in Anaria. A man she didn't recognize sat beside an arrangement of flowers near her sister and Vash. He winced as Sadi pushed his gray hair back, and Faye stepped closer, attempting to observe more details. His lip was split, and blood trickled down his scalp toward his temples.

"My queen," the man cried, scurrying away from Sadi. He rushed forward and fell to his knees, bowing his head. "They took Jeneane. Please bring my daughter back."

Faye knelt with him. "Who took her?"

"Men came to his village," Alister began, holding up an envelope between two fingers. "They took his daughter and claimed this was payment."

Rage coiled through Faye. They kidnapped her? She buried her fiery emotions and lifted the man's face. "We'll get her back—"

The man clasped her hand in his. "Thank you. Thank you." He sobbed, pressing his forehead to their joined hands.

Damian rubbed the man's back and helped him to his feet. "Take a seat, friend. We'll fetch your little bird."

Faye perceived Sadi's power rising as wisps of her magic circled the man. He went still and nodded with an unnatural calm, letting Damian lead him back to his chair.

She frowned and turned toward Sadi. "What are you doing to him?"

"Calming his mind," she answered simply.

Faye glanced back at Jeneane's father. Spelling his mind was better than letting him suffer, she supposed. Damian poured their guest a whiskey. Faye motioned toward the envelope Alister held. "Do we know what court did this?"

"Jeneane was abducted by the Court of Golden Scales," he replied. "I'll deliver the petition personally."

"No," Faye snapped. These dark-bloods came to her realm and stole one of her people. She wasn't going to leave her at their mercy for another day. She'd failed Cleo and Christine, leaving them to suffer with their captors for weeks.

She wouldn't fail Jeneane.

Sparrow bumped her hip against Faye's as she pulled on a pair of fitted leather gloves. "Let's go fuck their life, hooker."

If they hurt Jeneane, Faye would extract their pain as payment. She glanced up at Rune. "Do you know them?"

He shook his head once. "I have not heard of their court. I will have our travel arranged."

"Did you want all of us present, dove?" Damian asked from his seat on a sofa near the crackling fire.

"No," Faye said. Rune accompanied her anytime she left Hell. The two of them were enough of a show of force.

Sparrow called a harness and strapped two swords to her back. "I'm going with you. I need to protect my future niece and nephew."

Sadi glanced at Sparrow's weaponry, unimpressed. "Call us if you need assistance," she said, getting to her feet and vanishing.

Damian went after her. His scarf swayed as he gave a flourished bow. His disembodied voice lingered long after he was gone, circling Sparrow. "See you at dawn."

A small male with curly blonde hair stuffed under a fedora stood near the grand double doors in Faye's Hall. He removed his hat with shaking hands and placed it over his chest, bowing as they approached.

"Afternoon, my lady." The man's voice didn't waver, but his eyes lifted before dropping to the floor. He swallowed and pressed his hands together. "Traveling to the Court of Golden Scales?"

"Yes, thank you." Faye smiled, attempting to put the poor soul at ease.

His pale eyes darted behind her once, and Faye reached for Rune's hand. His reputation terrified most, and it would only be mended with time.

Their surroundings slowly faded as if the light in the room drained away. Sunlight suddenly snapped into place, stinging Faye's eyes. They'd materialized on a stone platform. Faye squinted as they adjusted.

They stood beneath an overhanging stained-glass awning,

shielding them from direct sunlight. It followed a winding pathway to a beautiful three-story home surrounded by manicured trees and hedges.

"The Court of Golden Scales," the man announced and faded from view.

Rune stepped off the platform and straightened his coat. "This is a court of vampires."

"How can you tell?" Sparrow asked as they walked toward the veranda.

The brick home itself was simple. The ornate metalwork over the glass awning and the home's shuddered windows were reminiscent of the expansive greenhouse Alister built for Prinia.

"The glass is spelled," Rune said, lifting his chin. "The metalwork designs are how my kind recognize it is safe to approach."

Faye glanced up at the colored curve of glass above them. The evidence of vampires left her chest tight, but Jeneane wasn't a woman in love with a man who saw her as a pretty bottle of wine. This court kidnapped a woman, and because she was Anarian they foolishly believed repercussions wouldn't follow.

Her sister snorted. "What happens if it's just fancy glass?"

"Have you seen a vampire in sunlight?" Vashien asked. "They don't disappear in a puff of smoke."

"My kind burn. I imagine they would subject their host to the same treatment," Rune said.

Her vampire walked in the sun, and Faye hoped their children would as well. She pushed her awareness over the white brick home and was met with nearly a dozen reservoirs of power. They were in separate parts of the home, and Faye's senses recoiled when she touched a familiar subconscious.

The tainted film coating this mind reminded Faye of a summer when she'd been selecting fruit in the market. She picked up a basket of strawberries to find another beneath it that had been crushed. It rotted, spreading mold to its neighbors.

That's what Delilah was, rotted goods, spreading her decay to anyone who encountered her.

"The Queen of Lace and Bone is with them," Faye said as she walked up the stairs.

A brass knocker depicting a snake biting its tail was at the center of each door. Rune's elegant fingers closed over the serpent's head. He knocked twice. The door clicked and opened, revealing a small hall.

Gothic standing candelabras lined either side leading to a black crystal throne beneath a smoke quartz chandelier. The Queen of Lace and Bone leaned back on the throne in dramatic movements, placing her hands on either armrest as she crossed her legs in a flourish.

The slit of Delilah's glittering black dress parted to her waist. A black lace mask studded with diamonds swept over her sharp features, red streaks trailing down her cheek from a smooth white stone.

Faye's stomach knotted. It was a cheekbone trailing blood down her face.

Movement beside the throne caught her attention. A woman with curly brown hair crouched on her hands and knees, pressed to the side of the crystal throne. She bowed her head, hiding her face behind a veil of hair.

"Jeneane?" Faye shouted, rushing forward.

The woman lifted her head, and Faye's heart seized. Half of her face sagged unnaturally, and Faye's predatory stare snapped toward Delilah. The sadistic bitch was wearing Jeneane's cheekbone.

Faye's power rose through her, flowing past her as wings burst from her back. Her strength radiated past her physical body, causing her hair and clothing to sway around her.

Delilah smiled and drummed her fingers on the black crystal. "Go back to your peasant realm. You are not my Queen, and your word is meaningless here."

Whispers slithered through Faye's mind. Seductive murmurs urged her to sink her claws into Delilah's awareness and drag her into the psychic chasm cradling the Darkness. She would dive, holding her close, and watch as the Darkness—her Darkness—destroyed every facet of her.

It was a feeling, Faye reminded herself. She took a steadying breath. These were instincts and desires. She could choose not to act on them.

The depth of her power grew, gathering at her feet. She longed for the crystalline spikes in Hell as her magic sparked beneath her fingers, a coiling bed of vipers just beneath the surface of her humanity, anxious for her to name their targets.

The presence Faye felt throughout the estate began to flicker and appear in the shadows of the hall. The sound of steel being drawn rang all around her, and Faye wasn't sure if her sister and Vash's swords were among them.

"Did you know fear sweetens the blood, Shadow Prince?" Delilah fisted Jeneane's hair, dragging her up as she wailed. Her court crept forward, surrounding them.

Faye wanted to kill them. To rend their bodies and let the bloody debris fall to the ground as the monoliths crashed in Hell. "No," Faye sighed, breathlessly as she floated a foot off the ground. She wouldn't kill them, but she would repay the cruelty they inflicted today.

Power lashed from Faye, her shadowed serpents striking Delilah and each member of her court.

"Prey." Faye smiled, uncoiling more of her power. Screams chorused, surrounding her in a sweet melody They thought they could take Jeneane because she was an Anarian. Her life didn't matter.

"You can't take my people and think I won't follow," Faye crooned as she walked toward Delilah.

Their terror fed her dark impulses. She felt each of them as they dropped their weapons. Laughed as they lifted their hands in a futile attempt to protect themselves. Faye fixated on Delilah's screams. Her shadowed serpent flared its hood and struck her mask, not once but twice, claiming the bone beneath her eye.

Clutching her ruined face, Delilah and her court fled. Their reservoirs of power blinked out one by one as they phased away. Her snakes arched high behind her as she heard movement.

Jeneane screamed, scurrying away as she sobbed uncontrollably.

Her fear-stricken face hollowed Faye. She lowered to the ground as her power ebbed. Sparrow rushed past her, and Jeneane crawled to her sister. She hugged her tight, turning away from Faye.

Hurt clawed at her throat as she backed away from her sister. Rune's strong hand met the small of her back, and she leaned into him.

"She's afraid of me," Faye whispered, her pain resonating deeper after saying it aloud.

His hand curved over her hip, pulling her closer. "Power is feared. It is the way of things, vsenia."

Faye didn't want to be feared. She wanted to be a safe haven to her people. Her heart twisted each time Jeneane looked nervously at her, confirming the truth. In her attempts of protection, she became the threat.

Jeneane ducked back into Sparrow's shoulder. Faye turned away, unable to see the reflection of her actions. "Ask Sadi to heal her please. We need to search the rest of this place. I can't feel Anarians."

"Yes, my queen."

Sixty-Nine

Faye stood in Rune's study. Her vampire held her loosely before the wrought iron glass. Sadi healed Jeneane, restoring the bone and tissue Delilah had taken. Faye had kept her distance even after Sadi calmed her mind. She had saved her, yet Jeneane shrank from her each time she approached. Stealing glances at her while she hid behind Sparrow as though she feared Faye might attack her next.

The afternoon weighed heavily on Faye, hollowing her until she was numb. Every move she made was in error.

Sparrow and Alister returned Jeneane to her family and Faye let Rune phase them to Hell. He held her in silence as she gazed down at the dark stone slabs arranged in a circle outside. Stark against Hell's glittering floor.

The faint glow from the sky, or possibly the crystals themselves, reflected against the carved rocks, illuminating the edges in pinks, purples, and blues. Her mate's realm was breathtaking, but all she felt as she stared at Rune's altar was Saith's dark magic slithered over her.

Was this the warning of death Sadi saw looming over the horizon? Faye had felt the woman die on Rune's stone as though it were her. Her hand dropped protectively over her twins. Was she meant to die there? Would her children?

They inherited Rune's vampiric blood. If binding them to Hell endangered them, Rune would understand. Faye leaned heavily on her mate and breathed, "I need to go to the Hall of Empty Eyes."

Rune canted his head and gently caressed her side. "What troubles you, love?"

"The stone scares me," Faye reluctantly admitted. "I need to make sure they'll be safe if I tie them to your realm."

Rune's hand splayed over her middle. "Our children are well. Their heartbeats are strong and steady."

For how long? Faye looped her finger through his belt loop, staring up at him. Please understand. "I need to be sure."

Rune drew her closer and she lingered in the safety of his embrace. "As you command," he whispered.

Faye's surroundings faded. The intricately designed window was replaced with tall double doors leading into the Familiar temple. Thunder rolled, and lightning streaked through the storm-cracked sky, casting harsh shadows against the blackened wood.

Rune released her and took a step back. "I await your return, vsenia."

Faye nodded and pushed the heavy door open. The creak of its hinges echoed through the corridor. She crossed the threshold and the mirrors blurred to reveal rows of ashen bodies. The beat of her heart echoed her steps as she warily strolled into the hall. She turned to face the vessels, meeting the vacant gaze of the woman standing directly in front of her. Dread seeped into her bones and Faye's hand skimmed over her abdomen.

She swallowed. A choice and a consequence. Rune dismissed their warnings as Familiar nonsense, but Sadi's words struck her. Phrasing was important. Crucial. Faye spent hours pouring over her previous visits. Writing down their responses and arranging them side by side.

Faye crafted her questions, hoping if she used the words they provided, they would recognize her meaning and answer her, instead of leading her in circles. Faye projected her first question into the expanse the empty-eyed vessels occupied.

Are the choices and consequences between the flesh made for temptation and ending The Crumbling one and the same?

The vessels stilled and leaned their heads back before gaping their mouths wide. Eerie voices slithered past their motionless lips, speaking as one all around her. *Made and fashioned. One and the same.*

Faye's heart raced. It worked. The vessels were like aging villagers whose minds deteriorated before their bodies. It was easier to walk with them through their memories than try to force them into the present.

She turned their words over in her mind. If she chose to follow Rune's traditions and died on the stones, the realms would suffer her mate's rage.

Faye projected her next question. *Show me the consequences of The Creator's son's choice.*

The glass rattled as thunder boomed inside the temple. Faye's breath caught as the sky fractured above the vessels, red and angry. They spoke as one, their voices circling her in a rush. *The Creator fashioned the maddened darkness. The Creator made death.*

What? Death and the maddened darkness? A chill ran down her spine as she searched the bleeding sky. There were no landmarks, no way to tell where this was. Faye rubbed her collarbone, and the scene dissipated. The vessels righted themselves and began swaying once more.

Was the sky their emotions? Had she angered them? Faye had one question left, and she came to see the death that would shape the realms.

A heartbeat passed. Two… and Faye forced her words into the endless void of Chaos.

Show me the Shadow Prince choosing to destroy the realms.

The temple dissipated, giving way to the room Faye shared with Rune.

Faye saw herself beneath her vampire. Her toned legs wrapped around his lean waist while he made love to her. Their sheets were a tangled mess, pillows strewn about.

None of this was unusual.

Faye expected to be outside, surrounded by the stone slabs Rune and the other Shadowmen were born on. How was this Rune choosing the destruction of the realms? Faye glanced toward his small desk and froze. The window was wrong. Narrow windows were evenly spaced along the exterior wall instead of the larger window he rebuilt for her.

Faye swallowed as she looked at Rune's desk.

A black skirt was tossed haphazardly over his books and documents. Tulle and lace made up the train, spilling over Rune's chair. Faye's mouth went dry, and a laugh she recognized so well sounded behind her.

Faye's heart constricted, and she turned, unable to escape the vision she no longer wanted to see.

The woman Faye desperately wanted to believe was her, dug her nails into Rune's shoulder. Hellfire glinted off the articulated ring covering Sadi's index finger.

Faye stared in disbelief.

A rush of tears collected on her lashes.

"Stop. I don't want to see this," Faye said, stepping back.

The vessels paid her no heed. It continued, and she hated the way he moved. Tension set in his shoulders, and bile rose in Faye's throat. He was close, watching Sadi affectionately—but the veined misted shadows Faye saw with him were completely absent.

"Offer me your throat."

Faye touched the back of her hand to her lips as her tears fell. This wasn't real. This never happened. He loved her.

"Stop," Faye cried, closing her eyes. The vision continued, playing behind her lids.

Rune lowered his head, and each of Sadi's moans cut Faye deeper than the last. Sadi came beneath him, and Rune purred, "The sounds you make, vsenia."

"Make it stop!" Faye shouted. Rune growled and thrust harder. His back tensed, and he stilled. Betrayal cracked fissures into Faye's heart.

This isn't real.

He didn't choose her. He wouldn't.

He loved her.

Sadi's night-shattering scream startled Faye from her thoughts.

The next instant a blinding light flared from Sadi's chest and struck Rune's. Faye couldn't breathe. Rune spasmed, his fangs lengthening in a silent scream. Sadi's wail thinned and went silent. The beam of light arcing out of her flickered, then went out.

Rune collapsed, and Sadi's hand slipped from his hair. It fell lifelessly off the edge of the bed. The Shard of Darkness in her articulated ring was shattered and destroyed.

No. No, this was wrong. Faye took a step closer, struggling to piece together what occurred. What she was being shown.

Rune's white-blonde hair began to sway suddenly as though he was submerged in deep water. He roared, clutching his head as he tumbled onto the stone floor. He writhed, screaming, and Faye's heart bled with his suffering. She reached for him and froze when her hand passed through his shoulder.

Rage and frustration collided in her as her power roused with her emotions. "Why are you doing this?" Faye screamed into the air. The vessels were here, they had to be. "Make it stop," she begged in a broken sob.

Faye's pleas fell on deaf ears. She was powerless. Could only watch.

After what seemed like an eternity, when Faye had no tears left to shed, Rune collapsed. His pale blue eyes stared into nothingness as his head lobbed to one side.

"Rune," Faye said in a hoarse whisper. She reached for him, but her fingertips met nothing tangible.

His hair swept over his face as though it was caught in a strong current. He stirred, and his pupils pinpointed to sharp points before widening. The current calmed into a gentle tide around him. Rune rose with the telltale mark of Familiar magic. His eyes dilated, swallowing the pale blue with black.

Voshki's shadows were nowhere to be found.

Faye took a step back as Rune levitated off the ground and floated back to the bed. He gingerly lifted Sadi's lifeless body and tucked her in. "Sleep, my queen. When I return, you can bathe in their blood."

His words gutted Faye. She couldn't move. Every breath pained as her vision of Rune and Sadi faded away. Whispers overlapped in the expansive dark, humming into a unified voice.

The Creator made death, reducing the realms to shadows… and ash.

Seventy

The Ra'Voshnik rose as Faye's heart rate spiked. "Vsenia?" Rune called as his queen backed away from the mirror. He knew Faye witnessed events unfolding, but a cold dread descended upon him at her stricken expression.

His magic couldn't penetrate the temple to pull her out. His chest tightened. A moment before he reached for Morbid's mind, Faye turned in his direction.

Her lightning-streaked midnight eyes cleared, as if seeing him for the first time.

"Faye," he said in a firmer tone.

She glanced at the mirror and shuddered, then strode toward him.

He took her hand and drew her to him the moment she stepped over the threshold. "Are you well?"

His queen nodded against his chest, wrapping her arms around him. The Ra'Voshnik's temper flared as it circled his mind. *Find who upset our queen, and rip their spine from their body.*

We cannot kill visions, calm yourself. Rune glanced down at Faye. What vision could have frightened his queen so badly? "Shall I return us home?" he whispered to her.

Faye shakily nodded, pressing her body to his side as she clutched his shirt. Rune phased to their room and lifted her into his arms. Tension riddled every inch of her. He clutched her tighter as he took a seat on their bed with his back to the headboard. "Some visions are difficult to see. It will pass, love," Rune murmured.

Faye pulled back to stare at him. Her dark eyes were glassy, but her relief struck him. She caressed the side of his jaw and paused, searching his eyes. She drew a shaking breath before her hand settled against him.

The Ra'Voshnik rose closer to the surface, eager for his queen's touch. Her heartbeat eased a fraction as she ran her thumb through the veined misted shadows Rune knew stretched across the tops of his cheekbones.

She still prefers me to you, Voshki snickered.

Rune ignored him and leaned forward. His forehead touched Faye's, and she closed her eyes, her breath warm on his lips.

He smoothed the back of his index finger under her chin, meeting her lips in a feather-light caress. "Speak with me. What has upset you?"

His queen's voice was hoarse as though she'd been screaming. "You can't sleep with her."

Rune's expression pinched. Who did she speak of? He would never be untrue to her. "I am yours, vsenia."

Faye flinched at the endearment he'd voiced countless times. She lowered her gaze, and her hand fell to his chest. "That's what you called her too." Faye shook her head. "I don't know if it's after I'm gone, or something happens to me." Tears wet the curve of her lashes. "You can never sleep with Sadi."

The Ra'Voshnik recoiled. *Over my dead fucking body.*

"I will never turn from you," Rune promised. "If your immortality does not seat, I will wait for your return."

"No... I need you to understand. The death Sadi feels is her own. I asked the vessels why Sadi and I looked nearly identical. We were made by The Creator to tempt you. Your choice leads to a consequence. I saw you chose Sadi. You slept with her—"

"I have never touched Sadi in such a way." Would never. He belonged to her and her alone.

Faye blinked as her tears fell. "I saw what happens if you do. The Creator made her for you to absorb. It kills her and changes your power to Familiar magic. It breaks your mind, and you destroy the realms. You can never sleep with her."

Morbid was all-seeing. He would never allow Saith to shape his daughter.

Unless it was her fate, Voshki added. *How many times have I told you she tastes of want and death?*

Rune exhaled, reflecting over the centuries. The Familiar King didn't participate in wars, but surely, he would protect his own daughter.

He didn't retaliate when Angelique was poisoned, the Ra'Voshnik reminded him.

Anger bristled though Rune's mind. *If he's all seeing, he left us in Sadira's court for one hundred and thirty-seven years.*

Rune pushed aside his rancor and pressed a kiss to Faye's forehead. "You are the only woman who will ever grace my bed. I will never be unfaithful to you." She clung to him, and Rune smoothed his hand over her back. "Your Voshki would never allow it. He is quite *perturbed* by her presence."

A short laugh escaped Faye, and she sniffled. "I thought the death Sadi felt would be me or our children when I give birth on your stone."

Rune tensed as images of her words surfaced in his mind. "What would make you believe such a thing?"

Faye shrugged her slim shoulders, and Rune waited. "I don't like the way it feels," she said in a small voice.

She'd said the same about her altar. If her deaths in previous lives warded her away from the locations of her demise… Had she died at her altar as well?

"If you do not wish to have our children there, we can move to another location."

Faye gazed up at him, worrying the inside of her lip. A nervous compulsion she did when she thought deeply. "But it'll weaken them if I don't tie them to Hell."

The corner of Rune's mouth lifted. "They are Pure Bloods, and coming from us, they could stand to be weakened."

His queen relaxed against him. He considered not asking his next question, but ultimately, he needed to know. "The feeling you get from my family's stone, did you feel the same way at your altar?"

Tension riddled her again, and Rune thinned his lips.

"My altar was much worse."

Seventy-One

Rune devoted his undivided attention to his queen the past few days. Faye's vision of Sadi had shaken her, and Rune had no intention of leaving her fears to fester. He silently wished he could speak to his mother or Belind. Questions regarding Faye's pregnancy plagued him, but with Lyssa as the only surviving Pure Blood to bear young, they went unanswered.

Faye's appetite for blood steadily increased, but her exhaustion remained constant. He'd remained with her while she napped, devouring books on pregnancy. There was no documentation on Pure Bloods. Turned vampires, while able to bear young, produced what they had been before they transitioned, not Pure Bloods.

Rune had slipped away as Faye dozed this afternoon. He stood before his long-neglected duty, The Crumbling, watching lightning arc within the churning wall of storm clouds. Much like Chaos, it illuminated dark shades of grays and purples.

We shouldn't be away from our queen, the Ra'Voshnik growled.

Separating from Faye went against Rune's instincts. They demanded he protect and kill for her until she bore his young.

My young, Voshki added with a laugh.

The corner of Rune's mouth lifted. He suspected the violent urges wouldn't subside after Faye gave birth. His instincts would sharpen, widening its scope to his family rather than his pregnant wife.

Rune exhaled with a soft smile. Wife. A title she denied him until her court settled. A milestone he traded to the Ra'Voshnik for every Hunter's Moon to follow. Rune didn't waste his time pondering his agreement. He'd struck a bargain and was true to his word. The Crumbling ground against the barrier Rune placed between it and his realm. The same magic protected his queen's realm. He wove a shield around himself, spelled to regenerate by consuming his reserve of power, and stepped into the destructive clouds.

Don't exhaust yourself with The Crumbling. We need a measure of strength to protect our queen from her enemies, the Ra'Voshnik grated.

His days of draining his power in an attempt to unravel The Crumbling were long behind him. Delilah and her rallying courts were a constant threat. He would hold enough of his strength to level an army, but he'd ignored The Crumbling for months. The bird king would soon be crowing at his queen for an update, most likely at the High Council meeting tomorrow.

Rune splayed his fingers and lifted his hand, as tightly woven glowing green threads materialized. The number of lines had grown in his weeks of absences. Rune's brow lowered, and he exhaled. Lifting the threads and angling them on agile fingers, he separated the glowing filaments. A new line stitched over the ones Rune held, and he frowned. This new cord layered complicated matters, pulling against the others and threatening to snap them.

Rune released the strands and began anew, only to have the same line appear again. With a growl, he began a third time, anticipating the new twist in this maddening puzzle. He caught it before it drew over the other filaments and finished untangling the first layer. The strands vanished, revealing the second.

He selected lines, waiting for the errant cord to appear. He caught it, dismantling the puzzle thread by thread.

When Rune reached the third layer, the Ra'Voshnik said, *Enough of this. We are half drained and in need of blood. Return to our Queen.*

"Be silent," Rune hissed, shifting a thread from his index finger to his thumb.

The Ra'Voshnik growled, prowling the edges of his mind. *You couldn't dismantle The Crumbling's before, yet you believe you will suddenly now? When the lines have doubled?*

The threads shifted and snapped, reforming once more beneath his hands. Rune cursed in High Tongue and walked out of The Crumbling as loose crystals ground beneath the soles of his shoes. This new development spelled doom. Morbid assigned him this task. He would not have appointed him if it were beyond his reach.

Rune reached for the Familiar King's mind, *Morbid.*

Prince.

I am in need of guidance. Do you have a moment? Rune asked.

The Familiar king's laughter filled Rune's mind. *For you, I could spare a moment or two.*

Rune phased to Morbid's ever-changing home in Chaos. Today it was a decrepit towering stone castle with a splintering drawbridge and moat. The lightning-filled sky and bones littered the ground around the structure, only adding to its menacing air.

Polished femurs shifted beneath his weight as Rune reached the bridge. He took note of the serpentine creatures coiling through the thick black liquid surrounding the castle and shielded himself. He'd never been attacked by the flora or fauna of Chaos, but fate had a way of twisting certainties if one grew too comfortable.

A large courtyard opened beyond the rusting gates. The sight would have been a beautiful garden had it been alive. The blackened skeletal remains of trees and bushes were painstakingly curated throughout the space. When noticing the scorch marks climbing the stone walls, he wondered if this was once an actual location lost to time and madness.

"Prince?"

Rune's eyes narrowed. His host and the furnishings had not been there when he arrived. The Familiar King slouched in a light pink chair adorned with white ribbons and ruffled trim. A round table matched the chairs holding a tea service. Instead of small hand-trimmed sandwiches, tiny cuts of raw meat were spread over the three-tiered display.

"Interesting choice of venue," Rune said, taking his seat.

A sleek white cat lifted her head from Morbid's lap and peered at Rune over the table. Her blue-gray eyes were reminiscent of the storm clouds overhead.

Rune inclined his head to Morbid's Queen, "Lady."

Angelique flicked an ear and bit Morbid's hand before turning to look at him.

"My wife rarely misses her afternoon tea." Morbid chuckled. He leaned forward, pinching a shred of meat between his thumb and forefinger before hand-feeding Angelique.

An odd description for the scene before him, but Morbid had always catered to his queen. His fangs sharpened as his throat burned with the power he'd exerted in The Crumbling. Did Morbid foresee the state he would be in and add blood to Angelique's array of refreshments out of kindness? Rune breathed in again, unable to discern which ornate teapot contained the blood.

"To the left, with the snakes painted on it," Morbid said as he brought another cut of meat to his wife.

"My thanks," Rune said as he poured the crimson wine into the dainty teacup placement set before him. The shadowed snakes decorating his tea set didn't go unnoticed.

Rune drank deeply, replenishing what he'd lost, and poured a second cup. "I need your guidance," he said as he arranged the teapot on the cluttered table. "The Crumbling is accelerating at an alarming rate. You assigned me this task. What is eluding me?"

Morbid lowered his drink, allowing Angelique to lap from it. "I said it would be in your best interest to look into The Crumbling."

Familiar non-answers. Rune sighed. He needed advice, and his patience was far too thin for riddles. "I am failing to unravel the magic binding it."

Morbid's midnight gaze met Rune's. "Everything you need stands before you, Prince."

You have no answers here. Return to Faye, the Ra'Voshnik pestered.

Rune ignored Voshki's tirade as the growing headache drummed at Rune's temples. He catalogued what he knew. What he had access to. "Is the answer I seek in the Familiar library?"

The Familiar King shrugged. "Can't say."

Rune rubbed his fingers over his forehead and stared up at the turbulent sky. Why had he thought Morbid would be forthcoming with information? "Thank you," he said before nodding at Angelique. "Lady."

Rune phased to the decaying library deeper in Chaos, materializing on the lower level. He'd read through three bookshelves, but there were dozens more. It was a small miracle the books didn't shuffle each time he returned. He called the five books he'd borrowed and slipped them back into their place.

He moved to the next bookcase and selected five more tomes from the top left corner.

The Ra'Voshnik prowled through his mind, growing more impatient by the moment. *Take them all. I'm tired of leaving our queen to collect books.*

Rune glanced over the plethora of tomes lining the bookcase. He'd never seen another soul on this level. Familiar seemed more preoccupied with their carnal desires than any meaningful research. Rune vanished all the books from the shelf so they would travel with him. If anyone required a book, he could easily return it.

He phased home and found his bed empty. Voshki's displeasure was evident as Rune listened but heard nothing in the surrounding rooms. He reached for his realm, feeling for his queen's location. Hell answered, revealing her in the courtyard with her sister, Damian, and Vashien.

Faye's laughter reached him as he strolled toward the hall. She sat on the iron benches near Vashien under the balcony overlooking what would have been the public gardens. The crystalline trees and shrubs glimmered around the tall fountains.

Sparrow and Damian circled each other in the open space set before the terrace. The blonde harpy caught sight of him and straightened, dropping her sword. "Back already?"

A sharp snap cracked, and Sparrow shrieked, holding the back of her thigh. She hissed, turning her murderous gaze toward Damian.

"Easy," Vash said loud enough to carry over Sparrow's anger.

"I used the flat end," Damian said, twisting his sword to reflect the light off his weapon.

Sparrow shook her leg out, giving him a soured look. "You

didn't have to hit me so hard."

"You dropped your guard," Damian lectured. He aimed his sword at her, holding it straight and tilted down. "Be glad I didn't use the pointy end, dove."

Sparrow snorted, and the two began circling each other once more. She thrust the sword with her dominant hand and twirled the other.

The blonde harpy would be formidable if she ever learned to focus. She was in Damian's capable hands. Rune never bothered to hone his skills. His will was far more destructive than a blade and had a much further reach.

Rune stood beside his queen, and the Ra'Voshnik purred at her proximity. "Have you eaten?" he asked.

Faye smiled shyly at him and said, "I was waiting for you."

"Were you now?" The corner of his mouth lifted as he offered his hand. "What would you like?"

His queen stood, intertwining her fingers with his. She waved at her sister as they departed and strolled silently until they reached the great room. She leaned closer to him and whispered, "I'm thirsty."

So are we, the Ra'Voshnik answered, growing aroused.

An ever-singular mind. Rune was more concerned with her timing and separation from her friends. Rune brushed his thumb over her knuckles and said, "You have not told your sister our young require blood."

A light blush colored Faye's cheeks, and she shook her head. "She'd want too many details."

Rune hummed his agreement. The possessive, volatile aspects of his nature reveled in the knowledge she only partook from his veins, while his rational mind didn't want her to starve in his absence.

If you don't leave her, she won't suffer her thirst, Voshki said as it floated calmly through his mind. Pleased to be in their queen's presence.

Remaining at her side every moment of the day was impractical. Rune brushed his lips over the back of her fingers and said, "I could collect my blood in a decanter. You would not need to wait for me to feed."

Her flush deepened, crossing over the bridge of her nose. "I like drinking from you and—"

Rune didn't wait for Faye to finish her sentence.

He phased to their bedroom, closing the door. Faye broke away, crawling into bed. He shrugged out of his jacket as Faye pulled her red day dress over her head and discarded the garment on the stone floor. Rune admired the way her dark hair tumbled across her breasts. Her light brown skin gleamed with golden undertones, begging for his touch.

He folded his jacket over the back of the chair at his desk, and his tailored shirt followed. Desire lit his mate's gold-streaked eyes, and a pang of guilt knotted in his chest. She'd longed for him, and he'd left her wanting, unable to give her what she needed.

Stay in the present, the Ra'Voshnik crooned. *Go to her and ground your thoughts.*

Rune approached her, silently chanting his mantra. He was home. In his room. With his queen.

Faye scooted back, making room for him and tucking the sheets under her arms. The blatant lust in her gaze dimmed, and she gave him a warm smile. Rune hesitated, contemplating stepping back. The Ra'Voshnik could rise and properly tend to their queen.

She wants you. Go to her, Voshki urged.

Rune joined her, and she outstretched her hand, caressing his face. She leaned closer, lovingly pressing her lips to his. Her kiss was soft and accepting. Kind and gentle. Her breath warmed his mouth, and she whispered, "Hi."

The same greeting he'd received the first time she curled up to him, in this bed no less, during their dreams.

Darkness, he missed her. He kissed the corner of her mouth and the underside of her jaw, moving lower to nuzzle her throat. Faye remained still, letting him take from her. He breathed in her scent. His night breeze through plum blossoms. His dark queen. The woman he waited lifetimes for.

"Lay with me," he purred.

She gave a small nod, and Rune gathered her in his arms. He laid them down, holding her back to his chest. His fangs ached as he hardened for her. The tip of his cock pressed against the curve of her ass, and Rune drew her closer before biting into his wrist. Faye's lips closed over the vein, and she shifted her hips as she drank, pressing onto his hardened length.

His memories shifted, and Rune felt Faye's nails scoring his back.

Voshki's memories with Faye. Her claws at his back. Her bite as she writhed against him. The burn he relished from her marks.

Voshki's voice purred through his mind. *Ground yourself with our queen. There is no need to linger on dead bitches.*

Rune tightened his embrace and tentatively shifted his hips. Faye whimpered at his touch, arching her back as his cock pressed against her ass.

Take her. She's wet and aching, the Ra'Voshnik said.

Rune scented her arousal and groaned. He brushed the side of his face against her long dark hair, and heated words slipped past his lips in a strained whisper, "Offer me your throat."

He ached to graze his fangs over the soft skin of her neck. To sink into the taste of her exquisite blood.

Faye dropped her shoulder and lifted her chin without hesitation. Her fingers intertwined with his as she lovingly stroked his hand while she drank. Her unspoken invitation to take what he desired. What he needed.

Rune kissed her throat and bit down. The length of his fangs sank into her giving flesh. Faye moaned, squeezing her thighs together as she rolled her hips. Her ass dragged over the length of his cock, and Rune's lids slid closed.

The rich dark taste of her blood coated his tongue. It left no room for anything but her as she writhed against him.

Fuck her, the Ra'Voshnik grated. *Spread her legs and bury your cock. We both know she'll come again once you're inside her.*

Rune opened his eyes and momentarily mistook the gray stone walls of his room for the dungeon Sadira confined him to. Remnants of his memories kept him from his queen. They lurked on the outskirts of his mind, waiting for him to lose focus.

Rune's lids slid closed as he inhaled deeply, focusing only on his queen. The scent of her blood and arousal. The feel of her body pressed against his. He listened to her breaths as she drank. His cock throbbed with each swipe of her tongue and suck of her mouth. He couldn't take his pleasure from her, but perhaps he could give it.

Rune's hand smoothed over her belly, traveling lower. Faye whimpered when his fingertips brushed the junction of her thighs. She hooked her ankle behind his calf, spreading her legs in invitation.

Rune lightly teased her clit, and she shuddered. He kissed his bite, drinking lightly as he moved lower, pressing a finger into her. Her grip on his wrist tightened, and she whimpered, rocking against his hand. He added a second and began a quiet rhythm, curling his fingers the way she favored. She tensed, arching her back, and he sank deeper, stretching and teasing her while he circled her clit with his thumb.

As she came, a breathless sigh slipped past her lips, and Rune held her through the pleasure. He clung to her while he worked her into a handful of gentle orgasms. When her pulse slowed, and the intimate fluttering around his fingers ceased, he descended into himself. He'd given her everything he was capable of but couldn't offer the connection and intimacy she deserved.

See to our queen, Rune said.

Voshki hesitated for the span of a heartbeat and circled him. *You haven't failed her. You're returning to her.*

Rune remained silent and relinquished control of his body as Voshki rose to their queen.

Seventy-Two

Fingertips brushed over Faye's scalp, sending tingles down her back. A groggy haze blanketed her mind.

"Rune," she called to him. She'd spent the night alone with him before Voshki rose. She pushed off his chest and lay beside him on the corner of his pillow while he played with her hair at this horrid hour of the morning. It meant Rune would get out of bed and take his warmth with him.

She stroked his cheek softly, and he turned to face her. "I liked being with you yesterday," she said quietly. He blinked, lowering his gaze, and her heart squeezed. She traced the corner of his jaw. "You don't have to say anything. I want you to know I'm here, and I love you."

Rune rolled onto his side. The quiet rumble of his purr settled over her as she lay content in the arms of the man she loved.

"You are everything to me, vsenia," he said as his lips brushed her temple.

Faye adored the deep rasp his voice took when he first awoke. She basked in his comfort and warmth until her eyelids grew heavy.

"Shall I let you rest until the High Council meeting?" Rune asked in a whisper.

Faye nodded, and her vampire pulled their sheets to her chin. Heat spread over the silk, and she couldn't help but sigh. Her attentive consort left her side, and water faintly tapped against the shower tiles in the bathroom, lulling her back to sleep.

The bed sank beside her sometime later, and her mouth watered at the scent of fried food wafting through the air. Faye wiped her eyes as the heavy fog of exhaustion lifted. Rune sat beside her in his tailored black suit, but her attention was centered on the bowl he held. Golden brown crisps of Vash's chicken fingers were sprinkled over the top like croutons.

"I thought you would be hungry," Rune said playfully.

Faye pushed herself up and peered into the bowl. A smile broke over her lips. "You put my chicken in the clam chowder."

"Vashien was kind enough to share the recipe," Rune said as he called a short bamboo tray.

Faye studied her breakfast. "Did you cook this?" she asked. Sparrow always burned his recipes, but these looked like Vash made them. Faye leaned forward and crossed her legs. "You magicked this, didn't you?"

Rune chuckled. "I did not care for another male cooking for my ravenous queen but feared you would crack my ribs if I stood between you and the meal you craved. Learning to prepare it seemed an adequate compromise."

"Good choice, big guy," Faye said with a smile.

She dug into her breakfast, and they laughed in quiet conversation. When she finished her meal, Rune vanished her dish and sat at his desk. He read while she stepped into her closet. An array of colors stood before her, and she swiped through articles of clothing. She slowed on a gray dress with a fitted bodice and flowing silhouette. The gauzy material with mock sleeves had caught Faye's eye in Necromia. She slipped her High Council dress off the hanger and dressed.

Faye stood in front of the full-length, free-standing mirror and adjusted the top. Rune stepped behind her, veined misted shadows stretching beneath his pale blue eyes.

"The dress suits you, love," he said in an appreciative tone.

Faye leaned against his chest and stared up. "You could wear the sweater I got you."

The corner of his mouth lifted, and he uttered a single word. "No."

She would get him to wear it, eventually. Faye accepted defeat and held her hand out. "Shall we?"

She phased them before the High Council, silencing the chatter of the early arrivals.

Rune pulled out Faye's chair, and Jareth laughed. He leaned forward, arching a brow toward his brother. "You accompany Faye to every meeting. Are you sure you don't want to be Hell's council member?"

Faye giggled. Of the three brothers, Jareth was the most *normal*. He tilted his head, and a few strands of his short white-blonde hair fell over an eye. He gave her a roguish grin before turning his attention to Rune.

"I have no taste for such things," Rune said dryly.

The High Queen's hollow laughter rankled Faye's temper. She folded her hands and turned toward Lyssa. Unfeeling hazel eyes swept over Faye, taking her measure as she'd done since their first meeting. Faye's power rose as the high bitch lingered on her breasts before dipping lower.

"You're carrying young." Lyssa's lyrical voice took an ugly edge as she met Faye's stare.

Faye held her head high, pressing a hand to her belly. "I'm pregnant."

Did all dark-bloods call babies young?

Lyssa's smile lit her eyes, and Faye softened.

The High Queen straightened her stack of documents and turned her attention to Rune. "Whatever will you do when your pet Anarian's young don't bind to Hell?"

Wrath fueled Faye's magic as her serpents surged to the surface. They rose behind her, unseen, ready to tear and claim pieces of her newly found prey until nothing remained.

Rune grasped her shoulder. Faye recoiled from the vicious impulse and calmed with his firm touch.

"Do not insult my Queen. I have told you time and again. Faye carries my young," Rune said with an unnatural calm.

Lyssa waived her hand. "We both know you are incapable of siring offspring."

"Just as we both know you're incapable of inspiring my consort's desire," Faye said in a feigned politeness. The High Queen attacked Rune with the only weapon accessible to her. It was time she learned Faye's words could be just as sharp.

Lyssa remained aloof, acting as though Faye hadn't spoken—a curated lie as tension set in the corners of her eyes.

Morbid's laughter broke the growing silence. He kicked his heavy unlaced boots on the table and crossed his ankles, leaning back to balance his chair on its two back legs.

Jha'ant adjusted his glasses and cleared his throat, taking a nervous glance at Rune. "Shadow Prince."

Rune nodded at the Artithian King and squeezed her shoulder before vanishing. Jha'ant began their meeting, and Faye's eyes wandered up to the private balcony Rune occupied. The corner of his mouth lifted when he noticed her watching.

Jha'ant called forward a list of petitioners, and Faye's brow lowered. They were all the same. Necromians expressed their fear of The Crumbling. Faye addressed concerns like this during each of her open courts. She glanced at the High Queen. Were the families coming to the High Council beneath their Queen's notice?

She waved each of them off, stating, "The Crumbling is being addressed."

There was no compassion in her voice. She did nothing to ease her people's distress. Lyssa was no Queen. Faye had been right to take Anaria from her.

Faye spent the next hour listening to complaints, announcements, and court formations. Jha'ant stood and spoke the words signifying the close of their meeting.

"Is there any additional business requiring our attention?" The Artithian King's spelled voice carried through the airy structure.

"Yes," a woman answered.

Delilah materialized in the center of The Eyes with a male a step behind her.

Faye tensed, her power rising, ready to rend flesh and resow from the Queen of Lace and Bone. The vampire queen held her head high. Her face was unmarked. Not a single visible scar to evidence Faye had taken her eye and the bone beneath it a little over a week ago.

Faye choked on the injustice of Jeneane's suffering. Sadi healed her, but she lived in terror while Delilah moved forward as though an Anarian's life was insignificant and beneath her notice.

"The Anarian Queen is imposing her will in Necromia." Delilah turned toward the High Queen. "I humbly request her banishment from Necromia."

Faye's wings stretched behind her, materializing from the Darkness rolling down her back. "I will free my people *regardless* of the realm they are stolen to," Faye hissed.

Fear flitted across Delilah's features, and Faye fanned her wings before settling them at her back, daring her to speak.

"You forget your place." Lyssa's cold, biting tone edged Faye's temper to a razor's edge. If the High Bitch aligned herself with Delilah, she would strip Lyssa of her realm to keep her people safe.

Faye turned, ready to proclaim war—but she wasn't the subject of the High Queen's attention.

"You believe I would oppose a sister court for you?" Lyssa's melodic laughter rang through the crowd. "Your court and bloodline are insignificant. Begone."

"High Qu—"

"Another word… and the banishment you requested will fall on your shoulders," Lyssa spoke calmly, and Faye wasn't sure if the veined misted shadows were an attempt at intimidation or her Ra'Voshnik calling for Delilah's head on a spike.

Delilah bowed her head and cast Lyssa a hateful stare before stepping back. She turned toward Faye, ran the claw of her gauntleted finger under her cheekbone, and pointed at her. Rune's growl emanated from above them, and the crowd grew silent.

Faye held two fingers up at Rune, refusing to break eye contact with the vampire queen challenging her. Faye's magic rose, enveloping her, giving her halo of serpents form as they materialized behind her wings. Delilah's rot had spread far enough.

It was time she separated the wheat from the chaff.

Faye stood, ominously spreading her Darkness-kissed, iridescent wings. "Come for my people again, and I will do more than rip the bone from your face."

Seventy-Three

Faye reclined on a lounge chair in her private gardens in Anaria. Sadi stood over her, blocking a portion of the golden rays. She smoothed her hand over Faye's middle, examining her twin's development. Faye closed her eyes, savoring what sunlight she could while contemplating the high bitch's strange alignment to her court this afternoon.

Faye wasn't blind. Calling her a sister court didn't translate into an alliance. Lyssa aligned with Rune, much like her evil-twin-turned-Familiar-midwife. Faye pushed her bitterness down. Lyssa refused to shelter Delilah in her realm.

It was a start.

Ornate metal and glass stretched over the space. It was a safe place Prinia could venture into without being burned. Faye's shoulders sagged. With her appetite for their father's blood, her children, at the very least, inherited Rune's vampiric side. She looked at Sadi, who stared into her belly.

"How did Rune learn he could walk in sunlight?" Faye asked. How would she know if her babies needed to avoid the daylight she loved?

"He's several centuries older than me. When I came to court, he was a formidable man," Sadi said with a smile as she straightened. "Your young are progressing well."

Faye's lashes lowered to Sadi's narrow, corseted waist. It was irrational; she expected to gain weight and inches around her waist. She was pregnant. But every other woman in the realms didn't have a double parading around as what they once looked like in front of them. Faye wondered if Rune mourned the loss of her lithe body.

"Will I start showing soon?" Faye asked. It'd been a couple of months. She could at least look pregnant.

"Another month, six weeks at the most. You'll need to be careful. You painted a target on all our backs with your outburst at the High Council," Sadi said in a clipped tone.

Faye's temper spiked. This was unbelievable. "You and Rune both wanted me to set an example. Now I have."

Sadi shifted her weight to her back leg and huffed a small laugh. "You think your display was an example? You made a threat—one Delilah will rise to."

Faye's cheeks heated as her power rose with her escalating heart rate. "I will deal with her if she takes any more of my people."

Sadi crossed her arms and ran the claw of her articulated ring along her jaw in a graceful motion. She tapped it against her bottom lips and said, "You're gambling eternal lives for mortals."

"They are equally important," Faye snapped.

Sadi blinked as the corners of her mouth lifted. "We'll see if you stand by your convictions when a price is extracted. The weakest members of our court will be targeted. Your sister. The winged male. Your young," Sadi said, outstretching her hand to Faye's belly. "Rune will level the realms if they are lost or injured."

Faye stiffened. No one would target babies. Not even darkbloods. Right? "I will protect my court and family."

"See that you do," Sadi said before vanishing.

Faye glowered where Sadi stood. "Do you guys like her? No?

If she's mean to you, I'll make you two Familiar totems to chase her with." Her stomach rumbled in mock answer, and Faye sighed. *Will you two stop,* she grumbled.

She craved sweets. Rune would bring her anything to satisfy her cravings, but she felt like she was suffocating him. He'd been so attentive, remaining with her while she napped and learned to cook her chicken strips. He deserved to have a few hours to himself even if he spent his free time with his nose in a book. Faye giggled.

Faye made her way to her sister's suite of rooms. One thing she could count on was Sparrow having a full spread of dishes at any given moment. She turned the corner and called, "Hooker."

"Bitch," Sparrow answered.

"You decent?" Faye asked, following her sister's voice.

"If Vash was fucking me, I would have said come back in a couple of hours—" Sparrow's words broke into shrieking laughter. "Put me down fucker! She knows we have sex. Quit being so boring."

Faye stepped into their den and covered her mouth to hold back a laugh. Vash effortlessly dangled Sparrow upside down by her ankle. Her sister flailed wildly, but Vash held his arm out. His reach was no match for hers.

"Did you need something before I drop Sunshine here into the nearest lake?" Vashien asked.

"I just set my curls. I swear to the Darkness, if you ruin my hair, I'm going to cut your balls off," Sparrow yelled, kicking Vashien in the chest.

Faye threatened to bite Rune occasionally, but their banter played out in private. Sparrow's threats were empty, but Faye couldn't imagine speaking to Rune or Voshki like that.

"Damian hasn't taught you how to escape an enemy if they grab you like that?" Faye asked. She seemed pretty helpless for training with a battle-hardened Familiar every day for months.

Sparrow clasped Vashien's hand when he offered it and righted herself. "He taught me to stab them through the pelvis, then open their fey-mortal artery."

"Femoral," Vashien corrected.

Sparrow snorted as she fluffed her blonde curls back into place. "Keep talking shit, and I'll show you my technique."

Faye paled. "Sparrow."

"What? The next time the high bitch comes at me, I'm going to be ready. Look." Sparrow beamed, calling in two beautiful short swords with emeralds embedded in the center of the guard. "I named them Fuck and You," she said, holding out one sword and then the other.

She twirled her swords in a flourish movement from side to side, and Faye took a step back. "Stop fucking around before you cut somebody."

"Oh, I've already done that," Sparrow said nonchalantly.

What the fuck? Faye's expression must have read on her face because her sister snorted and rolled her eyes, dropping her swords to her side.

"Damian said he's seen too many students cut down in their first battle because they froze when their blades met flesh," she said, mimicking Damian. Badly. She wiggled a brow at Vashien. "I can sever every major artery, and I know which tendons to cut to impede movement. Catching the heart was a little harder. Ribs and shit," Sparrow said, shaking her hands as though she were screaming, *surprise!*

"Are you slaughtering animals?" Faye asked, hoping they numbed the cows and pigs before giving them to her sister to practice on.

Sparrow wrinkled her nose. "Eww, no. Plus, livestock won't be attacking me. I practiced on Damian."

"What?" Faye choked out.

"Fairly common among immortals," Vash added as he sat at the dining table.

Sparrow vanished her swords. "Stop being a pussy. Your evil twin was right there healing his ass," she said before squeezing herself next to Vash and sniffing his glass. She turned up her nose and stuck her tongue out. "Water? I thought it was vodka."

"It's a glass woman, not a shot," Vash said before pulling her into his lap.

Faye leaned on the table's edge, peering at the assortment of dishes: roasted chicken, table grapes, spiraled potatoes, but the chocolate cake she saw yesterday wasn't anywhere to be found.

"You hungry, bitch?" Sparrow asked.

"I was hoping you had some dobash cake left over," Faye said as she sat down. She scanned the plates, searching for an alternative for the chocolate cake she wanted.

Sparrow called the ornate obsidian talisman and set it on the table before poking it with a finger. "We need a dobash cake, please. Or cupcakes. Cupcakes would be better."

"How did you get that from Rune?" Faye asked. He used it constantly, catering to her cravings.

Sparrow fluttered her hand. "This one's yours, and by yours, I mean mine. They sent it this morning."

"You can't rifle through your sister's mail," Vashien said in a firm tone. He reached for the talisman, but Sparrow snatched it.

"It's mine. She has Runey's," Sparrow whined.

Faye shook her head and looked over the boxes and new furniture scattered over the large room. "How's the unpacking and decorating going?"

"We're about halfway," Sparrow said before turning toward Vashien. "Do you have condoms?"

His brow pinched. "Do I need condoms?"

"Yeah, to protect your dick from my stomach acid," Sparrow cackled. Faye giggled as Vashien gave her a stern look. "Oh, come on," Sparrow whined, dragging out the words. "That was funny."

Hazel eyes, flecked with blue, met hers. "She's yours," Vashien said dryly.

"No, no," Faye said, raising a finger. "Five years. She's yours now."

"Fuck you both. I'm hilarious," Sparrow grumbled. She called a small stack of parchments and tossed half of them to Faye. "If you want to be serious, help me with these."

"What's this?" Faye asked, lifting the first letter.

"Coffin water gave me some of the petitions." Faye raised her brows and blinked at her sister. "What? Don't look at me like that. I'm a productive member of court," she insisted.

A chime sounded, and a tray of chocolate cupcakes appeared. Her sister put one on a small plate and slid it in front of Faye with a fork. She thanked her and cut it in half as she read the first petition. A day-blood stone mason requested raw material to renew the graveyard because she'd seen it done in a neighboring village.

This was the harmony she wanted for her realm, and seeing it come to life filled her heart. If everyone gave a little, they could create positive change—an example to live by.

She set the letter aside and took a bite of cake, savoring the spongey texture and decadent silky frosting. Alister would know who had the mason stone she needed. She finished her cupcake and took another as she read more petitions.

Faye's heart sank with the next one. It was from Jeneane's mother. She requested her daughter be admitted into the staff of Faye's estate. Jeneane shut herself into her home, afraid of being abducted again if she ventured outside.

"You took Jeneane home, right?" Faye asked, glancing up at her sister.

Sparrow nodded. "Met her parents and her little brother, too. Why?"

"She's been terrified to go outside since the attack. Her mom is asking for her to be brought here so she can work on the grounds."

She remained silent and leaned back to Vash, drumming her fingers on the table. After a few moments, she nodded to herself. "I can buddy her with Kimber. She's apprenticing under coffin water."

"Doing what?" Faye asked.

"She's working in the kitchen this month. I think she said housekeeping was next. Coffin water is teaching her how to manage an estate."

Faye softened. Alister didn't dismiss Kimber because she was Anarian. He didn't discourage her by saying most courts wouldn't want her to manage their homes. Faye couldn't guarantee Kimber would find work, but she was relieved Alister offered to teach her.

"Yeah, that sounds good. Can you get her?" Faye asked. Her voice felt hollow. "I think she's afraid of me."

Sparrow snorted. "She's not afraid of you. Now Delilah. That bitch is afraid of you and your hungry snakes."

Faye pushed her cupcake around her plate. She could still see the terror in Jeneane's glassy eyes as she scurried away in vivid detail like she was a beast in a fairytale.

"I'll grab Kimber, and Vash can take us to pick her up. We'll bring her family too. I don't want to separate her from her support system if she's that scared."

Faye nodded, studying the sweets she no longer had an appetite for. Sparrow kicked her, and she winced. "You have shoes on, hooker," Faye snapped, rubbing the sting from her shin.

"You are the biggest ball of stress. Is Runey not banging you because you're knocked up?"

"Sparrow!" Vashien growled.

She twisted around in his lap and yelled, "It's a valid question!"

"You're this close to being dropped in a cold lake from really high up," Vashien said, holding his index finger and thumb together.

Sparrow sighed loudly and turned to face Faye. "You need something fun, bitch." Her green eyes brightened as a toothy grin spread over her lips, and Faye groaned. "Baby shower! You have babies. You need a shower. You can announce to everybody you're naming them after your favorite sister." She blinked her lashes, posing with her hand under her chin.

Faye frowned. "It's too early. I don't want—"

"Ahhhhhh," Sparrow said, pointing a finger at her as she hopped to her feet. "You get no fucking say, grouch potato." She pulled on Vashien's sleeve and said, "Let's go to Aunty Clara's house to pick up Kimber."

Sparrow put another cupcake on Faye's plate. "*Aunty Clara* will be happy to host her favorite one's baby shower." She stuck her tongue at Faye, and the two of them vanished.

Seventy-Four

Faye phased onto the landing platform for Alexander with Rune and Sparrow. She equally looked forward to and dreaded this baby shower. It would be a nice evening with her family, but she was sure Sparrow planned something outlandish.

Her sister pulled her party together in less than a week, recruiting Vashien to make her cake. She asked him to incorporate a pink and blue sparrow, and he said no thankfully.

Vash had gone to Aunty Clara's house to set up the cake, and Faye wanted to pick up some candies the little ones could snack on during the week. A small tradition she carried for years. Faye made her way toward the candy shop she'd visited since childhood in the town center.

The setting sun cast hues of oranges and pinks over the sky. Two girls laughed, running to the brazier in the middle of their village.

They both tossed folded papers into the blue hellfire and ran off giggling. Their prayers to The Creator.

Saith was a disgusting man. Her people burned offerings to him, believing it made a difference, and Faye couldn't bring herself to diminish their hope. Instead, she focused on the girls as they whispered to each other, picking flowers. They reminded her of herself and Sparrow when they were girls. Of Kimber and Jeneane, now. During the past week, the two hit it off and quickly became inseparable.

Sparrow snorted, looking over the rebuilt village.

"You've been busy," Sparrow said, giving off a low whistle as she spun in the center of town.

"This is a testament to Alister," Rune said.

The villagers greeted her from afar. Some of them she'd known her whole life, while others shared her vision and migrated to her realm. All of them kept their distance from her vampire. Faye laughed softly. Rune's reputation was slow to change, but they no longer scooped up their children and hid in the nearest building.

Small steps lead to a mile. Eventually. Rune had many miles ahead of him.

She turned to her sister and said, "If you visited more often, hooker, you would have seen this a long time ago. I think Rune has been to Aunty Clara's house more times than you have."

Her sister snorted in response. "Doesn't count. He follows your pregnant ass everywhere."

Faye intertwined her fingers with his, beaming, and Sparrow made a gagging sound.

"You two are nauseating. I'm going to see what Aunty Clara is cooking," Sparrow announced as she broke away.

"Vanish your swords, or Aunty Clara is going to yell at you," Faye called after her.

Her sister spun on her heel, walking backward as she threw her arms in the air. "Can't. These are permanent accessories."

Faye shook her head and abruptly stopped as a young boy chased a piglet dashed past her. Faye leaned into Rune and whispered, "He's never going to catch it."

She felt a trace of Rune's power rise. He tracked the boy's path, and the piglet suddenly squealed. Faye's head snapped. The little animal was pinned on its side, kicking its legs desperately as it tried to right itself.

The boy grabbed it, yelling, "Got you!"

"I didn't see anything for the piglet to trip over. Did you?" Faye teased.

Rune glanced at her momentarily. "Hmm."

Faye squeezed Rune's arm to her side. "Careful. People might start thinking you're nice."

A low rumble rolled from him as he pulled her closer. "Doubtful."

Faye purchased the candies, and they made their way to Aunty Clara's house. Rune opened the gate. When they approached, the small children piled onto the porch, obeying Aunty Clara's rule. They couldn't play outside after they washed their hands for dinner, and the porch was still considered the house in their minds.

Sparrow opened the screen door and yelled, "Get back in the house, you little beasties. She'll be here in a second." The children eyed her until her hiss sent them scattering back into the house. "I need to visit more often. These little shits forget who I am."

"Stop scaring the kids!" Aunty Clara yelled.

A wooden spoon narrowly missed Sparrow's head and clattered to the porch. Sparrow turned and gawked before dodging another spoon.

"Should have caught that one, dove," Damian called from inside the house.

Faye climbed the steps and picked up Aunty Clara's projectiles. She thinned her lips and raised her brows, wagging the wooden utensils at Sparrow as she passed.

"Shut up," Sparrow said, snatching the spoons from her.

Garlic butter and fried chicken permeated the air. The adults were seated at the dining table, and the small children crowded around the kid's table with their Familiar totem toys. Damian and Vash sat together, but Faye didn't feel Sadi's reservoir of power in the house.

"Is Sadi running late?" Faye asked.

Damian quirked his lips and shook his head. "My kitten has been living in her visions of late. Something is bothering her, but I can't follow her into her creepy temples."

"I sent the High Queen an invite, too," Sparrow said, flopping into the chair beside Vashien.

He groaned. "Tell me you didn't."

"I mean, she didn't show." *Rude bitch*, Sparrow mouthed.

Faye glanced over the dishes on the adult's table and spotted Vashien's chicken strips at the kid's table.

"Bitch, I swear to the Darkness, if you pick overgrown chicken nuggets over *poached lobster*, I will fight you," Sparrow snapped as she set a succulent tail on her plate.

"You will lose," Rune crooned.

Sparrow's lobster vanished and reappeared on the serving plate. "Look, shadow dick, I'm food bowl aggressive," she said, stabbing the shellfish with her fork.

It vanished again, materializing on Faye's plate. "I'm doing it," Aunty Clara said, taking her seat at the head of the table. "Your sister is supposed to eat first. What's the matter with you?"

Faye wished the lobster was a strip of golden fried chicken. She cut off a small piece and ate it, allowing everyone to begin their meal. They passed around the dishes with laughter and conversation. Faye took a little of everything. None of the dishes were anything she ate growing up. She guessed Vashien came early to cook under the guise of setting up the cake.

Did you want me to bring you a few chicken strips, vsenia? Rune asked along a mental tether.

Faye nibbled on her braised short ribs and answered, *No, but thank you. Vash worked really hard on this. I don't want to offend him.*

Rune sipped his crimson wine and motioned to the corner of the room. "Is this another Anarian custom?"

"Their blessings for your babies," Kimber answered.

Faye hadn't noticed the column of colorful balloons netted in the corner of the room.

"We write our hopes and dreams for the little guys, roll them up, and tie them to the balloons. Then you let them go, and they float away to the Darkness," Kimber explained.

"I wished for them to be best friends," a girl chimed in.

"I wished for them to have lots of toys," a boy answered.

"You're not supposed to say what it is, or it won't make it to the Darkness," Bayle scolded.

The kid's table quieted with hushed whispers, and Faye stifled a giggle.

"That one's going to be trouble," Kimber said, stuffing another bite of lobster in her mouth.

"Only for people with horse booties," he answered.

Damian laughed deep in his chest. "That one will grow into an exemplary master of the guard."

They finished their meal, and Kimber took the balloons, leading the children outside. Aunty Clara illuminated the night with floating balls of hellfire as their hope-tied balloons were distributed.

Faye sat on the steps with Rune. A mixture of rabbits, birds, and foxes made of wood clippings and grass followed the children as they took their positions.

"Come forward a little more. You're too close to the hellfire," Bayle said to a boy who repositioned himself. A red-headed girl with a koi fish totem swimming through the air ran up to him and touched the fish to his chest. It changed the trajectory of its path to circle Bayle instead.

"I don't need it, Bianca. I know how much you like it." Bayle grabbed the fish and held it out.

She pushed it back toward his chest. "You always give me your turn. You keep it." Bayle blushed, and she smiled before running off.

"He's so sweet on her," Faye whispered.

"The young Bayle?" Rune asked.

Faye nodded. "He asked Aunty Clara how to send a request to Sadi. He asked for the koi because it's Bianca's favorite animal." She'd been surprised Sadi answered and brought colorful koi scales to craft the totem.

An explosion rocked the night as flames lit the skies over Alexander. The children screamed and ran to Aunty Clara. Faye rushed toward her aunt, and reservoirs of power flickered into the tree line before vanishing.

"Get in the house!" Faye screamed, ushering them toward the porch.

A man dressed in black appeared beside them. The lace mask over his eyes was adorned with a polished cheekbone.

"No," Faye shrieked as his blade swung.

Seventy-Five

The Familiar totems exploded into a barrage, whirling and slicing through the man. His sword dropped harmlessly, followed by his decapitated head and mangled body. The gore-covered children screamed and scattered across the field, followed by their living toys as a medley of balloons colored the night sky.

"Get in the house!" Faye yelled. She locked eyes with Rune. "Go to the village. Protect them." Veined misted shadows stretched beneath his gaze. *You're the only one strong enough to hold the village yourself. Go!*

Black light flickered over her, and Rune vanished.

Carnage and mayhem surrounded Faye. Aunty Clara managed to call most of the children to her and ran to the house with them. She stopped at the steps and called her meat cleaver as the little ones rushed past her through the screen door.

Faye's power rose in a rush as her wings burst from her back. Darkness pooled at her feet as her serpents rose. She phased Aunty Clara into her kitchen and shouted, "Stay in the house!"

She turned toward the battlefield, and a flash of blonde curls caught Faye's attention. Gray light flickered over a man holding a small boy by the back of his shirt. The shield cracked, falling around him like glass, and Sparrow's sword ripped through the man's chest.

Her sister raced to the next Court of Lace and Bone member. Dark churning mist coated her swords as her hair swayed around her.

Vashien appeared behind her, severing the heads of the males charging at her back.

Faye turned to the sound of screams. These cowards were chasing children, toying with them. She let her tendrils fly, naming her targets. Her magic struck, and Faye smiled as the impact reverberated through her. She pinned them, embedded in their cores, choking their magic so they could not escape.

Her vipers reared back and struck, claiming tissue and bone as they screamed.

Damian phased through the field, incapacitating men for Faye's serpents as he prioritized the children without totems.

Faye's predatory gaze shifted as the screams of her latest prey quieted. Bianca's red hair arced over her as she dropped to her knees, cowering before a man at the foot of the steps. He lifted his sword, and Faye named her target. Her serpent sang toward him, but Bayle barreled into Bianca the next instant, pressing the koi to her chest. Its glowing scales dispatched the man before her serpent could reach him.

Beside them, Kimber slammed her body into a male dragging a young girl by the hair. They tumbled to the ground, and Kimber scrambled to her feet, clutching the child to her chest as she raced for the porch.

Kimber screamed when a man appeared behind her and fisted the back of her hair. A male Faye recognized. He stood with Delilah in The Eyes. The little girl fell from Kimber's grasp onto the wooden steps. "Get inside!" Kimber screamed, lifting her hands to hold the grip on her hair.

"You look like a better catch," the man laughed, jostling her.

"Get away from her!" Aunty Clara rushed down the steps, raising her meat cleaver. She brought it down, aiming for the man's neck.

A gray light flickered over him as the butcher's knife met his shield. The man smiled, drawing the sword at his hip and holding it out. Time stopped as he angled his wrist and drove the sword behind him.

Desperation consumed her.

"No!" Faye screamed, echoing her sister.

Sparrow's image flickered, and she materialized in front of Aunty Clara.

The man's sword cut through Sparrow and into Aunty Clara's chest. The old woman's dark eyes widened, and her cleaver tumbled down the steps.

Seventy-Six

Faye's scream cracked the night sky as her power surged past her, igniting her wings and charring the grass beneath her.

The man twisted his sword in a swift motion. Faye couldn't breathe. Sparrow's head tilted back in a scream as Aunty Clara fell, crumpling to the ground.

"Sparrow!" Vashien charged at the male with a powerful beat of his wings.

Vashien's wing was twisted at impossible angles with a sudden burst of power and a sickening crack which sent him to ground. Faye's broken rage unleashed from her wailing chest, her serpents arching toward the man.

He flashed his fangs and vanished with Sparrow a moment before they reached him. Her shadowed cobras struck the ground with such force chunks of earth were strewn about in different directions.

Faye ran to Aunty Clara, dropping to her knees. Tears obstructed her vision as she pressed a hand to the wound in her chest.

No, no, no, no.

"Get the healer," she screamed through her sobs.

It's okay. It'll be okay, Faye thought, pushing Aunty Clara's white hair out of her face. Her dark eyes stared past her, lifeless.

Faye shook her head, holding her tighter. This was her fault. Her decisions caused this. Agony tore into her chest, breaking it in two. A soul-deep, splintering pain threatened to break her. Grief devoured her ravaged soul, taking more than she possessed. Taking, until all she could do was scream.

Hard muscles pressed to her back, and Faye blinked through her tears. Rune's strong arms wrapped around her, but she felt no comfort. She clung to her aunt, her body growing cold and heavy in Faye's embrace.

She'd lost her sanctuary.

The person she found her home in as a child.

Stolen with an unfeeling swing of a blade. Faye took a shaking breath. He had her sister. This man killed and took from her. A deathly calm blanketed Faye as her dark power crested through her, numbing her heartbreak.

They wanted an example? Faye would give them one. She pressed her lips to Aunty Clara's forehead and rose.

"Take me to the Court of Lace and Bone."

The night sky stretched overhead, darkening the ominous stone structure whose size rivaled Faye's estate. Narrow windows etched with wrought iron vines stood above her, clouding her ability to see inside. Tall gothic gables created a jagged rooftop while turret windows lit by candlelight added to the menacing air.

Faye marched down the spelled glass enclosure protecting vampires from the burning rays.

They would find no such protection from her.

Rune asked Morbid to retrieve Sadi. Sparrow would need a healer when they returned, and Faye couldn't allow herself to believe anything to the contrary. Her sister was alive.

She had to be.

Damian and Alister remained at the orphanage and village. Vash didn't bother repairing his wings. They dragged uselessly, scraping against the ground behind him as he and Rune followed her. Faye pressed her awareness over the massive structure and was greeted by dozens of reservoirs.

Music and laughter bled past the doors and Faye seethed. They attacked her village and were throwing a party?

Rune's voice slipped through her mind. *Delilah was not with them purposefully. She positioned herself to claim ignorance. Are we purging their court, vsenia?*

Yes! No. Faye clenched her teeth, tucking her wings tighter to her body. She wanted to hurt them. Listen to their screams as they writhed, begging for death. A mercy she wouldn't grant until their pain engulfed hers. A dark mist rolled at her feet with each step.

They killed Aunty Clara and took her sister. The man who delivered the blow would answer.

The doorway exploded into stone rubble and splintered wood with a flicker of Faye's mind.

"Where is she?" Faye demanded as she stalked into the Court of Lace and Bone.

Delilah sat on a throne constructed of polished black marble and bleached bones. Her slinky dress was reminiscent of Familiar fashion with her embroidered corset and exaggerated skirt.

Her court lined either side of the hall, some in elegant couture while others were dressed for battle.

Delilah uncrossed her legs, leaning forward. She glanced at a footman holding a tray of glasses filled with dark liquid and held out her hand. The man appeared beside her, slipping the stem of the wine glass between her fingers with shaking hands.

The Queen of Lace and Bone swirled the liquid and leaned back, spreading her legs as she looked at Rune.

"Where is who?" Delilah asked with a coy smile.

Burning rage circled Faye, constricting her ribs. She shook with effort, holding back her viciousness. She wanted to strike at every court member in attendance until they returned Sparrow and surrendered the male.

"Your court attacked my village! Took my sister!" Faye screamed. Her barely contained power charred past her, swirling impressions on the stone floor.

Delilah brought her hand to her chest and blinked innocently. She peered to either side of her hall, dropping the facade as she began to laugh. Her court followed with their own chortle.

Delilah's hand shot up, and her court silenced. She smiled and said, "We've been here the entire time."

Faye flexed her claws. She felt other presences deeper in Delilah's estate but couldn't be sure which one belonged to the male.

"A man led a group—"

"My son, most likely," Delilah said, tilting her head as she pouted her lip. "He enjoys hunting in the peasant lands."

"Bring him to me," Faye screamed. Her magic surged, cracking the stone beneath her.

Gasps and whispers broke out, and Delilah's court members flickered several times.

Rune tsked at them. "None of you shall leave until my Queen is satisfied, and you have returned the blonde harpy."

Delilah paled for an instant and recovered just as quickly, baring her fangs. "Get out of my court!"

The ground shook, and Faye struggled to keep her gaze fixed on Delilah as Rune's power sent fissures up the stone walls.

It intensified for a heartbeat.

Two.

"Deacon," Delilah hissed.

The male appeared beside his mother, and the ground quieted. Fury blinded her, and Faye's claws ached to be buried in his chest while she tore his heart from his convulsing body.

Faye snared his mind and phased him to her, fisting the larger man's shirt. He sneered, a curl of his black hair falling into his pewter eyes.

"Where is she?" Faye bit out each word.

Deacon flicked his wrist, and Sparrow appeared at her feet— bound, gagged, and beaten. Nasty bruises cover one side of her face. The swelling forced one of her eyes shut.

"Sparrow," Vashien said in a hushed whisper, gathering the petite blonde in his arms. His words didn't carry toward Faye, and he pulled her closer. His brow pinched and lifted as he rested his forehead on Sparrow's, drawing a shaking breath.

Her sister pried the only eye she could see out of offering Vashien a smile. Then she coughed blood. Her gaze shifted to Deacon's direction.

"Pussy," Sparrow muttered, scarcely audible.

Vashien phased with Sparrow, and Faye turned back to Deacon. She bared her teeth, and he leaned into her.

"Go back to your realm. We both know you're not going to do anything. You carry dark shards, but you're no dark-blood."

"You tried to kill my sister," Faye whispered with a deathly calmness.

He chuckled. "I was aiming for the old woman."

Maddening rage enveloped Faye. Her magic shot past her, and she drove her hand forward. It passed into his chest, and Faye's claws sank into his core. Deacon choked, struggling to pull away, but Faye held him in place.

She channeled power into the intangible part of him, housing his magic. Deacon screamed, bowing his back, and Faye squeezed harder. He would never hurt another innocent. Never touch another one of her people.

A final surge of her Darkness ripped into his core.

Shattering it.

Faye released him, and Deacon fell to his knees, clasping his hand and staring into the ring, holding a broken, empty soul shard.

"What have you done!" he screamed, shaking.

"Prey," Faye said, marking Deacon as her target.

Her nest of shadowed vipers rose from the Darkness, pooling at her feet. They struck, fangs sinking through each joint as another looped around Deacon's neck twice. It unhinged its jaw and stretched over his face, muffling Deacon's desperate wails.

They coiled, knotting their bodies before yanking back, tearing their prize free. Screams broke out over the crowd as his torso fell. Serpents struck, suspending his body as others fought for their share.

Ripping and tearing.

Faye's shadowed cobras devoured him, leaving nothing but a stain of blood leaking into the Darkness churning at her feet.

She gazed over Delilah's court and met the Queen's blistering stare.

"You are banished from Anaria," Faye shouted.

Delilah's court huddled into small groups, terrified. Cowards who condoned an attack on children. Her serpents lifted higher, surrounding her in a menacing halo.

"Step into my realm, and I will hunt you. Your death will be agonizing. Nothing will remain when I am finished."

Seventy-Seven

Faye clutched a folded shirt she'd taken from the laundry basket near Aunty Clara's dresser—clothes she'd never wear again.

She sat on her bed, twisting the buttons like the rage and sorrow inside her. Tears came, falling from her unblinking eyes. Grief fractured her soul, stealing her will to participate in life.

She hated the days for continuing, for leaving the person she loved behind in its inevitable march. Her turmoil begged her to unleash her power and bury the realms, striking at time itself and ceasing its constant momentum.

Bound to her hollowed sadness, her tireless companion, was an inconsolable rage.

But it was Aunty Clara who leashed her destructive desires. She'd been gone for over a week, and Faye could still hear her weathered voice when Faye's thoughts turned to devastation.

I'm old, you know. The Darkness can take me at any time. After I'm gone, don't cry. It's not good to cry, you know.

It was stupid advice. All she did was cry. It could have been worse. Faye swallowed thickly. Sparrow and Vash had been injured during the attack. She could have lost them too.

All of it was her fault.

A choice and a consequence. The vessels' words echoed, rippling through her life.

Faye drew a shaky breath and returned the shirt to the laundry basket. This was the third time she'd failed to pack up Aunty Clara's room. The space still smelled like her, haunting Faye with the lingering scent of cherries and almonds.

She opened the palm-sized tin containing the balm Aunty Clara used for her dry skin and inhaled deeply. She'd used the same scented lotion for as long as Faye could remember.

Rune waited for her in the hall. He'd offered to help her box Aunty Clara's possessions, but she didn't allow boys in her room while she was alive. Faye wasn't going to let a grown man in now that she was gone.

"Lyssa sent a package," Rune said as she approached.

He drew her into his arms, and Faye squeezed him close. She'd received countless parcels. Each of them contained Chrysanthemums for the funeral pyre and a sympathetic letter. She'd been too numb to read the letters, but Alister sent various correspondence of thanks on her behalf.

Faye doubted the high bitch had anything kind to say, and she didn't have the mental fortitude to deal with her.

Not today.

She pulled away from Rune's warmth and wiped her eyes. "If she's being a cunt in this letter, I'm going to set her on fire before we go to the funeral."

"If she is anything but polite, I will drag her into the sunlight myself," Rune said as a package and letter appeared in his hand.

Faye opened the letter and read. Rune guided her out of the emptied shell of her sanctuary.

I offer my deepest condolences for your untimely loss. I know we've had our differences, and I send these words in good faith. I understand the pain of losing a mother and have included memory crystals with flowers, our tradition in times like these. They are imbued with Familiar magic and will replay the memories stored within. They've brought me peace during my own dark times, and I hope it affords you the same comfort.

Lyssa's signature and wax seal adorned the bottom of the letter. She wasn't being a bitch. Faye stepped out onto the porch and opened the box. Three white chrysanthemums rested inside, one for each member of Lyssa's house. Nestled between them were two large clusters of quartz crystal.

Faye removed the flowers and vanished the box. The white blooms starkly contrasted her black gown. The cut was exquisite. The beading and lace in the bodice fed into the exaggerated collar. It lifted behind Faye's head in a halo of glittering black gems. The full-length sleeves and layered skirt flowed around her as she walked down the steps.

The Queen of Anaria would be attending the funeral. She wouldn't give Delilah the satisfaction of her pain. Faye waved a hand over her swollen eyes and puffy face, glamouring the appearance of youth and health.

She'd kept busy, throwing herself into her responsibilities to keep the weight of her grief from crushing her. The children from Aunty Clara's house were relocated to Faye's estate. Kimber had taken the reigns, helping Faye transition the little ones into a place where they felt safe. She'd become their caretaker, and the children flocked to her.

Not because she was a replacement for their beloved aunt, but because she was one of them, she thought to herself.

Faye focused on her list of tasks. Anything to keep her mind preoccupied. In those moments alone, her loss crippled her, splintering her spirit until she thought she would break.

Her priority was to create more Familiar totems. So many young lives would have been lost without them. Sadi taught her how to create them, and the children now possessed their own living toys.

She worked with Sadi to alter the spell guiding them, allowing multiple imprints on a single totem. Faye spent the week constructing a large Familiar totem in the middle of Alexander with a dozen sentries attached to it, wandering the streets.

The next set of hunters foolish enough to prey on her villages would find themselves on the receiving end of their intentions.

She had months of work ahead of her. Each of her villages would be protected, beginning with the children. Purpose gave her peace. Her emotions threatened to consume her if she sat idle, and it was time for her next task.

Faye turned to Rune and outstretched her lace-gloved hand. "I'm ready."

He nodded, lightly clasping her fingers and bringing them to his lips. Their surroundings faded, and they materialized in the private gardens of Faye's estate.

The crowd was much larger than she imagined. The villagers from Alexander and the children crowded around Kimber and Jeneane, as she expected. But what surprised her was the people respectfully grouped throughout the manicured space. Men and women Faye didn't recognize stood in line to bow their heads and toss blooms on the funeral pyre.

Faye held her head high and stepped over the stone border surrounding the structure. She tossed the flowers Lyssa offered at the foot of the woven branches. Aunty Clara rested on a bed of white silk over the braided wood draped in transparent red gossamer.

Guests laid their blooms at the bottom of the pyre. Friends and extended family added theirs to the top of the wooden base, and immediate family placed their chrysanthemums with Aunty Clara.

Vashien lifted the smaller children, helping them add their flowers and say their goodbyes. Sparrow's eyes were puffy, but she shed no tears as she surveyed the crowd. Sadi and Damian stood with Jamie Lyn. Faye hadn't recognized the Familiar at first. She wore a black gown made of satin and lace, covering her neck to ankle, much like Jamie Lyn's dress.

Faye waited until everyone had placed their flowers and paid their respects. She called the bouquet of chrysanthemums and approached the wooden structure. The white blooms tumbled across her view as a few fell onto either side.

She looked peaceful. Faye stroked her cheek beneath the crimson veil and whispered, "I miss you every day." She lingered, wanting to stay, not knowing if she could do what came next.

Faye moved to the head of the pyre, where Rune waited for her beside a stone rabbit that reached the middle of his chest. The bunny stood on its hind legs on a rock with lotus and cherry blossoms at its feet.

She touched the rabbit's forehead and channeled her magic into it, activating the spell tied to the stone. It would absorb the ashes and flowers as they burned, breathing color and life into Aunty Clara's memorial.

Hellfire would steal the only thing Faye had left of her. It would make her loss real. Permanent.

I can't do it, Faye cried in a broken whisper.

I have you, vsenia, Rune said gently through her mind. A shadowed hand caressed her spine and settled at the small of her back. *Shall I finish this for you?*

Faye gave a slight nod, and blue flames sparked, flaring to life through the woven branches. She couldn't watch. She didn't care about appearances. Not anymore, as the finality of her hurt, grief, and loss solidified in her soul.

Faye's heart cracked. White crept up the rabbit's hind legs, and she clung to Rune, sobbing into his chest behind her glamour.

Seventy-Eight

Rune found his queen in her private gardens. She sat cross-legged in front of the white rabbit statue amidst several plates. One was stacked with pancakes with tangerines neatly piled on another, and the last was a bowl of oatmeal and fruit. Tea and orange juice rounded out the meal Faye brought to the statue each morning. Though, she never partook in it.

He didn't understand Faye's rituals but honored her wishes. He purchased cases of tangerines so Faye could hunt for crucial characteristics he was blind to. Her methodical routine granted her a degree of comfort. There were days he held her as she cried, but they were outweighed by the days she brought breakfast to her caretaker's statue and lit three sticks of incense in prayer.

The orphans she cared for visited the statue as well. They spoke to it, hugging it as though some part of their beloved matriarch resided in the stone. The little ones had excitedly picked flowers to lay at the rabbit's feet. By the third day, they had plucked every bud and bloom.

Faye had franticly poured over her desk, planning an additional garden to sustain a steady supply of flowers. Rune had draped an arm over her shoulders and pulled her back to his chest. He'd kissed her hair and murmured, "I will make arrangements for the little ones."

He scheduled an array of blossoms to be delivered to Kimber, who distributed them to the little ones daily. Their habits were strange, but it allowed them to accept the loss they suffered.

Rune took a seat beside his queen as Voshki rose through his mind. He purred as Faye toiled over grass clippings, leaves, and flower offerings left with the statue from the previous day. Faye piled her materials into heaping mounds before weaving her magic into them. They clumped together and squeezed, bursting into a rabbit constructed from the trimmings.

Familiar totems of snakes and rabbits surrounded his queen. Smaller versions of the towering guardian she left in Alexander. She'd crafted a rabbit perched on a stone with three cobras rising out of the churning petals at its base. It stood taller than him and resided at the center of the village near the brazier.

One of Faye's snakes slithered over his shoe, and Rune turned toward her. "Have you eaten today, vsenia?"

He knew better than to ask her to eat a portion of the breakfast surrounding her. It was her offering to her favored aunt and would remain immaculate and untouched.

Faye gave him a weak smile and separated another pile of garden debris. "I'll eat after I finish one more," she said to the mound of flowers.

No, she's pushing herself too hard. She skipped breakfast again. We should have brought her a meal, Voshki growled as he brushed the surface. *Let me rise. She'll stop for me.*

Adding to her guilt was not the route he would be taking. Now or ever. She carried enough on her slim shoulders.

Rune hooked the bend of Faye's knee and pulled her between his legs. "You are carrying our young, vsenia. Please, share a meal with me. I will return you to this very spot the moment you are finished and remain with you until you are ready for your afternoon nap."

She slouched and poked the side of his knee before begrudgingly replying, "Fine."

Rune stood and helped Faye to her feet. She leaned back, petting the rabbit's forehead as though it were real. "I'll be back Aunty Clara."

He phased them to the kitchen when she straightened. The strips of chicken she favored and a pot of clam chowder with extra clams waited for her on the counter. Faye sat on the stool and propped her elbows on the counter. Her shoulders fell, and she dragged a small plate in front of her.

Rune stepped closer, confused. She typically consumed an alarming amount of chicken. He was positive he followed Vash's instructions to the letter. "Is this not to your liking? I can bring you something else."

Order her some choice cuts, the Ra'Voshnik added. *Or the chocolate oranges she likes.*

Chocolate is not a meal, Rune retorted.

Voshki scraped his claws over Rune's awareness. *What does it matter so long as she eats?*

Faye leaned against him, staring at her meal before whispering, "Nothing sounds good."

"Humor me."

She grumbled loudly before sitting up straight and breaking a chicken finger in half. "I'm pregnant. Be nice to me."

Rune chuckled. "Yes, my queen."

Faye bit into the golden-brown strip and pulled her lip back as her chewing slowed. Rune raised a brow when she spit it into her napkin. Did he miss an ingredient?

She hates your cooking. Let me rise, the Ra'Voshnik snickered.

"It tastes funny," Faye said as she reached for her pomegranate juice. She took a long swallow and choked, coughing into the glass. She wiped her mouth and recoiled from her meal. "Everything tastes like its spoiled."

Obsidian would not have spoiled juice.

Skin them! Voshki roared.

Calm yourself. Rune lifted her glass and scented the dark liquid. There was no smell of rot. He took a small sip and set it down, finding nothing amiss.

"Perhaps your cravings have changed?" Rune asked.

She pondered his words, and her expression suddenly dropped. *You've upset her,* the Ra'Voshnik growled. *Get her a fresh meal.*

Faye grasped his lapel and pulled him closer, leaning in. The warmth of her breath skated across this throat, and Rune hardened for her.

"Darkness. Why do you smell good already?" Faye pulled back to glare at him as though it were his doing. "I drank from you last night."

The corner of Rune's mouth lifted as Voshki purred. She had. Faye regularly fed from his wrist and offered him her throat. He drank from her, stroking his fingers into her until she came on his hand. Last night she'd pulled his hand away and thrust two fingers into herself. He toyed with her clit until she came, then she did something unexpected.

She brought her fingertips to his mouth. He'd licked and sucked the desire from her index before moving to the next.

He'd been so close to taking her, but the stone walls of their room closed in on him, reminding him of another room.

Voshki banished the memory. *Stay present.*

Rune focused on Faye and purred as he brushed his lips over her temple. "You chose me to sire your young. Our twins have the appetite of Pure Bloods."

My twins, Voshki interjected.

Faye turned toward him, whispering against his lips, "You don't drink every day."

"Fledglings need more blood to sustain themselves," Rune murmured. "I drank multiple times a day in my youth."

Faye sighed, leaning a fraction closer.

Kiss her. She wants you, Voshki urged.

Faye hadn't completely regained her balance after Delilah's attack. They had a long road ahead of them, and Rune would not take advantage of his queen. She would lead, and he would surrender anything she required.

Rune remained still as her lips met his. He moved with her in a soft and giving dance. She broke their kiss and nipped his throat, whispering words that heated his blood.

"I'm thirsty."

Seventy-Nine

Rune lifted her into his arms and phased into their bedroom. She wrapped her legs around his waist, deepening her kiss. He purred as her fingers closed over the front of his throat and she rolled her hips.

"Touch me," she breathed before slanting her mouth over his. Her tongue sweeping against his, and he groaned, palming the curve of her ass.

He scented her arousal. His night breeze through plum blossoms anchored him and he ached to have his cock deep inside her. Voshki replayed memories of their queen beneath him, moaning as he took her hard. Her touch caressing the side of his neck and slipping lower to his chest. The feel of her wet heat squeezing his cock as she came.

Rune used a flicker of power to nick his throat. His hand tangled in Faye's dark hair, and he made a fist. His queen relaxed, allowing him to guide her head back. He gazed up at his dark queen, powerful, willing, and his.

"Drink from me," Rune grated, releasing her hair.

Faye dragged her tongue over his throat. She moaned sweetly and tightened her thighs over his waist as her nails scored his back. Rune's eyes slid closed. The warmth of her mouth teased the side of his neck, and she bit down—holding him with her teeth while she drank.

Rune cursed in High Tongue, and she sucked harder, tangling her hand through his hair. His cock and fangs throbbed with the beat of his heart. Rune fumbled with his belt buckle before growing frustrated and snapping the leather. He tossed it aside and metal struck the gray stone floor.

His eyes snapped open, and he tensed. Gray stone walls closed in on him and tainted memories surfaced of their own accord, intermingling with Faye's touch. His breaths came faster as his memories haunted him. The feel of bodies dragging against him while he'd been chained to a metal chair beneath Sadira's court.

Stay in the present. Look at our queen, Voshki said firmly, banishing his memories.

Rune held Faye closer. Focusing on her as she drank and ground against him, but this room could have easily been one from Sadira's court. He needed more—a place his mind couldn't misconstrue into his previous enslavement.

Sunlight replaced shadows as they materialized in the shade of the two willow trees boarding the hot spring. Faye pulled back and stared at him. Traces of his blood colored her bottom lip. A wanton invitation to his kind.

He caressed the side of her neck and threaded his fingers into her hair, pulling her in. His tongue darted over her sweet lips, licking his blood away. He purred before kissing her, desperate to stay in the present.

He vanished their clothing and Faye pressed her hand to his chest. She broke their kiss and took in their surroundings, before glancing down at him. "Rune, we're outside."

"We are," Rune crooned. He tilted his head and nipped the underside of her jaw.

"Someone might see us," Faye hissed.

He began walking into the hot spring and shielded the outer courtyard. "No one," Rune whispered as he knelt on the stone seating at the edge of the hot spring. "Will." He lifted Faye higher and laid her over the stone border onto the grass. "Disturb us," he murmured as he trailed kisses down the inside of her thigh, settling between her spread legs.

Faye wrapped her legs on either side of his head as he tasted her delicate flesh. The scent of her arousal intoxicated him, devouring his senses until all he knew was her. He pressed two fingers into her, purring as he teased her clit.

"Darkness, Rune," she cried, dragging her heel up his back as her fingers tangled in his hair. A bite of pain radiated from his scalp, and Rune chuckled. His queen pulled his hair, pressing his mouth into her wanton flesh as she shamelessly rocked her hips.

He obliged her, roughening his purr. She squirmed as he pressed a third finger into her, stretching her to accommodate his possessive touch. Her legs closed around him as she came, but Rune did not relent. He drove into her harder, wringing orgasm after orgasm from his queen.

A trail of red spilled over his collarbone and dripped onto the stones beneath his queen. Rune withdrew and lifted her into his arms. His voice lowered as he purred, "Were you thirsty, vsenia?" He guided her legs around his waist and sat on the edge of the hot spring. A groan escaped him as he lowered her on his cock. Her inner walls fluttered, squeezing him intimately.

Faye panted against him as she took more of his considerable length. "Is this, okay?" she asked, searching his eyes.

Rune fisted her hair and gently guided her to the blood on his throat. Her lips touched his skin, electrifying every nerve in his body. He leaned back on his arm and grated, "Ride me."

Her teeth closed over his neck, and Rune rocked his hips, driving hardened inches into her. "Take it, vsenia. I want every inch of my cock inside you."

Faye dug her nails into his back. Her thighs tensed around him as she lifted her hips and took more of him with each fall of her hips.

Rune leaned his head back, letting her work his thick cock in and out of her body. He drew her hand to his mouth and bit into her wrist. The exquisite taste of her dark blood coated his tongue and euphoria blanketed his mind. He blinked slowly as he drank, letting this memory burn away every other.

The taste of her blood, the feel of her lips, and his queen bathed in sunlight as she rocked above him.

Possessing him entirely.

He cursed in High Tongue when she screamed against his throat. Her movements slowed as her inner walls squeezed him. She trembled as she came and Rune gripped her ass, flipping her onto her back.

He thrust into her, and Faye cried his name.

"Take it for me, vsenia," Rune growled, thrusting deeper. "Spread your legs and take me."

Faye parted her thighs, and he took her in a merciless rhythm—but Darkness, he needed more of her.

His body lowered over hers, jarring her with each punishing stroke. "Offer me your throat," he grated.

Faye lifted her chin and turned her head without question.

He bit down hard, sinking his fangs deep, and Faye bucked beneath him. She came around his cock, and Rune chased his pleasure, intent on joining her.

He pressed his lips to his bite and drank as his shoulders tensed. His cock ached with unbearable pressure. Then pleasure erupted through his senses. He drove into her, grinding his waist into hers as he emptied himself into her.

The feel of her consumed him, and Rune was dimly aware of her stroking his hair. He nuzzled her throat and lifted his head to brush the side of her face with his own.

It's good to see you back, Voshki purred through his mind.

Rune held Faye closer, languidly thrusting into her with gentle strokes. "You are everything to me," he murmured.

She held him close and whispered words that were a balm to his soul.

"I love you… and you belong to me."

Eighty

Faye loved this house. Without the constant chatter of children and clanging metal of meals being prepared—without its heart—her home felt like a grave, hollow and cold.

As Faye stared into Aunty Clara's room, Sparrow linked arms with her, and Kimber followed suit.

"You don't have to put anything away. We can do it," Sparrow said, stepping into the room.

Moisture clung to Faye's lashes, and she squeezed Kimber's arm to her side. Weeks had passed since the attack, and she'd visited this room dozens of times. It was always too soon.

Too final.

"Shhh. It's okay sweetie." Kimber hugged her, and Faye's tears spilled into her dark hair. "You should sit outside with Rune. We won't throw anything out," Kimber said, pulling away. She smoothed her tears and gave her a watery smile. "We'll put everything in the steamer trunks we got you, yeah? It'll all be there when you're ready to go through it."

Faye nodded absently, turning from the room Aunty Clara no longer slept in. Rune joined her in the kitchen, but the space became nothing more than four lifeless walls. The tables and chairs she once enjoyed family dinners on had already been taken to her estate with the children's beds. It looked strange without Aunty Clara's worn pots piled on the aged, white stovetop.

Rune led her outside, and she rushed down the stairs, too many memories crowded these steps, but the last one destroyed any happiness she'd once felt there.

She wandered to the swing set with Rune close behind her. The earthy smell of the forest quieted her mind. She faced the tree line and sat on the swing, gripping the chains on either side.

Rune crouched in front of her and held her knees. "I know it pains you to be here. The harpies can finish their task. I can shield the grounds if you want the space to remain undisturbed. You can leave her room as it was for as long as you wish."

Faye shook her head. It was so quiet here now. She didn't know how much time she might have had left with Aunty Clara. Would it have been months? Years? Her time had been stolen. She hated each passing hour. Raged as time continued without the person she needed. Casting her aside like she was insignificant.

Sorrow festered into an angry wound within her. Faye's voice broke as she whispered, "Why didn't she stay in the house."

"Come here," Rune said gently.

He lifted her into his arms and positioned her on his lap, setting them both on the swing. Faye's tears came harder. Rune offered his handkerchief, and when she opened it, he traced small circles on her back with his thumb.

He kissed her forehead and looked into the woods. "The two of you are cut from the same cloth. She loved her people and fell defending her court."

"She would slap you for calling this place her court."

"I asked for her blessing. The same permission is required from a court's queen when her members are pursued romantically," Rune said quietly.

He held her tighter, rocking them back and forth. She didn't answer, only swayed with the motion.

"Bitch!" Sparrow yelled from in the house.

Faye straightened, peering at the red and white house.

"She can't hear you. She's outside," Kimber snapped, shoving the screen door open. She rushed down the stairs, but all Faye saw was the bright red paper lantern with hanging tassels above her.

"Look what we found stashed in her closet," Kimber said, holding the balloon toward Faye.

A tiny scroll was tied at the base. Aunty Clara was always extravagant, masquerading superstitions within traditions. Faye took the string and pulled it down, gingerly touching the rolled paper. A final note from a woman who'd been a mother to her.

"Thank you," Faye whispered before turning to Rune. "I want to go to my garden."

Her vampire nodded to Sparrow and Kimber, her surroundings fading. They materialized in her private gardens. Aunty Clara's white rabbit statue basked in the sunlight.

Faye touched the rabbit's face and gazed at the curled paper containing the hopes she didn't get to release. Delilah's son had stolen them from her, and he'd paid. She stroked the rabbit's ears. She looked into the clear blue sky and back down at the statue.

"I want a house built for her... for when it rains," Faye said.

Rune nodded. "I will arrange for a shrine to be built to your specifications."

Delilah was a rot she'd cut from her land. She would destroy what remained of Aunty Clara if she realized what it meant to her. Faye bent to catch one of the Familiar totem snakes she'd crafted this morning.

She went to her knees before Aunty Clara's memorial.

Delilah would never be given the opportunity to try again, and anyone who tried would face the same fate Deacon had.

Faye drew her power, imprinting the snake totem on the statue, and paused. What was she doing? She didn't need living toys to protect her statue.

Not when she could create a totem capable of protecting itself.

Faye smiled, channeling her strength into it and binding her intent to the stones as she wove her magic through the spells within.

The rabbit's ears twitched, and Faye pushed harder.

When her power saturated the rock, Faye stitched it to her reservoir, and fur sprouted over the rabbit. Faye stared as it blinked and dropped down from its rocky perch. Her other totems were animals shaped by the materials she'd used. But this...

It looked so real.

Faye held her hand out, and the huge rabbit hopped toward her and nosed her palm. A small laugh escaped her, and she ran her hand over its back. She was covered in soft fur, but Faye felt the stone beneath it.

The rabbit climbed onto her rocky perch, and Faye noticed the cherry blossoms and lotuses had thinned, taking on the appearance of true flowers.

This was all she had left of her. Pain and regret accompanied her rancor, tearing at her. "I should have listened to you," Faye muttered. "If I made an example of her, Aunty Clara would still be alive."

Rune slipped a finger under her chin and lifted her face. "Let me purge her court, vsenia. Speak the words, and I will see it done," he purred.

Faye had her vengeance. Her shadowed serpents devoured Deacon. "If they trespass into my realm, you can have them."

She stood and drew Aunty Clara's balloon down. The red paper lantern would serve as her final goodbye. Faye took a deep breath and carefully removed the small, rolled parchment. She let the ribbon slip through her fingers and watched as the lantern drifted upward. It grew smaller as it rose higher until it became a speck and vanished into the sky.

Faye unrolled the scroll, and her tears fell with her aunt's shaky script.

I hope Faye's children bring her as much joy as she brought me.

ACT THREE

ENDGAME

Eighty-One

Faye leaned into the sunlight as her mind went blissfully blank. She dozed on a plush canopy bed in her private garden. A twin to the original Rune had commissioned after she'd complained about the ground hurting her back while he made love to her in the grass.

She comfortably laid on her side amidst more pillows than she cared to count, listening to the birdsong overhead as Rune massaged her feet. The past few months had been quiet. The example she'd made of Deacon silenced the courts who'd once rallied to Delilah. The Queen of Lace and Bone had withdrawn to lick her wounds.

Faye had searched the crowd during the next High Council meeting and subsequent meetings, but Delilah was nowhere to be found. Faye's rule went unchallenged without her constant opposition, and though she could scarcely admit it… She should have retaliated sooner.

The white-furred stone rabbit, the size of a large dog, sat on its haunches. A hint of a smile graced Faye's lips as the bunny cleaned her front paws before grooming her face and ears.

Choices and consequences.

Some days were harder than others, and she suspected they always would be. It was the still moments when her mind was quiet that she dreaded the most. When there was no action to take. No tasks to complete. When her mind turned on her and the memories came. The meals they'd shared. The way her light gray soul shard had glittered when she gossiped. The smell of her hand cream. Rune had held her while she cried—while her heart longed for a person forever out of her reach.

Some wounds do not heal, vsenia. They are injuries we learn to live with.

Aunty Clara would forever be a scar on her heart.

Rune's strong hands moved higher, and Faye moaned as he massaged her calf. He was the picture of devotion, fawning over her tirelessly.

"As much as I'd like to lay here all day, I need to waddle over there and get everything set up for Prin's visit," Faye said, motioning toward the small gazebo as she pushed herself up.

Rune chuckled and helped her. "My beautiful queen does not waddle."

Faye looked down at the belly encompassing her lap and exhaled before casting him a sidelong glance. "I feel like a house."

Rune purred and nipped the top of her ear. "You are radiant and carry my young." He splayed his hand possessively over their twins, and the little traitors shifted and kicked as though to greet him.

"Children," Faye corrected, tugging on a length of his hair.

Rune's purr pitched lower, "Minx."

She giggled at the mischievous glint in his pale blue eyes. If they were in Hell, she would have let him take her. Her vampire had become quite the exhibitionist, making love to her out in the open, but she didn't want her sister walking in on them or worse... Vash. Rune had added a door to the outer courtyard leading into their private gardens in order to ease *her* mind.

"You're the only person I know with an outdoor bedroom," Faye teased.

"Perks of ruling a realm," Rune rasped in her ear, patting her thigh. "Come, you will be tardy for Prinia's afternoon tea."

Faye groaned as she stood. "I should let Alister run Anaria, he does a better job of keeping it all together."

"My brother is tuned for war. This is merely a different battle-field."

Her vampire's words weren't inaccurate. When she'd expected Delilah to attack her villages as vengeance for her son, it was Alister who disagreed. He called the Court of Lace and Bone bullies. Delilah tormented weaker courts, and Faye had brought retribution to their doorstep. There was no avenue Delilah could emerge victorious after she'd stepped onto the battlefield.

Faye had been skeptical, creating as many totems as possible in the days ahead. As the weeks gave way into months, Faye slowly began to hope Delilah had given up her crusade. Alister warned her to stay vigilant. Delilah could not win outright in a battle against her. It did not mean she would stop looking for an opportunity.

Delilah thankfully stayed quiet, which benefited Faye. She wasn't sure how intimidating she would be waddling into a court to demand her citizens be released. Not to mention the further along she was in her pregnancy, the more Voshki wanted to obliterate anything unfortunate enough to breech her proximity or mildly inconvenience her.

Faye made her way to the gazebo and the iron-scrolled table inside it. She called the tea set she'd ordered. A rose-colored pot appeared, accompanied by a three-tiered carousel of pastries and almond cookies. She picked a few branches from the azalea bushes beside them. The icy pink and lavender blossoms lent a burst of color to the table setting.

"Stop holding my niece and nephew hostage," Sparrow's voice echoed from the hall. She rubbed Faye's stomach as she walked by and said, "Hi, guys."

Sparrow's skin held a dewy shine. A few unruly blonde curls framed her face, escaping her hair tie. She didn't bother taking off her gauntlets or unstrapping the swords crossing her back. Sparrow chose a pastry square and gave Faye a toothy grin. "Vash said he would spar with me. Want to watch me beat him up?"

"You can't wear all that. Alister is going to lose his mind," Faye said. Alister only recently allowed Sparrow to join Prinia's weekly visits, and with her outfit, she was sure this would be the last.

"Coffin water can suck it. He has three *big ass* swords, and Prin-Prin is just fine," she said, gracelessly falling into the closest chair.

Rune smoothed his hand over her side, leaving a tantalizing trail of warmth in his wake. "Enjoy your tea, vsenia." His touch became intangible, and Faye turned to find he'd vanished.

"I still vote we have Vash here," Sparrow argued, picking through the sweets until she found another baklava square. "I don't trust coffin boy."

Faye threw a napkin at her sister. "You need to be nice. *Nice*, nice when Prin gets here."

Sparrow snorted. "I'm so fucking nice." She pulled her teacup and saucer closer before calling a bottle of tequila.

"What are you doing?"

"Nobody's going to know," her sister insisted as she filled her cup.

"Prin is a vampire," Faye said, pointing at her nose.

Sparrow vanished her bottle and fluttered her hand at Faye. "Does she even know what tequila smells like?"

Booted steps echoed through the halls leading up to the garden. Faye turned toward Alister's unconventional method of announcing his approach. He turned the corner with Prin on his arm. His hair had remained short and black, but during recent months, he'd begun incorporating Jareth's style into his wardrobe.

Compared to Prinia, Alister looked plain in his trousers and simple buttoned shirt. Her dress was elegant and flattered her curves, but it was the flowers arranged in her intricate braids that caught Faye's attention. Crimson spider lilies nestled in her woven tresses like a crown, bathing her in their red aura.

Alister called a tin canister, and Prinia's doe eyes gleamed. She took it and rushed toward Faye. "Hello, little heartbeats," she breathed, tapping at Faye's belly like it was an aquarium, and she was gazing at fish. She straightened and held the tin out to Faye. "We brought you tea."

"We brought snacks," Sparrow added cheerily as she slid the three-tiered arrangement closer to them.

Prinia took a seat beside her and wiggled her fingers over the almond cookies before picking the one with the least number of cracks. She set the sweet on her plate and turned to the side. She leaned forward, her long braid falling over her shoulder. She rubbed her fingers together, clicking her tongue as if she was calling a dog.

Aunty Clara's rabbit leaped out of her shrine and hopped over to them. She pressed her nose into Prinia's hand, and she laughed, petting the oversized bunny.

Prinia straightened and smiled at Alister. "I like her. She feels like Onyx."

Faye nodded. She could see how Prin would compare her massive, shadowed wolf with Faye's stone rabbit. They both brought their owners a degree of peace.

Prinia took another cookie and held it to the rabbit sitting between them. Aunty Clara's memorial took the treat and bounded back to her shrine. Faye giggled. She didn't need to eat, but Prinia insisted on sharing their desserts with her.

"You should name a heartbeat after her," Prinia said, nodding as she bit into her almond cookie.

Alister prepared their tea and said, "We are named on the stones, sweetheart."

Prinia frowned at him, and Sparrow snorted, sipping her tequila.

"The stones can call her one name, and you can call her another," Prinia said to Faye. "We're allowed to name our legacy."

The thought warmed Faye's heart, lessening some of the ache burrowed deep inside her.

She placed her hand over her belly. Rune wouldn't object to naming their daughter Clara. Faye thought of the vision she'd seen in the Hall of Empty Eyes. *Clara*, Faye thought. She envisioned a little girl who inherited all her features but took on Rune's ivory skin, white hair, and pale blue eyes. Her lips widened into a smile made of hope and sorrow.

Clara Sacarlay—the name suited her daughter.

Eighty-Two

Rune strolled through the public courtyard with Faye. Her estate neared completion, and the only items left on the agenda were a few furnishings and landscaping options. His queen was always happier in the sunlight, hugging his arm and smiling. He supposed she longed for her realm as much as he longed for Hell.

"I'm so done with being pregnant," Faye complained, leaning against him and smoothing a hand over her belly.

Rune pressed a kiss to her hair. "Our young will be here soon enough."

"They can get out and take all of this with them," she grumbled, gesturing to herself.

Rune rubbed his hand over hers. She'd been crossed with her weight gain as the months passed, narrowing her eyes anytime he paid her a compliment as though he'd spoken untruths. Her dark hair shone with glossy luster. Her skin was radiant, lit with a soft golden glow. She could not be lovelier, and she carried his young. Pride warmed his chest.

We both know they're mine, Voshki purred. He urged Rune to take Faye back to bed and curl against her, enveloped in her scent.

The corner of his mouth lifted. He wasn't entirely against the notion, but his queen wanted to fit new bedding in the nursery. They'd converted the consort's room for the twins in Hell. In Anaria, Faye had chosen to have their young's room adjacent to theirs with French glass doors, which opened into a shared private garden. He grinned, knowing she'd readied individual gardens for them even if their twins needed a few years to make use of them.

Walking through Faye's estate, they arrived at their private wing overlooking the mountains. Faye slipped away as soon as they entered the brightly lit room. She opened packages delivered earlier in the day and went about arranging the two cribs for the dozenth time.

How many blankets do they need? the Ra'Voshnik asked, perplexed by Faye's endless fussing.

I believe she is nervous, and this calms her, Rune replied, admiring the room his queen curated for the young she would soon have.

The walls were painted in pale earth tones which complimented the animal caricatures and framed pressed plants adorning the walls. In addition to the typical furnishings, a pair of rocking chairs sat in front. Faye raised a brow at him when the chairs were delivered. He'd simply replied, "You will need assistance rocking the two to sleep."

Rune faintly heard a scream followed by a young female voice wailing for Faye. Voshki growled, rising to the surface as Rune phased. He materialized in the central wing housing the young from his queen's orphanage. Jamie Lyn burst out of the classroom and into the hall, followed by several other little ones. Each of them clutched handfuls of leaves and twigs.

Faye's voice slipped through his mind. *Where'd you go?*

The young are distraught, Rune answered as they ran to him.

"Something happened to Sadi," Jamie Lyn desperately cried, shoving the clippings toward him. Bits of dried leaves crumbled, catching the layers of crushed black satin and lace covering her from the neck down.

Rune picked up the girl and settled her on the bend of his arm.

None of the materials they held were the flowers left at their matriarch's feet—only the forest clippings Sadi used. A chill ran down Rune's spine, and he reached for Sadi's mind…

He found nothing.

Panic tore through him, but he forced his composure. They needed to prioritize the young and ease their fears.

Faye appeared behind him, and little ones flocked toward her, choiring their fears. She smiled and ushered them back into their classroom, but Rune could see the tension in her steps. They exchanged a look, and she asked, *What happened?*

I do not know, Rune replied. He set Jamie Lyn down to return with her friends and reached for Morbid. Thankfully, the Familiar King's mind was present. *Are we needed? I do not feel Sadi's mind.*

Silence answered him.

Morbid, Rune growled more firmly—to no reply. He cursed in High Tongue as the instructor collected the handfuls of debris into small bowls. She seemed attentive, but Rune hadn't made her acquaintance. His queen had selected her, and it was enough.

Faye calmed the little ones, and Bayle ordered them into a line. He stood at the back with Bianca while Faye reanimated the Familiar totems.

Rune stepped closer to the teacher and said, "I would appreciate if you brought Jamie Lyn to us after her lessons have concluded."

Sadi had unofficially adopted the girl. She returned in the mornings so Jamie Lyn could continue her education with her friends a few days each week. Sadi collected her at the end of the day, and the girl remained in Chaos otherwise.

Prince? Morbid's voice slipped through his mind like a silk ribbon.

Where is Sadi? Rune growled.

I'll meet you in your brother's office. Bring the court.

What has happened? Rune asked. The communication tether snapped, and his fangs lengthened. He brushed his mind to Faye's and said, *Morbid wishes to meet with the court. If you would call your sister and her male to Alister's office, it would be appreciated.*

Faye nodded and addressed the classroom. "Everyone's totem is fixed. I need to do some court business. So, I want you all to behave for Miss Vivian."

"I don't care about this stupid bird! Something happened to

Sadi," Jamie Lyn exclaimed from the back row.

Faye walked to the girl and crouched beside her desk. "Sadi is *really* strong, sweetie. She carries the Darkness. She was just doing a big spell, and these little guys got disconnected. She can remake your little bird when she picks you up."

Jamie Lyn squeezed her living toy to her chest and nodded.

Faye stood and left the classroom. She glanced up at Rune as they walked. "Sparrow and Vash will meet us there. I tried to reach Damian, but he isn't answering, and... I can't feel Sadi."

"I know," was all Rune managed to say. Delilah could not have attacked Sadi with any degree of success. She would have snared their minds and laughed as they butchered each other.

He silently hoped Morbid's unshaken demeanor meant Sadi walked among the living.

Eighty-Three

Faye stood near Rune, warily eyeing the display above the polished marble mantle in Alister's study. His swords were mounted in a false sense of security. The weapons arrived and vanished with their owner's comings and goings. Faye wondered how many people underestimated him because they believed they had an advantage due to his weapons being out of reach.

She waited for what remained of her inner circle and Morbid's arrival. It wasn't long before his footsteps echoed in a strange cadence. Morbid strolled around the corner, stepping to a rhythm Faye imagined was music only he heard. His low-slung leather pants displayed a hint of muscle, cutting diagonally beneath his hip. The Familiar King stopped before her and adjusted his bright green scarf over his bare chest.

"Where is Sadi?" Rune asked. His cultured voice held an edge of tension.

Morbid studied his scarf's embroidery and let it slip through his fingers. "In time, Prince."

"Does she live?" Rune bit out.

"In. Time. Prince."

"Wait, what happened to Faye's evil twin?" her sister groaned when Morbid remained silent. She kicked her feet over the armrest, balancing a plate of pastries on her stomach. "Why are we here?" she whined. Her eyes widened, and she clapped her hands. "Did you come to give my niece and nephew's fortune?"

Faye cut her sister a glance and mouthed, *What?*

"Pregnant Queens pay him to tell their baby's futures," Sparrow explained.

"I take payment in the form of favors," Morbid said with a feline grin.

Rune's hand closed over her waist, drawing her against him. "We will be offering no further blood debts. Where is Sadi, Morbid?"

"You have your father's patience." The Familiar King's grin widened into a smile, showing his less-than-subtle fangs. "And I need no further blood debts from you, Prince." He stepped closer to Faye, peering down at her swollen belly. His midnight gaze rose to meet hers. "But for the Queen of Chaos and Darkness, I would barter my services if you allowed me to babysit from time to time."

She laughed softly and leaned into Rune. Sadi couldn't be hurt if her father was being this lighthearted. Morbid was strange, but Faye had grown to like him. "You don't need to read their future to spend time with them. Just don't let them get into the bones covering your realm."

"Yes, he does, bitch! I want to hear their future," Sparrow said, righting herself. She pointed at Morbid. "And you don't get them when I want them."

The Familiar King's rich laughter filled the room. He lifted his hand to Faye's belly, careful not to touch her. "May I?"

At Faye's nod, Morbid rested his hand over the pronounced curve of her abdomen. She expected to feel his magic spread over her twins, but she felt nothing outside of the light pressure of his hand.

"Your daughter will be as terrifying as she is beautiful. She will carry your likeness but, unfortunately, inherit her father's coloring.

The two will be inseparable, and your daughter will safeguard your son."

Faye looked down at her belly, and she couldn't help but smile at Morbid's words. They would take care of each other, the white-haired daughter and the black-haired son she'd seen in the Hall of Empty Eyes.

Children she would soon meet.

Her family.

Morbid strolled to Sparrow, pilfering a small square pastry from her plate. "I have other news. Sadi has been injured. She will be… unavailable while she mends."

Faye's lips parted as a chill rippled down her spine. "What happened? Did the Court of Lace and Bone ambush her?" They'd been so quiet. Faye never guessed Delilah would shift her focus to a formidable member of her court. Sadi carried a shard of Darkness. How could she be injured?

Morbid chuckled. "If Delilah came for my daughter, she and her court would be strung from scaffolds throughout Chaos."

Because Morbid would intercept them before they could reach his daughter, Faye thought.

"There would be nothing for me to intercept. Sadist is more than capable of defending herself," Morbid crooned.

Faye's jaw snapped shut. The Familiar King winked at her, and her cheeks flushed.

Sparrow snorted, oblivious to her reaction. "Why did you name her Sadist? Did you foresee she'd be mean as hell and decided to give her a warning label?"

Morbid chuckled. "She'll grow into her name."

"Should we watch over Jamie Lyn until Sadi recovers?" Rune asked.

"No," Morbid answered. "I'll bring the young Jamie Lynx back with me. She belongs to Chaos now."

If Sadi was injured, Faye wasn't going to abandon Jamie Lyn to another realm. "I would like to go with her and check on Sadi."

Morbid remained silent, and Faye hoped he wasn't listening to her thoughts.

After a long moment, he asked, "Will you be joining your Queen, Prince?"

"I shall," Rune replied.

"Who attacked Sadi?" Faye asked. Was there another court, *a stronger court*, she needed to shield her village from? Morbid shrugged his broad shoulders, and Faye bit the inside of her lip. Sadi was formidable. If it wasn't Delilah...

"The empty-eyed vessels turned on her." The Familiar King gave a slow nod, confirming her suspicion. "What did she see?"

The mirthful glow retreated from his midnight eyes. "You know what she saw."

Her death under Rune. Faye swallowed and asked, "How did she escape?"

"Can't say."

"Can we be of assistance?" Rune asked.

"She needs time, Prince," Morbid answered, gesturing to Faye's belly. "Much more than you have remaining. I could introduce you to Ash. They delivered Sadi."

Faye looked up at Rune, and he stroked the back of his fingers down her spine. "It is your choice, vsenia."

"Will they be comfortable with my delivery in Hell?" Faye asked.

Morbid grinned, placing his hand over his heart as he leaned forward. "Hell is simply another realm to my kind."

Eighty-Four

Morbid phased Faye, Rune, and Jamie Lyn to his home in Chaos.
They materialized on the stone landing pad surrounded by
small, pointed bones. Faye narrowed her eyes at one with four prongs
and immediately averted her gaze. Jamie Lyn leaped down before
Faye could stop her and ran toward the front door. Faye's stomach
knotted as scores of teeth ground and popped beneath her shoes.

"Jamie Lyn wait for us," Faye yelled as the girl reached the door.
She focused on the less macabre facets of Morbid's realm. The dark
thundering sky and the Familiar King's ever-changing mansion. It was
a small cottage today. The humble building was reminiscent of the
home she once shared with her sister.

Jamie Lyn frowned at her bird totem, and her eyes glassed over
with tears. "It's not showing me where Sadi is," she said in a broken
whisper. She turned toward Morbid, and Faye's heart squeezed. She

gripped Rune's wrist, preparing to bend down to the little girl's level. How could she explain Sadi was injured without scaring Jamie Lyn?

Morbid stepped in front of her and held his hand out. The living toy landed on his palm, and he stroked it affectionately. "Sadi is no longer tied to your bird, little lynx, but I can weave some of Chaos into your friend."

Blood-red feathers sprouted into a crest, and the little bird returned to the girl. It circled her and fluttered through her sunset-hued hair as Jamie Lyn asked, "Where's Sadi?"

The bird chirped and flew into the cottage. Following it, she dashed up the stairs.

"Jamie Lyn, wait for us," Faye called once the girl reached the top and disappeared down a hall. She was too pregnant and too exhausted to chase children up and down stairs.

A warm hand pressed against the small of her back, and Rune took her wrist, offering his support. "I'm fine," she hissed. "Stop her before she finds Sadi. We don't even know if she's awake." Or what condition she was in. Faye couldn't stand the thought of Jamie Lyn stumbling onto Sadi while she was injured and unresponsive. How the image would stick with her.

"My daughter is awake. Her core is... damaged but mending." Morbid volunteered the information as he strolled past them. "Angelique requires my attention. The little lynx will find her dam."

"You're leaving her with Sadi?"

Morbid didn't slow or turn toward them as he spoke. "Sadist is far from helpless. Her core was injured. You should know a person's worth reaches beyond the shard they wear."

He turned down a hallway and continued out of sight. Faye respected her Anarians, seeing the value in their lives even though they didn't possess a soul shard. She'd never given thought to those who had magic and suddenly found themselves without.

She mentally shook herself. This wasn't about those with or without magic. This was about a little girl's welfare and whether Sadi could care for Jamie Lyn with her injuries.

The Familiar totem lead them through the house, but Faye felt them the moment she set foot on the second story.

Cracked reservoirs hemorrhaging power. Faye concentrated on Rune's strength, unnerved by the degree of damage she perceived.

They were in worse shape than Alister after he'd rushed into the Hall of Empty Eyes for Prinia. Sadi served Chaos. What happened?

The small bird stopped in front of a set of carved double doors, and Jamie Lyn stood on her toes to knock. "Sadi. Damian. Are you busy?" she asked, rocking back on her heels as she waited for a reply.

Seconds ticked by, and Faye wondered if Morbid might have been mistaken. They couldn't be awake with the condition of their cores. One of them stirred, and Faye blinked.

The door clicked open, and Sadi's hand reached into the hall. The elegant black lace sleeve hung from her wrist as she brushed a strand of hair behind Jamie Lyn's ear. "You're home early, lynx."

Faye stiffened. There was no strength in Sadi's voice. No ring of self-assured arrogance. No regal sophistication.

"Morbid brought me. I was worried about you," Jamie Lyn insisted.

The door opened wider, and Sadi padded into the hall barefoot. Her long, unruly black hair fell against her bare face. Faye couldn't help but notice how much smaller she was without her corset, exaggerated skirts, and belted thigh-high boots. She was so… *normal* dressed in a floor-length chemise.

"I'm well. The cooks are broiling candied beef sticks. If you want one, you should hurry." Sadi said, gently ushering Jamie Lyn further down the hall.

The girl took a few reluctant steps and turned, hugging Sadi's waist. "I'll get you one, too, okay?"

"That would be lovely," Sadi said.

Jamie Lyn released her and whispered to her little bird before and ran after it.

Sadi crossed her arms, turning toward Faye, but everything was wrong. There was no silent invitation for Rune. She hadn't even looked at him. Faye's blood chilled when she caught sight of Sadi's Shard of Darkness embedded in the first joint of her gleaming finger gauntlet.

The dark mist surrounding her shard was stagnant.

Sadi bristled and dropped her hand, ducking back into her room.

"Wait." Faye stopped at her threshold, but Sadi stalked through her lavish sitting room and continued through a bloodroot archway. She turned to Rune, unsure of what to do.

He exhaled but remained where he stood. "She does not wish to see me, love. I am not entering her bed chamber."

Faye wasn't sure if he stayed out for her benefit or Sadi's, but she was grateful. "I can't leave Jamie Lyn here. I need to know she'll be cared for." And Safe.

"Then speak with her," Rune said, motioning toward Sadi's room. "I will remain here."

Faye stepped into the opulent room decorated in black and maroon. The plush carpet cushioned her shoes as she walked. It reminded Faye of the brothel Rune had taken her to, decorated in rich tapestries and billowing fabrics. A decanter of red wine was placed between empty glasses, and an untouched plate of choice cuts with a long thin knife beside it.

She silently wondered if this was something Sadi always kept on hand or if it was a meal Morbid ordered for her.

"Sadi," Faye said, inching closer to the darkened archway. The black and maroon theme carried into Sadi's bedroom.

"Go away," she answered. There was a rustle of satin as she sat on her massive canopy bed alongside a black tiger with red stripes, sleeping on his front paws.

Faye leaned against the dark wooden beam and faced the sitting room. "I can't leave Jamie Lyn here without knowing she'll be cared for properly."

"My lynx has an entire staff seeing to her needs and education," Sadi snapped.

Faye's lips parted, and she shook her head. "Having servants doesn't mean she's safe."

"Safe?" Sadi scoffed. "Your home was attacked, not mine."

Her words struck Faye into silence, and she couldn't breathe.

A spiraling rage came next, and Faye stormed into Sadi's room. "Speak another word, and I'll put you in the grave you're begging for."

Sadi clapped slowly. "Finally acting like a Queen," she said. Her lashes lowered. "Now, get out."

"Why are you such a cunt?" Faye snapped.

"Get. Out."

"Cut this shit and come back with us."

"No," Sadi answered. Giving her back, she pulled the blankets back and got into bed.

This bitch was impossible. Faye splayed her fingers and walked in a tight circle before hissing an exasperated breath. "How are you going to defend her? You can't use your power!"

Sadi threw the blankets off and stalked toward Faye. "I'm not returning with you!"

"Why!"

"Because everything I believed was mine belongs to you!" Sadi panted, tears spilling over her cheeks. She looked away and drew a shaking breath. "Now go," she whispered, waving a hand at Faye as she trudged back to her bed.

"Sadi—"

"No," she hissed. A bitter laugh escaped her lips as she traced the corner of her bedpost. "You have taken everything from me."

Her pain cooled Faye's temper. "Rune... Rune was never yours. He's not a belonging."

"The Shadow Prince?" Sadi's voice was hollow and steeped in anguish. "You think Rune is the only thing you've taken from me?"

"You have Damian," Faye said, pointing to the sleeping tiger in her bed. "Don't you love him?"

"Leave!" Sadi spat, baring her teeth.

"You know it's safer at court," Faye yelled. "Why are you fighting me so hard?"

"Because I've lost my sight!" Sadi screamed. Her nails dug into the wooden post, leaving deep grooves.

Faye fell silent and took a step back. Words Sadi had spoken during their lessons replayed through her mind.

And a Familiar without their sight is no Familiar at all.

Sadi harbored doubt or went against fate. The empty-eyed vessels would have turned on her, ripping and tearing at her mind. "How did you survive?" Faye whispered.

Sadi wiped her eyes and glanced at her over her shoulder. "I've taught you our ways. If you're so curious, witness it yourself."

Eighty-Five

Kill her! Voshki roared. His claws raked over Rune's awareness, urging him to sever Sadi's head for daring to raise her voice at Faye.

Calm yourself, Rune retorted. Sadi's service to Chaos defined her. Without her sight...

Step into her room, and I'll break your neck, Voshki snapped.

He would never disrespect his queen in such a manner, but Sadi had been his closest friend for centuries. Loyal and steadfast.

And in love with you. Did you not hear her? Voshki asked.

Sadi stood beside him through many wars. He depended on her guidance and visions. Darkness... She'd liberated him from Sadira's court.

He wouldn't abandon her.

Sadi's voice carried to Rune's sensitive ears. "I've taught you our ways. If you're so curious, witness it yourself."

No, Voshki growled. *She is days from bearing my young. This is too dangerous.*

Rune remained silent, and Faye's footsteps approached.

She turned toward him. "Do you think Jamie Lyn is safe here?" Faye asked quietly as she peered down the hall.

Rune wondered if Faye would want to find the young Jamie Lyn and speak to the staff assigned to her. "I believe Sadi is of sound mind, and Jamie Lyn has lived here for the past five months."

Faye worried her bottom lip, and Rune spelled the space between them to keep their conversation from drifting past Sadi's door.

"Did you want to talk to her?" she asked, not meeting his gaze.

"No, vsenia. She will not be amiable to my presence."

She looked up through her long lashes. "Did you hear everything?" she whispered.

More than he ever wished to learn. "I expected one of you to shield the room, but..."

"She needs a friend, and I know you care about her."

"Vsenia, I harbor—"

Faye raised her hand. "I know you don't view her in a romantic light, but she's your friend. And... she's in a lot of pain."

She's hasn't begun to feel pain, yet, Voshki crooned.

Rune ignored the Ra'Voshnik's threats. "The preceding centuries I have known her does not excuse how she spoke to you, vsenia. I will send a letter and speak with her if she wishes. Shall we return home?"

Faye rested a hand on her belly and looked down at their twins. "I want to go to the Hall of Empty Eyes."

Alarm edged in a predatory need to defend his pregnant queen seized Rune's mind. "Vsenia, you are *days* from birth."

Faye looked away and pulled her arms to her side. "The vessels turned on her. They should have killed her. You saw what happened to Alister and Prinia. I need to know how she survived."

Rune thinned his lips, stepping toward her and splaying his fingers over their young. "Can this not wait, love?"

A whisper of a smile curled the corners of her mouth as her lightning-streaked midnight eyes found his. "They're fine. I've been in and out of the temple with them multiple times. The vessels showed them to me," Faye said, smoothing her hand over his. "I want to know how to walk every path leading back to you and our family."

Do not let her walk into that temple, Voshki growled. His agitation grew with Faye's insistence.

Everything he needed stood before him. Rune finally understood Morbid's words. Faye and their family were all he needed, and he would not risk them. He took her hand and pressed his lips to the backs of her fingers. There was a better way. A safer way. Sadi had taught her the Familiar ways.

"You can witness how Sadi survived without setting foot in a Familiar temple."

Eighty-Six

Rune took Faye's hand, phasing them to their room in Anaria. She finished decorating it last week. The cool gray tones complimented the simple iron sconces she'd purchased, but her favorite feature was the large bay window overlooking her private gardens. The pane's reflection framed her image in unfocused greens and highlighted with splashes of red and lavender.

Time leaves an impression, embedding memories within the land.

Sadi's words echoed, and she turned toward her vampire. "I haven't done this before. I'm not sure how long it will take."

Sadi had shown her Rune as Lyssa's consort. Faye knew memories could be accessed from any location, but Faye wasn't sure how to call them forth.

Rune's hand slid down her back, and he sat on the cushioned bench. "It will take as long as it takes, love," he said, gesturing to the space beside him. "I will await your return."

Faye nodded, sitting beside him. She descended into herself and stepped beyond her body. She ascended the physical plane, and her chest constricted, forcing her breathing to slow as the Darkness rolled across the ground.

She and Rune sat in the window, but instead of a garden bathed in sunlight, the window opened into a dark void.

Faye visualized the Hall of Empty Eyes as though she were preparing to phase. Smoke and shadow swept over her. When it cleared, she stood in the mirrored hall surrounded by rows of swaying ashen bodies.

She pressed deeper into her magic, willing time to roll back. The vessels stared through clouded eyes, and Faye gritted her teeth.

Maybe she was going about this the wrong way. Faye reflected on the past days, hoping time here would follow suit.

Nothing came of it.

Faye took a deep breath, recalling Sadi summoning Rune's line. How the strands moved, weaving his life in the present. Sadi had flicked her hand in order to view Rune's past.

She opened her hand, palm down before her. She called to this place and imagined a shining line made from the glass around her. A gleaming cord lifted from the Darkness, blanketing her feet and resonating with the hall. Faye flicked her wrist, driving the line past her. The vessels jostled rapidly, shocking her from her concentration.

The empty-eyed vessels slowed, watching her. A chill slipped down her spine, and she lowered her gaze, avoiding their jarring movements as she pushed time faster.

It obeyed, accelerating the minutes into a metamorphosis of change.

Faye stopped once a blur moved past her.

Time slowed.

Sadi entered the temple, closing the door behind her. Shadows weighed heavily across her face. With her eyes on the ground, she strolled into the temple. Her hand smoothed over the front of her corset, and she looked to the empty-eyed vessels.

The claw of her articulated ring dragged over the embroidered fabric of her fitted corset. "Show me my life… if… if Rune chose me."

She'd known Sadi wanted Rune. Her evil twin confessed as much earlier, but listening to it out loud —seeing it— made it real. Heat rushed to Faye's face, and her magic rose to meet her emotions.

She exhaled in slow, measured breaths. None of this mattered. Rune loved her. She was here to see how Sadi survived the empty-eyed vessels after they turned on her.

Sadi's expression softened, fingers reaching forward. Her nails clicked against the glass, and her lips parted as she blinked the moisture from her lashes.

Faye knew what she was seeing, and possessive anger rose through Faye. Rune and Voshki were hers, and she would crush anyone who attempted to take them. Her shoulders tensed while gazing into the mirror, but the vessels didn't part.

No future for Rune and Sadi was given.

The vessels revealed nothing to her, crowded in rows as they stood shoulder to shoulder, focused on Sadi.

"Rune." Sadi's voice was little more than a whisper as she watched her vision play.

Sadi jerked her hand away from the mirror like she'd been burned. Her features darkened, and she bared her teeth.

"No," Sadi growled. "This cannot be."

She turned to the vessels on either side and screamed, "This is not my fate!"

Faye's anger was forgotten as fear chilled her. The empty-eyed vessels tilted their heads back and opened their mouths wide.

Made.

You are not special.

Created to be consumed.

Fodder for the Shadow Prince.

You are nothing.

Sadi opened her mouth wide and hissed as the vessels tore into her mind. Faye brought her hand to her mouth and stepped back. She sensed magic welling within the mirrors all around them. Tendrils forced themselves from the magic, arching high.

Vipers ready to strike.

Faye's heart seized as the serpents struck through the glass, claiming chunks of Sadi's core and mind, leaving the power she contained to pool around her in shattered pieces.

Faye recognized this magic and its viciousness. She took another step back, unable to breathe. The dark mist covered the ground. Shadowed snakes... a mirror of her magic without Faye's conscious to temper it.

Terrifying, deadly, and efficient.

Sadi's eyes rolled into the back of her head as blood trickled from her mouth and the corner of her midnight eyes. She collapsed, and her body seized as the vessels repeated their hateful words. Her power spilled—broken beyond repair.

How could she survive this?

Faye frantically searched the hall. Where was Morbid?

The doors crashed open, and a male voice shouted, "Sadi!"

Faye jerked toward the sound. Damian stood in the doorway. His chest quickly rose and fell as he assessed the situation. An oversized harness appeared in his hand, and he pulled it over his head. It rested around his throat and hung across one of his shoulders.

He pulled a large spike from it and drove it into the stone entryway. Once it was embedded deep enough, he took a final look into the temple and backed down the steps. A cord stretched from the spike, connecting to the harness draped over Damian's throat.

A blinding flash of light consumed him and reshaped him into a larger form. A massive black tiger emerged from the fading light, and Damian charged up the stairs with the harness around his neck. He crossed the threshold in a powerful leap. More voices overlapped, blending into a horrific crescendo.

She doesn't love you.

You will fail her.

Animal.

This will end, and you will be alone.

Damian roared as his ears flattened and his lids fluttered closed. His paws remained outstretched, crashing over Sadi as the empty-eyed vessels ripped at his core and mind.

His claws sank into Sadi's ribs and thighs as he jerked and seized. A high-pitched sound whirled, and Damian was dragged backward by his throat, taking Sadi's body with him.

They tumbled down the stairs and fell in a heap over the bones littering the ground. Faye stared in shock. Sadi didn't survive on her own.

Damian saved her.

The shadowed serpents darkened. Sharp purple tendrils illuminated the churning black mist, retaining their shape. The cobras' forms slipped, cascading into the Darkness and seeping through the mirrors. The carnivorous magic shrank back to its master, greedy for new prey.

Faye's chest tightened. This was *her* power. The vessels spoke to her because she was tied to them, tied to the Darkness—what did that make her?

Airy notes startled Faye, and she turned toward the sound. Morbid whistled a cheery tune. He pulled the tangled harness off Damian and hoisted the massive tiger over his shoulder. Morbid appeared unbothered, draping the much larger animal like he weighed no more than a towel. He gathered his daughter in his arms next and stood.

Morbid's slowed in front of her, winking. Faye flinched and rushed forward.

"Do you see me," she shouted, calling out into the void. She was touched by a memory. Morbid's only response to her before he vanished.

It drew out her sister's laughter. Damian smiled ferally, answering a thousand and one of her many questions. Even Sadi had been somewhat pleasant within the memory, fawning at her mate as she purred, *"I need him to survive what's coming."*

Faye remembered how odd it sounded then. Her prediction had lingered in the air.

'What's coming?' Faye had asked her fated twin, unsure whether she wanted the truth—but Sadi only responded with, *"Death."*

The Familiar had used her visions, but only to save herself.

Faye returned to her physical body and let the Hall of Empty Eyes dissolve. Her vision shifted, adjusting to her surroundings.

Rune leaned forward as he came into focus and cupped her cheek. "Are you well?"

Faye nodded. "I know what I need to do."

Sadi's mate entered the Hall of Empty Eyes to save her at the cost of himself. Faye would make sure Rune never set foot in this temple.

Eighty-Seven

Faye reclined on the chaise in Rune's study. Her feet hurt after the day's excitement, and her joints fared no better. Rune sat at the far end with her feet on his lap, unlacing her boots and pulling off her socks, massaging her aching soles.

She lifted a foot and inspected her swollen ankle. "They need to get out," she said, dropping her leg onto Rune's lap.

"Soon, vsenia," he purred, possessively splaying his fingers over their twins.

The little traitors shifted and kicked beneath his touch, and Faye grumbled, "You can carry them since they like you so much."

Rune chuckled. "They are only pleased to hear from me because I dote on their mother."

A knock on the door caught Faye's and Rune's attention. He ran his hand along her shin as footsteps approached them.

A tall Familiar walked in front of the fireplace. The leather panels of their long skirt parted with each step, exposing the length of their legs. Tall, belted boots made them nearly as tall as Rune, and a leather waist cincher emphasized their hourglass figure. Instead of a scarf, they wore long lace sleeves, crossing over the backs of their shoulders, leaving the hard planes of their chest bare.

"My name is Ash, my King requested I oversee the birth of these two darlings." The Familiar grew closer, their bright lavender eyes kind and emphasized with dramatic sweeping lines. "I'll need to do an exam and check on the sweet kits. May I?"

Faye nodded. "Is this okay or should I get up?"

Ash swiped their hand at Faye playfully. "Only if it makes you feel more comfortable."

"I'd rather be off my feet," Faye said with a small smile. She was ready for a nap and would do so as soon as Ash told her the babies were healthy.

Rune withdrew his touch, and Ash smoothed their hand over her belly. "I'm just going to take a peek at the little ones," they said as their eyes became far-seeing. Ash's curled dark hair and garments swayed, and they slid the clawed point of their articulated ring along her belly.

Faye giggled as Ash pressed their hand over different areas, blinking each time they kicked. "They are quite active."

Faye tapped her foot to Rune's chest, meeting his pale blue eyes. "They riot anytime they hear his voice and wake me up at night."

Ash stepped back, and their hair and clothing returned to normal. "They will be keeping you up for different reasons soon. Your little ones are developing well. I'd say you have another few days—a week at the most. I'll visit daily to check on the kits. Do you have any questions for me?"

"No, it was very nice meeting you," Faye said.

"Well, alert me if you feel any changes," Ash said, leaning forward and speaking to her belly. "I'll see you darlings, tomorrow."

Ash straightened and bowed their head. The gentle light shone through intricately wrought iron windows, reflecting the purple dust highlights accenting their deep brown skin. "If there's nothing else."

"Perhaps you could advise my queen to rest during these last days. Limit her duties," Rune teased, turning toward her and raising a brow.

"I have found it's best not to question mothers-to-be," they laughed. "Life has no schedule, but a good queen compromises with her consort."

Faye slowly blinked at the gray stone walls while Rune checked and fluffed her pillows for the fifth time in the past hour. Her vampire had become unbearable the past two days, and Sparrow did nothing to save her.

Feminine laughter sounded from the hall, and Faye envied their ability to leave. Sparrow, Kimber, and Jeanene walked into her bedroom. Her sister and Kimber carried on, but Jeanene quieted and fell back a step, partially hiding behind Kimber.

Faye sat up, wincing as her back twinged.

Rune caressed the side of her face and lifted her chin until she met his pale blue eyes. "You should be resting, vsenia."

"My back hurts because you're trapping me in this bed," Faye argued.

"I mean, this is how you got into this mess. It's pretty fucking hilarious this is how it's ending too," Sparrow said as she emptied the bag's contents onto Faye's bed. She froze, and her eyes gleamed. "Can we call you *fang daddy*?" she asked with a toothy grin.

"No," Rune replied.

"But it's perfect," Sparrow whined, giving Faye her best pair of sad eyes. "He has fangs, and he's going to be a daddy."

Rune sat beside Faye and turned his attention to Sparrow. "Let me speak in terms you will understand, harpy. Get fucked."

Faye's mouth fell open, staring at him, but Sparrow burst into laughter.

"It's about fucking time you developed a sense of humor," her sister said, snatching his pillow.

She lifted her arm, and Faye pointed at her. "Sparrow, don't you dare."

"What? He started it," she argued, vigorously scrubbing Rune's pillow against her armpit. She threw it at him, and her vampire promptly swatted it to the ground.

Rune glanced at his defiled pillow, then back at Sparrow. "I shall have it burned… immediately."

Kimber linked arms with Jeneane and pulled her to the edge of the bed with the rest of them. "We got more birthing sheets you can pick from. Sparrow picked out baby blue—"

"Sky blue," Sparrow corrected.

"It's blue. Shut up," Kimber said, sticking her tongue out at Sparrow. "Jeanene chose one with autumn leaves," she added. When Jeanene didn't move, Kimber hip-bumped her. "Show her the one you got."

Faye smiled and leaned back onto Rune. The poor girl was terrified of her. She'd tried to see Jeanene as she and her family acclimated to life at court. She took to Kimber immediately, but the laughter and ease drained out of her anytime she caught sight of Faye. It hurt, but she gave Jeanene her space.

Faye's role as Queen meant her people were safe. They didn't have to befriend her.

Jeanene briefly met her eyes before averting her gaze. Reaching into her large shopping bag, she pulled out a bundle of sheets printed with pressed leaves.

"Those are beautiful," Faye breathed.

"Sparrow said you tend a garden," Jeanene said quietly. She took a measured step behind Kimber and tightly squeezed her arm.

"I said she loves her leafy babies," her sister corrected.

"I got you bunnies, but you can use these, and I can get these exchanged for crib sheets," Kimber said, pushing Jeanene's bundle closer and pulling hers out of the packaging.

White rabbits were stamped in different positions over the sheets with carrots. Faye smiled, wishing Aunty Clara were still with her.

"Could you exchange them for blankets instead?" Faye asked.

"Yeah. Of course," Kimber answered, stuffing the birthing sheets back in her package and placing them on the ground out of sight.

Faye sucked a breath as her back spasmed.

"Bitch, are you in labor?" Sparrow asked.

"No." Faye rubbed her lower back, willing the pain to cease. "I've been stuck in this bed for two days since *someone* insisted I should stay off my feet," she said, eyeing Rune.

Sparrow snorted and opened the pressed leaf birthing sheets. "I'm getting these washed. I'm betting you're in labor."

Rune waved his hand and said, "How have you survived for decades without learning simple hearth magic?"

Her sister bunched the sheets and shoved them to her face, inhaling deeply. "How did you get them to smell so good?" She pushed them in Kimber's face. "Smell this. It's like he stuffed Faye's garden in here."

"I'm not in labor," Faye argued.

Rune massaged her lower back and pressed a kiss to her hair. "Ash will be here shortly, and they can shed some light on your back pain."

Eighty-Eight

Ash had arrived and confirmed Sparrow's suspicions. Rune smiled. His queen was in labor, and his young would soon join the realms.

My young, Voshki purred, eager to meet their twins.

Rune had ceased arguing with the Ra'Voshnik. Voshki's diluted beliefs did not change facts. *He* had not been present during the Hunter's Moon, and Faye's young were his.

He ushered the three women out of their room, claiming Faye needed rest. Jeanene retreated quickly, visibly relieved to be out of his presence, while the blonde harpy argued to stay. Kimber had been a gift from the Darkness, pulling her away by the hair.

"If the harpy returns, I will shield our wing," Rune said as he strolled back to Faye. She lay on her side, cradled comfortably by an exuberant number of pillows.

He sat with her through the night, massaging her back through each contraction. He timed their frequency and how long each persisted. Faye said nothing, but he could feel the tension climbing up her back with each passing hour.

She dozed lightly between her back spasms, and Ash checked in with her periodically. They offered to shield some of the pain, but Faye declined. These were the beginning stages, and she wanted to wait until her labor progressed.

The Ra'Voshnik prowled his mind growing uneasy as the night passed. Faye's eyes squeezed shut as her lips parted with panting breaths.

"I need to bring you to the stones, vsenia," Rune said when Faye relaxed, taking deep breaths. She nodded, and he gathered her in his arms before phasing himself and Faye to his family's altar.

Ash had arrived before him, arranging the bedding and pillows Faye meticulously picked over.

"I have you," Rune whispered, pressing his lips to her hair. He tightened his hold and leaped onto the stone slab. Faye gasped, digging her nails into his jacket, and he chuckled. "Do you truly think I would drop you?" he asked.

"I'm going to bite you," Faye growled.

He hummed in agreement and knelt, lowering his queen onto the plush bedding. "Promises, promises."

Faye pulled her shoulders up and whimpered as clear liquid soaked through her skirt and bedding.

Ash made comforting sounds, smoothing their hand over Faye's wet skirt. "Your water broke. Nothing to worry about." The material dried beneath their touch, and Faye calmed a fraction. They walked around the stone slab and brushed Faye's hair away from her face. "Do you think you can get on your hands and knees?"

Faye nodded but struggled to lift herself. Her arms shook through the next wave of contractions. Rune sat back on his heels, helping his queen reposition herself. Faye draped her arms around him as he massaged her lower back with the heel of his palm.

Ash flattened their hand over the small of Faye's back, and their other hand slid over her belly. "I can dull your pain, but your labor will still exhaust your body."

Faye sagged against Rune, taking deeper breaths. She turned her head toward him and muttered, "I want my sister here."

"Have Vashien bring Sparrow," Ash said. Rune cut a glance, and they smiled. "Delivery takes time, Shadow Prince. Happy mothers have easier births." They rubbed Faye's foot and said, "I need you to scoot back to the edge."

His queen laughed softly against his throat. She leaned up and winced, cutting into his self-control. Her pain affected him as nothing else had in his life.

Why are they only dulling her pain? the Ra'Voshnik growled. *They might be more understanding if I break one of their bones every time she flinches.*

They saw to Angelique's delivery. They can see to our queen's, Rune growled through his mind as he lowered his head to whisper at Faye's ear, "Hold on to me."

Her arms tightened around him, and Rune stood, lifting her with him. Two steps brought him to the edge of the stone slab, and he knelt, placing her where Ash requested.

Rune reached for the winged male's mind. *Faye is requesting Sparrow's presence.*

She hasn't stopped pacing. We'll be there shortly, Vashien replied.

"Pardon my reach," Ash said, gathering Faye's skirt. They folded the flowing material over Faye's waist and cut away her undergarments with a small, hooked knife. They let the material fall to the floor, arranging Faye's skirt back into place.

Faye tensed, and iridescent wings erupted from her back. Her claws pierced Rune's jacket and bit into his back as she groaned. They sank deeper, drawing blood as she strained under her next set of contractions.

Rune soothed her, and the soft, lingering light of Hell's ever-twilight sky faded. Storm clouds swept over the stars, and the corner of his mouth lifted. He'd been so preoccupied with being caught when he'd invoked his blood all those centuries ago, he didn't notice Hell's sky darken.

Rune's voice dropped an octave as he whispered to her. "Hell is welcoming our young."

Faye bit down on the spot where his neck met his shoulder, piquing Voshki's interest. Rune smiled, his fangs lengthening.

"Children," his queen growled through labored breaths.

Rune chuckled, purring for her. "Yes, my love."

"Your sister has arrived," Rune whispered, his fingers brushing her side.

Faye turned her head, but she heard Sparrow before she saw her.

"Where are my niece and nephew, bitch," Sparrow yelled, drumming her hands on the stone slab near Faye's feet.

Vashien stepped toward Sparrow, and her sister shoved him back until he was behind Rune. "You stay back here," Sparrow hissed. "No boys allowed past here." She lined her hand with Faye's knee.

Rune chuckled, and Sparrow scowled at him. She pressed two fingers on either side of her windpipe before pointing at him. "You better take care of her fang boy. I'm watching you."

"You should keep a respectable distance, too," Vashien insisted.

Sparrow snorted, fluttering her hand at him. "I've seen her charcuterie board."

Faye laughed, instantly regretting it as another contraction seized her body. She breathed through the pain, trembling in Rune's arms.

When the pain subsided, Vashien asked, "Do you need anything?"

Sparrow made an exasperated noise and rolled her eyes. "Are you trying to get his shadowy highness to break your neck?"

"Do either of you need anything? Crimson wine?" Vashien cut Sparrow a look and grinned. "A gag?"

Faye leaned on Rune's shoulder and smiled at her sister. "I'm glad you're here."

"I wouldn't be anywhere else," she said, rubbing Faye's thigh. "Now quit slacking and give me those babies."

Hours passed, and the contractions increased in frequency. The muscles in her back began spasming with the effort it took to hold her wings up during the first hour. Her back ached, but when she let them fall limp over either side of the stone slab, the additional pressure worsened her labor pains.

Rune held her wings up with his will, using his phantom touch to massage the stiff muscles in her lower back.

Faye sucked a sharp breath as her pelvic floor cramped and pain shot up her back. She clenched her jaw, forcing herself to breathe. Her damp hair clung to her face, dragging over her sweat-slick skin anytime she moved.

Ash flattened their hand on the small of Faye's back and pressed against her lower belly with the other. "Your little ones are ready to make their grand entrance. Widen your stance. The Shadow Prince will help hold you up."

Faye curled forward. Pain and pressure blended together, clouding her mind.

"You are doing so well," Rune murmured. He lifted her, supporting her weight while he gently eased her thighs apart.

Faye panted, closing her eyes as Ash gathered her skirt and pinned it above her waist. They spread their hands over Faye's belly and said, "I'm going to move them to a better position. This will hurt."

Faye tightened her grip on her mate and nodded. She trembled, biting back a scream as her twins shifted, applying more pressure.

The sound of tearing fabric puzzled Faye. She twisted slowly to look behind her. Ash cut and ripped the leaf-pressed blankets and bedding between her legs, exposing the stone beneath it.

Rune purred, brushing the side of his face in her hair. "The blood from their birth will name them and tie our young to Hell."

Faye groaned as another contraction wracked her body. She dug her claws into Rune, shaking.

"When the contractions come, push," Ash instructed. "Don't fight against it."

Another wave of pressure and pain flooded her before the previous one abated. "It feels like one big contraction," Faye hissed.

"When they start, push. We're almost there," Ash said.

Thunder crashed above them, thick dark clouds covering the sky. Faye's eyes snapped open as she exhaled.

"Hell will welcome our son and daughter," Rune whispered to her.

The contractions came in unending waves, crashing against her, drowning her as they overlapped. Faye beat her wings unknowingly, writhing in Rune's arms as she pushed.

Her back cramped, compounding her pain. She screamed, claws gripping Rune's jacket and the muscles beneath, culminating until

Faye couldn't breathe. Couldn't think.

Her agony peaked—then *relief.*

Faye fell limp in Rune's arms, exhausted and thankful for the small reprieve.

"Bitch, you have a boy!" Sparrow yelled from behind her.

Faye smiled weakly. "I want to see—"

She screamed as another contraction sliced through her. Faye panted, leaning onto Rune for support. She thought she would have a break between the twins. Exhaustion clawed at her. Faye wasn't sure how much more she could take.

"He's really cute," Sparrow added. By the wobble in her voice, Faye knew her sister was hopping in place with her hands clasped.

Her son wailed, and Ash chuckled. "He seems rather upset to be separated from his sister."

Sparrow brought a swaddled bundle into Faye's vision.

Faye smiled, out of breath, resting on Rune's shoulder. Her son peered up at her with dark blue eyes. His full head of unruly black hair tufted out in different directions. He shifted and grumbled, pinching his expression.

He was perfect.

Eighty-Nine

Sparrow rocked Faye's son, patting his bottom. "Wasn't it supposed to rain or some shit?" Thunder crashed, and Sparrow said, "Never mind."

Faye didn't care if Hell welcomed him.

"His hair is quite unruly," Rune said, kissing her temple.

Faye curled forward, pain shooting through her. She forced herself to take longer breaths as she leaned up, posting herself on Rune's thighs. Pain culminated in her lower back and focused between her legs. Faye squeezed the hard muscles of Rune's legs and groaning through the new set of contractions.

A scream broke from her lips as the next wave of pain crested over her. She jerked when something wet struck her lashes. Faye blinked, and another drop hit her nose. She squinted, looking up as rain began to fall.

Lightning crashed, and Faye thought she saw a man and woman illuminated by the flash. They vanished with the flickering light, and Faye dismissed it to exhaustion.

"One more push, we're almost done," Ash said, smoothing their hand over the small of her back.

She pushed until the agony washed through her. Almost done, and then she could rest. Faye leaned harder, claws cutting into Rune's thighs.

Her little girl was nearly here.

Faye choked on her scream as the pressure reached its pinnacle and suddenly eased.

Rune's phantom touch held her up, and she relaxed against them fully, rain-soaked and exhausted.

"My niece is here!" Sparrow announced. "Darkness, her hair is white. *White*, white I want to see the high bitch say these aren't Runey's now."

Faye glanced back, short of breath. "Is she okay? She's not crying."

"Because she's a good baby," Sparrow answered.

"Good babies cry," Faye yelled.

Ash squeezed her calf. "Your little darling is fine." Faye nodded, closing her eyes. Her family was here.

Vashien outstretched his wing to herd Sparrow to his side. "Congratulation," he said with a broad grin. "I'll take her and give you some privacy."

Sparrow began to object, but she and Vashien vanished.

Ash laughed, strolling to Faye's side, holding her son and daughter swaddled in red cloth. Faye smiled. Their daughter took after her father with her ivory skin and white-blonde hair. Her deep blue eyes matched her brother's but would lighten over the coming months to match Rune's.

Her daughter blinked the rain out of her eyes, observing, seemingly too aware for a newborn.

Faye took the little bundles from Ash, holding them close. Her hair slid forward, wet from the rain. Faye kissed their foreheads, rocking her twins. She had her family. Everything she wanted in life was before her.

Faye met Rune's gaze, and his features softened as his smile met his eyes. He collected their son, cradling him. The rain had soaked him through. His black dress shirt clung to every cut of muscle, and Faye blushed. He'd never been more attractive than he was now holding their son.

"Tell me their names," Faye said, turning back to her daughter, eager to know what to call her twins.

Rune had never felt more content in his life. His Queen gifted him with young, and the depth of his devotion widened to encompass the small forms he and Faye held. Rune ran his finger along the underside of Faye's jaw and gently lifted her head. He kissed her, tasting her lips along with the warmth of the rain.

Faye giggled against his mouth, nipping his bottom lip. "I want to know the names your rock picked for our children."

"Yes, my queen," Rune said before stealing another kiss. He stood, sheltering his son from the weather, and leaped down.

His brow drew together as he read the names. The Ra'Voshnik mirrored his confusion.

A single addition was carved beneath Jareth's in liquid diamond. His daughter.

Kaeyos.

Ninety

Rune returned to his queen to find her laughing softly to herself. His daughter blinked and cooed, staring up at him through the dwindling rain.

"These little traitors," she said, adjusting the cloth swaddling their daughter.

Did she think our young wouldn't prefer me? Voshki chuckled.

The corner of his mouth lifted, but Rune didn't rise to Voshki's baiting. He smoothed his thumb over his daughter's forehead, and she closed her dark blue eyes.

"Our daughter is Kaeyos." Rune met Faye's gaze, then glanced down at his son. "You will have to choose a name for our son."

Faye frowned, rocking their daughter. "How do we know which one of them is named Kaeyos?"

He'd expected his line to bind to Hell as he and his brothers had.

Rune failed his firstborn and longed to offer a thing he could never grant. "Hell welcomed our daughter, vsenia. There is only one name written."

Faye touched their son's chest, and he wiggled in his blanket. "Your rock didn't name him."

She wasn't asking a question, and the sorrow in her voice ripped his heart from his chest. "Hell does not run in his veins, but he is ours—and he is perfect."

Unshed tears clung to his queen's lashes. Rune leaned closer, wiping them away. "Morbid foretold the two will be inseparable. Kaeyos will look after her brother."

Faye nodded weakly, down-turning her face.

This would not do. Rune curled his finger under her chin, lifting her face. "Being tied to a realm is bothersome. He will be happier as a Pure Blood, or perhaps he will sprout wings and fly about the nursery."

Faye laughed, and Rune brushed her cheek. Her wings darkened, fading as the sky cleared. "I was going to call her Clara... but our boy needs a name. How do you feel about Clarence?"

Rune brushed away Faye's tears, murmuring, "Clarence Sacarlay is a fitting name, vsenia."

Ash healed Faye and carried their young, allowing Rune to hold Faye. He phased them to their bedroom and lowered Faye onto their bed.

"You're getting our bed wet," Faye complained, tightening her hold and squeezing him closer as though it would stop him from setting her down.

"Lucky for you, I'm used to drying all manner of... let's call them 'things,' out of clothes and sheets. A little rain is nothing to be worried about," Ash said, strolling closer.

A pleasant breeze flowed over them, drying them thoroughly.

"They'll start getting fussy soon. You'll need to feed them every two to three hours for the first few months." Ash gave Faye their son and handed Kaeyos to Rune.

The Familiar went to Rune's desk next and proceeded to stack all his books and documents into a neat pile. A tray of bottles and a craft of white liquid appeared in the space they cleared.

"Feed them one ounce to start. If they fuss, give them two," Ash said. They plucked a small black blanket out of the air and walked toward Faye. It was hardly large enough to swaddle the twins.

"You will bleed for several weeks. This will help keep you comfortable and dry when you're in bed," they said. Faye pinkened as the Familiar winked and handed her the cut of cloth. "I'll give you two some privacy and stop by tomorrow to check on the babies and their proud parents. If anything changes or alarms you, I'm never far."

"Thank you," Faye said.

Ash smiled brilliantly and bowed before vanishing.

Faye kissed their son's cheek and placed him in the center of their bed.

"Watch him," Faye said as she gingerly got to her feet. She arranged the cloth on the bed and went to her closet. Rune placed the siblings together and left to assist their mother. Faye widened her eyes and pushed against his ribs. "You have to watch them, so they don't fall."

Rune leaned back on his heels, peering at his young through the doorway. "They are too young to right themselves. In the event they do, there is a barrier around them. They will not get far. Certainly not far enough to fall from our bed."

"Magic for everything," Faye muttered, pulling her dress over her head. She turned toward him, and Rune arched a brow. "I need to put stuff on. Get out."

He grinned, allowing Faye to shove him out of her closet. The Ra'Voshnik cackled when the door shut in his face.

I want to see my young, he said, lightly running his claws over Rune's awareness.

He begrudgingly relinquished control of his body with a sigh.

Voshki prowled toward the bed, shrugging out of his jacket. He held it before him, inspecting the tears in the fine fabric. *She has no idea she shredded our back,* Voshki said, letting the ruined suit jacket fall to the ground.

The pain was nothing compared to birth. *We are nearly mended. Do not make her feel guilty,* Rune warned.

Guilty? he replied. *I want her to bring this energy when I'm fucking her.*

Do not be crass, Rune growled.

"Crass," Voshki said, lying on his side to inspect the twins. "Well, that's how you two got here, isn't it?" They blinked at him, and Voshki carefully ran his black-tipped claws through their unruly hair. It tufted in different directions, midnight strands mirroring the white.

He purred, lulling the infants. "They are cute."

The closet door clicked, and he glanced up. Faye smiled brightly, dressed in one of the nursing nightgowns she had purchased. The soft beige material was pleated, gathering at the neckline. Small hooks could be undone, allowing Faye to nurse their twins.

"I keep telling the Shadow Prince you prefer me, vsenia. You might have to tell him. He doesn't believe me," Voshki teased.

Faye laughed, arranging herself on her side of their bed. She picked up their son and unfasted the panel over her breast. "I love you both equally."

Voshki glanced upward and said, "She's talking about my young, not us."

"You're awful," Faye said without looking.

Be useful or return my body to me. Rune laughed.

Voshki collected their daughter and went to the desk. He unscrewed the top of a bottle with one hand and wrinkled his nose as he poured a helping of the foul-smelling white liquid into it. "This smells terrible," Voshki said over his shoulder.

Faye narrowed her eyes, holding her hand out. He handed her the open bottle, and she brought her nose to it, inhaling deeply. Her lips pressed, and she handed it back to him. "It's formula."

Voshki leaned closer to Kaeyos and said in a hushed tone, "Your mother is making me give this to you."

She took one taste and grimaced, shaking her head. Voshki sat beside Faye, swirling the formula. "She agrees with me. This is awful."

"Here, give her to me," Faye said, trading infants with Voshki.

His son fussed at being separated from his meal but calmed once he accepted the bottle. Voshki leaned closer and muttered, "Why are you drinking this?"

Faye garnered less luck with Kaeyos. She squirmed after latching on for a moment and grew more frustrated each time Faye tried. Her little face reddened, and Kaeyos wailed.

She wants blood, Rune said.

I know, Voshki replied, pulling his knees up. He let their son recline on his lap and held the bottle with one hand. He bit into the pad of his index finger and held the bloodied pad near Kaeyos.

Her deep blue eyes stared up at the drop of red before she

began fussing again. Voshki touched his daughter's lips, and Faye knocked his hand away.

"Get your claws away from the baby," Faye scolded.

Voshki pressed a kiss to his queen's temple. "She's thirsty," Voshki said, motioning to their daughter sucking on her bottom lip. "Trade with me unless you want to nick a vein."

Faye exhaled. "Fine."

Voshki gathered his son and the now empty bottle, handing him to Faye. "Greedy little thing," he said, taking Kaeyos. He cradled her in the crook of his arm and nicked his wrist with a black-tipped claw.

Faye held their son against her shoulder, patting his back. She leaned against Voshki and tilted her head on his shoulder. "I'm exhausted."

"You should rest," Voshki purred, leaning his cheek to the top of her head. "I can take them to their nursery."

Faye peered up at him and raised her brows. "You're... going to watch them both?"

Voshki chuckled. "Armies flee from my approach. I won't be defeated by these two." Faye remained silent, looking unconvinced. "I also have the Shadow Prince with me. He can bore them to sleep if they get out of hand."

Rune exhaled. *Do not antagonize her. She needs to rest.* He considered retaking his body, and Voshki growled. Faye kissed his shoulder, oblivious to the discourse between them.

"Wake me up if they get out of hand," she breathed.

"As you command," Voshki answered.

Voshki floated Clarence off Faye's shoulder, and she snatched the small bundle to her. "No. Carry them. With your hands."

Voshki chuckled, spurring her mood. "I won't drop my young, love."

Darkness, was this what Voshki felt every time he earned Faye's ire? *Our queen is exhausted. Cease aggravating her.*

Faye warily handed over their son. "Don't magic them and be careful with your claws."

Voshki collected the sleepy bundle and leaned forward, nipping at her earlobe. "I've been careful with you, have I not?"

Faye met his gaze and cupped the side of his face. "Rune, please watch him."

He laughed, and Voshki prickled before growling, *Be silent.*

Being favored is simple from this vantage point, Rune mused. He watched Faye through Voshki's eyes. Her thumb brushed over the tops of his cheekbones, disrupting the veined misted shadows Voshki's presence unveiled.

"I love you," Faye said, smiling sweetly. "Both of you."

Rune could now understand how Voshki became so delusional. He felt Faye's love and devotion with every gaze, with every touch. Yet when she was upset, Voshki took the brunt of her displeasure.

Don't delude yourself. She prefers me over your company, Voshki muttered, gathering the twins. He looked at Faye and purred, "I love you, too."

Ninety-One

Faye sat in the nursery of her estate, staring out into the private garden as Clarence slept on her shoulder. The morning light filtered in through the spelled glass, casting golden lines onto the carved wooden cribs. It would have been a beautiful morning if she hadn't been up since the previous night.

Sleeping when the baby slept was sound advice for individual children, but Faye had twins. She loved them, but the little tyrants slept in shifts. She and Rune tried to separate them, but they wailed when they were apart and quieted when reunited.

Weeks had passed and gone in a blur. Kaeyos and Clarence had adopted the nicknames Kae and Ren during the first week. Faye had been worried about her upcoming open court, but Alister sent notices to all the villages in Anaria and the High Council. It stated she and Rune would be occupied with the newborns for the next few months.

Any documents or pressing issues would be rerouted to him while she and Rune concentrated on their family.

Faye stroked Clarence's black hair, rocking beside Rune in their chairs. She smiled at her mate. "How's our little vampire doing?"

"Our young Pure Blood Princess is delighted to be in her mother's company," Rune said while Kaeyos drank from his wrist.

Faye looked down at their son. He refused blood altogether, while his sister fed almost exclusively on it. When she fussed, Rune would offer her his wrist, and if she grew angry at his blood, Faye would feed her.

Rune glanced toward her and smiled, despite the heavy shadows lingering beneath his pale blue eyes. His customary tailored black suit had devolved as the weeks passed. The first two buttons of his dress shirt were undone, and he'd forgone his tie and suit jacket.

He stared lovingly at Kaeyos, and their daughter made what Faye imagined was a baby vampire growl. Rune lifted his arm, and a mess of drool and red smeared over his wrist. "We will need to work on your table manners," he said, plucking the handkerchief from his jacket folded over a nearby chair. He cleaned her face before wiping his wrist.

Faye giggled, lifting her foot into a beam of sunlight. Playing with the twins in the grass after the sunset was pleasant, but... the patches of turned earth in her garden longed to be in the sunlight with her children.

"How did you discover you could walk in the sunlight without getting burned?" Faye asked.

Kae gripped Rune's finger with her tiny hand and cooed, commanding the entirety of her vampire's attention. "Yes, love?" he said to their daughter, gently twitching his finger.

Faye tapped his leg with the side of her foot, and his pale blue eyes lifted to meet hers. "Apologies," he said with a smile. "I found I could withstand the sun through my lessons with Saith."

She immediately stopped rocking her chair. "Tell me that asshole didn't shove you into the afternoon sun."

Rune laughed, and Faye scowled. "I mistakenly placed myself in sunlight. I was young, seven, I believe. I practiced drawing what power I could, shaping my will. I lost my concentration, and my magic lashed past me, bursting all the windows."

"Would that have killed you if you were like other vampires?" Faye asked.

Rune stared past the spelled glass as though he were considering an enemy. "I would like to think I would have escaped the light if it burned me, but I am not certain."

"Kae is a little Pure Blood, Shadowman, woman. You know what I mean. How do we test her or him. I don't think he's a Pure Blood, but how can we be sure?" Faye asked. She wouldn't stand for someone holding their little fingers in the light to see if they burned.

"We will treat them as normal Pure Bloods. Alister has built extravagant atriums for Prinia, covering entire fields. We will do the same. If they are burned, Ash will be able to mend the damage. So will Sadi after she recovers," Rune said before glancing toward the door. He leaned into her and said, "Your little helper is coming."

Kimber entered the nursery with Jeneane in tow. "Is she finished eating?" Kimber asked. Rune stood, letting her take Kae. "You will have such a good nap after a nice lavender bath. I made a new batch with eucalyptus in it. These little chub chubs will be out cold by the time you return." Kimber collected Faye's son and whispered, "Give you a couple of hours of alone time."

"Thank you," Faye said. The sexual connotation amused her. Kimber would laugh if she realized Faye only wanted a few hours of sleep. She slid her hand into the crook of Rune's arm as he collected his jacket.

"Send for me if they need anything," Rune said.

Kimber and Jeneane nodded, taking the babies into the bathroom. Faye and Rune took a short stroll through the halls leading into the public garden in the courtyard. She cherished their quiet moments but felt guilty being away from her children. She knew she couldn't do everything on her own, and she wanted to give her children the family she never had.

This meant sharing her time with others like Sparrow, Morbid, and Kimber.

They entered the manicured grounds surrounded by roses, lilies, and azaleas. Rune called a sealed wax letter as they wandered the stone path through her handpicked plants.

Faye took it, flipping it over. "I thought Alister had everything brought to his office."

"The correspondence is from Lyssa," Rune admitted reluctantly.

The last package she got from the High Queen had been a letter of sympathy after Aunty Clara returned to the Darkness. She'd made use of the Familiar crystals Lyssa included. The thoughtful gift moved Faye. When she returned to the High Council, Lyssa wasn't dismissive, but they weren't friendly either. The two of them had mediated a cool civility during the past months.

Maybe she hadn't been able to replace the memory playing crystals and asked for their return. Faye wouldn't blame her, and she could witness any of her beloved memories on her own since mastering the Familiar skill.

She headed to a wooden bench and sat, cracking the wax seal.

The Court of the Black Rose recognizes and honors the heirs of the Court of Chaos and Darkness. Lyssa of the Creator's House requests an audience with the new heirs of the Sacarlay House.

The letter read as convoluted as the note Rune gave Sparrow when he wanted to court her formally. "I think it's dark-blood for *I want to see the babies*," Faye said, holding the page out to Rune.

Her vampire read it and nodded, confirming her suspicions. "Lyssa is requesting an audience to see our young."

"Ch-il-dr-en," Faye said, drawing out the syllables.

Rune chuckled, taking a seat beside her. He took her hand, and his lips warmed the backs of her fingers. "You will have to suffer my diction," he said softly.

"Don't say that in front of Sparrow," Faye said, casting him a sidelong glance as she laughed. "She'll twist it in eighteen different ways, and they'll all be filthy."

"Noted." Rune leaned back onto the bench, stretching his long legs in front of him. He asked, "How would you wish to respond to Lyssa."

Rune's former lover wanted to see his kids. Faye attempted to reign in her jealousy. They were centuries old. Her mate's circle was small. She supposed she should be grateful they *all* hadn't fallen into each other's beds during Rune's three thousand years.

Faye took Lyssa's letter and folded it in half. Rune was hers, and his history with Lyssa was lifetimes ago. It would be better to garner peace with Necromia than isolate their Queen.

"I'll write a letter to her tonight," Faye replied.

Rune nodded and held his hand out to her. "Come, we should sleep while Kimber and Jeneane have the twins occupied."

Faye slid her hand over Rune's palm, and he phased them to their bedroom.

Ninety-Two

Faye double-checked the tea setting and adjusted the three-tiered dessert tray. She stepped around the white-furred stone rabbit, meandering at her feet. It'd been almost three months since she'd had Prinia over for tea, but another visitor seeded her nerves.

The High Queen would arrive at sunset.

Faye hoped to establish mutual respect if there could never be a friendship, but her taste for Lyssa had firmly cemented during their first meeting. She'd begged for help when Rune kidnapped her, and Lyssa had been cruel in her dismissal.

Sparrow's sword clanged loudly on the chairback, drawing Faye from her inward thoughts.

"Kimber and Jeneane are hogging the babies," Sparrow muttered from her seat. The early afternoon light beamed down on them, highlighting her sister's golden curls.

"You could do bath time with them if you wanted to visit the twins," Faye said, pulling out her chair.

Sparrow snorted and stole an almond cookie. "I'll steal them when they can stand and hold a sword."

Faye laughed, but her heart quickly sank.

"Has Damian come back yet?" Faye asked. Sadi hadn't returned, but she'd hoped Damian would have recovered by now. His core was severely damaged, but Alister sustained worse injuries when he stepped into the Hall of Empty Eyes after they rescued Prinia. He was on his feet in a matter of weeks.

But Sadi had mended him, and Faye wasn't sure if Sadi could heal in her condition.

"He showed up this morning while I was going through my routine. We didn't spar. We're going back to basic drills. Fundamentals. He remembers everything, but... he's not as fast," Sparrow fiddled with her teacup.

Faye leaned forward and squeezed her hand. "He'll be okay. I'm sure it'll come back to him in a couple of weeks," Faye said, praying to the Darkness she wasn't wrong.

Booted footsteps echoed from the stone archway, and Sparrow rolled her eyes. "Hey look, coffin water is here."

"Stop calling him that," Faye hissed.

Sparrow widened her eyes, looking her up and down. "Not happening."

"Not in front of Prin," Faye whispered as she smiled, waiting for Alister to make his entrance.

Prinia turned the corner with her arm looped in Alister's. She had a ruffled nightgown on today, accessorized with a corset and a lace shawl. Faye stood and waved in greeting. She quietly wondered if Alister went along with what Prinia wanted to wear or if this was the compromise from her original outfit.

"Good morning," Prinia said. Her bright smile displayed her little fangs. "Allie brought our tea."

"We have your favorite almond cookies," Sparrow said, holding her half-eaten dessert up.

Gross, Sparrow spoke directly to Faye's mind. *I just realized my little nephew is going to look like coffin water.*

A laugh slipped past Faye's lips, and Prinia rushed to her before she stopped suddenly, her expression falling. She blinked at Faye and stared at her middle. "Where are the heartbeats?"

Faye scrambled for words. "They're outside now. They don't stay inside forever," she said, patting her navel.

Prinia's eyes brightened, and she searched the garden before returning to Faye. "Can I see them?"

Faye swallowed, unsure how to proceed without upsetting Prin. She met Alister's pale blue gaze, and he dipped his chin in a subtle nod. She pushed her senses over her estate, searching for Rune and found his distinct reservoir of power absent. He must have returned to Hell or was checking on The Crumbling.

"We can visit them, but they might be sleeping," Faye said.

Prinia nodded as she excitedly squeezed closer to Alister. "I'll be quiet."

They strolled through the halls toward the nursery, and Faye reached for her vampire's mind. *Rune.*

Instead of responding, he materialized in the hall—and Faye stuttered her steps.

Everything happened at once.

Prinia shrieked, and her wolf burst from her chest. Its massive paws touched the stones and leaped, ricocheting off the wall before colliding with Rune.

Faye held Prinia's consciousness, preventing her from phasing, and screamed into Rune's mind. No! *Don't kill it!*

Rune was on his back, holding the shadowed wolf's throat as it snapped its jaws, dragging him along the stone floor. Veined misted shadows poured from beneath his eyes as he snarled a single word. *Truly?*

Prinia screamed behind her, and Alister roared, "Release her brother, or I will kill you."

Faye had moments. *Hell-phase. Make it as extravagant as you can.*

Rune glared in her direction.

There was no time to argue. *Please,* she begged.

Rune vanished in a plume of hellfire embers, shadows, and ash. Prinia's wolf growled and sniffed the charred ground.

Faye turned to Prinia, linking arms with her. "Look how strong your wolf is. He chased the Shadow Prince away." Alister's hateful expression lessened a fraction, and Prinia blinked red tears. "His name is Onyx, right? He's a really good boy. He'll protect you," Faye added.

I swear to fuck, if that big ass wolf bites me, Sparrow said in her mind. She made kissing noises at the shadowed beast and said, "Come here, baby."

A red haze trailed after its eyes as it considered her sister.

Prinia sniffled and held her hand out. Her wolf's demeanor changed instantly. He whined happily and bounded toward her.

Faye could breathe again.

"You're a good boy," she whispered, stroking Onyx's muzzle.

"And Runey's scared of him. You don't have to worry about tall, pale, and scary anymore," Sparrow added as she continued down the hall, walking backward. "The heartbeats are up here. You want to see them, right?"

Prin wiped her eyes and took a small step forward. "Yes, I would like to see the outside heartbeats."

Faye glanced back at Alister, but all she could see were his twin swords floating vertically over either shoulder. They vanished promptly, and he studied her.

"Thank you," he said, guiding Prinia to face him. He called a handkerchief and wiped away her tear tracks. "He can sleep in the bed with us," Alister muttered.

Prinia lit up with excitement. "He can?"

"Yes," Alister promised. He kissed her forehead and eased her forward half a step. "Do you hear the heartbeats?"

Prinia nodded, and Faye led them to the nursery.

Kimber pressed a finger to her lips when they entered. She stood over the cribs with Jeneane. *They're sleeping,* she mouthed. Her eyes widened when Onyx trailed in behind them. Kimber held her composure, but Jeneane backed away as the wolf approached, retreating into the garden.

Faye bit the inside of her lip. Between the two of them, Prinia was more fragile. Kimber could smooth things over with Jeneane after they left.

Prinia tiptoed to the crib and leaned over the railing. Kae was asleep on the rabbit sheets with a gray blanket over her. Her white hair was combed down after her bath but would be an unruly puff after waking.

"They sound different," Prinia whispered, moving to the second crib.

She reached into the crib, and Faye touched her arm. "Be very gentle."

Prinia pulled her hand back and said in a hushed voice, "They are very small."

Alister stepped behind her and pulled her back to his chest. He leaned down and said, "Be careful with them, sweetheart. They're like flowers. You need to be gentle and not crush their petals."

His gravel-filled voice felt out of place with the tenderness in his words, but she supposed this was the side of him Prinia saw.

"We should let them sleep and have our tea," Faye said.

Prinia nodded and followed Alister as he led her into the hall. "When will we have heartbeats, Allie?"

Faye and Sparrow exchanged a glance behind them. Her sister made an obscene gesture and pointed at Prinia as she mouthed, *Is he trying to knock her up?*

"It takes time to make heartbeats," Alister said to his wife.

He is! Sparrow mouthed.

Prinia purred as Alister continued, "The Darkness will bless us when the time is right."

Ninety-Three

Rune phased to Hell and exhaled, stripping out of his tattered suit. Prinia feared him. While he understood why she manifested a hellhound to attack him, it did not make her aggression any less irritating.

Get the stench of her magic off us, Voshki growled.

Rune rubbed his hand over the gouges marring his chest. They'd stopped bleeding, mending slowly and adding to his thirst. He phased to his private garden. The door leading in from the outer courtyard closed and locked with a flicker of his mind.

A warm breeze ruffled his hair, carrying the sweet scent of black roses. Rune waded into the hot spring, submerging himself entirely before sitting in the shade of a willow tree. The spelled water accelerated his regeneration, and the edges of his wounds began to tingle as they knitted closed.

He called a decanter of crimson wine and a glass. The dark red liquid splashed onto the grass as Rune poured a heavy serving. He drank deeply, refilling it before leaning back on the stones. He inhaled deeply, focusing on the traces of Faye's lingering scent mingled with his own from their bed a few feet away. His night breeze through plum blossoms calmed his mind.

We should collect Faye and my young. She'd enjoy a day spent with her plants, Voshki said.

It was a sound plan. *She will summon us after her mid-day tea,* Rune said. He imagined lying beside Faye on her oversized blanket spread over the grass while their twins napped in the evening sun, protected beneath the enclosure of spelled glass.

A mental nudge brushed his awareness, and Rune pried his eyes open, accepting the communication tether.

Alister's consciousness hesitantly touched his. His brother's gravel-filled voice reverberated softly through his mind. *Thank you.*

Rune swallowed the contents of his glass and struggled for words to act as a bridge, instead of reinforcing the wall dividing them.

I am sorry I frightened Prinia. I hope your wife is well.

Faye reassured her that the wolf would protect her from you. She's clinging to Onyx like a security blanket. A touch of humor colored Alister's voice, reminding Rune of times long past. Apprehension reverberated across the communication thread, and his older brother added, *I would appreciate your continued cooperation.*

Of course, Rune replied. A truce between them would be welcome. *I would ask you to sheath your blades in Faye's presence. We can band our endeavor to make our queens more comfortable.*

Alister's smile rang through his words. *It's a bargain.*

The mental tie snapped, and Voshki prowled his mind. *He only lives because Faye would mourn his mangled corpse.*

The corner of Rune's mouth lifted. She had changed them both.

Rune finished his fourth glass of blood, leaning his head back on the stones. The heat soothed his muscles, lulling him into comfort.

Rune?

He opened his eyes to golds, oranges, and pinks coloring the sky. Rune cursed in High Tongue as he got out of the hot spring. He'd been a moment from phasing to their room in Anaria and stilled.

Is our bedroom unoccupied? he asked.

Faye's laugh twinkled through his mind. *It's just me and the babies.*

Rune materialized near his closet and dried off before selecting a fresh suit. He dressed quickly, buttoning his shirt as he leaned out of the doorway. Faye had their twins on their backs with a spiraled mobile slowly turning above them. Red, black, and white shapes hung from it, and his young stared up into it, bewitched.

Faye had several articles of clothing spread out neatly over their large bed. She picked up a rose-colored dress and draped it over Kaeyos briefly before replacing it with another small gown.

He stepped behind her and kissed her neck, smiling at his infants over their mother's shoulder. Voshki sluggishly rose through his awareness, brushing the surface of his mind, and veined misted shadows crept forward. Clarance's blue eyes routed toward him, and he erratically kicked his little feet while his sister stared at the shapes above.

"I don't know what to dress them in," Faye complained as she swatched a shirt over Clarence.

Voshki growled, provoked by their queen's irritation. *Tell her we don't care what Lyssa thinks.*

"This is an informal setting, love," Rune said gently. He took the shirt Faye held and began dressing their son.

"I'm kicking her out if she says anything mean about them," she muttered. She laid a red dress over Kaeyos's legs. Shaking her head, his queen removed it and replaced it with a pink and muted turquoise blend.

Rune finished dressing Clarence and handed him to Faye. "She will not be cruel," he promised.

She cradled their son and eyed him suspiciously. "How do you know?"

Because we would burn her alive, Voshki volunteered.

Rune slid Kaeyos's little arms through the two-toned dress and fastened the clips down her back. "She recognized our heirs, and Lyssa thrives on her social standing. Requesting an audience to insult our young would be tactless. Gossip will spread, and the other noble houses will frown upon her behavior."

Faye's shoulders relaxed, and she nodded. Her head lifted, and she turned toward him. "Lyssa's here. I asked for her to be brought to the nursery."

Rune followed her into the adjacent room and closed the door behind him. Faye lowered Clarence into his crib and activated the spiral mobile. He watched it turn slowly, completely engrossed by the colors and shapes. His sister was similarly fascinated until the click of heels approached.

"The High Queen," the footman announced, promptly vanishing as Lyssa stepped into the room.

She wore a gray satin gown tailored to her figure. Strings of diamonds were strung into her hair, glittering with each step. Lyssa stopped a few feet from the cribs, and while Faye wouldn't recognize it, she pinched her thumb and forefinger together.

A nervous tic she had developed as a girl.

Lyssa inclined her chin in a subtle motion and said, "Faye. Rune."

"Lyssa," Faye answered curtly as though she were preparing for her cutting remarks.

His queen stepped closer to their children, and Kaeyos turned her head to stare in the High Queen's direction.

"May I see them?" Lyssa asked.

Faye's back tensed as she said, "Please."

Rune settled his hand over Faye's hip, kissing her hair. "Their names are Kaeyos and Clarence."

"I call them Kae and Ren," Faye added.

Lyssa reached into the crib, and Voshki growled through his mind. Loudly. She brushed Kaeyos's arm, and his daughter grunted, kicking her feet in a fit of temper. Lyssa pulled her hand away and blinked. She recovered quickly. "They are lovely names. I remember when Gabriel and Morgana were this young."

She moved to his son and lightly rested her fingertips over his chest. Clarence cooed at her. Lyssa continued to smile at his son as she reached for his mind. *You look happy.*

I am, Rune replied. He'd been granted everything he never realized he needed.

Lyssa smiled as Clarence gripped her finger. She turned to Faye and said, "You and Rune look very happy together. May your reign last through the generations."

Ninety-Four

F aye walked through the private garden between her room and
the nursery as the sun set. She'd finished feeding Ren and made a
habit every time she burped him to tell him the names of each plant.
The days passed quietly, without incident, and her babies would be
three months old in two weeks. A day she looked forward to and also
dreaded. Rune volunteered to bring the twins to her meetings, and
she'd laughed at the time, but now she wondered if he'd been serious.

"Are the chub chubs ready for bath time?" Kimber sang, strolling into the nursery with Jeneane and Bayle close behind her.

Faye remained in the garden, and Jeneane retreated to the bathroom as Kimber collected Kae.

"You're never going to guess what happened," Kimber said,
shifting Faye's daughter in her arms so she could take Ren. "I got a
letter from a fancy shop in Necromia. They want to sell the baby bath

I make for the chub chubs to nobles. *Nobles.*"

Faye beamed. "That's great."

"Right?" she said with a laugh. "I'm going to call them *Kimber's Concoctions.*"

"Is Bayle helping you?" Faye asked.

"No," he answered too quickly, joining them in the garden. "Men know how to take care of babies, so I'm learning."

Kimber burst out laughing. "You're not a man Bay-Bay."

"I'm nine," he hissed.

Faye ran her fingers through his black curls, brushing them to the side. "Men are also nice to ladies."

"Yeah, so be nice to me," Kimber sneered jokingly. She turned, bumping Bayle's shoulder with her hip.

"You're a horse booty, not a lady. So I don't have to be nice to you," he barked, following her to the bathroom.

Rune joined her in the waning light and offered her his arm. "Shall we go for our evening walk, my queen?"

Faye took his arm, leading him through their bedroom to keep a comfortable distance between herself and Jeneane. They walked down the hall and turned the corner, gathering a whiff of the sweets being made. "I want to stop in the kitchen," she said. "There were some delicious, candied berries this morning. I want to take a bowl of them to bed."

Rune cocked a brow and grinned. "Do you?"

"Not for that," Faye said, flushed. She bit the inside of her lip, imagining him blindfolding her and sensuously running sugared berries over her lips before feeding them to her. Her blood heated, and she added, "Maybe for that."

Rune stopped and held up two fingers. Faye froze as he turned back the way they'd come. Her surroundings snapped to darkness before her nursery came into sharp focus.

"Rune!" Bayle's young voice bellowed.

Red handprints smeared the marble tub. "Kimber," she called, rushing into the bathroom.

Kimber was the first thing she saw, and her blood ran cold. She collapsed in a pool of blood, clutching her throat as red slid down her arm and dripped from her elbow onto the floor. Faye dropped to her knees, pressing her hands to Kimber's neck.

"Ash!" she screamed, reaching for the Familiar's mind. Tears blurred her vision as her gaze followed Rune's to the changing station. Faye's voice hollowed to a whisper. "Where are they?"

Ash appeared beside her, and Faye went numb. Their tendril seated in the center of Kimber's chest, and they covered her throat with the other.

Faye couldn't breathe. "Where are my babies?"

Screaming filled her ears, and arms held her, dragging her away from Kimber. They squeezed until her wings ripped free from their grip.

Faye fell to the ground and realized—the screams were coming from her.

Ninety-Five

Faye's power tumbled past her. It scorched the ground, climbing the walls. Rune held her and dragged her away from Ash as she screamed.

"Faye," he shouted over her desperate cries. "Faye!"

She wailed in heartbroken anguish, and her wings ripped from her back, breaking his hold. Her legs buckled, and Rune dropped to his knees, catching her before she hit the ground.

She clung to him, digging her claws into his arm. "Where are they?" she asked in a broken whisper through her sobs.

"I will find them," Rune promised. His hands shook with tremors of rage. "I will bring them back to you." His instinct clamored for a massacre. He would find those responsible and draw their deaths out for centuries.

"Shadow Prince," Ash called from the bathroom.

Faye released him, and her eyes darted around the nursery, searching for the young he knew were not there. He held her face in his hands. "I need a moment, love."

Faye didn't respond to him, and Ash yelled louder. "Shadow Prince, now!"

Do not leave her, Voshki grated.

One of them had to be calm and assess the situation. Rune kissed Faye's forehead and said, "I will return," before phasing to Ash.

"Rune, we have little time. Give her your blood," Ash ordered. Kimber's complexion grew sickeningly pale, and the deep wound on the side of her throat had ceased bleeding.

Rune went to his knees and opened his wrist. "Do you wish to be turned?"

Kimber nodded weakly. "I don't want to die…"

He pressed his bloodied wrist to her mouth. She drank, gagged, and went still.

"Is… Is she going to be okay?" Bayle asked.

"If she survives the transition, she will rise in a few days," Rune said. His canines lengthened as he inhaled, scenting the room to begin his hunt. He could recall the scents. Knew their names. His hands tremored as his mind reeled. He and Faye had been betrayed.

For months.

Hunt them and retrieve our young, the Ra'Voshnik growled, prowling his mind.

Rune drew back his seething rage and collected his thoughts. He turned to Bayle.

"Tell me what happened," Rune grated.

The boy nodded, a gash marking his face from forehead to cheek. Ash knelt beside him, beginning to mend his injuries. "Jeneane started coughing and choking on her own blood. She stabbed Kimber. Then I screamed for you. She… she swung at me, and her eyes… She looked like she was dead. I ran to stop her, but she took the babies and disappeared."

Rune should have seen this. Should have asked Sadi to look through Jeneane's mind for a beacon. Bayle described Familiar magic. It allowed the possessor to operate their host like a puppet but burned through their mind and killed them in the process.

Familiar had his young. This would be a time for finesse, not force.

Voshki growled his disagreement, *I don't give a fuck about finesse. I'm going to make every last one of them beg for death.*

"She has them." Faye's whisper turned deathly cold.

Rune turned toward his queen. She stood over Kaeyos's crib holding a letter and a lace mask attached to a polished bone.

Hatred sank through his soul, seeping into his bones. Delilah had taken his infants and dared to leave her calling card. She would stand beside Sadira in Standing Shadows and suffer for an eternity.

He read the letter.

The Shadow Prince will surrender to the Court of Lace and Bone. I expect you within the hour. If you do not comply, I will carve a piece off your young for each minute you keep me waiting past the appointed time.

—Delilah

Level their court! Voshki roared as he prowled Rune's mind, desperate to pay back his pain. Delilah lowered an impossible gauntlet. His obedience weighed against the lives of his heirs. She knew the moment he secured his young, her life would be forfeit...

Which meant she felt secure in their hiding place.

Faye's breaths came faster, too fast. Rune took her in his arms. "Vsenia, I need you to calm yourself. She will have our young in another location. They will be safe—"

"My babies are not safe!" Faye screamed. Her eyes watered, and tears slipped down her unblinking eyes.

Rune smoothed away her tears. "Delilah needs them to hold over my head. She knows as long as she has them, she can control me. Our young are safe because they are all that stand between her court and death."

Faye's expression blanked as she blinked more tears. "I want them back."

"They have a Familiar among them, but they do not know you have Sight. I need you to focus, love. I will play to her demand of surrender and buy you time. I need you to set a beacon to the bitch's mind and locate our young. Once they are safe, I will make them suffer."

We will do more than purge them, Voshki promised.

Rune pulled her closer and leaned down until his forehead

touched hers. He needed her closeness. Needed to believe she wouldn't look at him differently after Delilah was done with him and he purged the Court of Lace and Bone.

"Find our children and show me their location. I will do the rest," Rune murmured.

Faye took a calming breath and nodded. "I'll find them."

Rune brushed his lips over hers, a feather light caress, "I will buy you the time you need. Show no weakness when Delilah tortures me. Give her nothing."

Faye took a calming breath and nodded. "I'll find them."

Rune brushed his lips over hers, a feather-light caress, "I will buy you the time you need. Show no weakness. When Delilah tortures me, give her nothing."

He reached for Alister, Sparrow, and Vashien's minds next, and explained what had occurred.

"Contain this. Interrogate every staff member. It is likely Delilah's spies have fled, but if any have lingered, save them for me," Rune asked of his brother.

"Where are you going?" Sparrow asked.

"To wage war on the Court of Lace and Bone."

Ninety-Six

Rune phased himself and Faye to their bedroom in Hell. "If you cannot do this, I can go alone." He took her hands, pressing his lips to the back of her fingers.

Faye searched his eyes. "How will you find them?"

Rune swallowed. "I will offer myself in trade."

A kindling of fire lit in Faye's dark eyes. "No." She blinked, stabilizing herself as her features hardened. "She kidnapped our children. I will not reward her with your surrender."

Pride swelled in his chest. His queen was fierce, and they would lay waste to Delilah's court together. "Find their location, and I will purge them all," Rune vowed.

At Faye's nod, he went to his closet, vanishing his suit before selecting another. He'd spent the entirety of his enslavement stripped, chained, and shackled in a cell— or the metal chair Sadira used for her court's pleasure. Rune tensed.

At the very least, Delilah would have him bound and whipped, carving a bone from his face. At worst, Rune's fangs lengthened at the thought of Delilah's hands on his body. His stomach twisted, remembering how she'd held his gaze and spread her legs. A blatant invitation. She could very well demand he tend or fuck her.

Do not kneel for that cunt! Voshki roared. *Let me rise. I'll make her beg for death.*

You will get our young killed, Rune growled, fastening his pants. *Be silent and let me think.*

Delilah would torture him and delight in Faye's suffering. The Queen of Lace and Bone held them at a severe disadvantage. She held his obedience with his young, and they both knew it. Just as they knew, once she lost her leverage, her life would be forfeit.

Rune finished dressing and pulled his jacket on before turning to his dark queen.

"Do not flinch. Delilah cannot see your pain. It will only drive her to do worse," Rune said.

Faye took a calming breath and nodded.

"Are you ready?" Rune asked, extending his hand. "They are safe, love. Delilah knows her court is forfeit if she harms them. She has shown her hand, and this is our only play. I will distract her."

"Okay," Faye muttered.

"Do not fear for me, vsenia. Pain is trivial. We are old acquaintances."

"I'll find our twins. You do the rest," she said, placing her hand in his.

Rune phased them to the landing for the Court of Lace and Bone. *Do not react,* Rune said directly to Faye's mind.

A pathway lit from the landing to the tall, narrow double doors. Sounds of merriment and feasting carried to them. He was certain Delilah spied on them and offered his queen his arm. "Shall we."

Faye hesitated, then slipped her hand into the crook of his elbow. They walked through the doors as though they graced an event.

Reaching the top of the stairs, bile rose in Rune's throat. He kept his expression bored, ignoring the grand hall adorned with pillars and shackles.

I'm going to spend centuries drawing out her death, Voshki growled as

Rune took in every detail. The greenish gray stones. The touches of moss. The shackles on the ground where he'd been chained before Sadira's dais. Delilah recreated Sadira's court with a terrifying attention to detail she couldn't possibly have known.

Rune and Faye approached Delilah's throne. A woman with light pink hair sat on the arm to Delilah's right, holding a staff. Familiar by the look of her clothing and the articulated ring covering her index finger. Silence fell over the hall.

Delilah leaned against her Familiar and smiled. "Kneel."

"Return my young, and your death will be quick," Rune replied.

The pink-haired Familiar leaped up, her tall, belted boots clicking as she descended the steps toward them. "If only Sadi weren't broken, she might have seen this coming," she said in a sing-song voice.

The Familiar's image flickered, and she appeared beside Faye.

"Kneel!" she screamed, swinging her staff at the back of Faye's knees.

Rune caught the rod before she could land the blow. It blackened, spreading from his grip as cracks formed in the wood. The Familiar dropped her weapon, watching as ashes flaked away, drifting through the air.

"Touch my Queen, and I will do the same to your bones."

Kill her! Voshki raged.

Rune fought the instinct to reduce the Familiar to red mist with a flicker of his mind. He needed to play their game and buy his queen the precious moments she needed.

Delilah appeared before Faye.

"You killed my son. For what?" Delilah spat, grabbing Faye's face beneath her jaw, forcing her to meet her eyes. "We are eternal creatures. You destroyed a man who lived fourteen centuries for *Anarians*."

Delilah bared her teeth. "You have taken from me." She pulled Faye closer. "Now I will take from you," she whispered, shoving Faye away. "Kneel."

The Queen of Lace and Bone smiled as Faye lowered to her knees. Delilah's perverse stare swept to him next. "Strip."

"I decline your offer," Rune said the same moment he spoke into Faye's mind. *Stay down and set your beacon.*

Delilah adjusted her skirt. "You will obey, or I will carve up your young." Rune's fangs lengthened as she strolled back to her throne. He prayed to the Darkness Faye found their young's location soon. "I have two of them. Should I kill one now to prove my intent?" Delilah asked, taking her seat. She made eye contact with two of her guards and tilted her chin toward Rune. "Strip him."

Rune ceased the guard's approach with a growl, buying precious moments for Faye at the cost of his dignity. His mouth went dry as he unfastened a cuff link.

Delilah growled, leaning forward. "I said strip him," she snapped at her guards. "You will learn your place," she said to Rune.

Voshki rushed to the forefront, ready to tear Delilah's head from her shoulders. Rune stopped him before the veined misted shadows slipped beneath his gaze. *Calm yourself. Give them nothing.*

Release me after Faye secures our young. I will make a symphony of their screams, Voshki grated. He remained beneath the surface, hungering for violence.

Rune stood impassively as Delilah's guards tore his suit piece by piece. Delilah's gaze roamed his body, and the Ra'Voshnik's control rattled with a menacing rage.

"Kneel," Delilah ordered.

Rune's movements were deliberate and slow as he lowered to one knee.

A coy smile played on her lips, and Delilah ran the claw of her articulated ring over her armrest before glancing at Faye. "You will disband your court. The Shadow Prince will serve the Court of Lace and Bone as my executioner and blood whore."

The fuck we will, Voshki grated.

Delilah's smile turned vicious as her gaze returned to Rune, dipping between his legs to the flesh that held no interest for her. He fought to maintain his bored expression. To keep his churning rage and hostility hidden.

"You will tend and feed any member of my court who desires your company," Delilah proclaimed, glancing at Faye. "You may visit him for one hour on this day each year… To remember what you've lost."

Ignore her. Find our young, love, Rune spoke to Faye's mind.

"This should be an easy role for you since you were Sadira's favorite stallion for over a century."

You will share this kill with me, Rune grated. *I will take her memories piece by piece.*

Voshki purred in agreement.

"The punishment for rape is execution," Rune said plainly.

"Under Lyssa's rule. With you properly leashed, I will be High Queen. My will. My law." Delilah shifted. "Your queen isn't even fighting for you. Does he mean nothing to you, little Anarian."

The pink-haired Familiar took a seat on Delilah's armrest, stroking her thigh as a lover would. "My Familiar, Cora, showed me your time with Sadira. Sweet thing was so gentle with you, couldn't ride you hard enough. Now that we know you *can* breed, you will sire my next son."

Rune schooled his expression as revulsion knotted his stomach. "You seem to forget how many of Sadira's court I killed."

"I have your young. You will comply," Delilah hissed. "Now crawl here and tend to me."

Rune glanced at Faye.

"Look at me. I am your Queen!" Delilah sneered, snapping her fingers between her knees. "Crawl here and tend to me."

We are not licking her slit, Voshki growled. *You can burst every heart in a hundred miles.*

And if our infants are caught in the backlash? Rune asked. They were too young, too fragile. He could not risk them. The Ra'Voshnik growled but remained silent.

"If I must command you again, I will have one of my guards fuck you until you make me come," Delilah says, leaning back on her throne.

Whispers and murmurs broke out as Rune crawled to Delilah's throne. Excitement lit the queen's dark eyes. Rune fought to avoid vomiting as he sat back on his heels between Delilah's knees. He pushed her skirt up and pressed his lips to the inside of her thigh, near her knee.

Tear her leg off.

Darkness, he wanted to. He wanted to burst every heart for miles and collect them all as ornaments for Standing Shadow's grisly display.

But he couldn't. His young would be caught in the onslaught, either by his hand or Delilah's order. Rune had no choice but to obey.

He ignored the Ra'Voshnik roars, sliding his fingertips over Delilah's thigh. The scent of her arousal sickened him. *Faye needed time*, Rune reminded himself, and he would buy it with whatever currency Delilah demanded.

His queen would never recover if their young were injured… or worse.

The bitch's hand was tangled in his hair, and Rune stiffened. She pulled a blade from a sheath, still covered within the layers of her skirt. Rune waited for the bite of her blade.

She pulled his hair taut and said, "I prefer my males with shorter hair."

On the first swipe of her blade, short lengths of hair fell onto his downturned face. After the third, she held up white-blonde hair like a trophy for her court to see. They jeered, shouting as Delilah discarded her prize over the steps leading toward her throne.

Her nails skimmed over the back of his head, mussing his hair. Rune prayed to the Darkness Faye found their young soon as his kisses trailed lower. He hated the feel of her. The rotted taste of jealousy, tinged with excitement and fear.

"You've done this many times," Delilah said, gripping his throat and pulling him up to meet her eyes. "I know something you've never surrendered…"

"Offer me your throat."

Ninety-Seven

Faye fought to breathe evenly while she knelt. Slipping into Delilah's mind had been the simple part, but Faye hadn't been prepared for the multitude of memories centuries of living had compounded through her mind.

Delilah felt like a cluttered, filthy room compared to Rune's mind. She couldn't decern her memories from the fantasies and schemes. Worse, she saw Rune through Delilah's eyes.

She wasn't jealous in the same way Lyssa had been. The High Queen loved Rune in her own way. Delilah wanted to own him—destroy him. It made her nauseous.

Rune pulled back to meet her gaze, a subtle tension in his jaw only she would recognize. Darkness, she was going to make her suffer. He lifted his chin, turning his head to the side and exposing his throat. Perverse excitement slithered through Delilah.

"A pity she's not a vampire. She will never truly understand what I'm taking from her," Delilah murmured softly, fisting Rune's hair and pulling his head further. She held the gaze of Faye's physical body and sank her fangs into Rune's throat.

Faye looked away, unable to watch, but experienced it through Delilah's mind. Each new memory she uncovered was more depraved than the last. Pleasure rippled through Delilah. She moaned, drinking greedily. Her nails raked over Rune's back as she ground her body against him. Faye's stomach threatened to empty its contents.

Frustration churned in her as she moved through Delilah's mind. She was here and couldn't find what she needed to save her children and Rune.

She promised to protect him. Told him no one would use him again.

The feeling of helplessness suffocated her, stealing her breath. Her failure would strip her of her family, her mate, and the innocents who depended on her. With Delilah as High Queen, things wouldn't return to how they were. They would become so much worse.

Faye withdrew from Delilah's mind, descending into herself. A burn lit her back, and Faye held in the sensation. They couldn't see her wings, not yet. She stood at the depth of her power and took an adjacent step into the psychic void where Familiar called upon their most dangerous magic.

Her heart tightened, calling Kimber's thread. Faye witnessed the last moments of her friend's short life, how she tried to scream for her and Rune. The gurgling hiss from the wound of her throat.

Sadi warned her only to watch and never reach into a vision unless she wanted to be lost. Faye swallowed as Jeneane slashed at Bayle and took her babies. Faye drew on Jeneane's life thread next, but it ended before she stabbed Kimber.

Confused, Faye returned to Kimber's thread and watched as the events replayed. She couldn't follow Jeneane's thread because she died before she stabbed Kimber.

Faye steeled herself. Sadi would heal, and Rune would bring her back. Faye held on to the dark, roiling rage, letting it anchor her. The Court of Lace and Bone came to her home, took her children, killed her people, and thought to rape her consort and mate.

Her dark power rose, answering her rancor, coating her as her eyes dilated. The world fell away as she reached into Jeneane's mind. She witnessed her deeds, traveling with her as an observer when she phased to a well-guarded country home.

Three other women took her babies upstairs as armored males laughed over a meal. Faye laced her magic over their reservoirs of power and climbed the steps. Pressing time faster until it slowed to the present.

"Do you think he'll grow up to look like the Shadow Prince?" one of the women asked, leaning over the crib and holding her sleeping twins.

"I can't believe Delilah is having us babysit instead of watching the show. Can you imagine what she's doing to him?" another snickered.

The third waved her hand. "We'll have our turn with him when she's done."

"What are you going to have him do first?"

The third woman took a deep drink of her wine and smiled. "He's going to fuck me while I feed on him."

Faye's power raced through her. She grabbed the third woman's face and retracted her power over each of their reservoirs, strangling their magic. Their screams mingled as Faye tightened her hold, cracking and shattering their cores.

Wrath enveloped her like a lover, seductive and warm. Faye sealed the country home, locking her prey in. This was far from over. Faye had so much pain to repay. She leaned over the crib, gently touching the side of each of her twin's sleeping faces.

Faye should have listened to Rune. Thinking she could peacefully assemble her realm had been foolish on her part, and she nearly lost everything because of it. Peace would never work, not as long as dark-bloods like Delilah cultivated gardens of cruelty. The answer was so simple…

Faye wondered why she resisted for so long.

Violence was the only language a dark-blood understood, and she would speak it in volumes.

Faye shielded her children, cradling them against her chest. She turned to the babbling woman as they touched their broken soul shards. Their anguish fed Faye's rage, but she wanted more.

Set an example, Rune's words flowed through her mind, filling her with warmth.

She smiled, agreeing with her consort. Screams filled the home with wet snapping sounds filling the space. Faye held their minds, denying them the mercy of unconsciousness. They would feel every measure of pain they intended to meter out.

But her work wasn't done.

Faye opened her eyes, summoning her children to her. She stood, levitating a few inches off the ground. Her hair and clothing swayed around her as though she were submerged in deep water.

Shouts of panic spread through Delilah's Hall. Faye ominously stretched her wings behind her, protectively cradling her twins to her chest. Her gaze fixed on the queen who thought to strip her of everything that belonged to her.

Faye floated forward, reaching for every soul within the grounds. Mental barbs embedded into each mind, tearing and digging deep. Faye held their awareness, smiling as their pain became a chorus. Her magic whispered over their bodies, contorting them. Breaking bones.

Faye sighed as the orchestra of agony played around her. Rune stood fully dressed once more, lifting Delilah by her throat.

An anguished cry choked past Delilah's red-stained lips, blue embers of hellfire, smoke, and ash leaking from her mouth. Hell's glittering crystals formed around her terror-filled face, consumed her.

Dark fury filled Faye as she turned on the rest of the court. Her magic constricted over their cores. She squeezed in measures, drawing out their agony and terror, until she shattered every mind within her mental hold.

Faye stood, surveying the court she reduced to a writhing mass of flesh. Kaeyos stirred, blinking her bright eyes as she cooed in Faye's arms. She lowered her head, resting her cheek on her daughter's white-blonde hair.

"I will protect my court and family," Faye said absently. She lifted her hand and held two fingers up, lacing her dark power over the bodies she destroyed. "This begins and ends with me."

Faye curled her fingers down with a sharp bend of her wrist, and silence rang as their heads tore from their bodies.

Faye's power receded as her wings faded. "Take us home," she said, turning as she heard Rune calling her name.

From far above her.

She froze, shaking at the scene before her. Rune was on his

knees beside her, cradling her body and their twins.

Her body gazed into the distance, Faye's dark eyes clouded and unseeing.

Ninety-Eight

Faye glanced down at her arms, and panic seized her mind when she found them empty. Her twins were with her physical body and Rune. She relaxed her mind, waiting for the natural pull of her body to bring her back.

None came.

No, no, no, Faye thought, rushing to her family. She took a steadying breath and stepped into her body. It didn't accept her. It was as solid and as real as if she collided with another person.

Rune called her name. The anguish in his pale blue eyes gutted her.

She dropped to her knees beside him.

"I didn't mean to break my promise," she whispered, reaching for his face. Wishing she could comfort him.

Her fingers passed through him, and Rune drew a sudden

breath, turning to look in her direction.

Relief flooded Faye until he glanced down at her body once more.

"Rune," she cried, brushing her hand through his jaw, his throat.

He met her gaze, then searched either side of her.

He doesn't see me. He mouthed her name, but his voice didn't follow. Faye stared past him as a black mist crept down the walls, consuming them.

No. Faye rose to her feet and whirled, looking for an exit. The mist surrounded her, inching closer as it crawled over the mangled bodies.

"No!" Faye screamed. Chaos couldn't have her. She didn't fight this hard to be lost now.

Faye stood behind Rune, closing her eyes and stepping into him.

Voshki roared through his mind, screaming his anguish as Rune rocked Faye's body. He reached for her mind and was met by nothing. An emptiness mirroring his soul and staring back at him.

He murmured her name, holding her and his young. Her absence threatened to break him. "Please come back to me," he begged. "I need you."

His chest constricted when he scented his night breeze. *This must be madness finally coming to claim me*, he thought bitterly, but he swore he felt her awareness scratch at the very edge of his mind. He drew a sharp breath, looking toward the mental tug. Searching.

Rune glanced down at the shattered remains of his family. He was going mad.

His queen's awareness scrapped at his senses twice, and emptiness continued to meet him.

"Faye," Rune whispered. Terrified to hope.

Rune closed his eyes and dropped the first three mental barriers shielding his mind, leaving himself vulnerable. Moisture collected on his lashes, and a tear tracked from the corner of his eye. In a broken whisper, he said, "I am yours. Command me as you will."

A presence slipped into his mind, and his queen's subtle scent blanketed his senses. Voshki rushed to her, mingling his presence with her own.

His night breeze returned to him.

Faye, Rune said through his mind as his throat constricted.

Rune. Faye's voice carried through his mind. *Voshki, get off me.*

Rune laughed as the tension left his body. He could breathe once more. *I need you to return to your body, love.*

Faye was silent for the span of a heartbeat. *I did things to save our family. Now I can't get back.*

Rune got to his feet. He cradled his queen and secured his young's safety with a modified shield. He reached for the Familiar King's mind next.

Morbid, I need you.

He appeared in Delilah's throne, pulling on heavy boots. Rune had never been so happy to see him in his life.

"Prince," Morbid said, tightening his laces.

"I need your assistance returning Faye's mind to her body."

Morbid adjusted his pink beaded scarf and peered at him. "There's nothing I can do to help her."

Rune exhaled as his patience wore thin. Familiar and their incessant need for riddles. "How do I return Faye to her body?" Rune grated.

Morbid stood and skipped down the dais. "Nothing you can do either, Prince."

Rune glanced up for calm. "It has been a *tiring* evening."

"Yes, your queen sent dozens to my realm."

He didn't care that his queen sent this court's souls to madness with her torture. It was a mercy compared to what he had planned for them. Rune met the Familiar King's midnight gaze. "Tell me how Faye can return to her body."

Morbid gazed into Faye's clouded eyes, then stared at him as though he was looking into his skull. Rune waited precious moments under Morbid's scrutiny.

"Looks a bit crowded in there," Morbid said with a laugh before meeting Rune's steady gaze.

"How can Faye return to her body?" Rune asked again.

Morbid circled Rune, taking in the bodies as though this were a garden instead of a massacre. "Your queen already knows the answer,

Prince. She did it for Prinia."

We need to go to the Hall of Empty Eyes, Faye said in his mind.

"Yes," Morbid agreed.

"Carry her mind and take her body to the temple," Rune paused when the Familiar King gave him an apologetic look. "Please, Morbid."

"It's not a matter of wanting to, Prince. She was able to walk into your mind because you're fated. A part of you is threaded into her and a part of her is threaded into you. I hold no such bond with your queen. If she leaves your mind outside of my temples, she will be lost to my realm."

Rune exhaled. He was out of options. "Watch over my young," he said gravely.

Morbid brightened. "I've been waiting for you to ask me to babysit." He cradled the infants and sniffed his daughter's hair. "This one definitely has some Familiar in her."

Rune narrowed his eyes, unamused.

"I did a lot of thinking of your mother while she was pregnant with you. You're one of us, like it or not, Prince." Morbid laughed.

Rune dismissed the notion of Morbid with his parents, not wanting to know if it was true. He glanced at the Familiar King. "Will you join us to pull me out, at least?"

Morbid shrugged. "I suppose I could do that."

Rune, no. They will fracture your core, Faye snapped.

He ignored his Queen's words and phased to the Hall of Empty Eyes. He stood before the double doors as fear chilled him. Morbid appeared beside him, and the door opened in silent invitation.

Rune, do not go in there. We'll find another way. I am commanding you to stop!

He would do anything for her. Pay any price. He trusted Morbid to drag him out after Faye returned to her body. He wasn't certain he would retain his three Shards of Darkness. Rune looked down at Faye's clouded, unseeing eyes and couldn't fathom how Alister survived eight centuries of this. He squeezed Faye toward him and pressed his lips to her forehead. He whispered, "Our children need their mother," before stepping over the threshold.

Ninety-Nine

Faye screamed as Rune stepped into the Hall of Empty Eyes. He fell to his knees, clutching her body toward his chest.

She closed her eyes, letting her mind drift. Relief struck her like an arrow as the proximity of her body drew her consciousness from Rune's mind.

Rune collapsed as Faye opened her eyes. She panted, touching her chest. She was back. Thank the Darkness.

She scrambled out from under his dead weight as voices choired behind her.

She will wither and die.

You will lose her.

You cannot protect her.

Your strength is meaningless.

Faye screamed as misted serpents rushed past her, striking

Rune's mind, damaging his core.

Her power rose in a fury, tearing through her back as she lifted off the ground.

"You can't have him!" Faye yelled, letting her rage embody her. No one would take anymore from her. Not tonight. Not ever.

She unleashed her nest of vipers against the empty-eyed vessels. Her snakes moved faster, striking one after the other, snapping the serpents aimed at Rune in half.

They withered to nothing as they fell to the ground. It didn't matter how many she struck down. More erupted from the mirrors. Faye summoned more of her vipers as she outstretched her arms, sending them to attack the vessels.

Two of her shadowed snakes encircled Rune and dragged him past the threshold to safety.

The vessels closed their mouths, returning to rest, and Faye struggled to catch her breath. They may have abated, but Faye had not. She wanted to kill every last one of them. Destroy them for hurting her mate.

"If you purge Chaos, my vessels won't be there when you need them," Morbid warned.

Faye turned seamlessly toward his voice. Her vipers arched higher as she struggled to remember he was a friend.

He rolled his shoulders, still holding her twins. "It's quite foolish to challenge a Familiar in Chaos. Even more so to challenge their king."

Faye focused on her twins in Morbid's arms. Her anger drained away along with her power. She lowered to the ground, and her wings faded. "It's hard to focus when I call all of it."

Morbid shrugged. "It's your nature." Faye crossed the threshold, and he placed her children in her arms. "I'll trade you unless you'd rather carry the Shadow Prince."

Faye glanced down at Rune, the reservoir containing his power was cracked in several spaces. His power leaked out of a few small cracks, floating like raindrops.

"Can you heal him?" Faye asked, taking her children.

Morbid laughed, hoisting Rune over his shoulder. He patted the back of Rune's thigh and said, "He'll mend. I'd be more worried about getting him a proper haircut."

Faye smiled despite herself. Nothing phased the Familiar King, and it strangely calmed her.

"He is a little vain," she admitted.

"Hell or Anaria?" Morbid asked.

Faye bit the inside of her lip. "He'll heal faster in his realm, right?"

"You…" Morbid laughed. "…are a far better listener than your mate."

He phased them to the bedroom she shared with Rune. Faye placed the twins in their bassinet and helped Morbid arrange Rune.

He unbuttoned Rune's shirt and pulled it open. Faye flinched when he reached into Rune's chest, stopping halfway up to his forearm.

Faye narrowed her eyes. When Sadi was healing Prinia and Alister, Faye felt the edges of their cores grinding together, forced to fit.

What Morbid did to Rune felt more like hair encasing his core. It stretched over each drop of power floating nearby and drew it back into its housing. The threads curled, brushing over his core. Each filament found the tiniest cracks and filled them in with dark magic.

When Morbid withdrew his hand, Rune felt whole.

"He won't be able to exert the extent of his power for a few months. You saved him for the majority of the damage he was meant to sustain," Morbid said. "Should I send Ash to assist you? Rune will take a few days to wake."

"No, I'll take care of them. Can you bring my sister and Vash?" Faye asked.

"Of course. I'll send a barber as well."

Faye smiled, sitting beside Rune as Morbid vanished.

Rune woke to the sound of Faye's soft snoring. He opened his eyes and slowly realized his queen was draped over him with her head on his chest. Darkness, she survived. He hugged her closer, and needles stabbed through his mind, searing his nerve endings. He hissed a breath, and Faye stirred.

"Rune," she said, crawling up his body. "I was so worried."

She nuzzled his throat, and Rune wrapped his arms around her. "Where are the twins, vsenia?"

"They're in the nursery with Kimber and Sparrow," Faye replied.

The brunette harpy slipped his mind. She would have so many questions about her new nature. "I'll speak with her when she wakes. Explain the bloodlust."

"Lyssa has been answering her questions," Faye said.

"Truly?" Lyssa hadn't offered council to any turned in his memory.

Faye giggled softly. "After you get past her bitchy exterior, she's not so bad."

Rune pulled back, lifting her chin. He stared into her lightning-streaked midnight eyes and caressed her cheek. "I thought I lost you."

"I was so worried when you didn't wake up. Morbid said you would recover in a few days," she said as moisture misted her lashes.

"Shh, love. You will not be rid of me so easily," Rune said, wiping away her tears.

Faye sniffled and wiped her eyes. "I made Familiar totems for Kae and Ren. I'm not letting this happen again. I have a decree I'm passing during the next High Council meeting."

The meeting? Rune blinked. "How long have I been asleep, love?"

"Two weeks."

He'd lost so much time with her and their young. He pulled Faye closer and drew the sheets over her shoulder. "Tell me about the law you wish to pass."

"My people will be freed immediately, and if I need to collect them, they will find little mercy in my retribution."

One Hundred

Faye sat straight back, seated in her place within the High Council. The audience shuffled in, taking their seats. A few glanced around, murmuring to one other. She followed their stares to the balcony reserved for the Sacarlay house. Rune's styled mid-length hair had not gone unnoticed.

He sat with his ankle over his knee. His hand rested on the bassinet beside him. Her children were safe, and she would ensure they remained that way.

Dawn glimmered over the sky, coloring it golden pink. She'd summoned the High Council at this hideous hour to announce her decree, which would be recorded and distributed through the realms.

Faye pushed her chair back as she stood. Her dark soul shard twisted as she used magic to carry her voice through the large domed building. "I have attempted to rule as I wanted to live. I wanted to show you people are worth more than the sum of their shards," Faye began as the crowd silenced, finding their seats. "But you have proven time and again the only language you speak is violence. I am here to negotiate in terms you will understand."

Whispers broke out once more, and Faye cast her voice over the medley of chatter. "I am the Queen of Chaos and Darkness. You have until sundown to release any Anarians you hold captive. If you threaten my people, harm my court, or target my family, I will purge your entire court and destroy everything within their walls."

The crowd quieted, and Faye delivered her final warning. "Oppose me and I will make what I did at the Court of Lace and Bone look like a sweet mercy."

She phased to the walkway leading into The Eyes, met by Rune. Sadi and Damian materialized a moment later, followed by Sparrow and Vashien. Faye took her son, cradling him against her shoulder as she walked toward the exit.

Each step deepened the line she'd drawn.

Sunlight warmed her face as she stepped out of the domed structure, protected by intricately designed spelled glass. "We're returning to Anaria."

Faye phased to her study, her court a step behind her. She lowered Ren into his bassinet and unrolled a map over her desk. She paused as Alister appeared with Prinia and her shadowed wolf. Faye glanced at Rune, and he took a step back, inclining his head at Prin.

"Lady Prinia," he said.

Her shadowed wolf maneuvered itself between herself and Rune. Prinia folded her hands and held her back straighter. "I am part of this court."

Faye smiled. "Yes, you are."

She followed Alister to Faye's desk and watched as he drew lines over the map, dividing Anaria into larger territories. "We can each hold a territory until I assign guards and patrols for the villages," he said.

Prinia looked over the map. "I want this one," she said running her nail over a valley containing two villages.

"You don't need to fight, love," Alister said, taking her hand. "I'll protect it for you."

Prinia tilted her head and growled, "If they took her heartbeats, they could take ours when we have them. This was my valley. *We* will fight."

"As you wish," was all Alister said.

"We're really doing this bitch?" Sparrow asked.

Faye looked over her realm. She'd set an example, and now it was time to see if the dark-bloods would heed her warning.

For their sake, she hoped they did.

Delilah crossed a line, extinguishing any sense of mercy within her. She would hold her realm and protect it viciously. She looked over the faces of those who'd become her unlikely family. The court she'd built and loved. The court she would protect.

"This is my path. There is no going back."

YOU ARE CORDIALLY INVITED TO THE WEDDING OF
FAYE ALEXANDER,
QUEEN OF THE COURT OF CHAOS AND DARKNESS, AND RULER OF ANARIA
&
RUNE SACARLAY,
THE SHADOW PRINCE, AND RULER OF HELL.

EXPECT YOUR INVITATION IN 2024

Kalista Neith's
Dark Court Smut Bites

Take a deeper look into the realms
Of Chaos and Darkness with Dark Court Smut Bites
—a companion anthology best enjoyed after reading
Invoking the Blood.

Twelve spicy short stories featuring
your favorite characters, lore, and spice...

Acknowledgments

To my wonderful Muses: Kayla, Phyllica, Mandy, and Kellbell. Your support allows me to embrace my creativity and I appreciate you all more than I could ever say.

To my Chaos Demon, Jada. The way you put your whole ass Jadussy into helping me craft a beautiful story out of my hot-ass raccoon dumpster fire first draft will forever astound me. Your countless hours, late nights, and invaluable insight are nearly as important as your ability to send me songs you know will embody the vibe of the scenes I want to write. I worship the very ground you walk on, Holy Father.

To my Morally Gray Hoez, I love you, bitches. The support we feed each other nurtures my soul. You make the writing journey far less lonely.

To Erin, Delaney, and the entire crew at Tempe, AZ Barnes & Noble, I cannot express my absolute gratitude for letting my stray cat ass into your mansion. I adore you all. Don't tell anyone but you're my favorite store.

To Allie Shae and Corvin King, thank you for breathing life into my characters and giving them voices. Hearing them adds a new dimension to my story I never dreamed of. I can't wait to hear Rune and Voshki on Quigley.

And finally, to my war horse, thank you for your endless encouragement, even as the entire house transforms into my office. We've veered into my dreams, and the ethereal scenery is rushing past us in a blur. I never imagined we would arrive here, and while you stand patiently beside me as I stare in wonder, reliving the steps that brought us to this moment—I want you to know your presence has not gone unnoticed. You've been at my side every step of the way. Til death, baby.

About the Author

Love is sacrifice. What will you offer?

Kalista Neith is a Barnes & Noble and Amazon best-selling dark fantasy author who writes about love. What people are willing to endure to obtain it, and what they will sacrifice to keep it.

She lives in the Phoenix area with her partner and several four-legged creatures. When she is not writing, Kalista can typically be found buried in her digital art, or playing her favorite games.

Invoking the Blood is Kalista's debut novel in the highly anticipated dark fantasy series Of Chaos and Darkness.

Kalista Neith can be found online at:

KalistaNeith.com
Linktr.ee/KalistaNeith

*Take a deeper look into the realms Of Chaos and Darkness with
Dark Court Smut Bites.*
www.patreon.com/Kalista_Neith

Printed in the USA
CPSIA information can be obtained
at www.ICGtesting.com
LVHW041929290124
770209LV00014B/99/J

9 781957 30305